Artfully Annoying

Artfully Annoying

ANNIKA CHAMPENOIS

Sunny Laughs Press

Praise For Artfully Annoying

"Artfully Annoying by Annika Champenois should be at the top of every romance reader's to-read list. ... The chemistry between Surrey and Croft is palpable. An engaging read which is highly recommended."
—Readers' Favorite five-star review

"The humorous moments add spark to the clean romance between Croft and Surrey, offering a refreshingly different focus from the physical aspects at the forefront of many contemporary romances, honing in instead on what the characters actually admire and like about one another."
—BookLife

"A clean romance readers won't want to miss!"
—*InD'tale Magazine* Crowned Heart of Excellence Review

Prologue

HE ENTERED the house and smiled at the familiar surroundings. Cozy kitchen. Light wood furniture. Worn couches.

This was home. He moved through the living room, enjoying the smells of peach hand soap and paint. As he pushed open the door to the west bedroom, the smells welcomed him all the more.

He opened a closet and, for a moment, admired the dresses lined up inside. Then he reached in for a tiny object in the corner.

It hadn't done much good there, but that was okay. He knew exactly where to place it next. Some of the others needed moving, too, and he must take what they had found.

How he loved this work. How he loved *her*. She might never know all he did for her—his heart clenched at the thought—but he didn't mind, did he? Surely it was enough that he got to see her, wasn't it?

It had to be. He wasn't worthy of her. No one was.

He flexed his hand and shut the closet. His mind moved in circles, always centered on her, as he continued on with his handiwork. When at last everything was arranged to his satisfaction, he returned to the doorway of her bedroom.

He could leave now. He had a new batch of treasures. There was no need to linger like this.

Closing his eyes, he re-committed the smells and the feeling of the place to memory. A fleeting thought, however unworthy. A fantasy of more.

Vain fantasy. Setting his jaw, he forced himself to leave the room.

He let himself out through the glass sliding door and pulled a thin wire through the barely noticeable hole in the weathered woodwork, raising the inside hook and locking the door from the outside.

After a last prolonged look at the house, he made his way through the small backyard toward the car parked on the other side of the hedge.

Chapter One

You've seen the movies. Girl meets Guy. Guy is dating Wrong Girl. Eventually, he realizes New Girl is his true love, and the two of them find their way to happiness.

I am Wrong Girl.

Before you get me wrong, let me hasten to add: I'm not *Mean* Girl. I know you've seen her, too. Backstabbing woman, harassing New Girl, pursuing the guy for his popularity, et cetera. I may look like her—tall, blonde, and by all accounts gorgeous—but I don't do any of those things. I genuinely fall for the Good Guy every time, but when his true love appears on the scene and I realize they're right for each other, I let him go. I walk away. I let them live their happily ever after, and I'm left behind wondering if I'll ever find . . . well, *my* happily ever after.

* * *

I gingerly turned over the wedding invitation on my kitchen table. Brody and Hanna smiled up at me from the picture, happier than sunshine.

They had sent an invitation. To me. To go to their wedding reception.

Oh, Hanna was nice. It radiated from every particle of her, a fairy-tale goodness that surely went beyond human capacity. Without exaggeration, she was Nice with a capital "N" and a halo on top.

So was Brody. I had really, really hoped he would marry me.

He made me feel cared about in a way that made all the guys I'd dated before him fade away. He was sweet and mild-tempered, and he had a special talent of making a person feel at ease after said person had done something incredibly embarrassing—like, say, falling flat on her face and taking down a platter of food with her in the middle of a restaurant. No matter what I did, my face never burned with embarrassment for long when he was there. The way he handled my, ah, accidents wiped away my humiliation and left me happy to be in his company.

Added to this already outstanding gift was his ability to listen. My problems, big or small, mattered to him. He listened with a soft smile and found ways to be helpful. I still had my ringtone set to the recorded sound of my oven timer at his suggestion. When I expected an important phone call earlier this year, I had worried I would be engrossed in painting and would ignore my phone when it rang. Brody came up with the idea of the oven timer. My mind knew I must never ignore *that* particular noise, no matter how distracted I might be.

I knew some very nice people, but this couple took the cake. Truly, Brody and Hanna deserved happiness together, and being the wonderful people they were, I had no doubt they were happy to invite me to their reception.

But that didn't mean I was happy to go.

I dropped the invitation on the table, stepped into a pair of sandals, and left the house Gina and I rented.

My steps ate up the sidewalk of my Provo neighborhood off of Center Street. Tall, thick-trunked trees and uneven roads surrounded me, but I was blind to them. If postures could talk, mine was probably summing me up without mercy, yelling out: *Twenty-two-year-old BYU student, collects scars on her heart. Who wants to add the next one?*

I shook my head in frustration. Would my dream guy ever pick *me*? I didn't believe there was only one right person out there for everyone. In fact, I believed I had been as right for Brody as Hanna was and as right for Frank as Dinah was. Only, my dream guy always let go of his first dream girl —me—in favor of the newest dream girl. It was like a curse.

I slowed my steps and sighed. I had known Brody and Hanna were engaged. I just hadn't expected the card. It had brought back the familiar dull ache of loss and reminded me of the role to which I was always relegated, which was not the one I had dreamed of back when my little sister forced me to watch all her chick flicks and old movies during our shared high school years. And by forced, I mean she turned on the TV and called me over.

"Hi, Surrey."

Looking up, I found myself once again in front of my brick home. A skinny, eleven-year-old boy waved from where he sat on the front steps of the house next door, a graphic novel in his lap. I started to smile. Willie was out getting his daily dose of Vitamin D. The boy took his sunshine very seriously.

"Hi, Willie."

"Feeling better?"

"What?"

"You've circled the block three times," he said with a knowing grin.

I lifted my eyebrows, the right higher than the left. "You were spying on me?"

"I was out here in plain sight the whole time. I didn't call out, and you didn't see me." He picked at the grass. "You'd think an artist would actually go somewhere and look at nature, but when you're upset about something, you just walk around the block over and over."

I didn't say anything.

"So are you feeling better?"

"Yes." Or at least I would with a good distraction. "As a matter of fact, I think I'll go into town and buy some art supplies. Do you and your mom want to join me? I know she's been wanting me to point out my favorite paints."

"Nah, I have an appointment with Superman." He raised his graphic novel. "Maybe next time."

It was a strange friendship we had, but it was definitely a friendship. It felt like having a brother next door. My own little brother was two thousand miles away on the East Coast and halfway through high school, but I remembered the days when he was Willie's age.

"Next time," I agreed.

Wedding invite aside, it was a good idea to leave the empty house. My roommate was at work, and it was lonely with just me. Sometimes I didn't know who to feel sorrier for, me for being alone or Gina for working on Saturday mornings. *Early* Saturday mornings.

The late-morning summer sun had baked the inside of my car. I reveled in the warmth as I got on the road, ready to stock up on paints before the new semester began on Monday.

Turning on the radio, I sang along with one of the billions of musicians who seemed to have been crossed in love: Adele. While *Someone Like You* had definite similarities to my situation, somehow singing about it was easier than thinking about it.

As I drove down a small street, a commercial about wedding rings came on, and my hand shot out and turned off the radio.

I swear to you I was watching the road. I knew exactly where the radio buttons were. I didn't need to look down to fiddle with them.

As my car hit a bump I hadn't seen, I jerked forward in my seat—and I heard a scream of pain from outside.

My foot slammed on the brake, and the rest of me froze. Ice clotted my veins, crackling upward from my feet to my head. My brain was in cold shock, my fingers stuck to the steering wheel, my eyes to the rearview mirror.

A shout sounded, this one from an onlooker, and then someone moaned outside my car.

Red-hot fire raced through me, breaking through the ice and springing me into action.

In a split second, I was unbuckled and out of the car, slamming the door behind me and stumbling to the front of my vehicle.

No one was there. Falling to my knees, I looked underneath the car and saw a person lying—behind it—writhing in agony.

Oh. My. Word. He was all the way on the other side. I hadn't just bumped into him. I had *run him over*.

I ran to the back of my car and knelt beside the young man.

"Ohhhh," he groaned, holding his chest.

"Where are you hurt? Where are you hurt? Where are you hurt?" I heard myself asking while thick, red liquid squirmed out between his fingers.

All I could think as I watched the color spread from his soaked shirt was how could he still be alive?

"You're going to be okay," I whispered forcefully, searching my pockets, patting myself down. If this were England, Jane Austen time, I would have had a handkerchief that could stop the blood. Or maybe I could have torn the hem off my gown and used that.

Were people stronger back then, or did their clothes just tear more easily? I was pretty sure I couldn't tear a piece from my shirt.

The man who had been staring in shock on the sidewalk suddenly regained his presence of mind and dug a cell phone from his pocket.

"I'm calling 911," he told me and turned to speak into the phone.

Stupid. Why hadn't I thought of that? Of course, my cell phone was back in the car.

"It's okay, you'll be okay. Don't move," I told the man on the ground, stopping his twisting movements with my hands. Wide, blue eyes looked up at me above a cheek that was swollen and sporting a bruise. His face remained distorted with pain, and the sight of his blood might have made me gag if not for its almost cozy, pungent smell.

Sirens started up nearby, and I let out my breath in relief. An emergency vehicle must have been close when the call was made. Still, I needed to do what I could for this guy until it arrived.

"Okay. Um." I tried to remember my middle school health teacher's instructions. "If face is red, raise the head. If face is tail . . ." My mind was swirling . . . "No, *pale,* then raise the tail."

I stared at the wounded man. He gasped, and his eyes rolled into the back of his head.

"I don't know if your face is red. Does a cut lip count as a red face?" I cried, then stopped and took a deep breath. "Um. Right, if in doubt, leave flat." I held up my hands and reminded myself that panicking out loud was probably not reassuring to the patient.

"They'll be here in a moment," I told him in a mostly calm voice, but when he took up squirming again, I clamped down on him anew. *Please don't let his innards be hurt,* I prayed.

The smell of the blood grounded me, surprisingly comforting to my senses. I had never exhibited vampiric tendencies before, but I was seriously starting to wonder if I had a problem.

"We need to stop the bleeding. Don't worry." I spouted reassuring nonsense while removing a hand from his shirt and tugging at the bottom of my azure V-neck. I put both hands to my shirt and tried to rip the fabric.

Of course it wouldn't tear.

How was I to stop the bleeding? Now that the thought had occurred to me, it seemed imperative to keep him from losing more blood.

His moans turned to shuddering coughs.

In desperation, I leaned down across him, slapped his hands away from his chest, and pressed the bottom of my shirt against the wound, stretching it away from my skin and feeling the nice-smelling blood soak through the fabric while the man's eyebrows shot upward and he seemed to shrink into himself.

"Whoa, we better stop it right there," the man from the sidewalk protested.

I looked up, catching a glimpse of him from the corner of my eye and underneath the hair falling in my face. I didn't dare move from my precarious position for fear I would fall on top of the invalid. "Can't you do anything to help?" I huffed.

To my surprise, I felt someone move my hand.

The bottom of my shirt sprang back to its rightful spot, wetting my skin and clinging as though glued.

I started to protest as the man I had nearly killed sat up, but then I saw that the dazed look in his eyes was gone and his face no longer contracted in pain.

"You were pretty heroic," he said in a cheerful voice, reaching out a blood-stained hand as though to clap me on the shoulder, then apparently thinking the better of it as he caught sight of his hand.

As though my shirt wasn't already ruined. But what did that matter in the face of his . . . injury?

The man who had called for help reached in front of me, phone in hand, and pointed at a scraggly tree while the wounded guy stood up as though he were perfectly sound.

Cell Phone Guy then spoke two words that stole my attention from the invalid.

"Hidden Camera."

I stared at the tree.

He guffawed. "You were great."

I heard a noise and turned to see the bleeding man extract a white piece of gauze from his mouth, leaving his cheeks evenly matched.

"That's the best reaction we've seen," he agreed. "Deserves an Oscar."

No more swollen cheek. Just a touch of makeup creating a fake bruise.

Oh, and "blood" on his chest, but apparently I should never have been concerned about that.

I swung to meet Cell Phone Guy's dark-blue eyes full-on.

"How dare you," I hissed.

"What? Film your moment of glory?" His tan, square face held what looked to be perpetual dimples—dimples that mocked me.

"We were very careful," the other guy spoke up. "The bump didn't hurt your vehicle. I waited to crawl behind your car until I was certain you wouldn't move it."

"Yeah, no worries," his friend drawled. "No one—"

"How dare you," I shrieked, wanting these perpetrators to feel just a fraction of the fear I had experienced these past few minutes. "What gives you the right to make me think I've killed someone?"

The one who had faked his injury looked a little worried and perhaps guilty. Not so his friend.

"I know it's a bit of a shock at first," Cell Phone Guy began in a condescending tone, "but the others who went through this thought it was funny once they realized . . ." His voice was shaking—not with fear, but with repressed laughter.

"This isn't funny," I insisted. "It's a cruel joke. No, it's not even a joke, it's just plain mean. You can't—"

"Relax," he interrupted, choking with laughter. "It's been done to others, and I'm sure you'll survive it, too. It's a good thing we decided our video needed one more scene." He shared a grin with his friend. "It felt incomplete when we put it together earlier this week, but now, with your awesome contribution and some mad editing skills, we can air our video on time. You'll be a star on YouTube." He gave me a theatrical bow.

I stepped toward him, ready to give him a sound slap like women do in the movies. Or maybe I would push him into the gutter. Angry as I was, I totally had the strength to do it.

His expression changed as though he realized the danger. "Look, we would have let you know the accident wasn't real as soon as you realized the sirens hadn't grown louder. That's what we did with the others. They figured out something was up, and we stepped in."

I hadn't been given time to realize the sirens weren't real—mainly because I had been busy sacrificing my shirt, along with a little bit of my modesty.

A fact that would henceforth be broadcast on YouTube.

"And hey, you have to be glad to know Josh here isn't hurt," Cell Phone Guy continued, pointing at the man's shirt. "It's not blood, just paint mixed with a few things."

I sucked in my breath. Paint. That was why the smell had steadied me.

How could I, an artist, have fallen for that? Embarrassment mixed with anger, leaving me unsure of what to do. The countless church lessons I had grown up with on being Christ-like came to mind. I decided to take the high road and leave off scolding.

"You guys aren't worth it," I growled and turned away.

Semi-high road, I guess.

I stalked back to my Kia where it waited, humming, the engine on the way I had left it. I jerked out the handle by the driver's seat, but the door didn't budge.

I tried again, to no avail. It was locked.

Was this part of the prank, too? Tensing, I prepared to give Cell Phone Guy another piece of my mind. Then my shoulders dropped. Staring at the immovable door, I knew it was me who had locked it.

My mom is big on safety. She taught me to lock my door no matter which side of the lock I'm on, minimizing my chances of being either robbed or kidnapped. It's a good rule, too, except when you're in too big of a hurry to remember to take the key out of the ignition.

Now I was stuck.

Humiliation washed over me, and all my pathetic longing for Brody returned in full force. If he were here, he would have worked his magic, and in a minute I would be comforted, happily chatting with him, his arm around my shoulders.

Instead, I was blushing and wishing I could melt into the sidewalk, never to be seen again.

Cell Phone Guy approached from behind, snickering.

I spun around and snatched the phone from his hands, making him finally shut his mouth in surprise, though a crooked half-grin still stuck to his face.

Gina—blessed, blessed Gina—answered on the third ring. I loved her for being off work by now. I also kind of loved me for having memorized her phone number.

"Gina, can you get me the number of a Provo locksmith?" I asked.

I *didn't* love me for not having roadside assistance on my auto insurance plan.

"Um. Okay," she answered.

I suppose I could have looked it up myself, but I wasn't keen on surfing the Internet with the owner of the cell phone breathing down my neck. At my words, he looked from me to my car and back again.

I fixed him with a glare that should have made him back off. It should have made him run home, leaving his cell phone to its fate with a surety he would never see it again.

Instead, he mouthed something at me. I can't read lips, so I had no idea what his message was until he did it again along with a whisper. *"Locked out?"*

"Got it." Gina's voice saved me.

A second embarrassing phone call later, I slapped the phone into its owner's hand, spitefully glad to see that I had gotten red paint on it.

"So." His voice was suspiciously thick. "You locked yourself out, huh? That really wasn't part of the plan."

Meaning they hadn't expected me to be this big of a fool.

"Doesn't matter," I snapped. "Humiliating me was the plan from the beginning. It was the whole point of the fake wounded-guy scene."

Josh began in a placating tone, "Croft and I didn't mean . . ."

"Doctors agree a good scare now and then is healthy to the heart," his accomplice—Croft?—interrupted with a smirk.

"But not a heart attack and tons of stress and guilt packed into five minutes." My stomach hurt from the stress that had flogged it earlier. It was also itchy with dried paint. I heard tears in my voice and took a deep breath to stop them.

"Two." His voice surprised me. I looked into his mocking eyes. "It was only two minutes. It'll probably be at least five minutes before the locksmith gets here and undoes the damage, though."

I jerked up my hands. "This isn't how I planned to spend my day. I'm supposed to be *shopping*."

He rolled his eyes. "I'm sure your wardrobe can wait."

He thought I was going clothes-shopping. Obviously, the only thing this Croft guy saw when he looked at me was *blond*.

I didn't correct him.

He sat down on the curb, stretching his legs out in front of him. "Anyway, I'm not complaining, and I'm stuck, too."

"*You're* stuck?"

He pointed at a blue Mazda peeking out from the alley blocked by my Kia. "Your car's in the way. I have to wait for the locksmith and put up with an angry woman at the same time."

I gritted my teeth and crossed my arms, determined not to speak to him anymore. Josh joined his friend on the curb, but I leaned against my car.

Conversation lagged. Every two minutes or so, the dimpled jerk offered a satirical comment which I duly ignored.

When the locksmith arrived, it took him all of three seconds to unlock my car.

And the price of gas, my mind moaned, but I caught the thought and pushed it back inside. What was lost was lost. My dignity and fourteen minutes' worth of gas.

Croft sighed with an air of self-sacrifice and stepped forward. "You know what, I'll pay the locksmith bill."

No, thank you. I nearly elbowed him in the face as I handed over my credit card to be scanned. In another moment, the locksmith completed the transaction and returned my card.

Without another word, I got in my Kia, snapped on my seatbelt, and got out of there as fast as I could without breaking the speed limit.

I went home, of course. I couldn't waltz through the store with blood, or paint, on my hands and shirt.

Gina looked up from the table when the door closed behind me. Her first question wasn't why I had needed the locksmith. It wasn't even about the red mess that had ruined my shirt.

She put the card down, her brows knit in concern. "They invited you to their *wedding?*"

Chapter Two

THERE'S one thing you need to know right off the bat about Gina.

She's an angel.

Seriously, she's all that is good, sweet, and unselfish—a different brand of nice than Brody, a shyer kind. In fact, she insists her shyness is the reason guys don't ask her out. Back when we were in high school, she could barely string a sentence together when faced with a peer. I knew her only by sight back then. By the time she and I became roommates last year, though, she had improved by leaps and bounds. She could talk to girls with reasonable confidence, and if a guy were to spend enough time with her, she might eventually dare reveal her personality. Eventually.

She has a face I would love to paint: expressive brown eyes, arched eyebrows, and elfin cheekbones framed by light-brown hair. I finally sketched it onto a ten-by-eighteen-inch piece of canvas, and I can barely wait to put my brushes to it. But don't tell her. She would be embarrassed if she knew.

I suppose I should also tell you what I look like. It feels weird, but I guess it's the thing to do in narration. I've already given you my general descriptor, but here are the specifics.

My blond hair falls ten inches below my shoulders, thick and wavy as the ocean on a mild day. Round eyebrows arch above full eyelashes that void any need for mascara. In fact, I never use makeup. My eyes are emerald-green, my nose is Grecian with just enough of a button-nose to add a cuteness factor, and my high cheekbones color like a breathtaking sunset when I blush—Frank's words, not mine. Frank is a budding poet and the guy I dated and loved before Brody.

As for my figure, I used to admire it as a teenager, before I came to feel that people paid too much attention to my looks. I guess it had only grown more attractive since then. It was too bad I wasn't as graceful as I looked, but as you may have figured out, I was accident-prone. At the moment, I was also depressed.

* * *

"This is hard," Gina said. We sat next to each other at the dining table while I stared at Brody and Hanna's card as though it were an invitation to my best friend's funeral.

"Yeah," I replied. "I mean, I've known for a while they were engaged. He told me last month when we ran into each other, and she was so sweet to me when I saw her a week later, and she was nervous but felt she should show me the ring and make sure I knew . . ." My voice trailed off.

"But it's still hard to actually see the invitation," Gina concluded with feeling.

She was a good listener and an even better empathizer. That's why I rambled on about the engagement for another while. When I started going in circles, though, I knew it was time to stop.

"I've gotta go shopping." I jumped to my feet.

Gina bit her lip. "There's paint on your shirt."

"I know. I'll change first."

My Saturday errands kept me busy for the next many hours. By the time I came home again, I had decided against sharing the morning's incident with Gina. Talking about it would only raise my blood pressure. Cooking, on the other hand, would help me. Cooking meant having control.

I commandeered the kitchen in an epic takeover, and the ingredients accepted me unanimously. The jumbo pasta shells softened in subservience at my touch (and with ten minutes of boiling), and the ground beef sizzled in awe of my presence before leaping into a bowl of flavored cheese in a demonstration of allegiance to me. My phone added its voice of admiration with occasional beeps and dings, but I ignored each notification while I stuffed the reverential shells.

When the pan was full of pasta, I opened the oven door and blinked.

No heat came out.

I slapped my forehead. "I forgot to turn on the oven." As I set it to preheat, my phone beeped for the dozenth time since I'd started making dinner.

Shaking my head, I put my phone on vibrate mode and returned to the kitchen. I cleaned the counters and filled the dishwasher. Then, finally, my therapeutic masterpiece went in the oven while I silently yelled *Yes!* in my head and pumped my fist in the air.

Cooking always made me feel good. Even though my hand caught on the large utensil holder and knocked it over, I felt victorious as I picked up our ladles and spatulas.

"Smells good," Gina complimented when I returned to the living room.

"And I didn't break anything," I boasted.

We both jumped at the sound of my phone. I had placed it on the table, and as it vibrated, it sounded like a nest of angry hornets.

"Who is so excited to get ahold of me?" I exclaimed, letting my heart-beat settle back to normal before I picked up the annoying phone and opened my latest text.

You know you're on YouTube, right?

I froze. My Messenger app popped up, and I tentatively opened it to read another couple of messages.

I just watched Croft Taylor's hidden camera thing. You're hilarious!
Must've been scary to think you'd run someone over. Lol

Lol? I thought to myself. *Yes,* it was scary. *No,* it was *not* lol.

I threw the phone in the direction of the couch, but it landed on the floor.

Gina watched me with her brown eyes. She looked afraid to ask.

I unclenched my jaw and hoped I hadn't just ground deep grooves in my teeth.

"It doesn't matter," I said. "I got caught in some hidden camera thing today, and a few people texted me about it. Doesn't matter."

She nodded slowly, as though I had given a sufficient explanation. "Do you . . . wanna play cards while we wait for dinner?"

"Gina, I love you," I exclaimed. "I hope you know that."

"I have an inkling," she answered sweetly, and I laughed out loud. She never used to joke, but she was comfortable enough around me to do it now, and the glimpses of humor she showed were all the funnier for it.

By the time dinner was ready, my phone had gone off five more times, so I retrieved it and turned it off, determined not to read my texts or watch the video.

At least I get points for self-control, right?

* * *

The notifications on my phone blew up over the weekend. Who would have thought the scene would get so many views? That Croft Taylor or someone on his team must be a genius at movie editing and making videos searchable. For my part, I wished they had mediocre skills and fewer than ten subscribers.

That Monday, I was determined not to think of the disagreeable event or the media attention. It was the first day of school, which meant a new start with new classes and people to meet.

As I started off for campus, I waved at Mrs. Blaine's kitchen window where I could see a hand holding the curtain partially open. The eighty-year-old woman and her husband lived diagonally across the street from me and Gina, and she kept a close eye on our neighborhood at this time of day. If I were a burglar, I would warn my comrades not to come here between the hours of seven and ten in the morning—make that six and ten, just to be on the safe side—and certainly never to come on trash day until after the garbage truck had been by.

Above me, the sky stretched for miles and miles of uninterrupted blue. Purple, silhouetted mountains behind me and earth-colored mountain giants ahead emphasized the sheer size of the heavens. I liked my part of Provo with its unique houses and towering trees, though street parking was worse the closer I got to campus. Here, the lines of parked cars obscured the view of drivers at every corner. *Be ye masters at parallel parking,* the apartments on the south side of Brigham Young University proclaimed in ominous tones.

I ascended several flights of stairs and arrived in College World, classroom buildings and milling young adults all around me. A young man checked me out, but I ignored him, still admiring the majesty of Provo's landscape.

As I craned my neck to watch a bird fly overhead, I stumbled. Fortunately, I caught my balance in time. I didn't particularly want to attend my first day of classes scraped up from hitting the pavement face-first.

On the other hand, that would make me less recognizable. I frowned. It seemed to me there were more people than usual staring at me. Had they seen the hidden camera video, or was I being paranoid?

Taking one last breath of fresh air, I entered the Talmage Building, *my* building, a space dedicated to mathematics and statistics. The halls and spotted white concrete stairs were familiar and worn, actual concave spots in the stairs indicating their years of use. I entered my classroom five minutes before the hour and smiled at the white-haired professor.

"Hi, Dr. Phil."

"Surrey, good to see you."

The room was set up rather like an outdoor amphitheater, with the floor rising one wide step at a time from the front and on back, providing space for long, white tables at each of the three different levels. Five-wheeled ergonomic office chairs ruled the room, proclaiming that this was a classroom that understood the importance of physics—or maybe the facilities manager just wanted as little wear and tear on the carpet as possible.

I found a seat in the back and watched Dr. Phil set up the projector. As his assistant, maybe I should have offered to help, but electronics weren't my strong point. Instead, I looked around at the students and saw a red-haired boy turn to his neighbor and whisper. Both of them sneaked glances at me and hunched over to whisper some more. I caught the words, "Hot chick."

Fun. I didn't want to play the game of counting and calculating what proportion of the students were staring at me, but it was hard to miss them. Even as I tried to fix my gaze above the students' heads, I caught a girl with hair down to her waist gaping at me. When our eyes met, she started and looked away.

Then someone else walked in, and the air left my lungs.

No. No, no. Mocking, dark eyes. Square, cocky face. Dark-blonde hair with bronze highlights and a devil-may-care messiness to it. It couldn't be! But it was! Croft Taylor sat down next to the redhead and started talking to him.

I grabbed my notebook and held it up to block me from Croft's view in case he looked back. If he already had a stupid, successful YouTube channel, shouldn't he be out of school and enjoying his career? Also, who holds up a notebook in front of their face, especially on the first day of school before they have any notes?

The bell rang, causing a girl sitting near the door to jolt in her seat. I could sympathize. I had sat in the hall far too close to that bell at the wrong time, and the noise was terrible close up. At the moment, though, I would rather have been in the hall fighting deafness than in here waiting for Croft to notice me.

"Welcome to Stat 230," Dr. Phil's voice rang out, and I lowered my notebook, grateful that class had begun. Most of the students, including my nemesis, faced forward to listen. "Let me introduce myself . . ."

My shoulders fell with the realization that I was doomed. Introductions. Dr. Phil would announce me to the class as his Teacher's Assistant.

In a few minutes, he did.

"I'd like to introduce you to one of my TAs. Surrey Witherfield, if you'll stand and give us a wave back there."

I stood and gave them a wave but not a smile as everyone turned to look at me. The despicable prankster's eyes widened in surprise. My eyes swept the room, but by the time they returned to him, a taunting quality had entered his gaze, and his mouth was spread in a scornful smile.

Scorn? *He* scorned *me*? *He* was the one who had been a jerk.

He dismissively turned to the front shortly before everyone else.

"Our other TA is Tom Dorrick," Dr. Phil announced, not giving an introduction because Tom wasn't in the room. This particular class didn't fit his schedule. "Our TAs will be available to help you during the student lab hours shown on the syllabus."

I sat down as Dr. Phil kept talking. Unfortunately, now the students were talking, too, whispering among themselves.

"Dude, our TA is hot."

"Wasn't she the girl in that hilarious video?"

"I'm sure that's her. 'If face is tail' . . ." The comment trailed off into laughter.

Dr. Phil shushed the class and continued on.

I slumped in my seat. I had planned to attend this class all semester even though it wasn't required of me. It would be useful to review the material I would answer homework questions on, and I would be paid for my time in class.

Now I might have to rethink that plan.

At the end of the hour, I would have made my escape without seeing Croft again if it hadn't been for the girl just ahead. She stopped suddenly in the doorway and called out to a friend of hers in the room, making me jerk back to avoid running into her.

My head turned, and I caught Croft's eyes as he finished a conversation. He raised his eyebrows and looked askance at me.

His attitude left much to be desired, but I had zero interest in confronting him. Better to avoid him. I made it outside, cursing my bad luck at his being in this class. I hoped the jerk was brilliant and would have no need of the student lab this semester.

I should have majored in art instead of statistics.

* * *

MY OTHER CLASSES went much better, though I found to my chagrin that far too many people had seen the prank video. It was a relief to finish the day and walk home.

Willie sat on the porch when I arrived, a Wii controller next to him with its insides exposed.

I waved and tried to summon a smile. "Hi, Willie."

"Hi, Surrey. How was your day?"

"Meh." I didn't want to go into further detail than that.

"I saw that YouTube video of you."

That stopped me in my tracks. "You saw it?"

"Yeah. It's kind of all over the internet."

"Gah!" was my intelligent, well-controlled response. I raised my hands to my head in annoyance.

Willie looked at me with sympathy but said nothing else.

"Did I really look that dumb?"

"Of course not. You were panicked because you'd run over that guy. Anyone would be."

I paced my driveway. "People are laughing at me."

"People are trolls online," he said, not realizing I referred to comments I had overheard on campus. I hadn't even looked at the website that showed my video, much less the comment section. "Actually, a lot of them were okay. They didn't say anything about how you acted. They just talked about how amazing you looked." He rolled his eyes.

I winced. "I don't know that that's any better. I hate being ogled in person. I don't care to get ogled online, either."

His mouth twisted. "Sorry. Did people on campus recognize you from the video?"

I nodded grimly. "And get this, the guy behind the hidden camera thing is in my statistics class. Well, the class where I assist the teacher."

"What, really?"

"Yeah. And he wasn't sorry about it at *all*." I shook my head. "But my other classes were nice. It'll be a good semester," I said, my voice sounding unconvincing even to myself. I changed the topic. "How was your day?"

"Good. I hacked a government website and disassembled a foreign drone."

I raised my eyebrows at him.

"Okay, not really, but my computer and electronics classes were cool. I like my home-schooling gig."

"Your parents have you taking classes at the elementary school this year, though, right?"

"Yeah, Tuesdays and Wednesdays I have to go be with kids my age. Other than that, I'm free."

"I hope the students realize how cool it is to have a visiting undercover agent twice a week," I said in a serious tone.

"I hope they *don't* know." He smirked. "Wouldn't be much good if they knew I was a spy, would it?"

I laughed and headed to my house, feeling better than when I first arrived.

In my bedroom, I dropped my backpack on the floor and looked around, rubbing my hands together. I was ready now to tackle my list. The first day of school was the day I could officially start on my List of Ten Things to Do This Semester.

It was a new tradition as of last year, deciding on ten new things I would do each semester. The list was a mixture of silly, useful, and service-oriented tasks. One of my more fruitful projects had been to plant a berry bush, with my landlady's permission. This semester, the most exciting item had to do with prepping for a certain painting. I leaned over my desk to look at the small print I had drawn last month.

From the moment I'd had the idea, I was drawn to the image in my mind: A woman in a full-blown, elegant ballgown—with a camouflage pattern. It was a marriage of princess and military, refined and rough-and-tumble, ballrooms and hunting grounds.

I had sketched it out in detail and colored it with muted greens, blacks, and browns. I was still turning over the idea in my mind, however, certain I could make it better. The initial idea might have seemed silly, but I was determined the end result would be striking.

Sewing the princess camouflage dress was at the top of my ten challenges. The sewing project would help me decide exactly how I wanted the dress to look. Once completed, I would capture my evolved idea in a final painting.

Unfortunately, I didn't trust myself with the sewing machine alone. Accidents happened far too often for me, so I only used it when Gina was home. That way, if I cut off my finger or worse, she could call for help while I sat in shock or lay passed out on the floor.

I sighed. When school was in swing, Gina was rarely around. The girl worked too much. Thursdays would be my Gina-days this semester. That was the only weekday she wouldn't have work, and her classes that day ended at a decent time.

Well, no Gina at the moment meant no sewing. Ignoring the tempting fabric slung across my dresser, I opened my laptop and found a YouTube video with bird calls. The second item on my List of Ten Things was to learn to imitate an animal. I hadn't decided on the animal yet, but I was leaning toward either a dog or a bird. With little homework to do today, why not research animal noises? At least it should keep my mind off a certain someone who had the gall to take Stat 230 this semester.

"You and me, mourning dove," I muttered as I started the video. "Although I think I have more reason to mourn than you do."

Chapter Three

THE REST of the week was a struggle. I couldn't always tell whether people stared at me because of my looks or because they had seen the video, although sometimes they made it painfully obvious which it was. Gina was empathetic when I told her about the undesirable student in Dr. Phil's class, but there was nothing she could do.

When Croft made an aggravating comment on the way out of class that Wednesday, I really started to wish the classroom had two doors. We were able to ignore each other during instruction, but did we have to get stuck in the crowd near each other on the way out every time? It was a bottleneck effect I didn't care for.

Thursday morning, with my first class not starting until nine thirty, I took a ten-minute break from life and went to the small, drought-toughened backyard to dream and to sketch.

The clouds above me seemed alive. I could practically feel them breathing. I found pictures in their formations and drew the scenes I imagined they showed, blurring the lines from my pencil into wispy outlines to retain an element of the original clouds.

By the time the alarm on my phone announced the end of my ten minutes, I was relaxed. I returned inside to do homework for a while. Then I gathered my things and left the house.

Across the street, Mrs. Blaine sat in a green lawn chair, watching the streets like a hawk. A long-sleeved, floral-print shirt and a flat straw hat kept the sun at bay. The hat obscured little, if any, of her vision, and I was certain that was why she had picked it. She wouldn't have risked missing any activity on the street due to her headwear.

Although most of my neighbors, like me, were members of The Church of Jesus Christ of Latter-day Saints, some had solidified in my mind as Mr. and Mrs. while others had become Brother and Sister. The Whitmers and Sister James had insisted from the beginning that I call them Brother and Sister. Mrs. Blaine had never said anything one way or the other, and by now it was too late for me to change her title.

"Hello, Mrs. Blaine," I called, stopping in front of her house. "It should be about another hour, shouldn't it?"

She stared at the trash cans lining the street. "It should be, but you never know what time it will get here." Her gaze followed our street to its end as though she expected the garbage truck to round the corner this very minute. "If it's not here by twelve thirty-two, I'll call city services."

You may think that's an oddly specific time, not to mention it was strange for her to worry when it was only nine o'clock, but you have to realize, Mrs. Blaine took garbage pick-up very seriously. Once, she told me, the truck arrived at three forty-four in the afternoon even though it was supposed to be here around ten. Another time, it never came at all. Of course, she would add, that was in San Francisco, but it could happen here, as well.

I kind of adored Mrs. Blaine. I nodded at her. "Thank you, as always."

She nodded back and returned to scrutinizing the street while I headed to school.

New Testament Part I was a class I had looked forward to for a while. Even in the late-summer heat, I imagined I would feel like it was Christmas while I studied the Gospels. It had felt that way on Tuesday as we talked about the birth of Christ. A sense of anticipation filled me as I entered the classroom and started down a row of seats.

"Surrey," a surprised male voice exclaimed.

I snapped my gaze up and stumbled, throwing my hands out. An arm shot out and grabbed mine, steadying me. Flustered, I met Jesse's dark-eyed gaze.

"I didn't know you were in this class. Are you okay?" he added. The question came late not because he was insensitive but because he was used to this sort of thing from me. In fact, while we dated, I'd thought it tactful of him not to make a big deal out of it every time I had an accident, given how often that happened.

"Yeah," I gulped. "Um, good to see you."

"You, too." He beamed. "Why don't you sit here with me?"

I took the seat he offered, but not without regrets. "How are you doing?" I asked, glad to hear that my voice sounded sincere rather than half-hearted.

"Good. Maria and I are really happy. We found a duplex near the center of town, but she wants to move to Wymount at some point, just as soon as . . . well, as soon as we start showing signs of having started a family."

I stopped myself from saying "Oh" and nodded instead while my heart slid down inside me. Jesse was one of the guys I had thought I would marry. He had seemed just as smitten with me until a vivacious brunette showed up in his family home evening group.

That Monday afternoon, he and I had looked at Christmas lights on Temple Square and talked about what-ifs and our hopes for our future families. Following our meaningful conversation, we parted ways in time to attend our separate family home evening activities.

The next day, he had been a little distant as we cooked dinner together.

After that, our dates got a little less romantic, he became less willing to talk about the future, and his enthusiasm at seeing me waned. After three weeks, he started hanging out at Maria's place. Shortly after that, he stopped going out with me, and our four months of dating ended.

They got married last spring.

"She's studying to be a nurse, but I think you already knew that," Jesse was saying. "I'm feeling more and more certain about engineering, which is great because it would be rough on us both if I wanted to change majors . . ."

I was happy for them, I really was. They were both so nice, and they—it hurt to think it, but it was true—fit well together.

I had used to think *we* fit well together, though. I might still think so if I allowed myself to ponder it. Which I wouldn't, because I shouldn't.

Brother Deed stood and asked for a volunteer to pray, putting an end to Jesse's blissful updates. My ex gave me a friendly smile, which I managed to return. He closed his eyes for the prayer, and I closed my eyes, too, mouthing an "SOS" prayer of my own.

I hoped to avoid eye contact with Jesse during class, but then I remembered he was the kind of guy who whispered comments to the person next to him, sharing his thoughts with his seatmate rather than raising his hand and sharing them with everyone. I sighed and prepared myself for a long hour of listening and nodding at a happily married guy I had once loved.

The hour passed just as I expected. When it was time to go, Jesse nudged my arm to get my attention, as though he hadn't claimed it all along. "I saw that video of you."

I blinked. "You did?"

"Yes. It was funny, although it probably wasn't in the moment."

"No," I answered, struggling to keeping my voice neutral. *It still isn't*, I added in my mind.

"Well, you're famous now. I hope you get rich soon, too," he joked and clapped my shoulder. "I'll see you Tuesday. I'll tell Maria you're in my class. I wish she could be here, too."

"See you later," I answered and gave him a head start to the door.

* * *

THE NEXT DAY started out great. As I headed to my first class, birds chattered, leaves rustled, and I tipped my head upward to look at that great, blue canvas upon which God had put dollops of cream which—

The breath was knocked out of me, and I found myself held upright by the large guy I had walked into.

We both started apologizing to each other.

"Sorry."

"I didn't mean to . . ."

"No, it was my bad."

He broke off and stared at me. I realized I was still in his arms and stepped away. This was how Jesse and I had met. Not that it had done me any good.

"Sorry about that. I have to get to class," I excused myself and headed to the Talmage Building before he could recover his wits and maybe, I don't know, ask me out. He turned to watch me, his mouth still open. I imagined he would stare until after I entered the building, and the knowledge made my gait awkward, but I made it inside all right and walked upstairs, squaring my shoulders under my backpack.

You can see why I use a backpack. If I were to carry my books in my arms, I would have dropped them twice already this week—and incidentally, it would have made for an even more romantic scene out there with the guy picking up my books for me and thinking he would be my next boyfriend while I would worry about him being my next heartbreak.

Laughter rang out as I entered my classroom. It came from the guy next to Croft as he looked at the cell phone held out to him. "I can't," he moaned. "'Are you hurt? Are you hurt? Are you . . .'"

He caught sight of me and froze in the middle of wiping away tears. Croft noticed me, too, and his mouth twisted mockingly. My face hot, I marched toward the back, which unfortunately meant I was walking toward the two of them. While I would have loved to look away, keeping them in my line of sight was a must if I didn't want to face-plant onto the floor.

Croft seemed to have no problem with the arrangement. His stormy blue eyes followed my progress. As I watched, he raised a hand to his head and, with a precise and derisive movement, saluted me.

The gesture made me hopping mad.

I stopped and snapped loudly, "If you want to show everyone how stupid I am, the world is your campus." I swept my hand at the room and glared at him.

He blinked in surprise. Then he raised his eyebrows in a challenge, and his voice turned smug. "*I* thought so."

How I wanted to slap that expression off his face. Better yet, I wanted to slap off his actual face, but I was a civilized person, and civilized people didn't do that, so I just scowled and moved on to my nice, distant seat in the back.

The guy next to Croft turned around and mouthed something at me, looking apologetic.

Croft elbowed him.

"What? Dude, she's a babe," the guy said.

"So? Even babes can bite," Croft said. "Beauty doesn't mean she's one of the good ones."

I raised my gaze to the ceiling and kept it there. It kept me from grinding my teeth.

The other guy barked a laugh. "The good ones? What do you mean? Is she a bad one? How would you know what she's like?"

Why, with all the conversations going on around me, could I hear *this* one so clearly?

"I've picked up a few things." To my shock, Croft began to list off my perceived bad qualities. "Bad temper, no sense of humor, a temptation to every guy around, and way too good-looking for you."

The guy shoved him. Too bad it was in semi-friendly jest.

I *did* have a sense of humor. It was different from Croft's, but that was only a good thing. I was also justified in getting into a temper over how he treated me, though I did try my best to stay calm.

I fumed throughout class. Croft needed to leave me be. He had to stop baiting me. He was downright mean, and on top of the attention from people all over campus who had watched his video, his behavior was getting to be too much.

When class ended, I hung back, waiting for him to clear the room first. Inevitably, one of his friends called out to him and made him turn around. His eyes met mine, and he gave me a scathing look before answering his friend and disappearing through the door.

Just what had I done to make him hate me?

I stood and slammed my backpack onto the table. On the way up, one of the straps got caught on my chair, which fell back and hit me. Though the chair didn't strike with much force, it surprised me and made me stumble backward into the wall while the backpack fell off the table and hung dangling from the chair. Angry, I pushed off the wall and snatched my backpack, then stormed out.

The rest of my classes weren't enjoyable enough to dull my vexation.

* * *

WILLIE CALLED out to me on my third march around the block.

"What ho, Surrey."

I paused, and my lips twitched in spite of myself. I had only heard him say that once before. The first time, I had nearly laughed my head off in appreciation of whatever book he had gotten it from. This time, I wasn't nearly as ready to collapse with humor.

"What's wrong?" he asked from his porch.

I turned and stomped my way past his house again. "It's the guy in my statistics class. He's driving me bonkers."

"What guy?"

I whipped around and clomped the other way. "The one behind the hidden camera prank. He's been mocking me all week."

"Mocking? What do you mean, mocking?" Willie asked, suddenly alert.

I turned around again. "Monday, he saw me and totally dismissed me. Wednesday, one of the other guys caught me on my way out. The guy was flirting and telling me how impressed he was that I was majoring in statistics. Then Croft joined the conversation with, 'Well, she obviously wasn't going to make it as an EMT,' and the people around us all laughed at me."

"What?" Willie jumped up. "He's making fun of you for what happened on Saturday?"

"Yeah. And today he was showing the video to someone when I walked in. I told him he could show everyone how stupid I was, and he just agreed." I stopped and clenched my fists. I think I actually cracked my knuckles.

"That's so wrong," Willie exclaimed, clenching *his* hands. "Who does he think he is? Was he the guy on the ground in that stupid prank?"

"No, he's Mister 'I'll call 911.' Ugh."

"What makes him think he can crash your statistics 325 every morning and make life miserable for you?"

"230, and it's just three times a week," I corrected, but I felt a little better. At least Willie understood. My hands relaxed at my sides. "I don't think I'll go to that class anymore. I don't have to, you know, and with him taunting me, it's not worth it."

"But that would be the coward's way out," Willie protested. "You can't let him chase you out of your own class."

I shook my head. "I thought of that, but that's the wrong way to think of it. This is self-preservation. I can act out of some twisted sense of pride and let him torture me, or I can stop attending and have life be that much easier. I choose the second path."

"But . . ." Willie was so upset on my behalf that his face had turned red. Or maybe it was sunburn. I couldn't tell. I was still debating when he took a deep breath and sat down. "Okay. I guess that makes sense."

I didn't quite believe in his sudden acquiescence and felt the need to explain myself further. "I'm only giving him more power to bother me when I go. I don't have to take his punches."

Willie nodded, still looking annoyed. "Yeah, you're right. But Surrey?"

"Yeah?"

"The guy's a jerk of the first order."

I smiled. "*I* thought so."

Chapter Four

I MADE good use of my extra hour the following Monday morning, studying ahead and doing homework that would be assigned later that week according to my syllabi. If I couldn't attend Stat 230, I could at least be productive.

As I headed to school, I was tempted to skip along the sidewalk. How easy it was to avoid the torture that had been Dr. Phil's class.

The morning sun warmed my back as I reached campus. I began a daydream about my future professional life, complete with a statistics career that kept me fed while I dabbled in art on the side. Hopefully I'd get to have a family somewhere along the way, at which point I would quit my job to be a full-time mom. It was the toughest job of them all, but I wanted a family like the one I had grown up in. Actually, I had often wished I would get married and have a baby while still in school. It had been a fancy of mine ever since my first semester when I shared a class with a young mom. She had brought her girl to school and kept her in a stroller by the wall. While logically I knew it would be grueling, I couldn't help but romanticize the idea in my mind. Of course, *my* baby would probably scream through every class.

With only a year and a half left of school, it no longer seemed likely I would fulfill my class-disruption dreams. Worse, I was starting to worry I would never get married, period. Not because I had passed any sort of age limit at twenty-two, but because of my dating pattern.

Excited voices broke into my thoughts. In front of the lawn leading to the X-shaped Administration Building, I spotted a growing group of college students crowding together, their faces worried. Concerned, I joined them and peeked between two young women to see a motionless boy on the ground.

I gasped and pushed my way through. "Willie," I called, dropping to the grass before his still form. He was wearing a helmet and some knee and elbow pads, and a skateboard lay beside him. What was he doing on campus? Had he crashed? "Willie!"

His eyes popped open. "Surrey?"

"Willie, are you all right? What happened?"

"I'm fine," he hurried to reassure me, sitting up. "Sorry. I didn't mean to scare you."

"What?" I grabbed his shoulder, bewildered. "Then why are you . . ."

"I just wanted to teach *him* a lesson," he said and pointed past me.

Half wild with worry, I turned my head in the direction he pointed and nearly cracked heads with the guy on his knees next to me.

I froze, staring at the source of my torment for the past week. Croft Taylor gaped back at me.

"He, um . . ." Croft cleared his throat. "He crashed into me before I could get out of the way."

"How's it feel, thinking someone got seriously hurt because of you?" Willie asked Croft, putting his hands on his hips.

Oh. Oh, so that was why . . . That was how come . . . Oh.

"It's not so fun when you're in the middle of it, is it?" Willie pressed on.

"Um, well," Croft stuttered.

My thoughts slowly reconnecting, I sat back on my heels, looking at my neighbor friend. Was he really . . . Yes, he was okay, wasn't he? He had staged it, all for . . . And Croft was here, and he . . .

I stood and walked away several paces, my heart stuck in my throat, my head buzzing and drowning out whatever conversation Croft and Willie were having. Those who had gathered began to leave with backward glances.

I couldn't believe . . . I suppose it was nice, maybe chivalrous, of Willie to . . . I would have to be more careful about confiding in him. I had never imagined he would act on my complaints in this way.

I turned back.

"No, I'm her neighbor," Willie was saying.

I broke in. "Are you sure you're all right, Willie?"

He scrambled up from the ground and picked up his skateboard. "Yeah, I'm fine. My work here is done." He threw a scathing glance at Croft on the ground. "See you later, Surrey."

Willie walked away, and I watched until I was certain he hadn't gotten hurt. Then I spun in the opposite direction and quickly left Croft behind.

I shuddered. It had been a shock to see Willie lying there, pale and lifeless. Would Croft mock me for being fooled again? Or would he think I had asked Willie to get back at him?

It didn't matter what he thought, I reminded myself. I was avoiding him and Dr. Phil's class, and it had been only a stroke of bad luck that I'd seen him just now.

I went to BYU's arboretum. The sounds of a stream grew louder as I descended the stairs on the south side of campus and entered a path lined by plum trees on one side and a brook on the other. Crossing the narrow stream, I sat down on a flat boulder and set the ten-minute timer on my phone. Then I clasped my hands across my knees and looked at the greenery around me, ready for God's creations to soothe me.

Willie was okay. Croft had been taught a lesson, though I didn't dare hope it would stick. Still, I didn't need to worry. I could calm down now.

My body relaxed as I watched the water's meandering. Then my traitorous thoughts turned to Brody and Hanna, making my heart hurt. Their reception was coming up, and I needed to get them a gift.

My timer went off, and I straightened and turned it off. I would think about the reception later. "To each day its own," I declared and slipped off the rock, my feet landing in the water with a splash.

Oops.

Oh, well, it was a warm day. I sloshed out of the stream and headed to class.

* * *

WHEN I CAME HOME, Willie's doorstep was markedly empty. The next day, it was the same, and I stopped and narrowed my eyes at his house. Was he afraid to see me because I had caught him trying to teach Croft a lesson?

If I didn't see Willie tomorrow, I decided, I would go knock on his door. He couldn't continue avoiding me and the scolding I ought to give him. I wasn't sure I *would* give it, but I did feel like we should talk about it. It wasn't every day one's friend threw himself down in front of one's enemy, pretending grave injury. Besides, I was curious about how he had known where to find Croft.

I entered my own house, my steps quiet on the wooden floors. The refrigerator hummed and the A/C unit whispered, but the house seemed hushed as though it were holding its breath. I frowned and came to a stop in the living room where an itchy feeling swept over me, bringing goose-bumps with it. I waited to see if it got worse.

One, two, three—I counted the seconds, and then the back of my neck began to prickle and I grew hot with nervousness.

With a huff of frustration, I returned outside.

I dropped my backpack against the oak in the front yard and plopped down. The feeling of discomfort in the house was sadly familiar. Every now and then, our rented house gave me the creeps. It wasn't the only place that had done so, either. Lest you think it's all in my mind, Gina had felt it, too. We had actually asked priesthood-holders to come over several times to dedicate or bless the place, but even so, it messed with my senses every few weeks.

I buried myself in a biology assignment for a time. Then I leaned back and looked up into the branches of the oak. On further thought, I decided to lie down to get a better look from below. The plethora of brittle, wooden stems and newer, green twigs crisscrossing cheerfully with all their heavy foliage made my breath catch. Imagine creating something like that. How did the world get to be so beautifully complex?

I would paint this view just as soon as I could get my things from my room—and, well, after dinner, which would probably be takeout. It was getting too late to cook.

I caught sight of Gina's shoes walking toward me.

"Hey, welcome home." I turned myself right side up and stood.

"Hi." She joined me on the lawn. "That looks nice, studying outdoors."

"Yeah. It, uh, wasn't so nice indoors."

It took a moment for the confusion in her eyes to clear. She looked at the seemingly innocent, two-bedroom house that served as our mostly happy and wonderfully cheap student home.

"Seriously?" she asked, though her voice was a bit gentle for the word. Gina is too mild to express actual indignation. I'm rather in awe of her mildness at times. "Should we, um, go check it out?"

I nodded. "It's probably not so strong anymore."

When we walked in, I only felt a tiny stress-pressure on the back of my neck. It was so faint, it might have been my memory providing it.

Gina turned to me. "It feels all right," she said, but her uncertain gaze told me she was waiting for my verdict.

"Right," I said, clapping my hands together, my mind filling with mouth-watering images of dumplings and Chow Mein. "How do you feel about Chinese takeout?"

Chapter Five

THE NEXT DAY, Evan entered the statistics lab as I was getting seated. He had gotten help from me on Monday, so I remembered his name. I smiled in reply to his greeting and resisted the urge to rub my sore eye. An acorn had fallen into it while I painted my ant's-eye view of the tree last night after dinner. It didn't really show, or at least it didn't this morning when I checked in the mirror, but it still hurt. Worse, though, was the fact that I had indulged in imagining I was still dating Brody. I had daydreamed about him tenderly tipping my head back to check for any signs of injury. How I missed his gentle attention.

I forced away the thought and focused on Evan. "Did you get a chance to look at the new homework already?" I asked, my voice friendly in spite of my pathetic state of mind.

"Yeah," he said, claiming a five-wheeled chair beside me and fumbling with his book. The lab had the same ergonomic chairs and white tables as our classroom but without the amphitheater setting. A row of computers hugged the wall, and whiteboards surrounded us on all sides as though calling for our surrender. "Yes, um, and I, uh, wanted to look at question 15."

"Okay." I waited for him to find the page in his book. It didn't take long to go over the problem.

"Any other questions?" I asked.

"Yes. Well, no. But actually . . ."

Oh, here it comes. I suddenly recognized his nervousness for what it was.

"Can I take a picture of us?" he asked, his stammering suddenly gone and his gaze more direct than I liked.

Okay, so he wasn't asking me out. His question hung in the air for a few seconds.

"No," I answered. His face fell, and I cleared my throat and added, "but I appreciate that you asked." Believe it or not, I had had guys snap photos of me on the sly without asking for permission.

"Oh. Well. Thanks for the homework help," he said, jumping to his feet. "I'll see you later."

"Yes. Bye." His quick exit strategy underscored the awkwardness, but it also shortened it. He strode to the doorway, stepped aside for Croft to enter, and left.

Croft?

I nearly moaned out loud as he strode toward me, smiling like all was well with the world.

"Hi, Surrey," he called out in a merry voice.

I blinked. "Um. Hi, Croft." What did he have up his sleeve?

He plopped into the seat next to me, and I frowned. How about a little distance?

I should have known he would end up needing help with his statistics homework. Maybe he felt a need to be nice to me while I helped him. He must be busy during the times Tom held lab hours. I squeezed my pencil as though it were a stress ball and hoped this wouldn't take long.

"I want to apologize. I realize the car accident scene scared you, so, sorry about that."

Croft's voice was nonchalant, even amused. I looked up in amazement and found my ears hadn't deceived me. He *was* amused. His dark-blue eyes twinkled as though he still wanted to laugh at the reminder of my performance.

"And I want to invite you to dinner. An apology dinner," he finished with a grin.

No. No way. Where in the world had *that* come from?

Eyeing him as though he had gone crazy, I managed a strangled "No, thanks."

"Why not?"

"There's no need." He probably didn't even plan to apologize at this dinner of his. At least, the apology would likely be no better than what I had just gotten—words without sincerity.

"You should come. I'll redeem myself."

I held back a snort. "Nope, I'm good." I looked down at my textbook and turned a page, hoping he would get the hint and leave.

"How about Friday? Do you have plans?" He paused, but I didn't say anything. "Saturday, then. I'll pick you up at seven."

I frowned. "I'm not interested."

"You pick the place," he said, leaning back in his seat and sounding satisfied with himself. "You want Mexican? Chinese? Thai?"

I sighed and opened my notebook for a study of regression analysis.

"Seriously, anything you want, because this is my apology to you," he said in a magnanimous tone. "Cheap fast food or hundred-dollar steaks, you name it. You can clean out my wallet if it will make you feel better." Another laugh entered his voice at the suggestion as though he were oh-so-clever.

"Fine." I gave him an annoyed sideways glance and held out my hand. "Let me see your wallet."

He laughed so hard the table shook. "You can clean it out at our dinner. Not here."

"Then no, thanks," I repeated.

"Hey, it'll be fun. I just need your address, and we can call it a date."

I set my hands on the table. "You're wasting your time, Croft. You want dinner with someone? Go ask someone else. I can't help you."

"Hi, Dr. Phil," Croft said.

I looked over at the doorway with a start.

"I was just stopping by to see how the lab's going. Are you having trouble with one of the problems, Surrey?" Dr. Phil asked, looking at me in surprise.

I quickly replayed my last few sentences and realized how it would have sounded if he had caught only the tail end.

"No, we've got it. She knows her statistics," Croft answered almost too helpfully.

"Yes, I'm fine," I agreed, although I most certainly *was* having trouble with a problem, and his name was Croft.

Dr. Phil's face cleared. "Surrey was one of my best students," he praised me to Croft. "You can't ask for a better tutor."

"Yeah, she's great." Croft nodded.

Dr. Phil smiled and left.

I turned to Croft. "I'm great? Really? Last week, I was bad-tempered and had no sense of humor, as far as I recall."

His mouth twitched. "That wasn't very nice of me. I may have been wrong."

"You know what else wasn't very nice of you?" I asked, raising my eyebrows in schoolteacher-fashion. "Making that video of me public and humiliating me in front of your thousands of viewers, but I haven't heard you try to apologize about *that* yet."

"Tens of thousands," he corrected. "But I couldn't *not* have made it public. It was for a hidden camera show, and your reaction was classic. Now, seven on Saturday works for you, right?"

"The only way I'll go to your apology dinner," I said with an air of great sacrifice, "is if you're not present for it."

"That would defeat the purpose." He grinned and clasped his hands behind his head.

I bit back a groan. I provided amusement while he apologized for half of his crime, and I provided amusement while I refused to go to his blasted dinner. Clearly, it was time to get rid of him.

"Did you need help on the homework?" I asked with fake cheerfulness, only to continue before he could answer. "No? Okay, you can go."

He sat forward. "Actually, I would like some help. Can I see your book?" He grabbed the end and pulled it toward himself.

I grabbed the other end. "Where's *your* book?"

"I didn't bring it."

"You need help on the homework, and you didn't bring your book?" I summarized slowly, unwilling to pretend with him that he had come to the lab for help.

"Do you make everyone who needs help bring their own book?" he asked, all innocence. "Now, let me see." He moved his hand down the page, and I regretted keeping him from pulling it closer to himself. It was still mostly in front of me, and he was right up against my elbow.

"Yes, question 4," he said and proceeded to read it out loud. I was certain this was the first time he had looked at it.

I flicked a glance at my sheet of paper next to the book. "That's not part of the homework assignment. You were assigned questions 1-3, 5, 7 . . ." I stopped, not wanting to give him the rest of the list. It would help him ask valid questions when in reality he was only looking for excuses to stay.

"But the more of these problems I do, the better I'll understand the material. See, I don't believe in just getting a grade. I think it's important to learn."

Rather than respond to his convenient bit of philosophy, I began to talk through the problem. I stayed professional, making him look up the formulas needed and helping him figure it out rather than explaining it all up front. After all, though he was a pain, I was still a TA, and I would do my job well.

He stretched it out, looking at all perceived and non-perceived angles of the problem until we had gone over it so thoroughly that I felt terrible for whatever dead horses he had beaten in his life.

Then, beaming, he pointed out another problem in my book for us to tackle.

It was a true feat that I made it through the hour without conking my hidden camera perpetrator on the head. I hoped he had given up on taking me to dinner when my "no" was still a "no" at the end of the lab, but something about the cheery way he bid me farewell left me worried.

When I got home after my last class, Willie was in his usual spot outside.

"Where have you been?" I demanded.

"We were at Lake Powell yesterday, boating." I looked closer and realized he did look sunburned.

He shifted and stood. "Uh, I should go water the . . ."

"Sit," I commanded, and he sat back down.

I crossed my arms. "Tell me what you did on Monday."

He tried to read my expression. Then he gave up and shrugged. "I ran into that Croft-guy on my skateboard and fell and pretended to pass out."

"How did you know where to find him?"

Willie's smile was mischievous. "I got you to tell me the name of the class he's in and what days you meet. Then I looked up Stat 230 online. There was a Monday-Wednesday-Friday class at nine and one at eleven in the same classroom. I didn't even have to hack anything to see when or where they held the class." He looked a little insulted at the lack of challenge to his abilities, but I could see he enjoyed sharing his genius strategy. "I gave my mom an excuse on Monday and sneaked off to BYU. I was guessing I needed to find the nine o'clock class. Of course I knew from the YouTube channel what the guy looked like—you did tell me he was the one that pretended to call 911—and I hung around the classroom and followed him out of the building when the class ended. Then I came up behind him on the skateboard."

"Who'd have guessed it?" I murmured. "Not bad."

He acknowledged the compliment with a pleased nod. "He was being a pain to you. Someone needed to do it."

I paused. "Thanks."

He shrugged.

"We're not allowed to skateboard on campus," was my only admonishment.

Willie grinned. "I'll keep that in mind. He's not still mocking you, is he?"

"No-o." Unless one counted the fact that I was a big joke to him. Everything I said and did was a cause for amusement today. Still, he hadn't seemed scornful the way he had last week. "I actually saw him today, and he acted different this time." It was the truth, although I was being evasive about the details. Croft's half-baked apology might even have been delivered because of Willie's prank, although I had no idea what had made Croft try to ask me out.

"Good. Just so long as he's not bothering you."

* * *

YEAH, that would have been nice.

The bell had just announced the beginning of my lab hour the next day when, guess who, Croft walked in.

"Hi, Surrey," he again greeted me with enthusiasm.

I stared stiffly at him.

He scooted out the chair next to me and plopped down by my elbow. "Look, I brought my book," he said, putting it on the table.

I looked at it and back at him, annoyed at his closeness. "Are you planning on opening it?" I asked with a faint hope he might have come to get legitimate homework help today rather than to torment me.

"No, but I brought it. Aren't you proud of me?"

I narrowed my eyes. "I'd be prouder if you didn't show up."

"But I *had* to show up." His expression was too serious to be sincere. "I had to tell you Café Rio's special yesterday was chicken tostada." He paused for effect. "Unfortunately, I have no idea what it'll be on Saturday when we go."

"I'm *not* going to an apology dinner, so drop it already," I said angrily.

Croft leaned into my space to look past my textbook. "You draw?"

My notebook lay open, one page full of formulas and the other showing a sketch of a woman in buckskin clothes.

I reached out and flipped over the page, not caring for Croft to see the drawing and learn anything about me.

"Nice," he said, leaning over further still, and I became aware that the page now exposed was a drawing of maple leaves blowing in the wind.

I growled and picked up the notebook, closing it so that only the undecorated cover was visible.

"What types of art do you identify most with?" he asked, as though I were open to discussing my passion with him.

"Gee, I don't know, maybe the Bell curve." I tapped his statistics book with my finger. "Speaking of which, what homework do you need help with?"

Croft got more comfortable in his chair. "What I really need help with is finding out what kind of food you like."

"I'm not going to your pity dinner, so stop wasting your time," I said in exasperation.

"Apology dinner," he corrected, his eyes sharpening. "But fine, we can make it a dinner date instead."

I threw my hands in the air, and my pencil went flying. "I'm *definitely* not going on a date with you." I ignored the castoff, which landed near a computer.

He gave me a curious look. "Why not? I promise you would have a good time."

I shook my head at his audacity. "I only date nice guys. And *you* are *not* a nice guy."

His expression didn't change. "I admit my performance wasn't stellar last week, but you'll find I'm not that bad."

"You don't understand. You're not my type. I date guys who are *nice, kind, good*," I told him.

"Ouch," he said, but a grin grew on his face, and he straightened in his seat. "Okay, so you've dated nice guys. But here's a question: Where are they now?"

Talk about ouch. I didn't know the exact whereabouts of Killian at the moment, but Brody and Jesse were in town with their fiancé and wife, respectively; Frank the poet was on his honeymoon; and Keaton was somewhere in Hawaii with his wife and baby. Not that Croft needed to know any of that.

"Obviously, none of them have worked out so far," Croft said, the epitome of sensitivity, if you'll excuse my sarcasm. "I think it's time you tried someone different. 'Nice' might not be your type at all."

I stared. How could he be so obstinate, rude, and presumptuous all at once?

"Hey, are you the TA?" asked a girl's voice.

I looked up in relief. "Yes. Stat 230?"

"Yes."

"Come on over," I invited, barely keeping myself from jumping up to hug her.

I gloried in the time I spent helping her. She was a model student. She had brought her book, she knew which problems were assigned, and she had already struggled with the questions she needed help on. Of course, normally I would have expected all three of any student, but today, I felt like she deserved an award.

When she left, there were only a few minutes left of lab time. I inwardly praised her to the heavens and wished she might have stayed just a little longer.

"That was enlightening," Croft said. "I think I'll do very well in this class."

I sucked in my breath. He wouldn't keep coming, would he?

"Don't hijack my lab hours," I ordered, my mind whirling as I tried to come up with a way to stop him. "You can do fine in this class without coming here. I dare you." My mind caught hold of the idea. "Right. I challenge you to prove it."

He sat up with interest. "You're into dares?"

I blinked. "No. Yes." That was beside the point. "I'm daring you to ace the class without coming to my lab. Remember, I'm grading your home-work. I'll see how you do."

He grinned. I was beginning to realize he had a very limited repertoire of facial expressions. I had seen little besides a grin on his face yesterday and today.

"You should dare me to do something else," he told me. "Something worthy of a good, entertaining hidden camera prank."

My temper flashed. "I'm serious, Croft. I don't want you around."

Miraculously, he was standing—although maybe it wasn't that miracu-lous, with the bell about to ring. "I gotta go. But I'm serious, too. You've been dating the wrong type."

I opened my mouth but couldn't get a word out in my anger as he walked from the room.

Livid, I scrambled to my feet and rushed to the doorway. Croft was still visible down the hall.

"I'm not interested," I yelled after him. "So drop it!"

He gave me a shrug and a smile, and then he left.

I turned back to the lab and remembered to collect my pencil from next to the computer. By the time I had gathered my things, I felt calmer. In fact, I wondered if we hadn't reached some sort of closure or truce. Maybe Croft would take me up on my dare. Even if he didn't, there had been something in his last words that seemed final. My blood boiled as I remembered his words. *You've been dating the wrong type.* But if that was his parting blow, maybe he would leave me be from now on. He probably thought I would stew over the words, turn them over in my mind, and start thinking he might be right. He would want to give me space to think about it. He might even expect me to seek him out once I decided he was right.

Fortunately, he wasn't right. What girl shouldn't date a nice guy, unless she herself was nowhere near nice? If he meant to imply I was mean, well, that was just . . . just another thing that shouldn't shock me, coming from him. I gripped my backpack's straps until my knuckles turned white. He was the worst kind of jerk. He was the jerkiest jerk. The most obnoxious . . .

Okay, I needed to calm down. Blowing out my breath, I left the lab and the building for the outdoors. Sitting down on a stone wall overhung by a weeping beech tree up against the Knight Building, I set my alarm to go off in ten minutes. Ten minutes to stare at the ivy hedge and fall foliage across from me. Ten minutes to breathe deep. Ten minutes to pick out smells in the air: wood chips, grass, and faint smoke. California's wildfires were going strong, sending their smoke across the mountains to Utah.

I heard kissing nearby just as my alarm went off. Embarrassed, I kept my head down while I turned off the sound.

"See you soon," said an enamored, masculine voice.

"Love you," a sweet, womanly voice replied.

"Love you," repeated the masculine voice which, I discovered to my displeasure, sounded familiar.

I looked up as he walked my way after saying goodbye to—what was her name again?—oh, yes, Sage. His wife of more than a year.

I gave him a small wave.

"Surr," Killian said in surprise. He was the only one of my boyfriends who had taken liberties with the length of my name, and I had loved it. He looked just as I remembered, his jaw giving him a certain confident quality, his lips full . . . not that I should notice *that* at this point. I flushed as he continued, "How are you?"

"Good." I mean, I sort of was. My ten minutes had done me good. Still, I wouldn't mind slipping away from him. He had once bought me a ring, after all.

"Did you decide to stick with statistics?"

It had been a while since we'd dated and nearly gotten engaged. I had declared my major shortly before we met.

"Yes," I answered, realizing he was set on having a conversation. Friendly to a fault, as always. "I didn't know you were still on campus. Did you decide to go for your master's?"

"I did." He smiled. "Are you still dating Jesse?"

I winced. "Um, no."

"Oh, really? I thought for sure you two would make it."

"Yeah, no. He found someone else." I shifted awkwardly. Why did I seem to have this conversation so often?

"Sorry." He looked at me for a minute, and I shifted again. His silence wasn't that of a person who couldn't think of what to say next. It was the silence of someone who was uncertain as to whether to share their next thought. I remembered with a pang several instances when he had looked at me like this, and I had been honored every time he decided to trust me with what was on his mind.

He shook his head. "I was just thinking . . ."

When he didn't finish his sentence, I prompted, "Thinking what?"

He bit his lip. "Just . . . can I give you some advice?"

My eyes nearly popped out. Advice? What for? *Dating* advice? What was I doing wrong?

"Your no-kissing rule . . . You might want to relax it," he said, leaving me blinking.

"Relax?" I asked weakly. This was the rule that would have me kiss no one but my husband. I'd made the rule when I was ten and the Klepperts spoke at a church fireside and shared their love story. The Klepperts were a short, elderly couple in my ward back home, and I adored watching them on Sundays. They were so sweet with each other. When I learned they had waited to kiss until they got engaged, I decided to do the same.

"Yes." He looked nervous. "See, I, uh, don't think I was as into you as either of us thought. And I think it's because we never touched. We never kissed. That binds you together as a couple, you know."

"We *did* touch," I protested.

He gave me a blank look. "No, we didn't."

"We hugged. Didn't we?" I waited for him to realize I was right. We had hugged at the end of dates. We had sat close when we were next to each other. Sometimes he had touched my arm while we talked. Sometimes I had touched his.

"That's true. But just think about it, maybe. I didn't realize it then, but now I do." He looked sincere, if uncomfortable. "You can only go so far in a relationship without the kissing."

Well, my mind was spinning now.

"I thought—I thought you were fine with me not wanting to kiss until I got engaged," I said, not quite sure why I was pressing the issue. It would be easier to end the conversation. But his comment had come out of left field, and I couldn't reconcile myself to it. He had agreed to my rule, and I had never known it was a problem for him.

"Right, I thought so, too, but I realized later I really wasn't." He sounded apologetic. "The idea of not kissing until you get engaged, it's— it's very sweet and romantic, but it really only happens in Disney."

I bristled. "And in the eighteenth century, you forgot to mention that." He had just called my standard fictional. I had to bring up the eighteenth century before he also called it hopelessly old-fashioned. At least I beat him to it.

He grimaced, aware that I wasn't happy. "It doesn't work in real, modern life."

That wasn't true. I remembered Brody had been pleased when I told him my rule. In fact, he himself had wanted a rule like that.

At least that was what he had told me. Doubt niggled in my mind. Had he been pretending? Or, like Killian, had he believed he wanted this rule, only to later become discontent with it?

"Just, when you date the next guy," Killian said, "maybe try it. I think it'll help."

I bit my lip, unhappy that he had made me question Brody's positive reaction, not to mention question the fact that any guy might be okay with my rule.

No, I thought, setting my shoulders. I refused to be swayed. *I* liked my rule, and that was what mattered when it came to *my* dating life.

"Thanks for the tip," I said slowly, meeting his gaze. "I probably won't follow it, though."

It took another moment for him to speak. "Fair enough," he said lightly to break the tension. "Sorry if I pushed my nose in where it doesn't belong. I guess I'll see you around."

Unfortunately, he probably would. As for me, I was getting tired of being on the same campus as most of my exes.

Chapter Six

In case you were wondering, I didn't re-think my life that weekend.

I didn't change my mind on the no-kissing rule, as Killian had tried to inspire me to do. I also didn't decide I had been dating the wrong kind of guy, as Croft had tried to convince me.

What I did do was paint my heart out, get a bunch of homework done, and bask in the wonderful idea that Croft Taylor had left me to make my own conclusions and wasn't coming back anytime soon.

That illusion was shattered on Monday.

"Do you have any food allergies?" was his greeting as he walked in at the beginning of lab hour. "No, I know." He stopped and snapped his fingers. "You're vegetarian. No, you're *vegan*." His eyes widened in horror, and he continued in a pleading voice, "We don't have to go to dinner, you know. We could go roller skating in Orem instead."

That's when I knew he wasn't giving up.

I had lab hours on Mondays, Wednesdays, and Thursdays, and somehow Croft's schedule happened to be clear at all three times. Let me tell you, being badgered by him three times a week would test the patience of a saint. Although he didn't try every time to talk me into a date, it was annoying just to have him around acting like we were friends.

Fortunately, the other parts of my weekly schedule kept me sane. I stayed on top of my homework (mostly). I made great progress on my camouflage gown. I managed to paint Gina's cheeks in her portrait so they looked just like hers did in real life. This was a step forward for me. While I could paint people who looked real, for some reason, I struggled to make them look exactly like whoever acted as my model.

I also knocked several items off my List of Ten Things, although mimicking an animal took a backburner as I still couldn't decide which animal to imitate.

I know, I'm faced with such tough life decisions.

The semester progressed, and dating—well, didn't. I got cornered once and almost said yes to a guy, but a friend of his interrupted, and I escaped. I probably shouldn't have been avoiding men, but I still wasn't over the loss of Brody, and besides, I wasn't keen on falling in love again only to add another guy to my growing list of exes.

Hey, I'm a statistician. I've noticed the pattern in my dating life.

I could have made a timeline graph of my heartbreaks, but that would be self-pity overdone.

As the statistics 230 homework became more involved, more students made regular use of the lab. It was almost cozy when we had a group working together, like the Monday I found myself helping two girls and one guy besides the ever-present Croft.

As usual, Croft had come early enough to snag a seat by me. The other guy, Rick, sat on my left side, and Alicia and Jen were opposite us. The girls' arrival had brightened up the place, or so it seemed to me.

"I just never thought I'd find myself doing computer programming, but here I am, coding in R, and it's not that hard," Alicia was saying.

"That's because the teacher lets us use his code," Jen noted with a smile.

"Yeah, but still, we have to change things to make it work. It's just really cool. Now, which part of the table is the mean square error, again?" She squinted at the two-way ANOVA table in her textbook.

"It's next to the sum square." I pointed it out and tested her by asking, "Do you have enough information to calculate it from the other numbers?"

She studied it for a bit. Then she brightened. "Yes. I just divide the sum of squared errors by the degrees of freedom for the error. Right?"

"Right." It was fun to see her figure it out.

"I don't think we'll be doing these calculations by hand once we're out in the field," Rick said. "Everything will be done on the computer."

"Unless you're a teacher," Jen pointed out.

"True, then you'll really have to know everything," he agreed.

Croft joined the conversation. "I keep wanting to do a classroom sketch for my channel, something where the teacher doesn't know he's being filmed, but I can't come up with an idea for what should happen."

Alicia giggled. "Your sketches are really good. *You* were great in that accident scene," she told me. "I would have been in shock."

I *had* been in shock. That's why I had done dumb things like ask, "Where are you hurt?" three or four times in a row. It was one of the quotes I still heard from people on campus when they snickered about me with their friends.

The girls left after a while, but Croft and Rick stubbornly stayed behind, and the conversation quickly took a personal turn.

"Do *you* plan to be a teacher?" Rick asked me. "You're great at explaining things."

"Thanks. I don't think I'll be a teacher, though. There are a lot of statistics jobs out there to choose from." If dating ever did lead to my getting married, I still hoped to become a full-time mom.

"Which of those jobs would you choose?" Croft wanted to know.

I wasn't keen to answer questions from him, but I couldn't ignore him with Rick present, so I said, "Scientific research sounds interesting."

"Science is cool. Do you like being outdoors?" Rick brought my focus back to him.

"And do you like outdoor sports?" Croft's question made me swivel my head in his direction.

"I know a great outdoor ice skating rink," Rick said, and I felt like I was caught in a game of ping-pong as I faced him again. I also felt like I knew what was coming as he asked, "Do you skate?"

"Do you play ice hockey?" Croft broke in, grinning as he asked the ridiculous question. Not that it was ridiculous for a girl to play ice hockey, just for *me* to do so, what with my propensity for accidents.

"I don't," I said, facing him again.

"You don't what? Skate?" Rick demanded, returning my attention to him.

"I don't really do either." Next time Rick came, he had better sit on the same side of the table as Croft. Turning my head from side to side for this conversation was driving me crazy.

"But I'm sure you could." Croft turned in his seat to face me. "There's a skate night in the basement of the Wilk on Friday. I think they're holding it just for us."

"I can teach you to ice skate," Rick said after frowning at Croft.

"I'm not much of an athlete," I protested, trying to think of how I could get out of his fast-approaching invitation. He seemed nice enough, but he wasn't Brody.

"If I'm holding you, you won't fall," Rick promised, his voice a little deeper as he leaned in. "I'll teach you, and we can get ice cream after. What do you think?"

I bit my lip, my mind working frantically to buy time. The problem was that my time had run out. The invitation had been issued, and I couldn't in good conscience say no when Rick looked so hopeful.

"Surrey isn't really dating right now," Croft said, leaning in from the other side. "She's nursing a broken heart."

I jerked in shock and stared at Croft, my mouth opening and closing. He must have made that up on the spot. *I* certainly hadn't told him any such thing.

"Really?" Rick asked, sounding uncertain for the first time. "You're not dating right now?"

I was still gaping at Croft, whose eyes were dancing, but I had the presence of mind to answer, "I'm not."

"Oh. Sorry. If, um, you want to talk about it with someone . . ." Rick's voice trailed off.

With great effort, I turned my head in his direction. He didn't get the chance to finish his thought, though.

"Yeah, it's bad." Croft sighed. "I was hoping a skate night would do her good, but it just isn't happening right now."

Rick looked to me for confirmation. My throat tight with the things I wanted to say to Croft, I nodded.

"Okay. I'm sorry and, uh, happy to help if I can." He stood, gave me a last searching look, and left.

I turned on Croft. "How dare you say such a thing!"

"Well, aren't you?" he asked innocently.

"Aren't I what?" I demanded.

"Nursing a broken heart?"

I gripped my pencil with a chokehold. "The reason I'm not dating you is because I don't *want* to date you, and the reason I'm not dating *him* is because I don't *want* to date him." Or rather, the reason I wasn't dating him was because Croft had given me an excuse.

Croft shrugged. "Good thing I got rid of him, then, right? And how's this. We go out for hot chocolate tomorrow, and then we go skating. What do you say?"

Dr. Phil popped in before I could give Croft a piece of my mind. Now, this would have been a prime time for me to tell my professor that one of his students was harassing me. Trust me, I had considered complaining to him on more than one occasion. However, something stopped me from mentioning it during the brief conversation that ensued.

Maybe it was because Croft *had* in fact spared me from agreeing to a date with Rick, although his method made me fume. For that matter, his constant presence at lab hours had likely stopped other guys from asking me out, asking to take pictures of me, or asking whatever else they might think of. The only guy who hadn't given off romantic vibes so far was Walter, who always wore a striped shirt and a friendly smile. I was pretty sure he already had a girl in his life.

If Croft hadn't been at my side every Monday, Wednesday and Thursday, I would probably have been asked out by several guys from the class by now, and though I was nervous about dating, I might have said yes in case it led to something. Or I might have said yes to spare their feelings. Croft, on the other hand, I had no qualms about saying no to. Nothing held me back from rejecting him over and over again, and so his presence, while annoying to the fullest, was at least safe.

Dr. Phil left after some small talk, and I let out a long sigh.

"How about a walk on the beach? Meaning, of course, Utah Lake." Croft was back at it already.

"An apology walk?" I asked sarcastically.

He chuckled. "No, just a date walk. I'd like to get to know you better, maybe in a different setting."

"Why?" I certainly wouldn't be any nicer to him in a different setting.

He paused, looked at me—and cracked up. "Because you make me so happy," he said, wiping away tears.

Obviously, he just wanted to spend time with me so he could laugh at me. "Do you know how much women despise Mr. Collins from *Pride and Prejudice*?" I asked. "He refuses to take Elizabeth's no as a no."

Croft smirked. "There are other things about him they don't like. If that was his only flaw, he wouldn't be so bad. I'm not so bad, either, and I improve upon acquaintance."

Would he take nothing seriously?

"You could improve five, ten percent, and you'd still be terrible," I growled, trying to drive home the point that he had problems.

"Ouch," he said, but he was holding back laughter. "I'll improve at least eighty percent. A hundred," he upped it.

I shook my head in frustration. He still didn't get it. "I'm not sure percent is even the right mathematical term to use," I huffed. "In order for you to improve percentwise, there needs to have been something good to start with. Zero times one hundred is still zero."

"Ouch again," he choked out, but now he was really laughing—full-throated, eventually body-rocking laugher—and something strange was happening. Instead of the mean satisfaction I had expected to feel as I impressed upon him how much of a jerk he was, his reaction made me feel . . . clever. Entertaining. It was disarming.

Well, I wasn't sticking around any longer. From my sitting position, I grabbed my backpack off the floor and placed it on the table with a thump. "I'm leaving."

"You can't go. This is your lab hour."

I pointed at the clock. "The hour's almost over."

"Almost," he repeated. "There's still half a minute. What if someone needed you in that last half a minute?"

I stood. Or rather, I pushed out my chair and shoved my feet against the floor to stand, but the chair slid out from underneath me, and the floor rushed toward me.

Croft caught my arm and helped me regain my balance.

I took a moment to catch my breath. "Uh, thanks," I said and pulled away.

"It's a sign that you're not allowed to leave early." He choked back his amusement. "Fifteen seconds left."

I scowled. "Do you think *everything* is funny?"

"Almost everything."

At this point, I couldn't imagine anything not making him laugh.

"What things do you not find funny?" I demanded. If running someone over with a car was humorous to him, I hated to think what *wasn't*.

His eyes opened wide. "Is that a personal question? You want to get to know me?"

The bell rang.

"Time's up," I said and demonstrated my complete disinterest by leaving without a backward glance.

* * *

THAT WEDNESDAY, I attended Dr. Phil's class for the first time since the beginning of the semester. The room called to me, whispering about an increase in my paycheck and the opportunity to review the material I was helping the students with. I could handle Croft being in the class, right? He might be more annoying than a drummer at a headache clinic, but at least he no longer treated me with derision.

He didn't sit near the front like he had that first week.

"Hey, you're back," he exclaimed, and I looked up in time to see him move my backpack off the wheeled chair beside me. Before I could say anything, he took the seat for himself.

"You can't take that spot," I told him.

"Why not? No one was sitting there." He opened up my notebook in front of him and started flipping through it. I had spread my things out nicely, reserving the spot next to me so no one would take it. The guy had no respect for anything.

"Give me that." My voice wasn't angry or annoyed or scolding. I heard nothing but long-suffering in it. Croft was exhausting. I considered slapping his hand away from my notebook, but I couldn't seem to muster the energy. Instead, I took hold of my notebook, gave him a moment to let go, and then pulled it back to me. What were things coming to when I couldn't fight back or chastise him like he deserved?

"It's nice to see you here. How's your friend Willie?"

I looked at him with tired suspicion. "He's doing fine." In fact, Willie had been quite animated during our last conversation as he talked about the space mission simulator he visited last week. The thought made me smile.

When I realized Croft was watching me, my smile faded. "I didn't send him after you, you know, when he fooled you with his skateboard stunt."

"I know. The kid has a mind of his own."

"Yeah, and in his case, that's a good thing."

"What do you mean?" he protested, laughing. "You don't think it's a bad thing in my case, do you?"

I faced forward and prayed for Dr. Phil to start the lesson.

"I have lots of good qualities, Surrey. Spend time with me, and you'll find out."

"I *have* spent time with you. Tons of time. Endless time." My tone of long-suffering was back, but this time, it was accompanied with a little more fighting spirit. I wasn't broken yet.

He laughed and started to say something, but just then, my prayer was answered, and Dr. Phil welcomed the class.

"For example, I can be very attentive in class," Croft whispered to me.

"Then be," I whispered out of the corner of my mouth.

"I will. You'll be impressed."

He pulled out his notes and began to write. I watched Dr. Phil, but in my mind's eye, I saw again how highhandedly Croft had stolen the seat next to me after I had prepped to keep anyone from doing just that. Again, I couldn't muster up a sufficient amount of anger at the memory.

Croft ripped out a sheet of paper and pushed it under my arm.

I gritted my teeth and stared straight ahead. I believe I held out for at least ten seconds. After demonstrating my incredible self-control, I looked down.

At the top of the page, he had written the title "Good attributes of Croft" and underlined it. The rest of the paper had bullet points, with just the first one filled out: "Can pay attention."

As if to prove it, Croft hardly took his eyes off Dr. Phil during class except to take notes. I was glad since it gave me a breather.

He had put far too many bullet points on his page. *I* certainly wouldn't fill them out with good characteristics even if he had that many. I was tempted to write "blank," "nothing," "still nothing," and so on, but it seemed a little too mean. In the end, I let it be and pushed the paper back to him when class ended.

"No, that's for you," he said, "because I'm . . ." He bent over the paper to write, then straightened and read the word out loud, "generous."

"Hnnh," I said, rolling my eyes at the ceiling and making a noise you normally only hear when someone is constipated. I was definitely ready to get away. I needed a break before I would have to face him again in the lab two hours from now.

Stuffing his list in my backpack along with my other things just to get him off my back, I left, ignoring his cheerful goodbye.

How was I going to keep doing this?

Chapter Seven

Fortunately, the next day was Gina-day!

I guess it was also Jesse-day, but sitting with him in my New Testament class had turned out not to be as bad as I had feared. I still appreciated the insights I gained from class and from my home-study and especially the Spirit I felt as we moved toward the poignant end of the Gospels. Plus, half the time, I managed to sit somewhere that wasn't next to Jesse.

And when I came home, it was Gina-day!

"You're here," I exclaimed as I entered the living room.

"Of course." She looked up from her homework with a smile.

Now, don't get me wrong. Gina-day didn't mean we partied or went somewhere fun together. Usually, it meant doing homework side-by-side, though if I needed a break, I might paint while she worked. The point was, I didn't come home to an empty house for once. I wasn't alone until dinnertime or bedtime.

And I did like my roommate.

I was slapping folders onto the table when Gina cleared her throat. "Um, you've never shown your art publicly, right?"

I paused. "No. Why?"

"I was thinking you might be interested in something I heard about today. I could be wrong, of course," she hurried to say, squirming over her presumptuousness.

My heart sped up as I imagined the stress of putting my art out there. While I did hope to show it at some point, I wouldn't know where to begin when it came to advertising and legalities. I didn't want to deal with any of it yet, not while I was still a student and could pretend not to be an adult.

"It's a fundraiser in Phoenix," Gina said. "They're hosting a national fundraiser to help children in low-income families make it to college and to provide them scholarships once they make it there. They'll auction off paintings, and anyone can paint and donate their work to the auction—both professional and amateur artists. Everything is practically guaranteed to get sold for the cause."

My breath hitched, and I dropped back on the couch. "Really?"

"Yes. What do you think?"

"Do they have a website with more information?"

She lit up at my interest. "I'll look it up now."

We huddled around her computer, looking through the event summary.

"It's in January." I may have bounced a little. "I could do that. I could create at least two paintings by then. Maybe three or four. But what should I paint? It says anything goes. What would be better, do you think: Painting children so that whoever buys it will have a special reminder of who they helped, or painting something totally different to appeal to whatever interests the buyers may have?"

Gina pursed her lips. "I don't know."

"Because if it's going to be children, well, then it's children, but if it's anything, I might come up with a couple of world-contrast pictures, like the woman in the camouflage dress."

"Couldn't you do a contrast piece with a child?" Gina asked. "For example, paint a boy with part of him dressed in hand-me-downs and the other half in graduation robes?"

I cocked my head, imagining it. "Maybe so."

"Or maybe not," she hurried to say. "Maybe it's too close to home, or insensitive or in bad taste, to target directly what the auction is for."

"No, I think you may be on to something," I said. "I'd make it an acrylic. But I definitely want some oil paintings, too. I'll have to think about this."

"Didn't Mr. Claw have a painting in his room of a girl who wore a dress that melted into rags at the bottom? That's sort of the same thing, right?"

Mr. Claw was our high school art teacher, but I struggled to remember the painting. "Do you mean the one with flames at the bottom?"

She frowned. "I thought it was rags."

"No, it . . . Hold on. I think you can see it in the yearbook."

I dashed into my bedroom and returned with my copy of our senior yearbook. Rooming with someone from my high school meant it was worth it to have a yearbook on hand for occasional reminiscing despite the hated picture of myself on page 22.

Flipping past the picture of *Sexiest Senior Girl*, I found the page that showed our high school art teacher leaning back in his chair with his arms out as if to show off the classroom behind him. The message he so often repeated to his students was written below the picture in quotation marks: "If you can't see something, try closing your eyes."

I pointed at a painting on the wall behind him, and Gina leaned in. "Oh yeah, it *is* flames."

I looked closer. "Actually, it could be either. I guess it's up to the interpretation of the viewer."

Gina nodded and looked at me with twinkling eyes. "Do you remember when the art room was on fire?"

"Oh my, yes. Paper flames all over the floor."

"And on the desks."

"And taped to the walls."

"All because Mr. Claw praised someone's papier-mâché fireplace so highly."

"I'm so glad he let it stay for a while. It fed the imagination, being surrounded by fire." I sighed with pleasure at the reminder. Then I straightened and jumped to my feet. "We should do something like that here."

Gina hesitated. "I'm not sure I want to pretend the house is on fire."

"Water, then." I waved a hand and turned in a circle. "We could fill the room with waves."

Gina giggled, which was all the encouragement I needed. I ran to my room for paper, came out with my arms full, turned and ran back to stack markers on top of my armful, rushed out to the living room, then realized I needed tape and scissors and flew back to my room, stumbling in front of my bed and dropping everything on it.

I might want to take it slower this time, I told myself. Gently stacking everything together, I walked from my room. The doorbell rang, and Gina went to answer it while I kept my steps small and pretty and my back straight, dropping nothing and stumbling over nothing. Maybe I should add this to next semester's List of Ten Things: Learn to walk like a Victorian-era lady.

"Come on in," Gina's voice said, and I looked over to see our ministering brothers follow her inside. Now, in The Church of Jesus Christ of Latter-day Saints, members are all assigned to minister to a few people in their ward, which means being there for them and helping them live their covenants with God. Gina and I, like most BYU students, attended a ward full of young single adults. One of our ministering brothers was a freshman, and the other had recently graduated.

I had forgotten we had invited them over, but no matter. Now, how would a Victorian lady welcome two gentlemen into her home? Curtsying?

My gaze fell on the yearbook on the couch. Oh, book of mortification! I threw my things in the air, and as they rained down around me, I grabbed the book and stuffed it under a couch cushion, then sat down on top of it and looked up at Larry and Gordon. A marker rolled under the table, noisy in the now nearly silent room. Gordon gave me a weird look, and Larry glanced at the craft paper strewn across the floor in front of me.

At least I had kept them from seeing my yearbook and possibly asking to see our pictures. It would be just my luck for them to come across page 22.

"How did you like soccer night last Monday?" I asked brightly and stopped another rolling marker with my foot.

* * *

I ALMOST MANAGED to not sit with Croft in class the next day. Almost.

After wrangling the seat next to me, he wrote out another couple of good attributes on his list, and I scoffed and ignored him as much as I could. Since I hadn't brought back the first list of his attributes, he started a new one, which he put in his own backpack at the end of class.

When I wandered outside with an hour to spare before my next class, I hoped to find a quiet place where I could dream up ideas for the art auction fundraiser. First, though, I would have to wait for the between-classes stampede to end. I felt like Mufasa as the wildebeests—I mean the students—carried me to the Joseph F. Smith Building, where I managed to stop next to a low wall surrounding an island of foliage. Several of these islands dotted the area in front of the JFSB, giving students a place to sit and relax. A few people stood around the island chatting or, like me, waiting for the crowds to thin. The person in front of me stepped into the fray, clearing my view of another guy, who now turned around.

I caught my breath as I found myself facing Brody.

"Surrey," he exclaimed. "It's good to see you."

Somehow, I managed a smile. "Hi, Brody. Hi, Hanna," I said to the girl next to him, who returned my weak smile with a bright one of her own and a hop of excitement.

"How are you?" she asked brightly, her attention on me in a way that made me feel like there was nothing on her mind but me at the moment. I don't know how they did it, but it was a special talent both she and Brody possessed.

I almost felt embarrassed to answer simply, "I'm good." I sort of wanted to offer more information, just because she was so eager, but I could think of nothing else to say besides the fact that I would have liked to be in her place, engaged to Brody.

"How are your classes? Do you still live with Gina?" she persisted.

"I do. We live in the same place as before." I looked at Brody and back. "I got your wedding invitation."

"Good." Brody stepped closer, and I was struck with memories of sitting on the wall of one of these very islands with him, watching his animated face while we talked, his arm behind me in the grass, his gaze softening whenever he looked at me.

"I'm actually really glad we saw you," he told me. "The reception is getting postponed. We don't know when it will be, but we wanted you to know."

"Oh. Okay."

"We'll send you another invitation when we know the new date," Hanna said. "Or Brody will call and let you know."

"Not that you *have* to go, of course," Brody hurried to reassure me. "It's completely up to you, but I'd really like it if you came."

"So would I," said Hanna, her voice warm.

I nodded, trying to shake the feeling of being wanted when I knew we could never be close in the way I wished to be. "Um, why is it getting postponed?"

Hanna hugged herself, and Brody put his arm around her in concern, his attention now fully focused on his fiancée. Oh, it almost slayed me to see him look at her the way he had used to look at me. That gaze had made me think he was completely devoted to me and that nothing would ever separate us.

"It's my uncle," Hanna began before her eyes filled with tears and her voice broke. "He's a pilot. He got in an accident. He's out of his coma now but still in bad condition in the hospital. He's always been like an older brother to me." She steadied her voice. "It may be a while before he's well enough to attend, but we want him there."

"Of course you do," I said, my voice small. I couldn't help but notice how she leaned into Brody. I remembered him holding me on a frigid but sunny winter day last February while I cried after seeing Willie's cat get run over. Brody had stroked my hair and murmured comfort to me. I had felt loved, adored, treasured.

My head cleared in a flash, and a wave of guilt rushed over me for thinking about myself instead of Hanna's heartache. "I'm so sorry, Hanna," I exclaimed.

The next moment, my eyes widened in shock as she flung her arms around me.

"Thank you, Surrey." She stepped back, wiping her eyes. "At least he's past the worst of it. Or . . . he's survived. I think he has a long, hard road ahead. Anyway." She took a couple of deep breaths, and her voice returned to about half its usual cheer. "We'll send you a new invitation if we have time to print them up when we decide on a new date."

"Otherwise, we'll call," Brody said, his hand resting lightly on Hanna's back. Was it because that was what she needed, or was it because he didn't want to make me uncomfortable by being more touchy with her? Or was I merely imagining it, suffering from a sick sense of hope that he wasn't as committed to her as he seemed and that there was still a chance for us?

It was an awful thought that I might be hoping for their engagement to end. Hanna didn't deserve that at all. I did hope for things to work out between them. Didn't I?

"What's your favorite class this semester?" Hanna asked, at last sounding like her usual sprightly self. I was relieved for her, which must mean I did want her happiness, which made me relieved for me.

Figuring she needed the change in topic, I answered, "Oh, I don't know. I really like the math and statistics classes when I don't get stumped on the work. I love my art class, but I'd better, since I'm taking it for fun. We just learned about Japanese ink paintings." My enthusiasm grew with my answer. "And New Testament is so good."

"She likes school and learning new things," Brody summarized with a laugh, his eyes dancing. "I've always liked that about you. I sort of like school, but you do a better job of liking it than I do."

"Oh. Th-thanks," I stammered. I'd never considered myself more "anything" than Brody when it came to good traits. He was kind of up there on a pedestal. So was Hanna, who nodded and chuckled at his compliment to me.

I suddenly remembered the conversation with Killian that had led me to worry about Brody's sincerity. "Brody?"

"Yeah?" His blue eyes held mine, questioning.

Oh, great, there it was again. I wanted to bask in the attention he gave me. But his attention didn't mean he was into me, and maybe he never had been.

"I have an awkward question," I prefaced it and stopped.

His hand dropped from Hanna's back. "You can ask me." His voice was both kind and curious.

"Do you think it's wrong to wait to kiss someone until you get engaged?"

He looked startled. "Are you rethinking your rule?"

"No-o," I hedged. "No, it's more like I'm wondering what you really think of it."

"Well." He relaxed back into a smile, and then he and Hanna exchanged looks like a couple that knows how to communicate without words. It was the first time I had seen them do that. "Like I said when you first shared that rule with me, I'm all for it," he declared. "I had wanted a similar rule for myself, but I was afraid it wouldn't be popular with the girls I dated. When you told me your rule, it gave me the courage to decide I wanted the same thing."

He had told me all that before, but it helped to hear it again. That ought to mean it was true. Right? Or had he just not "realized" yet, as Killian eventually had, that it was a problem for him?

He looked at Hanna again, both of them grinning, before he turned back to me. "Hanna has a rule that she won't kiss until she gets married," he revealed.

I blinked. I couldn't imagine waiting that long. I didn't think it *advisable* to wait that long. Even so, all of a sudden, I couldn't help but grin back.

"Since her rule is stricter than mine," Brody continued, "that's the one we're going by."

"Don't let anyone change your mind," Hanna told me. "If it's your dream to wait to kiss him, then wait."

"Yes, it's up to you," Brody agreed. "If you personally want to change your rule, then do it, but don't change it because of someone else's opinion."

How could I not like these two? They made me feel special and warm and—and if I had married Brody, he would have always made me feel that way.

But his making me feel good now didn't change the fact that he had found someone else. I had to learn to be friends with him. Just friends.

I could do that. Eventually.

Chapter Eight

It came to me halfway through the semester that while I had successfully (in a manner of speaking) endured six weeks of Croft's annoying personality, there were still another seven and a half weeks to go—and that was just this semester. If I were a TA for Stat 230 or any other class next year, as I hoped to be, and if Croft found out my lab hours, I bet he would go, never mind that he might not be in that particular class.

I saw the future stretch before me, with Croft tormenting me several times a week until my graduation more than a year from now. It painted a bleak, disheartening picture.

In Monday's class, Croft pulled out two loose pieces of paper. I was used to the one with his good attributes, which he liked to add to and get me to read, but I didn't know what to think of the second one, titled "Good attributes of Surrey." The top three bullet points were already filled in: "Friends with kids," "Good neighbor," and "Determined."

"After we have dinner tonight, I'll fill in a few more blanks," he said, as though I had agreed to any such thing.

I pulled the paper in front of me and raised my pen, but he quickly whisked the page away, protesting, "No, no, it's cheating if you fill it out. I have to fill it out myself while I get to know you on our dates."

"You forgot to write bad-tempered, no sense of humor, and a temptation," I pointed out.

His dark-blue eyes turned a little darker. "I was completely wrong. I didn't know you or even try to get to know you, and I made some stupid assumptions."

I blinked. That was actually a good apology, certainly the best I had heard from him so far. Not that he had used the words "I'm sorry," and he hadn't apologized for badmouthing me to his friend, just for thinking poorly of me himself. Even so, he had sounded regretful, not to mention serious for once.

He rubbed his hands together, the serious expression gone so quickly I could have imagined it. "That's why I'm doing my research this time. So, dinner tonight? Candlelight and music? I need to fill out your sheet." He held it up and dangled it in front of me.

I groaned and resisted the urge to put my aching head in my hands. I couldn't go on like this, not for the rest of the semester, then the following semester, and then finally through my last one. There had to be a way to stop him.

Mr. Collins from *Pride and Prejudice* was looking pretty good to me about now. After some thinking, he had realized Elizabeth's *no* meant *no*. How could I get Croft to that point?

Arguing with him did no good. Ignoring him did no good, although it seemed a better route than trying to reason with him, as it gave him fewer things to laugh at. Still, my efforts never made him go away. What else could I possibly do? Stuff his lists down his throat and push him bodily from the room?

Lists. Maybe I should take a page out of Croft's book.

Come Wednesday's lab hour, I had a sheet of my own ready for Croft.

"Surrey, are you ready for our big date?" Croft asked, dropping into the chair next to me.

I had a feeling he would be my only visitor in the lab today, as everyone had just taken the midterm test and was lulled by a false sense of security that they could relax. For my part, I was making use of this hour to study for my other classes.

Without a word, I slid a loose sheet of paper over to Croft and bent over my notes for Bayesian Statistics.

"What's this?" He picked up the sheet.

Lab Hour Consent Form

In order to attend the lab hours of Surrey Witherfield, I agree to the following items:

-I will not ask any personal questions of Surrey Witherfield.
-I will not ask Surrey Witherfield out.
-I will not act as though Surrey Witherfield has consented to a date.
-I will not act as though Surrey Witherfield and I are a couple.

Student name (in print): Croft Taylor
Signature: ______________Date: _______

CROFT LAID down the paper and laughed long and loud.

I took a bracing breath. "Why are you laughing?" I asked, trying to sound calm instead of irritated to the moon and back.

"This is hilarious. You wrote this?" He looked at me with sparkling eyes. Was it just me, or did he look . . . admiring?

I gritted my teeth and returned to my notes.

"It's great," he chuckled, "just great. But I'm not gonna sign it."

My mouth tightened. "Then I can't help you with your homework."

"I'm afraid you have to. You can't refuse to help students just because they haven't signed a disclosure statement."

I pointed my pencil at him and glared. "I can if I don't like your face."

His eyes widened in dismay, and he clutched said face. "*This?* But of course you're teasing. No one can resist my beautiful—"

"What's your question?" I interrupted. *"On the homework."*

He fingered his face another moment and then gave it a consoling clap before he opened his book. "Hmm. Let's start with question 3."

I winced at the word "start."

"Also, will you go to dinner with me tonight at seven?"

"No."

He cocked his head and looked down at the book. "Really? I didn't think question 3 was a yes-no question. But okay, if you say so. And what's your answer to dinner?"

I dug out a pen and added to the statements on my consent form: "I will not misinterpret Surrey Witherfield's answers." I paused and added yet another, long overdue item. "I will apologize for the consequences of my prank on Surrey Witherfield and will never again hurt someone in a similar manner."

"I didn't hurt you, did I?" he asked, frowning. "Look, I *am* sorry it scared you," he began . . . and then his mouth pulled into a grin. "But I can't deny it was a funny scene." He covered his mouth. "I'm sorry, I just can't stay serious around you."

"That's funny," I replied coolly. "I dated a guy who was great at being serious, and I really liked him."

"Where is he now?" Croft asked, his eyes still dancing.

"On his honeymoon." The words slipped out before I could stop myself from sharing *that* piece of painful information.

"Ah. I'm sorry if that brings back bad memories." Again, his consoling look only lasted a moment before he beamed and held out his arms. "But hey, *I* can still take you on a date."

I grabbed my head in exasperation. "You're the last guy I would *ever*—" I began but stopped short.

Where was Frank? Where, indeed? On his honeymoon in California. Where was Keaton, the first guy I fell in love with? Somewhere in Hawaii with his wife and baby. Where was Killian? On campus, running around kissing his wife goodbye and telling me to drop my no-kissing rule. Where were Jesse and Brody?

And the million-dollar question: If I were to date Croft, where would he be a year from now? In Croatia, madly in love with his new wife? He would probably be engaged six months from now, maybe sooner. Hopefully sooner.

"Surrey?" Croft's questioning voice nagged at me, but I wouldn't be distracted from my thoughts.

Was I seriously considering going on a date, possibly even multiple dates, with Croft? Spending more time with him in the hopes that he would find someone else and finally leave me be?

"What are you thinking?" Croft asked, cocking his head.

What *was* I thinking? The idea of helping him find true love while I stayed single and lonely was painful. He didn't deserve that kind of help from me. I mean, he probably *did* deserve happiness—everyone did—but surely this was too much to ask of me when he had been such a pest ever since we met.

"Sooo, are you thinking about it?" he asked. "'Cause I could make reservations today. Pick you up at seven on Friday. Wanna give me your address?"

I shut my eyes as he pushed a pen and a sheet of paper over to me. He obviously wasn't about to go away on his own. As annoying as it would be to spend time with him outside of school, it was the surest and quickest way to get rid of him. And for once, it wouldn't hurt to lose the guy I dated.

"Digit-digit-digit something Avenue, I'm guessing," he said, holding the pen above the paper. "Or is it something Lane? Help me out here."

"Fine, I'll go on your stupid date," I snapped and took the pen from him.

I know, even I was impressed by my own graciousness. Of course, he already knew I wasn't eager to go, and I saw no reason to pretend otherwise.

He looked on in seemingly breathless silence—probably another joke of his—while I scribbled out my address for him.

"Can I have your phone number, too?" he had the gall to ask.

I was so ready to be done with this. Without a word of argument, I wrote it out at a furious pace. Too bad it was still legible.

He picked up the paper quickly, as though afraid I would change my mind and tear it up. "Well, thank . . ."

"Six o'clock," I interrupted.

"Tonight," he said.

Again, I didn't even argue. The sooner the date, the sooner he disappeared, right? "Guru's Café," I said, naming the restaurant.

"Sweet."

"Now, get out," I told him.

For once, he paid heed, grabbing his things and running out the door with his coerced goods in hand. He seemed to have taken the consent form with him, as well, though he hadn't filled it out.

My eyes hadn't left the doorway before he popped back in.

"If it's a fake address, I'll know where to find you tomorrow at lab hour." He waved the paper in his hand.

"I said, *out.*"

He disappeared, his laughter sounding all the way down the hallway.

I put my head in my hands and rubbed at my temples. "It will be worth it. It will be worth it," I mumbled.

I looked up at the clock. There were ten minutes left. Ten glorious, blessedly Croft-free minutes of lab hour. Could it really be?

I basked in it for four beautiful, almost tear-wrenching minutes.

I came off cloud nine and, more calmly, enjoyed the next few minutes. Was this what lab hour without Croft could be like? Mmm. Nice.

To be honest, the last three minutes, I was just plain bored.

Chapter Nine

Since the dinner-date was later that same day, I wouldn't get a chance to tell Gina about it before I left. She was due to arrive home half an hour after Croft picked me up.

I greeted Willie when I got home. Then I hesitated, wondering if I should say something about tonight. Over-sharing about Croft taunting me in class had resulted in Willie's surprise prank all those weeks ago. I had learned from that experience to be careful about what I told Willie, but if he were to look out his window and see me leave with Croft without prior warning, who knew what he might do then?

"School was good?" he asked from his spot on the porch.

"It was all right. Um. Yeah, it was fine." I was still struggling with my decision.

His expression turned curious. Obviously, he could tell something was up.

"Well. Gotta go," I said and walked to my door. Actually, I walked into my door. My head bounced back, and I rubbed my forehead and nose with one hand while jerking the door open with the other hand. Giving a wave, I shut the offending piece of wood behind me. I was tempted to kick it, just a little bit, but was afraid it would find a way to retaliate, meaning I would hurt myself further.

Hmm, I had nearly an hour and a half to prepare for the date. I tapped my fingers on the kitchen counter. What to do, what to do . . .

Catching sight of a notepad on the counter, I ripped a piece off. Gina ought to know why I wasn't here when she came home. I wrote, "I'm on a date with Mr. Annoying" and signed my name with a flourish.

My date-preparation done, I put away my backpack and pulled out my List of Ten Things.

* * *

THE DOORBELL RANG ten minutes before six. Pausing YouTube, I went to open the door and frown at Croft.

"You're ten minutes early," I told him.

He smiled wide. "I'll add that to my list of attributes. 'Punctual.' I believe that 'on time' is late, and 'early' is on time."

"Well, I'm not ready. Would you like to wait out here, or do you prefer to come in the house?" I asked, pained as I mentioned the second option.

"I'll come in." His grin widened, and he entered. "How many room-mates do you have?"

"One."

"Will I get to meet her?"

"Probably not. Now, hush. I'm busy until six."

I returned to the couch and clicked play on my laptop, releasing a series of tweets and trills from the Northern Cardinal. Pursing my lips, I whistled along, stopping and adjusting to match the sounds in the video. I had finally decided on which animal I wanted to learn to imitate.

Croft looked around at the paper ocean waves that adorned the walls and furniture. Then he sat down in an armchair across from me and watched, unabashed. I ignored him.

"What are you doing?" he asked, a muted smile on his face. I had a feeling he was waiting for the punch line, at which point his smile would grow to its usual obnoxious size.

"Practicing," I broke off to say before returning to my task.

He listened for a few minutes, then asked, "What kind of bird is this?"

I didn't answer. It wasn't my fault he had come early. He would just have to wait for me to finish.

"Let me guess. It's a . . . woodpecker."

"Wee-thur-wee-thur-wee-thur-wee," I mimicked.

"A finch," he suggested. "A yellow-bellied, um, chaffinch."

"Wee-thur-wee."

"A red-chested . . . robin." He nodded knowingly.

"F-r-r-r-r-r," said the video, and I repeated, "F-r-r-r-r."

He snapped his fingers. "A long-billed, crook-chested, blue-top hawk."

I broke off into a snort-giggle, which I turned into a cough. The video continued, but after a few seconds, I stopped it and stood.

"All right, you win. We can go now." It was still four minutes till six, but I wasn't going to practice any longer, not with him making me laugh. He might get the wrong impression.

"Aww, I was enjoying the show," he protested, standing. "Why are you practicing imitating a bird?"

I shrugged.

"Is it homework? If it is, you have *got* to tell me which class it's for."

"It's not homework." I put on my shoes.

"Is it a dare? I remember you extending a dare to me not so long ago."

"Nope."

"Come on, tell me."

"Nah."

"You're a bird-lover? You'll use this as a spy, as a warning signal?"

"Nothing so exciting as that." I locked the door behind us.

"Seriously, why are you imitating a swoop-feathered blue jay?"

"Now you're making up birds again."

"Come on, your house is swimming and you're communing with birds. What am I missing?"

We stopped in front of his car, both of us on the passenger side of a pretty, blue Mazda with a couple of scratches in the paint. Croft hadn't unlocked it. He stood looking at me, bursting to the brim with curiosity, his eyes alive. As I returned his gaze, I was reminded suddenly of one of the rules of romance stories. Guys were drawn to girls with a mystery, weren't they? He looked more interested than ever: interested in uncovering the why of my practice session, yes, but probably also interested in me.

That wouldn't do. I would have to give him the answer and burst whatever aura of mystery was hanging over me at the moment.

"I make a list of ten things to do every semester to make it different from all the others," I explained. "It's kind of a short-term bucket list. Learning to imitate a specific animal is one of my items."

"That's brilliant. And the waves in your house?"

"They're just for fun."

He looked no less excited than before I'd told him, but he did unlock the car doors and open mine for me. Probably something he did so he could pat himself on the back for being a gentleman and add it to his list of attributes.

"Now, why Guru's Café?" he asked as he pulled away from the side of the road. "You like their food?"

"I don't know. I've never been there before."

"Gotcha. You like trying new things."

I didn't correct him. Guru's was simply the next place on my list that I hadn't visited and embarrassed myself in. None of the waiters would recognize me as an accident about to happen, so it should be safe until after tonight.

My list of waiter-enemies grew quickly when I chose to eat out.

"What other items are on your bucket list?" Croft asked.

"List of Ten Things," I corrected. "That's what it's called."

"Okay, List of Ten Things. What else is on there?"

"Other funky, silly things." I dismissed his question.

"Who writes the items? Can I get a turn?"

"At writing them?" I stared at him.

"Yes. I want to put one on there for next semester." He waved a hand at the windshield. "Once you've mastered this warbling swallowtail chirping, you'll have to use it as a signal for someone out in the woods. Warn them through whistles and chirps about some unknowing passersby or other. We could come up with a story and film it."

"No. I write my own lists," I said forcefully.

With any luck, I would be rid of him by the end of this semester. It made no sense to commit to do something with him next year.

"You have to make use of your newfound talent," he insisted.

"There are only so many things you can get me to do, Croft."

"The camera wouldn't be hidden this time. You would know you were getting filmed."

"While knowing someone is using a camera is better than not knowing, it's even better when someone asks permission—and then *respects my answer*."

He nodded, his gaze flicking between me and the road. "It's just hard to drop the bird-signal spy idea when I could see you were excited about it."

My mouth dropped open. "*Me?* You think I was *excited*?"

"You definitely looked interested when I first mentioned it. That's another thing I'll have to add to your list—your list of good attributes, not your List of Ten Things," he clarified. "You have imagination."

I tried to look as unexcited about the whole thing as possible. While *maybe* there was something *somewhat* cool about coming up with a secret agent scenario and acting it out, I hadn't for one moment imagined giving in to his idea. I certainly hadn't been excited about it. Who did he think he was, dictating my emotions to me?

I schooled my features, trying to look as bored and uninterested as I could. Uninteresting, too, if I could manage it.

I am not a mysterious girl, I repeated inside my head like a mantra. *I am transparent and boring. You are not interested in me.*

Unfortunately, along with that last sentence, I imagined myself moving my fingers in front of Croft in a Jedi mind-trick, and the thought nearly made me laugh, ruining the bland expression I wanted.

"There we go, that's my happy Surrey," he said, pulling into a parking space.

"You don't have a happy Surrey." *And you never will.*

"Sometimes I have an amused one, and I vow it'll happen more and more often."

I opened my door and jumped out before he could pretend to be chivalrous again.

He kept talking as we entered the restaurant, but I was shaking my head, the words "happy Surrey" echoing in my mind. The words were so sappy and comical and dumb that I struggled again not to laugh.

His vow didn't sit well with me, though. That was another thing the stories showed: the guy always worked hard to coax a smile or a laugh from the girl he had fallen for. If Croft saw me as a challenge, he would remain intrigued. Yet what was there to do about that? I couldn't possibly start simpering and laughing at his jokes in order to take away the challenge. I would hate myself for it, and he would think I liked being with him.

I reminded myself of the facts. I didn't necessarily need him to lose interest in me. I just needed him to find the girl that would steal that interest away. That meant I could be myself and do whatever I wanted, whether it turned out to pique his interest or push him away. And, since nothing seemed to have the power to push him away so far, I should prob-ably—sigh—forget that possibility entirely.

"Tell me about your family," he said as soon as we had ordered our food and sat down.

"Tell me about yours," I countered.

"I'm an orphan," he lied.

"I'm a foundling," I shot back.

With an effort, he kept back a laugh. "I have no siblings," he said, again with a look that told me he was making it up, giving me short answers so he could turn the conversation back to me.

"My adopted brothers are half elves," I told him without blinking.

"You, of course, are a full-blood elf," he said, nodding sagely.

How had we gotten into such an easy banter? If I didn't stop this, I might give him the wrong impression. Again.

"Sooo. Is this supposed to be an apology dinner? Because I haven't heard any apologies yet." I folded my arms across my chest in a universal gesture of waiting.

"Oh, yes. Yes, go ahead." He beckoned at me and folded his arms as well.

My eyes widened at his audacity. I felt myself turn red, the sunset color that had inspired several of Frank's odes.

I put my hands on the table and leaned forward. "Sorry you're a cad."

His eyebrows rose and then fell. He looked at me in expectation, waiting for the next blow, his expression spurring me on.

"And I'm sorry I have to spend the evening with a pompous jerk," I finished.

His brows rose again, but his eyes were dancing. "I don't think 'pompous' quite fits me. Maybe 'cocky' is the word you're looking for."

"You try apologizing yourself, then," I challenged.

He leaned forward like I had done. "I'm sorry you took so long to agree to go out with me."

I sat back. "This is the worst apology dinner ever."

"That's because the food hasn't arrived. Ah, there it is. ... Nope, that was for someone else." He strained to see the next dish as another server dressed in a black Guru's T-shirt passed by. "Maybe that plate . . . Nope, guess not."

I pressed my lips together, not wanting to show any humor as he followed each plate's progress. Finally, our food arrived. I lost no time in applying my fork to it.

Croft sighed in regret. "I can't think of any more apologies. Can you come up with a few more?"

I took another bite.

He unfolded his napkin. "We'll just have to call this a date, then, since the apology part is already over."

"Poor me," I mourned.

He grinned. "I just thought of another apology."

I changed the subject again. "Willie tells me several of your hidden camera pranks are as mean as the one you subjected me to."

"He subscribes now, does he?" Croft looked pleased.

"If you ever feel like doing the world a service, you might consider changing your ways. Just throwing it out there," I said, ignoring the question.

"I wouldn't call my show 'mean,' exactly. I know it's uncomfortable for the people involved until they find out it's fake and the shock wears off, but otherwise it's funny, and my audience loves it."

I widened my eyes and spoke in mock pretense. "Just like that, you have convinced me."

He reached out with his fork. "That looks good. Can I have a bite?"

"Oh, no." I grabbed my plate off the table. "No. We are *not* sharing food."

"It's okay, I won't do the lady-and-the-tramp thing," he chuckled. "This'll only be *half* as romantic."

I turned sideways on my cushioned bench and held my plate in front of me with one hand, handling my fork with the other.

"Oh, come on, you can't turn your back on me." Croft's voice shook with laughter.

I couldn't, but this was as close as I could get.

"Okay, I won't take any of your food," he conceded. "You can turn around now."

"I have absolutely no reason to trust you," I said and continued to eat.

He was quiet a moment. "Well, I prefer having you face me," he said, weighing his words. "You can trust that I realize if you put your plate on the table again and I take something, you might turn away for good, and I don't want that."

I paused. He sounded sincere, and he was right. If he snatched something when I let down my guard, I would walk away or sit facing away from him no matter what. I wouldn't be fooled a second time.

I turned to the table and set down my plate, grumbling, "I don't know why you want me facing you, anyway."

He smiled broadly. "You're right. Your side is really pretty. But I like your front better."

I made a face.

"This is great. I'll have a lot more attributes I can write on your list after tonight," he told me.

"Just cross out the word 'good' and then go crazy filling it out," I advised.

"No, I'm done imagining up bad qualities in you," he said, as though citing a solemn vow. "I'm looking for the good in you now, and there's a lot."

"Not that *you've* seen," I argued.

"Yes, that I've seen."

"So, what, you've been spying on me?"

He shook his head. "For starters, how many college women are friends with grade-school boys? That impressed me."

I stared. It had *impressed* him? As in, not just caused him to apologize, but made him want to spend time with me?

"Are you saying," I spoke slowly, "that it's Willie's fault you went from holding me in derision to harassing me about a date?"

"Yes. You've inspired loyalty in that kid, and that's worth a lot."

I couldn't believe it. Sure, Croft's behavior had changed drastically after Willie's stunt, but I hadn't realized it had had this sort of effect on him.

"I'll kill him," I said.

Croft winced. "See now, maybe don't say that out loud. It's actually your fault, not his, for being friends with him. It's just his fault I found out about it. By the way," he brightened, "we should totally have dropped by and said hi when I picked you up. Does he know we're on a date?"

"What do you think he'd do if he *did* know?" I asked pointedly.

"That's a really good question." Croft tapped a finger against his chin.

"Maybe he'd approve. Or maybe he'd punish me with another prank. I bet he would come up with something worthy."

I bet he would. Pushing the thought aside, I looked at Croft and wondered if he was ready for any sort of negotiations now that we were finally on his oft-requested date. "So, Croft. How about you stop coming to my lab hours?"

"Oh, honey, I can't do that."

"Don't call me honey," I snapped.

"Sweetheart? Icing. Cinnamon." He tried each word in turn. "One never knows when I might need help with statistics."

"You're acing the class," I pointed out in exasperation.

"Because of you."

"Because of *you*," I corrected him.

He grinned, raising my blood pressure. "I just said that."

"No!" My hands flew out expressively, and one of them hit an arm. The plate cradled in that arm flew upward. The waiter who had been passing by struggled valiantly to keep his balance and his hold on a second plate but inevitably lost both.

Crash!

Ker-rash!

I shut my eyes for a moment and then stood, although I wanted to curl into a corner and hide from the sudden silence and gazes all around.

"I am so, so sorry," I said and dropped to the ground to clean things up.

Two notes of laughter rang out from Croft before he managed to stifle them. Then he was on his knees as well, reaching for pieces of food and broken dishes and speaking cheerfully to the employee I had assailed.

"I'm sorry, my man. What kind of bribe will you need? A ten? A fifteen? I don't have a fifteen, but I might have a ten and a five." He chuckled as we both helped in spite of the waiter's protests. People nearby laughed along and turned back to their tables, some of them mumbling in sympathy but with smiles on their lips. Croft and I continued to help until two more employees arrived on the scene to mop things up.

Once the floor was clean, Croft handed the waiter a couple of bills and raised his voice. "Now, who else wants to tip our friend?" He looked at the guy's name badge while those at nearby tables looked in our direction again with giggles and appreciative smiles. "His name's Peter. Just remember that if you're looking to tip someone extra."

Peter shook his head, red-faced, though something in his expression cleared as he realized he just might make bank tonight. Already, people were whispering his name to each other, memorizing it with chuckles and smiles. Croft gave a flourishing bow to the room, and several onlookers clapped and laughed before he seated himself.

I had already sat down so as to keep out of the limelight, but I wasn't planning on sticking around. "I'm ready to—" I began in a whisper.

"Hold on. You have a . . ." Croft came around the table, and I paused while he leaned down and picked something from my hair. How embarrassing. He held it out in front of me.

"Do you like broccoli?" he joked.

I eyed it with distaste. "Not at the moment, no."

He shrugged and dropped it onto my empty plate. "Wait, there's more," he said as I started to rise.

"More? In my hair?"

"Yes. I'm afraid there's dressing."

I groaned. "I'll go clean it up."

"I'll get it. I can see it much better than you, even if you use a mirror," he reasoned and sat down next to me.

I looked at him in apprehension as he picked up a clean linen napkin, wetted it with the water from my glass, and reached up. Rather than stare awkwardly at his armpit, I turned my head and faced the table, closing my eyes in humiliation as he dabbed at my hair.

His movements were gentle but thorough. It was probably my imagination, due to the horrible circumstances, that made it seem like it took forever. At least those nearby didn't seem to be watching. I heard them converse with each other, and no one laughed more than usual.

Finally, I opened my eyes as Croft dropped the napkin.

"All right, what do you want for dessert?"

I picked up my purse and stood. "I don't want dessert. I'm going home."

Croft hurried after me as I strode outside. "Wait up," he panted. "What do you think of Crumbl cookies?"

"I'm done for tonight, Croft."

"We don't have to go inside anywhere if that's what's bothering you. I could buy ice cream and we could sit and eat in the car."

"No dessert," I said firmly. "Either you take me home now, or I'm walking."

He quickly unlocked his car and opened my door. "I'll take you home, then."

I hoped we would drive in silence.

However, Croft was as talkative as ever. "It wasn't that bad, was it? I thought you handled yourself great in there."

"I sure hope I don't handle myself great in *here* and hit *your* arm," I said, exasperated. "We'd get in a car accident. You do realize I caused an accident in the restaurant, right?"

"Yeah, but it was just that—an accident." He chuckled. "And it was funny. It really did seem to happen in slow motion, like in the movies. Did you see that food go flying?"

"No wonder you wanna stick around me. I'm bound to make you laugh like nobody's business."

He laughed harder.

As we turned onto my street, he spoke again. "Maybe it's better this way, going home without dessert."

I stilled. Did he regret having been out in public with me, after all? Was he glad to have been spared further embarrassment?

"That means we're splitting our date in half. I'll pick you up on Saturday for dessert. What time is good?"

I leaned my head back against the seat. *Seriously?*

"How about four o'clock?" he asked, slowing the car to a stop.

I opened my door and walked out. His door opened, and I heard his quick steps as he rounded the car.

"Four o'clock it is," he called from behind me. "What do you like? Chocolate? Ice cream? Surrey?"

He was only halfway to the front door when I locked it.

"See you Saturday," I heard his muted voice call.

I rolled my eyes heavenward and entered the living room.

Gina, on the couch, looked up from her computer. "You're home early. Well, assuming it was a dinner date. Maybe I shouldn't assume that," she backtracked. "Um, how did it go?"

I put my hands on my hips and huffed. "Just great. He plagued the life out of me while I spewed insults at him. I made an enemy of another waiter and estranged myself from a new restaurant, and Croft picked food out of my hair." I paused to draw breath and held it for a moment.

Then I expelled it in a burst of laughter, surprising myself. I tried to speak but couldn't stop laughing. I shook my head helplessly.

"So it was good?" Gina asked with humor when I quieted.

I shook my head again, but I was smiling. Why was I smiling? "I don't know." I pulled a hand through my hair. My damp hair. I had never come home from a date and laughed like this. Until now, I hadn't realized I thought the whole situation was funny.

"Did he ask you on another date?"

I pursed my lips. "He said he would pick me up on Saturday to get dessert." I paced to the glass door and looked at the backyard, where shadows settled across the berry bush and the lawn like a blanket. The lighting was sleepy and comforting. I thought to myself that I had never seen a better rendition of dusk. Could I paint something like this?

My eyes narrowed on the silhouette of a fallen leaf. I turned and looked at Gina. "I'll make him rake leaves instead. He may as well do some good, and I still have a couple of items left on my List of Ten Things."

Gina snorted and covered her mouth. "You do that. Make Mr. Annoying work for his pay, if he's still bad enough for you to call him that."

"Trust me, he is."

Chapter Ten

THE NEXT DAY was my last lab hour of the week but not the last time I would see Croft. It was terrible of him to force not one but two dates on me in a week, but hopefully the more often I saw him, the sooner he would find his true love.

"You weren't able to sleep all night, were you?" Croft greeted me. "Butterflies and all that? I tend to have that effect. Sorry, I can't turn down my charm."

I finished writing out the answer to one of my regression problems. "No, I just couldn't imagine why I didn't take advantage and clean out your wallet yesterday."

"You can give it a try on Saturday, but you'll to have to eat whatever you order, so I would advise against twenty scoops of ice cream." He leaned back in his chair and rolled away from the table.

"We're not getting dessert on Saturday," I told him.

"Of course we are. I owe you."

"No dessert."

He rolled back toward me. "Does four o'clock not work for you?"

"Seven thirty," I said. "Bring a rake and gloves."

He blinked and then smiled. "We're raking leaves?"

I let my eyes widen. "How did you figure that one out?"

He coughed but recovered quickly. "It'll be dark at seven thirty."

"I know." I didn't elaborate.

"Ah, I see. A romantic date, outside in the dark." He nodded. "I'll bring candles."

I rolled my eyes. "You can bring whatever you like, but if you start a fire and end up in jail, I'm done with you. I'd get a restraining order rather than see you again."

He shook with mirth. "Fair enough."

* * *

ON SATURDAY, I found the perfect shirt—a white, lacy shirt that was just the right style for my camo dress.

My design had changed repeatedly as I worked on the dress, causing me to scrap some of the pieces I had sewn, but once I bought that shirt and took it home, I knew what I wanted.

The shirt fit to a curvy figure. I would sew my camo-patterned, trailing sleeves into the insides of the shoulders to make them protrude from the lacy white. My camo skirt would be overlaid with white lace, the lace portion being shorter so that the green-and-black cloth would peep out at the bottom.

I could hardly wait for the day the dress would be finished, and I could wait even less for the day I would complete the painting that had been on my mind for so long. I hunkered down to grade the latest stack of Stat 230 assignments, but as soon as Gina came home from work, I turned on the sewing machine and kept going until dinnertime.

"Are you still raking leaves today?" Gina asked after we said a blessing on the food.

"Yes. I told him seven thirty, so he'll probably be here at seven twenty." I took a large helping of stew.

"He likes to be early?"

"Apparently. It's one of his 'great attributes.'" I made air quotes with my fingers.

"Isn't there anything about him that you like?" She sounded both hopeful and anxious. I was pretty sure she regretted calling him Mr. Annoying two nights ago, even though I was the one who had come up with the name. Gina wasn't accustomed to using judgmental words about anyone.

"I'm sure *you* would find something nice about him," I answered. "You see the good in everyone."

"Well, if you spend time with him . . ."

"He'll move on to another girl and I'll be rid of him," I finished for her.

She frowned. "I know that's your plan. But I was thinking, if you go on enough dates with him, you might start to like him a little."

I pursed my lips and, after a long moment, conceded the point. "There's probably some good in him. But I'm not interested in noticing it. He has been an absolute pain, and that's *after* he stopped looking down on me."

"Right. Okay." She nodded. "So you just want to get rid of him quickly."

"If he finds his dream girl tomorrow, I'll sing praises to the heavens."

There was no point in either painting or sewing after dinner. With only minutes left before Croft might show, I put away the dress and halfheartedly opened a textbook, gazing at a picture of Descartes and turning it this way and that to see if I could make it look like he was smiling.

I was slow to answer the knock when it sounded but quick to address Croft. "Only eight minutes before seven thirty. You're late."

He held out his arms. "I'm early, which means I'm on time, as always." He stepped inside. "What bird are you imitating tonight?"

"None." I turned in time to see Gina's bedroom door shut behind her. I guess Croft wasn't getting introduced to her. "Let's go," I said, pushing at him.

He picked up the rake he had brought. "I think it'll take all of five minutes to take care of the leaves in your yard. Obviously, you just wanted an excuse to be alone with me in the dark."

I picked up my own rake and the roll of black garbage bags and proceeded down the sidewalk without sparing him a glance.

"I was kidding," he protested, laughing as he followed. "Where are you going?

"We're not raking *my* yard," I said into the cool evening air.

The Blaines's front yard was already neat as a pin. I probably couldn't have raked their yard without Mrs. Blaine catching me in the act, anyway. Bypassing her home, I stopped in front of widowed Sister James's house and turned to face Croft.

"I realize this will be nearly impossible for you, but you have to be very quiet," I said in a low voice. "I don't want her hearing us and knowing we're doing this for her. I *especially* don't want her to hear us and get scared and call the police."

Croft held back a smile and looked thoughtful for a moment. Just for a moment, and then the smile returned. "We're helping your neighbor. Anonymously."

I stepped onto the lawn, which was far more leaf-strewn than my own.

"That's cool. Also," cockiness filled his voice even as he spoke quietly, "one of my good attributes is that I can follow directions."

I raised one eyebrow. "You usually pay zero heed to mine."

"Not tonight. Scout's honor." He raised his hand in a three-fingered salute. "Why are we doing this at night? Couldn't we just have found a time when she wasn't home?"

I moved my rake experimentally through the leaves, listening to the rustling noise and looking up at the nearest window. It was closed, and I was pretty sure Sister James was asleep. She probably wouldn't hear us.

"Because it's on my List of Ten Things," I answered. "'Rake leaves in the dark.' I told you my items tend to be silly."

"You've turned it into a service project. Sweet."

I gave him a look, though he probably couldn't see its severity in the faint light.

"As you'll find out tonight, one of my good attributes is that I can be quiet when I need to be," Croft said and promptly shut his mouth.

He was true to his word. It reminded me of the day he had shown me he could pay attention. We worked in silence, trying to keep down the swishing noises of maple and walnut leaves as we worked our way through a yard twice the size of mine and Gina's.

When three large piles littered the yard, we brought out the bags. It was almost comical as Croft held the bag and I pitched in the leaves, all without either of us speaking. We switched positions with the next bag. I bit my lip against a growing urge to giggle. Was it a nervous giggle? Was I uncomfortable or simply amused with the ridiculous silence?

As we started on the last pile, my struggles made themselves known with little choked noises.

Croft straightened and threw a leaf at me. It didn't even make it halfway before it began a slow, side-to-side descent, which made me want to laugh harder.

He made an exasperated noise and picked up several leaves, which made it no farther. Still, I paid him back by picking up a few of my own and shoving them at him, not letting go until they touched him. At least mine made contact, I thought in satisfaction, just before he shoved a few at me.

I slapped a new handful into his solid frame and received another one on my arm. Stepping out of reach, I covered my mouth with both hands and giggle-snorted.

"Incoming," Croft whispered, and this time, leaves flew upward as he dived into the pile like a dog.

He turned onto his back and pushed up through the leaves. At his reappearance, I scrambled to grab armfuls and re-bury him, heedless of the dry, rustling noise. Sister James would hardly hear it through her closed window, anyway.

Croft raised his arms in the air and panic-whispered, "I'm drowning."

I rolled my eyes. "Do you always—"

He grabbed my hand and pulled me into the pile of crunchy, chilly foliage. "Always," he answered, covering me with leaves.

I sputtered and sat up with a scowl.

He helpfully picked a leaf from my hair. "You know you've raked leaves correctly when you come home with a few on your person."

I tried to brush myself off. They were on my arms, my pants, my back. I stopped an extra scratchy one from making its way down my shirt. Croft was still cleaning himself off when I indicated the pile and the sack and asked pointedly, "Shall we?"

We bagged the rest of our plunder and moved it to the curb. Croft breathed out as though declaring the end of a job well done. The thought occurred to me to prolong the raking just to make him work more—and possibly because I was having a good time—but before I could say anything, he asked, "Whose yard is next?"

I guess I shouldn't have been surprised at his eagerness to continue. Did he suggest it to spend more time with me or because he liked the activity? I looked around at the neighborhood and pointed to the Petersens' yard. "That one."

I had thought his leaf-frolicking was over for the night, but as soon as we finished raking, he pulled me into the leaves and jumped in.

"Ohhh, you scoundrel," I hissed while he laughed in subdued tones. I picked up the bag as he burrowed deeper. A warning went off in my mind that giving in to mischief would only make things harder for me, but in that moment, there was no stopping me. I pulled the bag over Croft's head and down to his waist.

The black mass deliberately bumped into me, dropping me into the pile. I scrambled away and was several yards out of reach by the time he got the bag off and looked around for me. When he found me, he advanced with an ominous chuckle.

"I think you better fill these bags yourself," I said, walking backward.

"All on my own? You wouldn't make me do that, would you?" He laughed quietly.

I covered up my apprehension with sharpness. "I would, and I'll lock my front door on you, too, if you don't stop moving toward me."

He stopped. "I'll be good. Come help me."

I crossed my arms. "I'll stand here and watch. Or I'll go home now."

He watched me. "All right." He set about filling a bag, silently at first, and then with increasing gusto and whispered comments in spite of the difficulty of holding and filling the bag all alone. His enthusiasm growing with each paltry addition to the bag, he looked to me for approval, his efforts punctuated by sentences such as "Do you see this?" and "I'm doing an impressive job, aren't I?"

I took pity on him and helped him fill the last bag. It was definitely a two-person job.

"That's it for tonight," I concluded, dusting my hands off after we lugged the bag to the curb.

Croft's eyes twinkled at me. Suddenly nervous, I hurried to cross the street. If Croft was going to get me back for catching him with the garbage bag, now would be the time. Or he might go back to joking about us being alone in the dark. Either way, I was ready for our "date" to be over.

"Just a minute," he called. "You're forgetting dessert." He ran ahead and unlocked his car. My steps slowing, I made to veer around him, but he held out a theatrical arm and continued, "With my brilliant knack for deciding on the most appropriate dessert to go with an activity, I brought steaming mugs of hot cocoa. However, as they're totally frozen by now, we'll have these instead."

I shook my head. He hadn't, either, brought cocoa, and while the air was cool, it was nowhere near freezing. I watched as he brought out "these," a cylinder-shaped package of cracker sandwiches with chocolate filling.

Ohhhh my, I appreciatively stretched out the words in my mind. I hadn't had these in a long time, but they had been one of my favorite snacks on family outings when I was small.

"Wanna eat them in my car? In the house? On the porch?" Animated, he listed off the options as though offering me Christmas and Easter together, all wrapped up in a pretty Dr. Seuss package.

I swallowed and shook my head. Things had been way too friendly tonight already. "Will these keep until Friday?"

He looked confused. "Yes?"

"Then how about we have our next date on Friday, and it'll be our dessert date. You come by, we eat these, you leave." Nice and short—*very* short—and it would be almost a week from now.

His laughter rang out. "I accept," he said, and my hopes spiked in surprise and then plummeted as he continued, "if I can add a few items of action to that list."

"You know what," I said, reaching for the package. I considered taking the whole thing and running inside with it, but he seemed to anticipate that and held on, so I just ripped the top off and took out a sandwich.

"Never mind," I said. "Let's have these now." Oh, they looked good.

"You like them, don't you?" He was thrilled.

I brought it to my mouth and stopped short. Turning it over in my hand, I tried to get a good look via the light from the nearest lamppost. "You didn't put anything in this, did you?"

His face pulled into an uncharacteristic frown, and he searched my eyes. "You really don't trust me, do you?" he asked in the most serious tone I had yet heard from him.

"You play pranks on people," I pointed out. "The first time we met, I got caught in one of your pranks, and so far as I know, you're still happily showing my demise to the online world. It's not a stretch by any means to think you might have done something to ruin this for me." I held up the snack.

"Well." Again, there was no smile in his voice. "I guess that makes sense. I do like my jokes. But I didn't do anything to this. Look." He took the next sandwich from the package and bit into it. "Try it. It's just chocolate and cracker."

I took a bite. Yes, it was exactly like I remembered.

"I'll work on the trust thing. We'll get there," he promised.

"I trust you enough to take a second one." I pulled another sandwich from the package.

"That'll do for tonight. Now, what great qualities have you discovered in me tonight?" he asked with a grin.

I rolled my eyes. If I could see his grin in the darkness, he could probably see my eye-roll.

"*I've* discovered *you're* service-oriented. Very commendable," he said with a nod.

"I'm gonna stuff my face with these and end this discussion," I threatened, taking three cracker sandwiches from the package.

"As it's currently a one-sided discussion, I don't think it will change things much," he mused, "just my expectation of your eventual answers. Now I'll expect your replies to sound something like *mmmf mgrmm mpm.*"

I nearly choked on my large mouthful. (No, I had *not* stuffed all three in my mouth. Just, um, one and a half, which was bad enough.)

"Besides combining fun with service, you're a good sport, Cinnamon," he continued. "You didn't get mad at being pulled into the leaves. You certainly don't have the temper I once accused you of."

He's calling me Cinnamon again?

I struggled to break up the biscuits in my mouth while he thoughtfully added on to my list of good attributes.

"You live in a nice neighborhood. Good taste." He shook with laughter at my helplessness. "You do yard work, too. That's great."

I managed to swallow the mess. With a glare, I turned and stomped up my driveway.

"Whoa." Croft caught my arm and gently turned me around. "Now you can talk back. Don't you want to contribute to the conversation?"

I was tempted to tell him exactly what to do with his list—both lists, in fact—but as my throat was dry and my mouth still full of crumbs, I shook my head, again glaring daggers, and pulled away, slamming the door shut on him.

Leaning against the wall, I tried to catch my breath. My mind reviewing the last few minutes against my will, I felt the corners of my mouth curl up. Ridiculous.

I made for the kitchen and poured a glass of milk. Ahh, that was just the thing. With my mouth clean and the tickle in my throat gone, I felt myself chuckle.

Sheesh, what was Croft's problem? I jammed another half cracker sandwich in my mouth to prevent a laugh but refrained from adding the last sandwich at the same time. I had learned my lesson.

Drawn-out, swishing noises reached my ears. It was the sound of raking.

I leaned toward the kitchen window and looked through the gauzy curtain, guessing it before I saw it. Angling myself so that he couldn't see me, I watched Croft's silhouette gather up the leaves in mine and Gina's front yard until it was bare.

Chapter Eleven

I WISH I could say Croft stopped being a pain during lab hours.

That Monday, he badgered me about watching his next hidden camera scene.

He leaned in with a mysterious air. "Tomorrow night at seven. Meet me at the Marriott Hotel."

"No, thanks," I replied airily, ruining the atmosphere he was trying to create. This was one event I had the power to avoid. When he talked about picking me up for a date, there wasn't much I could do to get around it unless I were to hide out in the bushes or beg someone to let me hang out at their place. However, if he was asking me to meet him somewhere, I could most certainly get around it by not showing up.

Or could I? Sudden doubt entered my mind. The bushes and a friend's house suddenly sounded good.

Croft sat back and twirled a pen in his hands. "You'll get to see my next prank, live." He spoke as though it were a real treat.

"I don't like pranks, Croft," I said, my mind focused on my quandary. Would he show up to take me to the hotel if I refused to meet him?

"You'll like this one. Or if you don't, you can tell me right then and help me see why."

I raised my eyebrows. "Well, what is it?"

He grinned. "I can't tell you that."

"Fine. Have fun with it," I told him but immediately reconsidered my words. If he had fun with it, that would probably mean someone else would suffer for his amusement.

"Come on," he pleaded. "I need to help you learn to trust me. What better way than to have you attend one of my pranks?"

"Are you serious? What part about inviting me to a hidden camera prank and refusing to tell me about it beforehand sounds trustworthy to you?"

"I won't be pranking *you*. You'll be next to me, watching the camera."

"I was practically next to you the day I ran over your friend. We were both on film together," I reminded him. "No, thanks, Croft. If you want me to trust you, you'll have to tell me in advance what will happen."

"And spoil the surprise?"

I sighed. "Obviously, we're at a standstill. Now, which homework problem do you need help on?" I jabbed a finger at his closed textbook.

* * *

THAT AFTERNOON, I found Willie straddling a branch in his maple tree, dangling a measuring tape toward the ground. This wasn't usual Vitamin D fare.

"What are you doing?" I called up to him.

"Measuring."

"What and why?"

He scribbled something on a piece of paper. "I'm going to engineer and install a swing for this tree."

"And you need to measure for that?" I asked in surprise. If it were me making a swing, I would just find a way to attach ropes to a board or a tire, and then I would tie said ropes to a branch. Eyeballing it should be enough, right?

Willie raised his chin. "I have to make sure it won't break under the weight of a person. That means taking into account weight, durability, everything. It takes physics."

I nodded, not sure if all that was necessary. Maybe it was. Did people get hurt on swings if the builder hadn't applied physics?

"Well, cool. Does that mean I'll see you on the swing from now on instead of on the porch?"

"Nah. I'm more interested in making it than swinging in it. But once it's done, you can use it whenever you like."

"Really? Thanks. That sounds great."

An image of Croft coming by to force me through another annoying date popped into my mind. Before I could stop my thoughts, they jumped ahead to a new scene, an image of Croft pushing me in Willie's swing.

I looked up at the tree in sudden horror. Croft would cajole me into the swing as highhandedly as he'd cajoled me into our dates if he knew I was allowed to use it. He wouldn't be able to resist.

Ugh, now he was invading my mind in the middle of a conversation with Willie. Couldn't Croft leave me be at least when he wasn't around? Still, it was about time I gave my neighbor an update on the state of things.

"Um, Willie?"

"Yeah?" He climbed down the trunk.

"Remember Croft?"

"Of course. What about him? What's he doing?"

"Taking me on dates," I said in a grumpy voice.

Willie narrowed his eyes. I could practically see the wheels turning in his head, and I hoped he wasn't coming up with another punishment for Croft. Not because Croft didn't deserve it, but because Croft would see it as extra incentive to get to know me because it further proved my friendship with someone younger than me. Go figure.

"Anyway, I just thought you should know. You might see him around sometimes."

"Do you like him now?" Willie asked.

I made a face. "When you get old enough to date, Willie, promise me you won't torment any girls."

"Ugh, I don't want to date," was his immediate answer. "I mean, I want to be a dad someday. But I'll stay away from dating as long as I can. I don't care for girls."

"Well, thank you very much," I said and turned as if to go.

"Not you," he laughed. "Come back."

"What, I don't count?"

"That's right."

"You don't think I'm a girl?"

"Oh, come on," he groaned. "You don't count because you're not annoying. Okay? And you're not my age, so no one would ever expect us to date."

Aha, I wasn't a threat. I struggled with laughter. Willie was quickly growing embarrassed.

"Sorry," I said. "You're right, and I'm glad we're friends. Anyway, I wanted you to know about Croft. He hasn't been mean to me since the day you played your prank." He had been annoying, rude, cocky, and more, but he wasn't *mean*, and I couldn't have Willie come after him again.

"Really?" Willie looked pleased. "But you still think he's annoying?"

"Ye-e-es, but I can live with it," I hedged. At least, I hoped I could live with it until he found his dream girl, which I sincerely hoped would happen this semester.

"If you're sure," Willie said.

I most certainly wasn't sure.

I pointed at his measuring tape. "What calculations have you made so far on that swing?"

That proved to be the right distraction. He was eager to show me, and I was interested in seeing what he had come up with. I hoped his "physics" were every bit as correct as he thought they were. If he had calculated wrong, I just might end up with my bum on the ground the first time I tried his swing.

* * *

THE NEXT DAY AFTER SCHOOL, I lay in the cool grass in my backyard, staring up into the wide, blue expanse. It was a semi-warm November day, and though the soil had nearly frozen last week, it was soft underneath me now. To my joy, Gina would be home any minute, her last class of the day having been canceled. Until then, I had a date with nature.

I imagined putting layer upon layer of blue paint in that sky, then adding fragile wisps of white with a different brush to match the beginnings of clouds that broke the expanse at its corners.

The glass door behind me slid open. I let out a deep sigh and spoke before Gina did.

"Isn't it amazing how deeply blue the sky can be? I don't think I can ever match it with my paints. It's God's canvas. I can't get over it."

"No, indeed, it looks like you're below it," joked an all-too-familiar non-Gina voice. "In fact, I'm afraid the sky will always be over *you*."

I sat up quickly and faced Croft. "What are *you* doing here?"

He gave me an angelic smile. "Your roommate let me in. Gina. I saw you through the glass door and knew you would love for me to join you. Shall I look at the sky with you?"

He came over and sat down, making me scoot away with a glare.

"You're right," he said, looking up. "It *is* amazing. You love beauty, don't you?"

I chewed on the inside of my cheek while debating whether to give a sincere answer. "Yeah," I said, relenting and gazing back up at the sky. "There's so much of it," I breathed. That was why I painted. Trying to capture the beauty of the earth was exhilarating and gave me yet another way to appreciate it.

Croft nodded, hiding a grin. "Well, it's all right to love yourself. Take it from someone with experience."

I blinked rapidly. This was only the second time he had referred to my being beautiful. Last time, it had been a warning to his fellow classmate. This time, it was a joke, but if I understood him right, he was also making a joke about himself being self-absorbed.

My voice turned cool. "I don't recall inviting you here today. Are you going to make a further nuisance of yourself by coming by at all hours?"

"You will notice I haven't made a nuisance of myself by calling or texting you." He sounded proud of himself.

"I *have* noticed." Having worried he would abuse the privilege after I gave him my phone number, I still couldn't believe he hadn't done so.

He cocked his head. "Then why haven't you said something about it? 'Croft, one of your good attributes is that you don't bug me on the phone.'"

"I was afraid bringing it up would remind you of the possibility."

He held up his hand. "I solemnly vow not to bug you on the phone. And I keep my promises. That's another of my good attributes."

"Coming by unannounced, however, is not." I stood, dusting myself off. "I'll leave the sky-gazing to you." Apparently my roommate was home. It was time to hang out and do homework. Croft was welcome to stay in the backyard and burn in the sun.

"Wanna go on a hike? You can get some more sky-gazing done," he suggested, standing.

"I have things to do."

"After the hike, we can go to the hotel so you can watch my newest prank."

I gave him a smug smile. "I can't. I'm having dinner with my ministering sisters tonight." Talk about ministering people being there for you. I was grateful the girls had agreed to have me over for dinner on such short notice.

He matched my smile. "Why do I get the feeling you scheduled that after yesterday's lab hour?"

"Maybe because I've made it clear I don't want to go. *And* because you make a habit of overriding my decisions about not wanting to do something. The only course left for me is to make sure I have another appointment."

He smiled wider. "A battle of wits and strategy. This is getting more and more exciting."

"I would rather there wasn't a war at all."

"Maybe there isn't. I have a feeling we're on the same side. You just haven't realized it yet."

"I have a feeling I'm your prisoner of war," I retorted, "but at some point, Croft Taylor, I will break free."

He took my arm. "Well, not today. I planned the hike in case you stayed firm against the hotel prank, and I have a couple lined up to join us. I'll text them now, and they'll meet us here. What do you say?"

"Oh, glory." I threw my hands in the air, forcing him to move away to avoid getting clobbered.

"I'll make sure you're back in time for that dinner," he reassured me.

"You had better, or I'll write you out of my books. I mean it."

"Yes, ma'am." He saluted. "We'll be back around six. Does that work?"

"Yes." At least I'd gotten out of attending his show tonight. And I did need to date him so he could find his dream girl.

I slid open the glass door and entered the house, giving Gina a pained smile. "Hey, Gina. I'll be back in a couple of hours."

"Where are you going?" she asked while Croft shut the door and bent over his phone.

"On some hike or other," I answered. "Do you want to join us?"

She shook her head and shifted on the couch, glancing at Croft. "Sorry. Too much homework."

That was the answer I had expected, but it had been worth a try. I looked at Gina's glossy hair and delicate face and thought again of the painting of her I had started over the summer. My auction paintings and queen-warrior portrait had put it on hold.

Croft put away his phone and clapped his hands together, looking at me and Gina. "What are we going to do for the next few minutes while we wait for them?"

An idea flashed through my mind and, going against all things decent, I went with it.

"*I* have something I need to do first, but hey, did you meet Gina on your way in? Gina, this is Croft. Croft, Gina."

Croft's smile was devoid of mischief for once, as though he recognized what a genuinely sweet person Gina was. "It's nice to meet you."

"Um, you, too."

I turned to Croft. "Gina's the best roommate I've ever had. Excuse me for a bit. Why don't you two talk?" I steered him to the couch. Surprised by my antics, he allowed himself to plop down next to Gina.

"Thanks for entertaining him, Gina." I moved away quickly. "She's great. You should get to know her," I told Croft, whose surprise turned to a look of disbelief and then reproach as I hurried away.

The last thing I saw before disappearing into my room was Gina's wide eyes pleading with me. I leaned against my closed door and let out a slow breath.

I kind of hated myself for what I was doing.

Gina deserved the best. She deserved much, *much* better than Croft. But what if she was somehow his match? After all, she would be the first person to find good in him. Maybe she would even fall for him. Maybe he would fall madly in love with her during their first conversation.

He was a pain, but he had raked our leaves for us. He had helped me out at the restaurant. If he hadn't actually been decent those couple of times, I would never have subjected Gina to this.

The memory of Gina's wide eyes seared into my mind. I had just thrown my friend to the wolves—or at least to one cocky wolf. She must be panicked at the prospect of entertaining him.

I really hated myself right now.

But I stuck to it. Grabbing a book, I lay back on my bed to read, trying not to think about what was going on in the other room. I heard voices for a time but tuned them out.

After a few minutes, I decided I'd given them long enough. I creaked my door open. The living room was terribly quiet.

Oh, no, what had I done?

In a panic, I ran out to check on them. They were still on the same couch, though Gina had moved to the very end, increasing the distance between them as much as she could.

Guilt lodged in my throat. I had caused my poor, sweet roommate to be uncomfortable for five long minutes. Gina looked extremely sorry, even apologetic, as she met my gaze.

She was apologetic towards *me*? *I* was the one who had done something unforgiveable.

I looked at Croft then, and my heart stopped. He was grinning as widely as ever, a heavy dose of victory in his expression, but what caught my attention was the book in his hand. My high school yearbook. Held open.

But how? I stared. He couldn't have stolen it from my room . . .

Oh. The memory came to me, clear as day, of my shoving it under the couch cushion and then forgetting about it.

He stood, stretching. "How was your escape—I mean, your room?" he asked, both eyebrows raised in a smug challenge.

"That's my book," I said with a steely calm I didn't feel.

He looked at it as though just now noticing it. "Oh, yeah. It does have a couple of pictures of you," he tossed out in a casual voice.

Gina crossed to me. "I'm sorry. I couldn't stop him," she whispered.

"It's not your fault," I managed.

Gina fled to her room. I turned back to the perpetrator.

"Who were you posing for?" Croft asked, turning the book so I could see myself, my lips pursed as though I were about to kiss someone, my eyes gleaming, a hand on my beguilingly cocked hip, and my body at an angle that showed off my figure.

"I wasn't." I bit out the words and snatched the book from him, slamming it shut.

It was true. To this day, I had no idea how someone had snapped that picture. I wasn't even sure where it had been taken. The wall behind me could have been from any number of places in my hometown.

I had tried to talk to the yearbook people about the picture, but Mike said no one knew who had sent it in—it just happened to show up in their pile of photos—and Jack said it was too late to remove it from the book. Everyone had already received their copy.

Croft's continuing grin made me uneasy. I wished I could wipe it off his face as easily as I had closed the book, but the truth was, he had just found the worst bit of blackmail imaginable on me.

"You obviously made an impression."

I raised the book threateningly, and he pretended to cower.

"Okay, okay. I'm just glad I get to hike with—what did they call you again?" he asked, stopping short of quoting my picture's subtitle, *Sexiest Senior Girl.*

"I'm warning you, Croft," I began.

"How about we make a deal?" he asked, much too sure of himself. He had all the cards in his hand, and he knew it. "You don't try to set me up with another girl tonight, and I don't tell anyone about your wonderful picture tonight."

Tonight? He wouldn't tell anyone *tonight?*

I threw the book behind me and stepped forward, then winced at the sound of a crash. A glance revealed that my missile had knocked the lamp off the table. It looked like it had survived the fall, though.

"Leave it," I ordered as Croft started toward the lamp. He stopped, and I became aware of how close we now stood together. Fine. I would work that to my advantage.

I reached out a finger and jabbed at his chest. "You will not talk about, think about, or remember that stupid picture. No conditions."

He grabbed my hand, folding my finger inward. "Yeah, you see, that's not how deals work."

I tossed my head and watched my blond hair nearly smack Croft in the face. Would that it had. "I don't know when, where, or how that picture was taken, but know this, Croft: I don't like hidden cameras. I'm tired of getting caught on camera and tired of people not asking for permission."

To his credit, his bluster faltered, and he frowned. "All right. I'll drop it," he said in a low voice.

Relief enveloped me, but I had no time to savor it before he led me toward the hallway, still holding my hand. "But don't try to set me up with my friend's date," he teased. "He wouldn't appreciate it, and I don't think she would, either."

"She couldn't appreciate it any less than I appreciate you setting yourself up with me," I grumbled.

"Hey, I thought we were beyond that point," he protested as we stepped outside, his friends nowhere in sight yet.

"What point?"

He raised our hands in a gesture. "The point of blatant dislike. *And* the next point of feigned dislike."

"*Feigned?*" I pulled his hand across me, making him stumble a step. This was fun. Maybe I could make him fall next. Nah, that would be too mean. "You think very highly of yourself."

"Yes." He beamed, catching his balance. "But not only that, I also think very highly of you. Highly enough that I'm sure you've already progressed to where you can admit to yourself, and sometimes to me, that you at least *sort of* like my company." He ignored my scoff. "Like I've told you before, no one's immune to my charm, and you're already becoming aware of its effects on you. I'm irresistible."

"You're several things that end in 'ible,' but that isn't one of them."

Croft pretended to be offended. "Inconceivable."

A white car pulled up, and someone inside it waved at us. I pulled my hand from Croft's and headed over to meet the couple as they got out. Better get this group date over with.

Chapter Twelve

To be fair, it was nice that Croft had invited two other people. Although I had been alone with him in his car on our first disastrous date, safe dating rules implied I shouldn't go on a hike alone with him. A double date was a good idea. It also gave me someone to talk to besides Croft.

I took full advantage of the opportunity. As the four of us drove together in Croft's Mazda, I joined Tristan and Jane's discussion and ignored Croft as much as possible. Unfortunately, once we reached the Slate Canyon Trailhead, Croft held me back while the others started across the parking lot.

"We'll join them soon, but first, I have something to say." He waited as they disappeared from sight.

I looked at him, my annoyance piqued.

He spread his arms wide. "How do you like it?" I frowned at him. "The scenery?" he clarified.

It wasn't half bad: a view of part of the city below with all its trees, my beautiful skies overhead, and majestic mountains looming up huge right behind us.

I crossed my arms. "Why can't we look at the scenery *with* your friends?"

"We could have, but that's not why we're staying behind. We're staying so I can apologize."

My eyes widened. Only that morning, a group of no less than five people had pointed me out on campus with snickers and quotes I was beyond tired of hearing repeated back to me. I could use some contrition from the culprit.

Then I remembered Croft's "apologies" at our dinner, and I told myself not to expect much. He wasn't about to wax poetical in earnest apology, that was for sure.

He cleared his throat, stepped back, and spread out his arms again. His voice rang out, pursued by an echo.

> *"Surrey, I'm sorry.*
> *I know you don't trust me.*
> *I'll remedy that.*
> *I want to change that."*

I couldn't believe it. He *was* waxing poetical—and his poetry was awful.

> *"While I may have blown it,*
> *I want you to, ah, known it"*

I snorted before I could stop myself. He grinned as though he were so clever.

> *"I'll help you to see*
> *I'm a guy you are free*
> *To trust."*

Yeah, right.

> *"I promise I'll never poison your crackers . . ."*

He broke off with a cough that could only be covering up laughter. I felt myself tense in frustration.

> *"Nor will I . . ."*

He stopped, laughing too hard to say any more.

"Why are you doing this?" I asked tightly. Bad poetry mixed with another apology that rang of insincerity, peppered with laughter—this wasn't helping one bit.

"Because . . ." He was still chuckling. "I want to make things better. If you can't even accept snacks from me without getting suspicious . . . I had this grand idea to prepare my words of contrition, but then my mind took off with the idea, and I just had to do this—recite a poem for you out in nature."

"Of course you had to." I rolled my eyes. "Forget about apologizing, Croft. You'll never manage it with a straight face. Everything is funny to you."

"Not everything," he said, reminding me of an earlier conversation.

"Everything," I repeated and threw my hands in the air. "Name *one* thing you've never even been *tempted* to make fun of."

I stared at him in defiance. He put his hands in his pockets, the humor draining from his face until he looked pained. I counted the seconds and grew confused. It was unusual for him to stand around this long without breaking into a smile.

When he finally spoke, his voice was quiet. "I actually should tell you about it. After all, it's why I treated you the way I did at first."

I was so surprised that I couldn't think up a snarky comment.

"I like to dwell on the funny things, though," he said with a ghost of a smile and a tiny shrug. "You're the one who helped me get back to that."

I blinked. I did? And he had, what, stopped finding things funny for a period of time?

His gaze sharpened. "Would you really like to know what I've never been tempted to make fun of?"

"Um." Suddenly, I wasn't sure. We seemed to have entered uncharted, terribly personal territory. Then again, how could I say no now? I would forever wonder what it was that had weighed on his mind.

His expression cleared. "I'll tell you. I'll tell you about it when you no longer think you hate me."

I mouthed the word, *Think?* The gall of him, even now while on the cusp of some deep confession or other.

He continued, "Once I've heard you say three completely sincere, completely nice things to me or about me, I'll tell you my secret."

I frowned. "Is that what this hike is for? Giving me time to think up compliments?"

He shook his head in amusement. "No, I don't expect it to happen today. And I'm the judge of whether what you say qualifies as substantial enough," he warned. "Once I've heard three real compliments, I'll tell you my story, and the telling will come with the sincerest apology you can imagine from me."

Honestly, that wasn't saying much at this point.

I shook my head. "I don't know what to think of you, Croft."

He took my arm and started toward the trail. "Think handsome, charming, and world's best sense of humor, darling."

"Not darling," I countered.

"I like 'Cinnamon' better, anyway."

* * *

SERIOUS CROFT MADE no return for the duration of the group date. He was as playful and pompous and laughing as ever. After seeing just a few moments of his serious side, I sort of preferred him laughing. Not that I preferred him. In any way. At all.

I was rather intrigued with the thought of Croft's "secret." Though it sounded like it would be painful to hear about, I was curious. I had little hope of earning my way to it, though. Coming up with nice things to say just for the purpose of satisfying my curiosity wouldn't be sincere, and he would be able to tell, I was sure.

Croft made bird noises as we ascended our dusty trail guarded by autumn-colored trees.

"Coo, coo. Come on, Surrey, let's hear your wood-chested, spotted-billed peckcracker noises."

"Her what?" Tristan asked.

"Surrey is an up-and-coming bird imitator," Croft told him. "Cheep, cheep," he called and finished with a whistle.

Jane joined in with some good imitations of her own. She and her date got excited about Croft's idea to play out a scene in which we communicated via secret bird calls, and they were quick to expand on the scenario. I wasn't surprised to find out they were part of Croft's hidden camera crew.

Even so, by the time we returned to the car, I was comfortable with both of them.

"All right, I want you to focus on the road, Surrey, while I take in the scenery," Croft told me as he drove.

"Watch your own road," I retorted.

"Fine," he sighed. "Surrey's an artist," he said heavily to the others. "I guess that means I should let her enjoy the fall colors."

"I guess you'd better," Jane told him. Then she offered, "I'll watch the road for you."

Tristan laughed.

"If you guys are part of this YouTube show, how involved were you with my scene?" I forced myself to ask, although I was afraid of the answer.

"I was part of an earlier planning session," Jane answered, "but I wasn't in town when it happened. It was still summer vacation. Tristan was involved, weren't you?"

"Yep. I helped figure out the logistics," he answered, "but the idea was Croft's. The initial ideas often are."

"Ooh, what if we lend Surrey the crumbling parchment we used in our ant-infestation prank?" Jane spoke up. "She could pass it to one of us fellow spies in her movie."

"Yeah, after we call back and forth with our bird noises to make sure the coast is clear," Tristan said, perking up.

It was all I could do not to smile at their suggestions. If Croft weren't around, I would have been tempted to make this silly movie with Jane and Tristan, but I couldn't let him know his idea was growing on me.

"Thanks for coming, you guys," Croft told them when he pulled up in front of my house.

"Thanks for inviting us," Tristan answered.

"See you soon on-set," Jane said.

"Are they actually dating?" I asked Croft in a low voice as they walked to Jane's car. I had my suspicions after watching their easy camaraderie.

"Not really. They're friends. But they were happy to be each other's date for the afternoon, so I was truthful when I told you about them."

I let it go with a shrug, since I was glad they had joined us.

Croft followed me up the walkway. "Let's see, you're missing out on tonight's event," he began as though thinking out loud, "but the week is still young. I think I'll come on Thursday and take you on a surprise date."

"Thursdays don't work."

"Twist my arm, will you? I'll come tomorrow, then."

"You seriously don't need to come that often." I was alarmed at the thought. "I have homework. I have a linear algebra test in a week and a half. I'm busy."

"It's either tomorrow or Friday. Which will it be, Cinnamon?"

"How about we don't see each other for a month?" I tried.

"Sounds good. I like the idea of tomorrow best, too."

"Don't hold your breath that I'll be here."

He turned to me at the door. "Aren't you glad I came today? Your day was so much better with me in it."

I rolled my eyes.

"You're welcome," he said magnanimously.

I shut the door on him.

Then I remembered the leaves he had raked and bagged for me and Gina. I hadn't thanked him for that. I hadn't even mentioned it.

Having been raised to express gratitude, I opened the door and stuck my head out. "Th—"

I stopped short and looked at him. He waited while I rethought expressing my appreciation. He was still a pompous cad, and he would have known I would know he had been the one to rake those leaves. He might have done it in hopes of getting some sort of reward.

I pulled my head back in and locked the door.

On the other side, Croft's laughter rang out. I could almost hear the swagger in his footsteps as he returned to his car, satisfied with the afternoon. He was insufferable.

Chapter Thirteen

My tender mercy the next day was that I had finished dinner by the time Croft knocked. At least I didn't have to eat with him joining me or looking on and making silly, arrogant comments.

I opened the door and sighed deeply at the sight of him. Until that point, there had been the faint possibility it was a salesman or a neighbor.

"Today is our dessert date," he announced cheerfully and proceeded to the dining room, where he placed a bag on the table. "Wait for it. When I prepare dessert, I go all out. Crème brûlée," he pulled something from his bag, "chocolate ganache cake, and an elegant dollop of vanilla ice cream to please the taste buds."

He placed two baby-pink plastic objects on the table. Two spoons followed, along with two forks. I stepped closer.

"You can still choose to go out for dessert if you want, but my vote is that we eat what I brought, because that was a lot of work," he said, setting out cloth napkins.

The pink objects were toy plates. Just as Croft had said, there was crème brûlée, chocolate cake, and white ice cream—all part of the plate and as plasticky as the rest of it. I hadn't seen plastic foods like these since the last time I stepped foot in the nursery at church back home.

"Oh, I brought the hot cocoa from last time, too," he remembered and took out two large toy cups nearly filled to the brim with plastic cocoa. Pulling out a chair with a flourish, he indicated for me to sit.

My face went into a series of convulsions. My lips twitched and twisted as I tried to keep them turned downward. I had laughed after our dinner together and even after we raked leaves, but I was determined not to laugh *in front* of Croft over one of his jokes.

My hand went to my face. I stopped my smile with it, then rested it on my chin, then blocked my mouth again, then pressed my hand semi-innocently against my cheek, trying to look unaffected. I finally thought to turn my back on Croft to keep him from seeing the struggle, but by this time, my shoulders were shaking.

I let out a chortle that sounded like a sob. Croft's hands settled on my shoulders from behind.

"I didn't imagine you would be so moved," he said with feeling.

I burst out cry-laughing, covering my face with my hands.

It was an experience, laughing my head off while Croft patted my back at intervals.

Finally, I regained a measure of control, wiped my eyes, and turned to him.

"Stop it," I pleaded, a chuckle making its escape.

He held up his hands and backed off as though I had meant he should stop patting my back, when really, I was referring to his joke with toy plates and food. And drinks.

"I'll stop. I need to get us extra cups, anyway. We might want some water with this."

He went to the kitchen, and I worked to compose myself, taking deep breaths and eyeing the plastic culprits askance where they sat on the table, tempting me to laugh again.

I could hear Croft looking for the correct cupboard and then filling cups with water from the sink. He was seriously going through with this. He would force me to spell it out for him that I wanted to go get dessert somewhere before he would drop this charade of eating what he had "prepared" for us.

Now that I thought about it, I did have a decision to make. Stay here and play pretend with the plastic, or ask to go out? Which was the better option? Though I was inclined to stay and keep our interaction as little like a date as possible, I might find myself laughing again, which would only encourage him.

"Hey, I know this guy," Croft's voice called from the kitchen. "Brody's in one of my classes. You went to his and Hanna's reception?"

I flinched. My fingers closed into fists and then reopened. With a fortifying breath, I walked to the fridge, where Croft stood looking at Brody's announcement.

I swallowed and said, "No, but I'm going."

"Time-traveling?" he grinned. "This took place last month." He pointed out the October date.

"It got postponed." It was finally happening this Saturday. Hanna had called me Monday, super happy with the news that her uncle was out of the hospital.

"Gotcha. Hey, that means I can go with you. Now you have your plus one," he beamed. "How do you know her?"

I scowled at his antics. "She's getting married to him."

It took him a moment. Then he backtracked. "Sorry, I shouldn't have assumed it was her you knew. How do you know *him*?"

My eyes stayed on the invitation, the picture of Hanna holding on to him from behind, both of them looking so happy. "We dated."

Croft was quiet for a time. "Wow," he finally said.

I kept looking at the picture. When I realized an unusually long time had passed, I turned to Croft, who was staring at me. "Wow, what?"

"Your heart *is* broken. And you weren't kidding when you said you dated nice guys. I don't think there's a creature in this world who's as nice as Brody." He looked impressed.

"Hanna might be," I said, and I'm pretty sure my words came across without any bitterness. Sadness, maybe, but no resentment.

"Well, it's a good thing I'm not competing with him for your attention," Croft said as he looked at the picture.

My shoulders dropped in surprise, and I barely stopped my jaw from doing the same. Just how insensitive could Croft be?

"Like I told you," he continued, "you don't need nice. Maybe you could be happy with a guy like Brody, but you could never be *deliriously* happy nor one hundred percent you. He's not your type."

Now my jaw did drop. *"Croft Taylor,"* I exclaimed, wishing furiously that he had a longer name more conducive to scolding. His first name needed more syllables. Or he needed a middle name. *Croft Jamison Taylor.* That would be better for scolding.

Lest you think my forage into pondering the length of names distracted me from the situation at hand, let me assure you I was burning holes in Croft with my gaze at that moment.

"No, he's not my type at all," I said loudly and sarcastically. "I don't need a Prince Charming, do I? Of course not. No nice, sweet, or thoughtful for *me,* thank you very much. What *I* need is someone *arrogant, pompous, cocky, self-absorbed* . . ." I spat out each successive word in italics. Then I stopped, blinked rapidly, and widened my eyes at Croft as though seeing him for the first time—square face, dark, messy hair and all.

"Here you are," I whispered as though I had just received a revelation. "My Prince Big-Head."

I would have gone on staring at him in pretend awe, but he smiled and took my arm. "Let's go for a walk, Surrey."

"No, thanks." Why did he have to ruin my scene? He hadn't even gotten properly offended.

"Yes, I think it'll do us good." He was already steering me outside.

I wasn't sure how it happened. One moment, I was giving him the best, most theatrical setback I had ever given anyone, and the next, I had grabbed my keys and was wearing my shoes, strolling through the neighborhood arm in arm with my tormentor, my righteous indignation wearing off.

"Why are we walking?" I asked, half annoyed and half curious about the answer.

"Blowing off steam. Feels good, doesn't it?"

"I just called you self-absorbed and a whole lot of other mean things. Doesn't that bother you?"

"I'm not worried." He tucked my arm closer into his. He was acting like we were a couple. Not only that, but it almost seemed like he was comforting me following my outburst.

"You're crazy," I told him, but my voice was quiet. I guess I was a little tired after my roller coaster of emotions and my tirade.

"As much as it pains me not to talk about myself," he said with fake anguish, "I was thinking we could focus on something else for now. Like the breeze touching our faces. The smell of burning wood from someone's backyard. Mmm. The trees all around us going to sleep for the winter."

Wow, he was being poetic. He didn't do great with actual poems, but he sure could spin something with his words.

"There's hardly a breeze," I said, just to be contradictory.

He winked and continued on, changing the theme a little. "The snow that blows across the street. The biting, sharp wind that threatens to over-turn us at every step." He staggered unevenly as if fighting the wind. "The frost in our eyebrows," he panted, "as we struggle to survive on our journey."

I turned away to hide my smile and caught sight of Brother Jackson, one of the men who had helped me and Gina move in last January. He stopped pruning roses to give me a wave, and I waved back.

"I didn't mean you don't need someone nice," Croft said suddenly, and I turned back to him. "You do. I just don't think you need someone whose strongest character trait is that he's nice."

"Oh." I didn't know what else to say. It was still heavy-handed of him to think he could dictate my type to me, but at the moment, I didn't feel upset.

Croft changed the subject. "How many siblings do you have?"

"Um. Three," I said before remembering how we had both evaded answering that question honestly on our earlier date.

He grinned. "What's the worst prank you've ever pulled on one of them?"

My mouth twitched in reply to his grin. I answered willingly. "Kent and I were hiding in the bushes by the front porch when London's date brought her home one night. We waited until it sounded like they were just about to kiss, and then we jumped out at them with Indian war whoops. She screamed really loud." I giggled. "We rushed off to a safe place inside before that scream ever ended. We had food storage ready for two days and a lock on the door so we could hide away that long if needed."

Croft laughed heartily. "And you say you don't like pranks?"

"I . . . don't . . ." I squirmed. Children's voices piped up nearby, and I recognized the Petersens as they rounded the corner up ahead and walked toward us. They were the second family Croft and I had raked leaves for. The parents nodded and smiled at me, and the littlest girl called out, "Hi, Surrey."

I waggled my fingers at her, grateful for a distraction. "Hi, Mace." It was a while since they'd had me over for dinner, but I must have remembered the name right, because Mace skipped past without correcting me.

Croft looked at the family with a glint in his eye before returning to our conversation.

"That sounded like a great one. That was the worst thing you've done to one of your siblings?"

"Probably not. It was just the first thing that popped into my mind."

He laughed again. "London, Kent, Surrey," he noted, ticking the names off on his fingers and ending with a decisive nod. "I could give my kids Australian place-names, too."

I fought a smile, silently giving him credit for being more creative with his reaction than most people when they realized how my parents had named my siblings and me.

"What's the nicest thing you've ever done for someone?" he asked.

I shrugged. "Raked leaves."

He shook his head. "You're saying the first thing that popped into your mind again."

"I can hardly go through all my memories and pick one that was more 'something' than any other."

"Hello, Surrey," called Sister James, her elbows moving back and forth as she power walked. I noticed a set of ankle weights strapped to her ankles and made a note to myself never to underestimate elderly Utah women.

"Hi," I called back.

"Especially on this particular question," Croft said, watching us. "I'm willing to bet you've done a lot of nice things, to your siblings and to others you meet. Last Saturday, you had me help serve your neighbors, and I've seen you greet people on these streets no less than three times within the last two minutes."

I actually blushed. Croft sounded admiring, and I didn't know what to do with it.

"I don't do much," I muttered. "A lot of them invited us to dinner after we moved into the neighborhood. Some, I invited to dinner myself so I could get to know them."

"Sweet. I think you should invite me to dinner, too."

I scoffed. "Nope. I don't need to get to know you."

He stopped and leaned in close, making me blink. "That's what *you* think," he said while I stared into eyes that reminded me of the sky at its darkest blue. Croft pulled back and continued, pretending to ponder, "Or rather, that's what you *think* you think. But you don't actually think that." He patted my hand with his free one. "We'll work on it. Do you ever go to this park?"

His spiel about my thinking deserved a chastising reply, but I forewent scolding him and turned my eyes to the park ahead. A dog barked, tugging on its leash in the parking lot as it tried to get to a group of teenagers. Children yelled on the playground behind them, and someone sat on a bench nearby with earbuds in his ears.

"Oh, I can interpret for him. I've got this," Croft said beside me, rubbing his hands together.

"Who?" I asked, confused.

"The Golden Retriever. You know what he's saying, don't you?" The dog pulled against its leash, whining in excitement, and Croft cried in a goofy voice, "Ooh, ooh, let's go say hi, come on, let's go meet them, I know they'll be my best friends, I just *know* it."

"Come on, Baby, we're going home," said the owner, a man who seemed intent on winning the tug-of-war.

"The owner is oblivious to the fact that he's dashing the hopes and dreams of Baby," Croft narrated in a near whisper, his eyes wide with sympathy. "Completely unconcerned with the feelings of his dog."

"Croft," I protested, shaking with mirth.

"Ooh, ooh, let's go see *them*, look at that group, do you see them? Can we go say hi, please? Please?" Mr. Goofy was back as the dog lunged in the direction of the playing children.

"No," the owner said, tugging. "No, Baby." His *no*s were interspersed with Croft's pleading. "Please?" "Stop it, Baby." "Come on, please?" "No."

The dog jumped impressively high. "But they *love* me," Croft spoke for him, and I cracked up, leaning against Croft, my arm still hooked in his.

"Oh, oh, let's go see *them*," Croft continued as Baby turned his attention to a strolling couple. "Oh, please, come on, please," the words came fast while the dog tripped, lifting his paws in quick succession and looking so excited I thought he might pee. "Come on . . . "

"No, Baby."

"Let's . . ."

"We're going home."

The dog crouched, gathering his hindquarters to jump. "But *they* love me, *too*," Croft exclaimed, timing his second word with the dog's leap.

My eyes started tearing up as I laughed.

"I have to—Oh, are we going home?" Croft's goofy voice perked up as the man unlocked his car and Baby ran to the vehicle, forgetting how badly he had wanted to go after someone else. "Oh, oh, I love home, especially when you're there with me. This is just the best day ever."

The door shut. The owner walked around and let himself in. Croft was silent beside me as the engine turned on and I squeezed out another tear.

"Open-the-window, please," Croft's bright voice rang out, sing-songy. "I wanna hang my . . ." Now *he* was laughing. ". . . head out . . ."

He broke off, guffawing, and held me more or less upright while I laughed against him.

"Okay, let's go home," I finally said, wiping my eyes not for the first time since Croft had arrived at my house today.

"To your home or to mine?" he asked.

"Our *respective* homes."

"All right, but first, I'll walk you home."

"I didn't imagine otherwise," I muttered under my breath.

"We haven't had our dessert yet, though."

I avoided a low-hanging branch from someone's front yard. "I think we've had more than enough. You've met your quota for tonight."

"My quota for what?" He cocked his head.

"For making me laugh."

He puffed out his chest. "I will say, it has been a delightful date. By all accounts."

I wanted to say something about asking to hear *my* account before making assumptions, but as I had just recovered from a laughing fit—my second of the night—there wasn't much I could do to naysay his assessment.

Croft spoke again, his voice kind. "Go ahead. You can say it."

I sighed. "Say what?"

"You think I'm funny."

I shook my head. "You . . ." He waited in expectation. ". . . have a big head."

He inclined said head, looking gratified. "And?"

"I'm not planning on making it any bigger."

His smile grew wide. "It sounds like you're holding back a compliment to keep my head from growing."

I remembered suddenly his secret, the dark story he was keeping from me until I gave him three sincere compliments. Well, as I had already concluded, I couldn't very well give him a compliment just to get him to start counting.

"It seemed to *me* you thought the 'big head' comment was a great compliment," I said. "I can hardly add on to that, now, can I?"

"There are always more things I can be complimented on." He gave a royal wave to an invisible crowd.

It was quickly growing dark as we returned to my home. Croft, of course, had to come inside and pick up his plastic food and dishes.

I unlocked the door and walked in to find Gina studying. "Hi, there," I told her.

"Good to see you, Gina," Croft greeted.

"You, too."

I bit my lip and hoped she didn't feel awkward around Croft. I had apologized profusely to her for my moment of insanity in putting the two of them together, but Gina was a people pleaser. If someone felt bad about something, she would do everything she could to reassure them it was fine because she didn't want them to feel bad. I had had to end my apologies and act like I didn't feel guilty in order to help her feel better. Go figure.

"Well, goodbye, Croft," I said unceremoniously.

He picked up his bag from the dining table and put the cloth napkins in it. "I think it'll take me a couple of trips," he said, considering the table before him. "Maybe three or four." He started toward the door, leaving behind the plates, cups, and cutlery.

No way would I let him delay his exit like this. I grabbed up his things and ran after him.

"I'm pretty sure you can do it in one," I insisted, but his only response was to speed up. Lengthening my stride, I caught up to him and tried to get to the bag, but he managed to get ahead of me again. A blast of cool air hit me at the entrance.

"What's the big hurry?" I called, my mischievous smile growing as I strode after him and tried not to drop the plastic plates or cups in my arms. My fingers were curled around the utensils he had left behind. "Come on, take these. You're a big, strong man. You can't carry it all at once?"

He put his bag in the car and turned to me. "Thank you very much for bringing those, Surrey."

"There's no need to waste trips to the house," I said pointedly while he took the objects, one at a time, and put them in the bag. I raised my eyebrows. "Wow, somebody's slow."

"But I'm big and strong." He grinned. "You said so."

"I retract that. Obviously, there's not a big and strong bone in your body." I relinquished my hold on the last fork and watched him put it away tenderly. The goofball.

He turned and picked up my hands next. "I wanted so to prolong our time together."

"Enough." I pulled my hands away so he couldn't put *me* in the car next. "I told you, you've already met your quota. But I suppose I should be impressed you can hold *two* hands at once."

He sputtered with laughter. I turned and headed back to the house. His steps sounded behind me, making me tense and speed up.

Maybe I shouldn't have saved him the trips. Now I was outside with him, and I was suddenly nervous about him trying to say good night to me on the doorstep.

"What's the hurry?" he asked, laughter in his voice as we both neared the door at an alarming pace.

I put my hand on the knob, but the door just rattled in place.

Oh, no. I had locked it on my way out.

I checked my pocket and was infinitely relieved to find I had my key with me. I wasn't sure which would be faster, though, unlocking the door myself or ringing the bell and having Gina open it.

"Thanks for tonight, sweetheart," Croft's cheerful voice said behind me as I scrambled to insert the key.

"I'm not a sweetheart." I hoped I wasn't scratching the metal. There, the key was in.

"You might be interested to know I have a thing about kissing." Croft paused for effect, and my stomach dropped. "I won't kiss a girl until I get engaged. You don't need to worry about the ol' doorstep scene."

I stopped and looked at him in surprise. Really? That was great. And almost funny, seeing as I had the exact same rule—although I wasn't about to tell him.

He gave me a compassionate smile. "I know it's a disappointment, but keep a stiff upper lip."

"My eyes will fall out if you keep making them roll like this," I told him.

"So, hug?" he asked brightly, holding out his arms.

I quickly turned back to the door and began working at the key again. "No."

One step brought him right up behind me. "What, no hug?"

"No."

"Fist bump? High five?" Out of the corner of my eye, I saw him reach out. I twisted so only one of his hands made it, putting a warm weight on my shoulder.

"Pat on the back?" he asked, clapping me with the hand that had landed on me.

By that time, I had gotten the door open. I jumped inside and locked it behind me.

Pat on the back? I could still feel his hand on my shoulder and hear his concession to the downgrade from a hug. When had I ever ended a date—or anything resembling a date—with a clap on the back while I was turned away from the guy?

The ridiculousness of the whole scene caught up to me, and I doubled over laughing for the third time that evening.

Chapter Fourteen

HE SLID the glass door open. As soon as he entered, the tension left his body. Oh, how he needed this. He couldn't fathom another week without walking through the house where she walked, touching the things she touched.

He hadn't used to need that. The pictures had been enough. For so long, the pictures had been enough.

Pictures. The cameras needed rotating, and he must see what they had captured. He went straight to his favorite spots, craving whatever stimulation they could give him.

Ten minutes later he was kneeling on the floor, laughing softly as he looked through the latest harvest of photos.

In one of them, her expression showed such attitude. In another, she appeared to be laughing for all she was worth. He stared at it for a long while. What did that laughter sound like? His eyes rested on the creamy throat she exposed, and he swallowed. What did the base of her throat feel like?

The back of his own throat burned. Once more, the pictures mocked him with their one-dimensionality. He wrenched a book from its shelf and ran his hands across it, putting his hands where he imagined hers had been, hoping to feel the connection. Did she ever feel his presence? His constant thoughts of her?

Clenching his teeth, he returned to the photos. When he moved on to the next one, he forgot to breathe.

Slender fingers curled around a paintbrush. A delicate hand hovered near the wood of the easel. A boy's face had come alive on the canvas, but he was nothing compared to the masterpiece that stood before him.

The usual adjectives didn't apply. "Ethereal" wasn't enough to describe the vision of her. "Queenly" or "elfin" didn't even come close. She was breathtaking. Exhilarating.

How did the others not see it? They dated her, and then they let her go. Fools, all of them. He closed his hand into a fist. No one deserved her. No one adored her like they should. If it were him, he would never let her go. Never.

If it were him . . .

Chapter Fifteen

I wasn't laughing when I arrived home from school the next day, only to be welcomed by that familiar, uncomfortable feeling.

I took a deep breath and felt a shiver trickle down my spine.

I didn't want to deal with this. I should be free to move around in my house. I *would* move around freely. Maybe if I pushed ahead, I would finally discover the problem and put an end to it.

My eyes settled on my bedroom door. I would walk to my room, I told myself. Today, the bad feeling wouldn't stop me.

As though unfreezing from a spell, I moved into action, my steps fluid and speeding up, my stomach hurting with anticipation. I was making a big deal out of nothing. My imagination was overactive, making the bad feeling worse than usual.

I reached the door in no time and, stomach cramping, opened it.

Everything looked fine—but it didn't feel fine. Still, today I was determined to face this problem. My heart thumping, I stepped inside.

Nothing looked out of place. There was no reason to feel strange. No visible reason, anyway.

Could it be bad spirits?

I struggled with discomfort, annoyed that this feeling kept creeping into my home. Still, maybe I had made progress just now. I had taken a step toward conquering this thing by venturing further into my house than usual.

I bit my lip. Or was I making it worse?

Either way, the step I had taken would have to be enough for now. I couldn't bear to stay any longer, so I hurried outside, shut the door in relief, and started walking.

The breeze Croft had mentioned yesterday nudged at my face and made me smile. "Biting, sharp wind," I murmured. Croft's stagger had been convincing. He should have been an actor.

My smile dimmed as I remembered his role in that long-ago prank on me. What was the prank I had managed to avoid attending this week? Had Croft truly watched from the sidelines, or was he in the video again, acting a part?

I shook my head. Apparently I couldn't even go for a walk without him intruding on my thoughts.

After circling the block a second time, I found Willie standing under his tree. Perfect. He was just the informant I needed. I approached and saw that he was putting rope through a wide board with holes in its ends.

"Ooh, is that the swing?"

"Yep. I'll tie it with constrictor knots. No one will be able to undo them."

I watched as he looped the end of the rope around itself in a figure eight. Eventually, he spoke. "Did you want to ask me something?"

I cleared my throat. "Is there a new video up on Croft's channel? Something that took place at the Marriott Hotel?"

Willie looked up swiftly. "He didn't film you in another one, did he?" I could see the avenging angel coming out in him.

"No, no, I was just wondering. I don't watch his things, but I know he did something yesterday."

"Oh." Willie turned back to the swing and finished the other knot, still frowning a little. "No, there hasn't been anything since a couple of weeks ago. Do you want me to tell you when there's a new one?"

"Sure." It hurt my pride to show interest in anything Croft did, but at least Croft didn't know. "Just this next one. I don't need to see more than one."

"Okay. Will you help me get the ladder?"

"Of course."

We grabbed the clunky ladder from his family's garage and started across the lawn.

"You said you're going on dates with him, right?" Willie asked.

"Croft? Yes. But they're only *sort of* dates." We stopped under the tree.

"How are they 'sort of' dates?"

"Why are you asking?"

He pursed his lips. "I've gone through all his videos and studied them from all angles. I had to do my research, you know, after you told me you were going on dates with him."

"Right. I guess. And?"

"I could be wrong," he said in the tone of someone who was pretty sure he knew exactly what he had figured out.

"What?" I asked impatiently.

He picked an old leaf off the ladder. "I feel like he picks on blondes. Some of those pranks, they get meaner when the person on film is a blonde."

I blinked. "You . . . you think so?"

"Just watch out, okay? And tell me if he gets mean again," he ordered, pointing at me.

His stern command made my mouth twitch in humor. I cleared my throat and nodded. "I will." If Croft *did* return to his previous behavior, I would have no qualms about letting Willie punish him. "Just don't break any laws if you go after him."

Willie's smile was secretive. If only I could imitate that expression myself. Or paint it.

"We'll see," he said.

He took the ends of both ropes and scurried up the ladder, and I quickly grabbed hold to keep it steady for him.

My mind turned over Willie's words. Was it possible? Did Croft have a thing against blondes?

He certainly had held a grudge against *me* for no reason at the beginning of the semester. Still, doubts about Willie's observation clouded my mind. Utah had tons of blondes. A good portion of the population had Scandinavian roots. Maybe Willie had misinterpreted what he thought was a pattern.

However, now I was even more curious about yesterday's prank. Part of me also itched to watch the earlier ones in order to make my own conclusions. It would probably be the wise thing to do, as it would help me find out more about this guy I was spending time with.

Then again, the whole point of my dating him was to get rid of him. Why should I try to learn more about him?

"Incoming," Willie yelled. My eyes widened, and I jumped back as he came sliding down the ropes until he dumped onto the swing. There he sat and bounced, the strong branch above him barely swaying with its new weight.

"Okay, you try now. Test it with your weight first," he said, jumping off. "According to my calculations, it should be able to carry someone of several hundred pounds, but one never does these things without testing it."

I turned to sit, then jumped at the sight of a girl standing on the sidewalk, watching us with a finger in her mouth. I recognized her as one of the Whitmer girls, the youngest in the family. She had been four years old when the Whitmers invited me and Gina to dinner last semester. I smiled at her and sat on the swing.

"Bounce," Willie told me.

I giggled and obeyed. Everything held.

"Okay, you can swing," Willie said generously.

I backed up with the board behind me until the ropes were taut. Then I let go, swinging forward with a rush. The motion tickled my stomach.

"This is great," I called out. "Nice work, Willie."

He beamed like it was Christmas.

"Hey," I said in a lowered voice as I swung by him. "Can she swing, too?" I asked as I passed him again and put my feet on the ground to slow down.

Willie turned to look at his guest. "Oh. Yeah." He frowned, as though unsure of how to go about inviting her.

I jumped off the swing. "Do you want to try it?" I asked the girl.

She nodded quickly, pulling her finger from her mouth and trotting toward us.

"Willie made the swing."

Her eyes widened. "You did?"

"I did." He shifted his weight awkwardly.

She ran to the swing and plopped down. "Can you push me?"

"Sure." His smile returned as he took on the duty of swing-pusher. He started out nice and slow but sped up when he noticed her kicking her heels in excitement, undaunted by the height and the tempo.

"Hold on tight, Bella," he encouraged. She squealed as she swung higher.

I couldn't stop grinning. I had a feeling Willie was about to become popular in the neighborhood. In fact, I was suddenly very hopeful of it. It would be a new thing for him.

So much for him not liking girls.

* * *

MY STEPS WERE light and bouncy as I headed to campus the next day. I had invited Gina to try the swing with me after dinner last night, and I had played on it probably more than I should admit. It meant less homework time than I had planned for, but all work and no play makes Jack a dull boy, right?

My future home would need a swing. And maybe a treehouse? But for sure a—

"Hi, Surrey." A familiar voice pulled me from my daydreams on my way to the Talmage Building. "You look happy."

"Hi, Jesse." I smiled at my ex. "I guess so." Had he noticed my discomfort from sitting with him in New Testament class, after all? Apparently I was more chipper this morning than he was used to.

He started to say something, stopped, then cleared his throat. "Are you dating someone new?"

Like Croft?

I couldn't help it. I burst out laughing. The idea of Croft having made me happy like this was ludicrous.

"No, it's not a guy," I said between chuckles. "I'm just happy. There's more to life than dating," I added saucily. "Anyway, I have to go to class."

He looked confused, but he lifted his hand in a wave. "Okay. Have a good weekend."

Seriously, I thought as I entered the Talmage Building, *life is great right now, and it has nothing to do with dating.* School was going well, I had my painting time, I had a swing next door, and I was surrounded by good people.

I sat down and didn't have to wait long for my eternal pest to take the seat beside me.

Strangely, I felt no flash of annoyance as he claimed his chair. In fact, I had a sensation akin to pleasure, as though a friend had just arrived and I was looking forward to a friendly chat.

However, that illusion was sure to shatter as soon as he opened his mouth.

He opened his mouth. "How come you didn't tell me Brody's reception is tomorrow?"

I blinked. "How did you know it was?"

"I have my ways," he said, aiming for a snobbish tone before dropping the charade in favor of his usual grin. "I told you I have a class with him. I asked him when it was."

Croft was turning out to be a veritable spy. Not a very discreet one, but someone who knew how to get his information, nonetheless.

"You told me it had been postponed, but you didn't tell me it was this weekend," he persisted, looking wounded.

I thought back to when we had conversed in front of the fridge. That entire evening had been a mishmash of laughter and anger. "Actually, it slipped my mind."

"Ah." He looked appeased. "Well, lucky for you, I'm available and ready to take you tomorrow."

"Not that I wouldn't have kept it secret if I had thought of it," I added, ignoring his offer. It wasn't an offer at all, I knew. He assumed I would let him join me. The strange thing was that the idea of going together didn't bother me. Was there something in me that had come to like . . . bantering with him?

"That's my Surrey," he chuckled.

"No," I said, pained. "You don't *have* a Surrey."

He just beamed. "I'll pick you up at eleven thirty. What'll you wear at the reception? I think we should match."

"I don't think so," I told him. "Just wear something nice, and we'll be good."

"Everything looks nice on me." He looked thoughtful. "Maybe I should wear a sack so I don't outshine the happy couple."

"Maybe you should wear a gag so you don't outtalk the other guests," I muttered.

Chapter Sixteen

I WAS at the dining table buttering my toast the next morning when it hit me. It was Saturday. Brody's Saturday.

My hand shook, so I laid down the knife.

This was it. He was getting married. By the time I showed up at his reception at noon, he and Hanna would have been sealed in the temple.

My appetite gone, I stared at the table. All my feelings for Brody, all my daydreams—they had to go.

Breathing through my nose, I asked myself, Do *I still have feelings for him?*

I pondered the question, letting my toast grow cold.

I honestly wasn't sure. No tears came to my eyes, but my heart did feel heavy. Memories of him warmed me. He had taken a bigger piece of my heart than anyone before him, and I had never gone for so long after a breakup before I gave love another chance. Even now, the thought of trying again wearied me.

I pushed away my food and went to bury myself in linear algebra homework.

Several hours later, I had the answers to fifty math questions and part of my life's conundrum.

What I had had with Brody was good, it was true, I acknowledged as I pulled on a flowing, lilac dress. Well, I would look forward to finding that with someone else. Somehow, someday, I would find someone to love more than I would have loved Brody. Heavenly Father wouldn't have taken Brody and the others from me if there weren't someone even better for me out there.

A knock at the door interrupted my musings.

Cue in Croft, I thought to myself, and the corners of my mouth lifted. *My Prince Big-Head.* I went to open the door.

Colors and dimples greeted me along with the brisk November air.

Croft wore dark-green slacks and a light-green, collared shirt, which was fine—but from there, things went downhill. His pocket-square was checkered red, white, and purple; the bowtie at his throat had enough tiny blue and yellow stripes to mess with one's vision; and the belt was orange. *Orange.*

"I thought if I wore enough colors, one of them would be sure to match yours," Croft said. "And just look. We're both wearing purple."

It took me a bit to find my tongue. "Croft. You look a mess."

He beamed. "And *you* look like a dream. Are you ready to go?"

I shook my head and leaned against the doorway. "I can't be seen with you."

His face fell. "But . . . purple?"

I rolled my eyes. "Look, I don't want to cause a scene at Brody and Hanna's reception. They don't deserve that."

"Okay, I can accept that." He turned over his belt within its loops, and I was relieved to find that the belt was a nice, woodsy brown on this side. Then he reached into his pocket, pulled out a tiny gray . . . bowtie? This he stuck on top of his striped bowtie with a pin.

"Better?" he asked.

I stared at the offensive mini-bowtie.

"It's funeral gray," he explained.

I moaned and stepped up to him, plucking the gray bowtie off his person. "You're not wearing this," I said, holding it up.

He gave me a sad look.

I pointed at the other bowtie. "You're not wearing *that.*"

He grabbed himself, hugging his shirt and his pants. "Please don't make me take anything else off."

I coughed and tried to give him a pointed look. "Either the pocket-square or the bowtie has to go."

He sighed deeply and replaced the square with a brown one to match the belt.

"*Much* better," I proclaimed. He looked good now. Well-dressed good, that is, not handsome good. Okay, maybe he *was* handsome, but that didn't matter.

"I knew I picked the right outfit," he bragged as we started down the driveway. He strutted to his car before realizing I hadn't followed. I was unlocking my Kia ten steps behind him. He quickly backtracked.

"Oh, no worries, you can follow me," I told him, getting into the driver's seat and waving at his blue Mazda. "Or not. You don't have to go at all if you don't want to."

"Nice try." He pulled at the doorknob on the passenger side. I giggled at the look on his face when the door didn't open.

"Surrey, you adore me," he said, looking at me with cow's eyes. "You're ecstatic that I'm coming today."

I shut my door.

He knocked on his. "You can hardly wait to show off your new boyfriend to everyone there," he called, the words difficult to make out through the glass.

I unlocked the door and waited for him to climb in. "You're not my boyfriend."

"Feel free to pretend, though," he said, chipper.

* * *

Ten minutes later, we arrived in front of the church building Hanna's family had reserved.

I turned off the engine, took a deep breath, and turned to Croft. Before I could say anything, he spoke up in an eager voice.

"Yes? Let me guess. You're eternally grateful I'm here. You're glad our clothes match. You can't live without me." He paused and nodded. "I already know."

Yeah, that deserved an eye-roll.

"Let's go." I opened my door.

"Whoa, whoa, whoa." He hurried around to my side as I got out. "I should be opening the door for you when you're in a dress."

"Not necessary."

"And when you're wearing purple, I should be helping you in and out of the car."

"Lilac," was my response. He had called it purple one too many times.

"Huh?"

I stopped and held up the skirt of my dress. "Lilac."

"Right. Artist. You'll have to teach me the different shades of purple."

"You can do a Google search on them."

"But not everything you find on the internet is true," he exclaimed, looking horrified at the thought. "What if you were to quiz me on the colors, and I failed because Google taught me wrong?"

We entered the building and were nearly bowled over by a group of kids playing tag in the hallway in their nice clothes. Noises sounded from the kitchen, but inevitably we approached the gym and stepped inside.

The round tables that filled the room were decorated with white tablecloths and strings of light. Chocolate fountains at either end of the refreshment table added to the ambiance. We were early, but there were already people sitting at some of the tables, and I tensed when I caught sight of the bride and groom.

Hanna glowed in her embroidered white gown. A wreath of pale yellow roses encircled her hair. Brody—I swallowed—looked celestial in his three-piece suit. The two of them stood in front of a display of photos and flowers, with several friends lined up to talk to them. The room felt too warm all of a sudden, and my stomach felt funny when I saw the couple sneak a kiss between greetings.

Of course. Their no-kissing rule had met its end—and they seemed pretty happy about it.

"Magenta. Violet. Lavender," Croft listed off, slipping his arm through my elbow. "Umm, periwinkle. And puce? What else is there?"

"There's a lot." My voice came out strained.

Croft leaned in and kissed my cheek, leaving it cool. "If you paint each shade of purple for me, I'll learn them." He looked heavenward, bringing his hands together as if in prayer without letting go of my arm, and continued, "just because I'll cherish the very canvas you touched."

I raised my eyebrows at him. "I don't know what I've done to deserve you," I said, but my mouth was twitching its way toward a smile.

"Well, I wouldn't worry about it." He patted my hand.

I huffed and dragged him toward the happy couple as though I would rather face them than his ridiculous obnoxiousness.

It didn't take us long to make it to the front of the line.

"Congra—" I began.

Hanna squealed and hugged me. "It's so good to see you, Surrey. I'm so happy."

Good thing she hadn't been *trying* to choke me, I thought when she let go.

"-tulations," I finished. "You look beautiful."

She nodded, happy tears appearing in her eyes.

"Is your uncle doing well?" I hurried to ask.

"He's getting stronger, and he's holding up so far today. He's over there." She pointed at a man who looked about ten years older than her and wore a body brace. After waving at him, she clasped her hands together as she beamed first at him and then at Brody.

Brody. It was time to face him. He gave me a hug, which fortunately didn't last long, but I felt flushed when I stepped back. Before he could say anything to me, Croft stepped forward.

"Brody, you lucky man. Congrats," Croft exclaimed as they pounded each other's backs.

"Thanks. It's great to see you here, Croft. And Surrey, I'm so glad you came. I hope you'll have a good time. You'll have to come visit us later."

Hanna nodded with enthusiasm while I said thank you. When Croft was about to steer me away, she threw herself at me for the second time, and Brody managed to get in a small clap on my shoulder before I said goodbye and walked away.

I worked on keeping my breathing steady as we headed toward one of the chocolate fountains. We probably shouldn't go there. I could just see myself sticking my head under the running chocolate and drowning my sorrows. Or whatever it was I was feeling. *Did* I still love him?

"This way," I said, taking charge and pushing against Croft's arm to change directions. "I want to say hi to her uncle."

He agreed without argument, and we approached the man who sat among his family, restrained pain in his eyes.

"Hi, there. Who's the famous uncle?" I asked, looking around and mustering a big smile. I locked gazes with the only child in the group, a six or seven-year-old boy. "Is it you?"

"No, it's him," the boy giggled, pointing.

"So it is." I faced the pilot, whose tired eyes were now twinkling. "I'm so glad you're here. Hanna would have cried her heart out if you hadn't been."

"Hanna has a heart of gold," he said with fondness. "What's your name?"

"Surrey."

"I'm John." He extended his arm for a gentle handshake. "And you?"

"Croft," my sidekick said, shaking hands as well. "Whose butterfly makes the biggest statement?" He critically eyed the other man's houndstooth-patterned bowtie.

"Is that a challenge?" John asked, amused again.

"For sure. The question is, did you choose it, or did someone else? I have to know who to fight."

"You might wanna leave off the fighting and turn your attention to your charming companion. Don't wanna ruin her day with a brawl, now, do you?" John asked, laughing.

Talk about charming. The man nearly made me blush.

"I find myself suddenly distracted," Croft said, gazing in obedience at me. As he was holding onto me, that meant our faces were close. "Come on, Surrey," he said in a worshipful voice. "I'll go wherever you go."

"Dork." I turned from him. "It was good to meet you, John and family."

They chorused their goodbyes, and we walked away, Croft staring dreamily at me.

Enough was enough. This newest joke of his needed to end.

I pulled him to a stop and looked down at our arms. "You know, I wasn't expecting to be on your arm all day."

"Honey, I'm just glad I can make a dream come true that you didn't even know you had."

I breathed slowly. "You can't call me honey. Or cinnamon," I rushed on as he tried to speak. "Maybe I should start calling *you* something."

As I freed my arm from his, he took the opportunity to give me an at-your-service bow. "Feel free to call me honey. Darling. Heart of my . . ."

"I'm thinking along different lines, as you well know," I said and paused to consider. "How about 'scoundrel'?"

He looked thoughtful. "It has a nice ring to it, for sure, but I think 'Your Highness' makes more sense."

"I'm afraid you can have nothing to say when it comes to judging sense."

"Oh, no, I'm most sensible right now. For instance, I noticed another good attribute of yours that I'll have to write down as soon as I get home." He looked over his shoulder at the group we had left behind. When he looked back at me, his gaze was warm and affectionate. "That was sweet, how you greeted her uncle. Giving him a nice dose of humor, too."

I flushed.

"What do you want to do on Tuesday?" He changed the topic.

"Go home to my family."

Croft clapped a hand to his chest as though wounded. "You're leaving me? For Thanksgiving?"

"Aren't *you* going home?" I asked in surprise.

"I am, but not until Wednesday. That's when sensible people leave. Not to mention those who have a heart." He gave me a pointed look.

I rolled my eyes. "You mean those who don't drive their families crazy. I see it now. If you go home Tuesday, they'll kick you out before Thursday's dinner, but if you go a day later, you'll be able to hang around for both dinner and pie."

"You don't think my family appreciates me?"

"I'm hoping for their sakes that they can handle you. Otherwise, I feel bad for them." I couldn't help a wicked smile as I said the words.

He grabbed my hand and cried, "Feel bad for *me*."

"Scoundrel." I wriggled my hand free.

"Your Highness," he reminded me.

I laughed out loud, and when he looked wounded, I laughed harder. "Let's go get some food."

"Food? That's all you care about?" He trailed after me to the refreshment table. "What about Gina?"

"What about her?"

"Is she going away for Thanksgiving?" Croft asked, piling food on his plate and following me along the table.

"No. She felt like Virginia was too far away."

"Where's *your* family?"

"Virginia."

"Then of course you must have grown up together," he surmised. Before I could protest—because while we *had* grown up together, being from the same state didn't mean one could assume we had—he continued, "I happen to know everyone from Colorado. We all recognize each other on campus."

I checked my earlier response and instead answered, "Funny."

"*Did* you know each other?"

"Ask Gina." Telling him we had gone to the same high school might remind him of the yearbook, and I wasn't eager to reintroduce that subject. Instead, I led him to a table where we could eat and continue our banter.

Banter. "His Highness" came up with the most ridiculous things to say, leaving me little time to dwell on what I was or wasn't feeling. I found myself laughing more freely than usual, and when we stood to leave, Croft put a hand on the small of my back, giving me goosebumps.

That was when I knew I needed to get away—not so much from Brody, but from Croft.

When we arrived at the house, I stepped out of my car and held up a hand as Croft tried to follow me. "You can clap me on the shoulder here, Croft. No need to walk to my door and back."

"What?" He was appalled. "Then how will I ever get my five hundred steps a day?"

I laughed before I could stop myself. "Wow. You need to set some serious exercise goals."

"That's what I'm doing. Five hundred steps a day," he repeated. "That's for Tuesdays and Saturdays," he then confided in a whisper. "The other days, I get off."

I was shaking my head. "Pitiful, Croft. Pitiful."

"Besides, I was hoping we had graduated to a hug by now," he said, taking my judgment in stride.

"Don't stress yourself," I said in a kindly tone. "We'll stay at shoulder-patting for now, for your sake. You can't kiss until you get engaged, right? I get it. We'll take things slowly." Oh, but it was fun to tease him for his no-kissing rule, especially when he had no idea I was of the same mind.

I headed up the walkway, Croft's laughter behind me as he shadowed my steps. My mind was turning over possibly telling him thank you for today. His presence had made a very real difference at the reception. I would have greeted Hanna, Brody, John, and the friends I recognized with or without Croft, but everything would have been much harder if he hadn't been there, cracking jokes and trying to get me to call him "Your Highness."

At the door, Croft cleared his throat dramatically. "Now that we've been to a formal event together, I think it's time for another one. BYU's holding a ball on December first. Maybe we can match this time. I have suits in several different colors, you know."

I sighed. "Did anyone ever teach you you'll be safe if you just wear black and white?"

"Where's the fun in that?" He looked at me as though he couldn't comprehend what I had just said.

"Wear your colorful decorations from today, then."

"Where's the fun in *that*? I can't wear the same things to both events."

I glared at him. "Then find a pocket-square that blinds people with its optical illusion patterns, but don't be upset when I snatch it away and drown it in a glass of punch. A girl has to have her standards."

Croft burst out laughing. "Are you trying to say you were embarrassed today, in spite of my tame, brown belt?"

I opened the door. "No." *Thank you for being here today,* ran through my mind, and I spoke quickly before I could stop myself. "I-appreciated-you-being-there-today-Thanks-Croft."

Before he could register my sincere tone, I shut the door in his face and locked it. I smiled to myself and leaned against the door. Then I jerked and stepped away, not wanting him to notice the lack of a sound of footsteps and to guess that I was leaning against the door.

Rushed though my thanks had been, I was glad I had managed it.

I had also managed to get inside without getting so much as a clap on my shoulder. *"Ha,"* I said out loud, and I didn't care whether he heard *that*.

I headed to my room to continue the search for a book I had been reading last week. As I checked behind my bookshelf, I frowned.

It was worrisome that I had enjoyed Croft's presence enough to be thankful for it. When I agreed to date him, I had been certain I would never fall for him. Now I was less sure.

He had to find his dream girl before I reached the point where it would hurt to lose him. That meant a new battle plan.

He must meet other girls—preferably in a setting in which he would get stuck talking for a time.

I imagined a pert waitress taking our orders, starting a conversation in which Croft soon found himself absorbed. That, combined with whatever accident I ended up in—hopefully one that would finally make him rethink hanging around me—might be just the thing.

There was no way around it. I would have to brave another restaurant.

With that decided, I set my chin and grabbed my paints. It was time to forget about Croft and immerse myself in something I loved.

It was the strangest thing, though. I could still feel the cool spot on my cheek where he had kissed me at the beginning of the reception.

Chapter Seventeen

I ONLY SAW Croft two more times before Thanksgiving, and I made it through both events—the statistics class and my lab hour—with notable suspicion. Croft *grinned* less and *smiled* more. But if he thought those genuine-looking smiles could fool me into believing he would wreak less havoc on my life going forward, he had another think coming. I didn't trust him one bit.

When I got home that Monday, Willie called me over from his yard, a Kindle in his hand.

"Surrey, the new video's out."

What new video? I wondered as I approached.

"Did you want to see it?"

"I, uh, guess."

Willie narrowed his eyes at me. "I'm talking about Croft's video."

"Oh." I slapped my forehead and regretted it when I hit my eye. "Ouch. Yes, let's see it."

The clip started off showing the inside of an elevator, catchy music playing and fading into the background. The elevator was empty except for a box. The camera zoomed in on the cardboard, showing what was written on it: *Free.*

"Uh-oh," I muttered. Whatever was in that box wouldn't be good.

Ding. Someone stepped inside. Music played again, and the video showed the point at which the man decided to pick up the box and take a look. Something large and dark remained on the floor behind where it had been, and when I recognized it for what it was, I clapped a hand to my mouth while Willie let out a gasp of laughter next to me.

The man rattled the box and took out a keychain while we waited for him to notice the tarantula. He shook the box again and started to put it down.

"A-Eh-Oh!" He scrambled backward, the box flying from his hands and crashing to the floor. Hugging the wall behind him in terror, he suppressed several more screams.

"The poor guy," I exclaimed.

The elevator dinged, and a new victim stepped into the reset prank scene. As soon as she picked up the box, she noticed the tarantula and reacted with a bloodcurdling scream, accompanied by a burst of horror music that made me hiccup and clap a hand to my mouth.

As expected, I felt bad for the victims. Still, I found myself struggling with laughter again and again.

Willie had fewer inhibitions than me. When he found it funny enough, he laughed openly.

The woman who tried smashing the tarantula with the box tickled my funny bone even though I knew she wasn't having fun herself. By this time, I knew the tarantula was a toy, although it still looked real.

I was startled into giggles when a new scene showed the tarantula inside the box before introducing us to the next string of victims.

All in all, the video was well done. No less than twelve victims had been filmed, and with variations in the placement of the tarantula, people's reactions, and the music, it never got boring.

"Well, that was that." Willie sighed. "As usual, it's kind of mean but pretty funny."

"I'll admit Croft's crew is talented," I said. "Otherwise, people wouldn't watch their videos. But I still don't like that they scare people." I should try talking to Croft about it. Not that he usually listened to me—except, sometimes he did. There was the time I made it clear to him how little I cared to be reminded of the despised photo in my yearbook. There was also the time he had agreed not to steal food from my plate, although that wasn't nearly as touching an example. Still, maybe I could do some good while I had his attention.

"I'll talk to him after Thanksgiving," I decided. Looking around, my gaze caught on the swing. "Has Bella been over recently?"

Willie groaned. "She wants to swing all the time. Her older siblings started showing up, too. I didn't mean to turn my yard into a regular playground." He sniffed. "It's a good thing it'll get too cold for that soon. I'll have my yard and my privacy back."

I thought he looked a little down at the thought. In fact, I was pretty sure he liked being bothered by Bella and the others.

"Maybe there's something else they could come and do," I suggested.

He looked up. "You think so?"

"Yeah, like . . ."

When I couldn't think of anything, he squared his shoulders and said, "Nah. It's better without them overrunning my place."

"What about when there's snow?" I asked. "You could play in the snow with them."

"They probably have others to play with. Anyway, who cares? I'm a genius and an international spy. I don't have time for babies and kids my age."

I hid a smile at his statement. I'd have to find a way to get him and the Whitmers to play at least once this winter.

"We'll see," I said.

* * *

THANKSGIVING. Did I *ever* give thanks for my break the next few days.

From the time I arrived in breathtakingly cold Virginia and was received with warm hugs and loud laughter at the airport, I was in heaven.

My older sister London, who was graduated and moved out, had arrived the day before. My younger brother Kent, currently in high school, and my little sister Fairlee, having finished a mission several months ago, both lived at home. All of us with our sunny heads of Scandinavian hair and similar facial features contributed to the boisterous atmosphere in Dad's car on the way home.

"Dad's treat," said Kent, handing me a can of soda and taking a swig from his own.

"Don't tell Mom," Dad warned from the driver's seat.

"Where *is* Mom?" I asked, popping the lid on my contraband. I had tried asking earlier, but no one had heard me as we all spoke at once.

"Home, preparing our bread-and-water meal," London said from the front, and we all laughed. Mom always said the food and work that went into Thanksgiving meant we ought to live on bread and water in the days leading up to it. However, she never followed through but instead cooked delicious meals for us all week.

"I think she's killing the fatted calf for your homecoming," Kent told me. "It smelled amazing when we left."

"Surrey, why do you have to live all the way over in Utah?" Fairlee complained. "You should quit school and come home. It'd be a lot more fun with you here."

London shoved Fairlee in the head, making her hair go static. "Don't talk her into moving home. Surrey's got a good head on her shoulders half the time. It'd be *none* of the time if she lived with you and Kent."

Fairlee and Kent broke out in loud protests. I decided to take the "half the time" comment as a compliment and didn't object.

It was nice to come home to our large, red brick house hedged by fir trees. It was even better to walk inside and see Mom puttering around.

"Welcome home, love." She came over to give me a hug and to press two decorative wooden blocks into my hands. "Find somewhere for these, okay?"

"Home is where the heart is" said one of the blocks in beautiful cursive. The other said "TURKEYS BEWARE."

"Sure, Mom." I sniffed the air. Something smelled spicy and southern. "Ooh, what's for dinner?"

"Bread and water," Mom said forcefully, her expression daring me to comment further.

Dad winked at me, London began to whistle a tune, and Kent started a conversation with Fairlee about the Star Wars saga to keep them from laughing at the obvious lie.

Silence had no part in the rest of our day, and there was certainly no space for loneliness. I didn't know how tired I was until I lay on the mattress that had been hauled into Fairlee's room for me that evening, the lights turned off and our bickering—uh, sisterly conversation—tapering off.

When I turned my head toward the window, our partially drawn curtains gave me a view of white Christmas lights twinkling on the eaves of the house across the street, declaring the next holiday before this week's had come to pass. Fairlee's room was warm and quiet, and my blankets were soft and cozy. Gravity pulled at me, closing my eyes and putting me in such a delicious state of sleepiness that for a time, I just enjoyed *being*, until at last my mind left behind the world of wakefulness.

* * *

THE NEXT MORNING was rife with vocal exercises in the shower, as was typical of the Witherfield household. No, I'm not talking about singing.

"Noooo," I yelled when my water turned cold. From the bathroom down the hall, London's voice responded with a merciless cheer.

The water turned pleasant again, and a shriek sounded from the other bathroom.

I let out a "Mwa-ha-ha-ha," and so it went, our "How could you?"s and other morning endearments continuing with each turn of the tide.

After everyone had completed their ritualistic morning routine, showering at the same time as someone else, it appeared we had all calmed down from yesterday's family reunion. London sat around reading a mystery book. Kent doodled, creating what looked like one of his graphic novels. Mom took a break from prepping tomorrow's foods and asked me about my paintings for the fundraiser, and I was happy to show her pictures on my phone.

All of us were in the living area, as we were under strict orders from Mom that whatever we did, we had to be in the family room while we did it. Now that we were finally under the same roof for a few days, she wouldn't allow us to hide away in our bedrooms or elsewhere, missing out on each other's company.

Fairlee walked around singing first a bunch of Broadway songs and then a flurry of Christmas songs. Some of us were going bonkers, but Dad, who sat at the dining table working from home, joined in, declaring that singing along was the only way to stay sane. London decided his definition of "sane" didn't match hers.

Fairlee stopped behind me to peer at the pictures on my phone and broke off from singing long enough to inform me that if I were to live at home, I would have more time to paint.

"School would still keep me busy," I argued.

Fairlee sighed in exasperation. "If you lived at home *and* stopped going to school, you would have more time to paint."

"Fairlee, I don't want to paint full-time."

She arched an eyebrow. "Are you sure?"

I rolled my eyes and expounded on my answer. "I don't want to live in a cardboard box while trying to make a living as an artist." It was far more practical to get a degree in statistics and enjoy painting on the side. We had been over this before, but try explaining practical to Fairlee. She thrived on spontaneous and taking flight with your dreams.

"You could live in this house," she offered, all graciousness.

Kent sniggered. "How nice of you to give her the run of Mom and Dad's place."

"They would let her live here before they would ever let her live in a cardboard box," Fairlee said, putting her hands on her hips.

"Yeah, but she wouldn't meet as many guys if she stayed here," London jumped in. "No, Provo's the place for her."

"That's right, who are you dating these days?" Fairlee asked. Kent's pencil stopped moving, and he looked up in anticipation, hoping to find out who he might get to meet and torment "for my own good" next.

"No one. I'm taking a break," I said, rationalizing the truth of my answer to myself. I wasn't actually dating Croft. I was allowing him to spend time with me because there was no way around it, but that was different than dating.

"A break?" London's laughter rang out. "How do you keep the hordes of guys away?"

I raised my eyebrows. "This may come as a surprise to you, but they're not exactly beating down my door."

"Surely you have guys asking," Dad said, "like you did in high school. And haven't you had a string of boyfriends at BYU? There are *always* guys asking you out."

"Well, no," I faltered, "there are always guys *noticing* me, but a lot are too intimidated to ask me out. Or they won't ask because I'm taller than them. Only *some* of the guys ask me out."

Mom was frowning at me. "Exactly how long have you been taking a break? I haven't heard of anyone new since Brody, and it's been at least five months since that ended."

I winced. Somehow I had been fine since the reception, but until then, my pain had been very real. "Five months isn't that long."

"It is when you'd only known him for four months before then," Mom insisted, overly logical. "Sweetheart, I'm sure it isn't easy, but you mustn't let it get you down for too long."

I tried a new tactic. "I'm not swearing off dating altogether. If a guy asks me out, I go out with him." At least, I was doing that with Croft. "I'm just not *looking* right now." That last part wasn't what Mom wanted to hear, so I hurried on, cutting off her protest. "I mean, I'm not tying myself down to one person just now." Sure, Croft was the only one taking me on "dates" these days, but I most certainly hadn't committed nor would commit to being his girlfriend. "That's okay, right?"

Mom swallowed whatever she had been about to say. "Yes. Just don't . . . wallow too long. I don't want you to give up hope just because you haven't found him yet. You're only twenty-two years old."

"Maybe you'll reconnect with some guy from your mission and you'll both fall madly in love," Fairlee suggested, clasping her hands together and effectively drawing Mom's attention.

"Is there someone in particular from your mission you would like to tell me about?" Mom asked in suspicion.

"Was hast du gesagt?" Fairlee responded innocently in the language she had been immersed in for the last year and a half. "Hey, London, you should have served a mission. We could all four fall in love with someone from the spiritual journeys of our youth."

London rolled her eyes. "I would have been sent to the England London Mission for sure, and it would always be a big joke."

"No one would know your first name while you served," Kent pointed out.

"*You* would all tease me mercilessly, and so would my friends and anyone who ever asked me where I served. I couldn't risk that, now, could I?"

"Aber du hättest ein spannendes Erlebnis gehabt," Fairlee insisted.

London spoke in tongues right back at her. "Nǐ shuō shénme?" She had studied Chinese for three years in college as she prepared for the business world, and I could see now that she would use it in battle against Fairlee whenever she pulled her German on us. I promptly joined the conversation in my own mission language, but since I had served in Oregon, English-speaking, no one knew the difference.

* * *

THANKSGIVING DAY WAS busy and full of heavenly smells. I made the apple pie filling and, fortunately *after* scooping it into the pie pan, dropped the bowl with the remaining batter upside down on the floor with a splat.

I had just finished wiping the floor clean when my phone rang, momentarily bringing my mind back to the kitchen in Provo, as my ringtone still mimicked the sound of the oven timer there.

Noting the caller ID, I shook my head. How had I ever thought I would be Croft-free all week?

It seemed suddenly strange to me that I had saved his number under the name *Croft Taylor*. Settling onto the couch near London, I waited until my phone went to voicemail. Then I opened my contacts list and edited Croft's information, deleting his name and replacing it with *Seriously?!*

I had barely saved the change when, surprise, it rang again. This time, I picked up.

"I miss you," Croft said disconsolately in my ear.

"Hahaha," I laughed at him.

"Why are you laughing?"

I stopped. "Wasn't it a joke? You, exaggeratedly feigning your state of hopelessness? Oh, sorry, I didn't realize I was supposed to play along."

"You're heartless," he moaned. "Here I am, pining away over our long separation, and you think I'm acting? Not only do I not get to see you for nearly a week, but to be away from you on a special holiday like this . . . Surrey, going forward, we'll have to spend every major holiday together. Maybe the minor holidays, too."

I considered for a second. "Nah, I have other people to spend them with."

"But, Surrey." He sounded horrified. "I'm dying to be with you, and I know you can't live without me, either. You must be positively wilting away right now. Tell me, how's your Thanksgiving?"

"It's great."

"Cinnamon, this is me. You don't have to pretend."

"That's Surrey to you. Happy Thanksgiving." I hung up, more out of my habit of rejecting him than out of annoyance. To tell the truth, the nickname Cinnamon was growing on me. Spicy and sweet—not bad.

Before I could put down my phone, it lit up again, the ringtone started up, and *Seriously?!* flashed on the screen.

I picked up and started our new conversation with a riveting topic. "Hello?"

"Icing, I need more details than just 'great.' Without details and proof, I refuse to believe you're okay."

"Icing is worse than Cinnamon," I said and hung up. After all, I couldn't let him keep giving me nicknames without asking if I liked any of them.

Two seconds, and my screen lit up.

"Come on, Sugar, I just need to know—No, Sugar sounds bad somehow." His voice went from cajoling to disapproving. "Kinda creepy. Okay, well, *Surrey*, if you don't mind my asking, what are you eating today?"

"Turkey, potatoes, and pie," I listed off blandly. "And you? No, let me guess. The same. Wow, we're so alike it's frightening."

I heard laughter in his voice. "Yeah, but my turkey's bigger than yours."

"How would *you* know?" I countered, rising to his ridiculous challenge. "I can assure you ours is five pounds bigger than yours."

"With a confidence interval that encompasses seven pounds in both directions from the average, and with my turkey being average, I'm afraid a five-pound increase is not significantly different from the weight of my turkey," Croft said prudishly.

My laughter started out quiet but gained momentum as his unexpected application of statistics sank in. Although I could imagine him grinning on the other end, my reaction feeding his ego, I couldn't stop. I sneaked a look around my dining room full of curious eyes and wished I could sneak off to somewhere else for this conversation, but Mom's rules were law.

"You're causing a scene in my living room," I finally scolded breathlessly.

"What? Is your family around?" His voice perked up. "How about you put me on speaker?"

"How about not." I wasn't that stupid.

"Okay," he said good-naturedly, and then he raised his voice to a yell, making me jerk the phone away from my ear. "HI, EVERYONE, I HEREBY DECLARE MY UNDYING LOVE TO YOUR . . ." I frantically turned down the volume. "DAUGHTER, sister, niece . . . whatever she is to you."

I clicked End Call and rubbed my ears. Scowling, I changed his name in my contact list from *Seriously?!* to *Scoundrel*. Then I chanced a look at my family.

Their gazes were interested, but there was none of the reaction I would have expected had they heard him proclaim his "undying love" to me. Phew. He hadn't been loud enough for them to catch the words.

Having punished Croft for his declaration, I called him back to give him my two cents. Only, I kept smiling as I tried to project a tone of impatience. "Are you done yet?"

"Could they hear me?" he asked, and I snickered because the volume was so low that his voice was tiny in my ear.

"Nope."

"Oh." He sounded disappointed. I strained to hear his next words. "How about you tell me your address, and I'll take a plane to Virginia tomorrow?"

I rolled my eyes. "No address, so good luck wandering through a forty-three thousand square-mile state. How about I just see you on Monday?"

He sighed. "Monday." His dejection was apparent in spite of the low volume.

"Yes, see you Monday." I repeated the words as more of a goodbye this time.

"See you then."

The call ended.

"Who was that?" Dad asked, looking at his computer screen as though it were far more interesting than the question he had just asked. I might have believed it if he hadn't been smiling.

"Just someone I'm helping."

"What are you helping him with?"

Yeah, they had probably heard enough of his yell to catch the fact that he was a guy.

I sighed. "I'm trying to help him find the right girl."

"What?" Kent gawked at me.

"You're trying to help him find a girl?" Mom asked, her words laced with disbelief. "Did he ask you to?"

Oh, he had asked for it, all right. He had pestered and pestered me about going out with him, and my going out with him would lead to him finding his dream girl, so by extension, he had asked and asked me to be instrumental in his finding his girl.

"Yes," I said simply.

"Maybe *you'll* end up being the girl for him," Fairlee suggested, and I inwardly cursed her romantic ideas.

"No," I began, trying to think of how best to deny it without making them think that "the lady doth protest too much."

"I haven't heard you laugh like that in ages," Mom noted, and my eyes widened with the fear that my mom of all people would read something into mine and Croft's relationship despite my denials.

"He incorporated statistics into a joke," I scrambled to explain and then proceeded with forced calmness. "If you guys would learn the wonderful language of statistics, you could make me laugh like that, too."

"Is he a statistics whiz?" London asked, giving me no time to recover and recoup.

"He's in a statistics *class*, and I help him with his homework. As the TA."

"A minute ago, you were helping him find a girl," Fairlee pointed out. "Which is it?"

"It's both, and incidentally, neither involves my falling for him, so you can scratch that idea from your mind. He's pretty arrogant, actually, but I'm sure we'll find someone for him."

"Either way, I'm glad to hear you laugh again," Mom said.

I stared at her. "I always laugh and tease when I talk to you guys." I did. It's true.

"Give Surrey a break, dear," Dad said mildly, coming to my rescue.

"Thank you, Dad." With some relief, I jumped to my feet. It was time to end this conversation. "Who wants to go for a walk?"

Chapter Eighteen

I RETURNED to Utah Sunday evening, where I hugged Gina, unpacked, and hunted around for my lip balm. Utah had welcomed me back with open arms and dried me right up, but was my lip balm where it was supposed to be? No. I finally gave up the search and resigned myself to buying a new one the next day. I hated when I misplaced things. I didn't use to lose them, you know.

The next morning, I marched into the Talmage Building with purpose. Croft and I needed to talk. Entering our classroom, I found him with his redheaded friend. I walked right up to them.

"Surrey." Croft threw his arms around me, and I disappeared into a strong, firm nest of Croft. In my complete surprise, I let him hug me.

He stepped back and turned to his friend. "I'll talk to you later, Eric."

Putting his arm around my shoulder, Croft walked me to our usual seats at the end of the third row.

I was still dazed by the warm welcome as I sat down. Something inside me had melted. I think it was my common sense, followed by about half of my defensive wall. Without that wall, what was I to do?

Croft's dark-blue eyes perused my face. "It's so good to see you again."

I just sat there blinking like an owl.

His gaze turned impish. "Tell me you missed me," he said, and the order helped bring me back to my senses.

"Missed you?" I shook my head and pushed my confusion aside. It was time to get stern with him. "I have a bone to pick with you."

"Ooh, this should be good." He folded his arms and leaned them on the table, facing me.

I folded my arms forbiddingly and leaned back in my chair. "We need to talk about your pranks."

"My pranks?" He looked nonplussed. "I haven't pranked you since the day we met."

"Not just *my* prank. *All* of your pranks. Your hidden camera scenes. They're mean."

"Mean? Wait, does that mean you've watched them?"

"That's not the point." I had only watched the one with Willie, but Croft didn't need to know the details. "The thing is, your pranks aren't fun for the people involved."

"I admit that's often true while it happens, but after they find out what's up, they usually think it's cool."

"Well, make it so they have fun during the filming, too."

He appeared to think seriously about my request. "I don't think our pranks are mean," he said at last, "but whatever they are, they're popular. People want to watch them. They're funny."

I huffed in frustration. "Funny isn't good enough, Croft. Are you saying you can't come up with ideas people would watch that *wouldn't* involve the victims being uncomfortable or getting scared?"

He could. I knew he could, if he was willing to make the effort. He had made *me* laugh more times than I dared count, and while I was usually annoyed with him, I'd never been uncomfortable or scared in those moments.

He opened his mouth and closed it. Intrigue slid across his face. "You're challenging me, huh?"

"I'm asking you to be a decent human being while you run your show."

He winced. Then he looked thoughtful. Then he broke into a grin. "How about you join us on Thursday to run through some ideas? You can help guide us."

Another excuse to spend time with me? I narrowed my eyes at him. "Are we still going to that December Ball on Wednesday?"

"Of course."

"I hardly need to spend two evenings with you this week." Though he had already set the standard for multiple dates in a week, I wanted to fight that particular standard and regain some freedom in my schedule. And some freedom in my thoughts, too. Croft crept into them far too often these days.

"Three," he corrected. "I haven't seen you for a whole week. We need to do something tomorrow."

"Three nights in a row?" I cried. "You've got to be kidding me."

"Welcome back to Utah," he said brightly as Dr. Phil started class.

* * *

WE CONTINUED our discussion during lab hour amid student requests for my attention. Now that Thanksgiving had passed, people were beginning to panic over finals.

"Flash mobs," I suggested, writing it down with a Yoda bobblehead-pencil I had found among my things last night. One of my siblings must have sneaked it into my bag. "People realize their reactions are probably getting recorded, but they enjoy it, anyway."

Croft frowned. "Flash mobs aren't funny, though."

"They can be." I tapped my paper. "You could put on a comical performance set to music."

One of the girls at the other table raised her hand. "Hey, Surrey. We have a question."

I walked over to check out the homework problem. Normally I would have enjoyed the chance to stay at the other table, away from Croft, but I was invested in our conversation, so I came back as soon as I could.

Croft picked up where we had left off. "Maybe if my whole crew was musically talented, but . . . Hold on." He sat forward, his dimples coming out in full force. "I've got it. Picture this: We're sitting in a public dining area, eating lunch. I get up, and a flash mob starts singing and dancing as I propose to you."

My shoulders fell. "Seriously? No, no proposal."

He cocked his head at me, half smiling. "Don't you want it on camera when I do?"

I groaned. "I want you a hundred miles away the day I get proposed to."

"Now, now, I have to do it in person."

"You don't have to do it at all. Not to me, anyway." I shook my head as if to rid myself of this last minute of conversation. "But back on topic. If you don't want to do a flash mob, then . . . How about animal videos? You could do something like that day at the park where you narrated the dog's thoughts."

"I suppose I could make some videos with that, but . . ."

"Hey," a guy broke in from where he stood opposite us. "Sorry, can I ask really quick which formula I'm supposed to use here?" He held up his textbook in desperation. "I get so confused on T score versus Z score."

I gave him the answer and reiterated the need for T scores when the population statistics were unknown. Hopefully he would get that straight in time for finals.

Croft was frowning when I turned back to him. "The thing is, our show's based on people. Unsuspecting people."

We were getting adept at holding a conversation amid interruptions.

"Unsuspecting is bad," I told him. "You have to come up with a scene that's so different that people know something funny's going on." I flicked Yoda's green head and racked my brain for an idea. "Someone dressed up as a movie character shows up—maybe more than one person from the same movie, and there's a confrontation? A comic con scene? The onlookers would be entertained, and their reactions will be fun for your audience to watch, but no one's a victim."

Croft's eyes lit up. "You really should come to some of our meetings. You're definitely giving me something to think about."

I dropped the pencil. Was he really contemplating changing his pranks?

He put a hand on mine on the table, giving me another of those genuine-looking smiles from before Thanksgiving. "You'll like the next prank we put together. I promise. And then we'll see how I like doing it your way. Now, what do you want to do for our date tomorrow? Raid the candy store? Go skydiving?" He rubbed his hands together with glee at both prospects.

I was staring. That had actually been sweet, his promise and the hand-holding. I had never seen Croft be sweet like that before.

Not that it mattered. I pulled myself together and answered, "Dinner." There was still my latest plan to carry out. I needed to get him talking with a cute waitress.

"Why dinner?"

I shrugged. "I want another chance to clean out your wallet."

His mouth twitched. "All right. Where?"

I named a restaurant I had been to last year, hopeful that my long-ago, small-scale incident there would have been forgotten by now even if the same people worked there.

"Surrey!" Eric, the red-haired guy, leaned across the table with despair in his eyes. "I can't figure out half the homework assignment."

"That's what she's here for," Croft said in a tone of consolation, though I could tell he was struggling not to laugh.

* * *

WHEN I STEPPED OUTSIDE after my last class of the day, it was quickly growing cold, and I was grateful for the scarf and coat I had thought to bring that morning. I walked home under a thick, gray cloud-cover. Close to home, my phone started beeping.

I picked up and let out a misty breath. "Hi, Mom. Miss me already?"

"*Yes.*" She feigned a hassled tone. "I'm turning the guest bedroom into your new room, and I've bought a plane ticket for you to come home and stay. Please, *please* come home. Maybe you'll have a calming influence on your little sister."

I snorted and brought a hand to my nose to warm it. "Fairlee? Not a chance. You forget that after she and I have been together a few days, we meld into one personality and get into mischief together."

"Oh, yes." Mom sighed. "Sometimes you're the ringleader. Fine, I'll see if I can get a refund for the ticket." I snorted again. "But anyway, how was your Monday?"

"It's been good."

Mom waited a moment, then asked, "How was your Monday *meeting* with that boy?"

I stopped dead in the middle of the street. "Excuse me?"

"Well, did you have a good time? What did you do?" I know it sounds impossible, but I could *hear* Mom's smile grow with each question. "What's his name?"

"*Mom.*" My footsteps started up in an angry stomp. I passed my house and kept going, unaware that I had started my characteristic upset walk around the block. My voice rose. "Croft spends *far* too much time with me as it is. I'm going to see him tomorrow, and Wednesday, and Thursday, and I'm sure he'll come up with something to drag me to either Friday or Saturday. I need a break from him. Can we please talk about something else?"

Mom was silent for so long that I feared the answer was no.

Finally, she asked, "Have you signed up for next semester's classes?"

She sounded happy. I decided not to ponder why. "Yes. I'll have four big classes for my major. It looks intimidating, but I'm excited."

We discussed my upcoming statistics classes and the art course I had chosen. I was on my third round of the block when we hung up.

By then, I was freezing. I put my hands in my pockets to warm them but felt sad as I approached my house with all the lights turned off inside.

There was no Willie outdoors, and I couldn't blame him for that, but I wished I had someone to talk to instead of an empty building to sit in for the next two hours. I wished I had a Keaton or a Jesse to spend time with without fear of them leaving me. They weren't as funny as Croft . . .

I blinked and pushed the thought away. The point was, things had been simpler with those first two boyfriends, back before I feared I was destined to have another girl chosen over me again and again.

The lighting out here was strange. The sun shone on the other side of the clouds, resulting in a bright, yellowish shade of gray on my side. As I watched the sky and my neighborhood, my gaze was drawn to the lone swing my friend had made. After a moment, I smiled. I would take ten minutes. Just ten, and then I would work.

My loneliness dissolved as I ran inside, found a warmer coat and mittens, and hurried back out. I took a seat and began to move, back and forth, back and forth, the swing creaking underneath me and cold air filling my lungs, making me feel alive as I rose higher and higher.

And then something magical happened.

Little white flakes appeared in the air, floating, shying away from me to find a place in the grass. The first ones disappeared without a trace, but more kept coming, and the yellowed lawn began to turn white. I rubbed my fingers together inside their mittens to keep the blood pumping. As I moved with the swing, I felt like I was dancing with the now more numerous snowflakes.

I slowed my momentum to take it all in. Adjusting my scarf, I listened to the silence of the snow and pondered how anyone could capture such a moment. The Master Artist had created a wondrous scene that used all my five senses, plus however many other senses I might have.

Little pleasures. I didn't need a grand-scale miracle like a husband to cheer me up right now. I could get by on this, the reassurance that God was here and the world was beautiful.

I may have stayed out on that swing a little longer than ten minutes.

Chapter Nineteen

LET ME TELL YOU, some waitresses are very nice, but a lot of them are feisty. I could imagine Croft with either type of girl, but it was easiest to imagine him with a feisty girl, one who wouldn't let him get away with anything but would give him tit for tat. Tonight's date was probably the best setting for finding her.

That's why I was so disappointed when a teenaged male server greeted us and took our drink orders.

At least, he tried to take our orders. He started to ask but never finished the question, trailing off to stare at me.

"Water," Croft told him twice without getting any sort of response.

"What would you . . . what . . ." The guy was still trying to ask. He was clearly not ready to hear the answers yet.

"What would you like to drink, Surrey?" Croft asked me gently, trying to make it easier for the poor guy.

I cleared my throat and looked at our waiter. "Water. Thanks."

His cheeks turned red, and I realized too late it might have been better not to make eye contact.

He finally seemed to grasp that we had both given our answers. Tottering away on unsteady legs, he looked back at me, causing me to fear he would get into an accident, one that for once wasn't caused by my clumsiness but was nonetheless connected to me.

I rubbed my face, embarrassed to have Croft witness the effect I had on our server. It had been a while since I had seen anyone get that flustered over me. When the young man returned, looking anywhere but at me as he handed out our drinks, I took a sip to calm my nerves.

"Don't look now, but he's staring again," Croft whispered as the guy walked away.

"How's your water? Can I have a taste?" I reached for his glass, changing the subject with a joke.

Croft quickly covered the top of his glass. "No, no. I seem to remember a woman who wouldn't share her food. I can't possibly share my drink." He moved his hand to peek at the water before covering it up again. "You shall never know what this tastes like."

A short young woman with black hair piled on top of her head arrived next to take our food orders, and I found myself hopeful for the fulfillment of tonight's plans.

Nothing happened as we told her what we wanted from the menu. I had expected Croft to be charming and joke around while he ordered, but he kept his comments tame and to the point.

I frowned over my menu, looking between Croft and the waitress. How could I get him to speak with her? She would leave in another few seconds if I didn't stop her, and then who knew whether she would be back or be replaced by another server—a male server again, if we were unlucky enough.

I cast around for something to say and settled on, "Your hair is beautiful. I like how you put it up."

She shrugged. "I find all sorts of 'dos to get it out of the way. Otherwise, the cats will mess it up."

"You have cats?" I turned to Croft, feigning excitement. "Don't you just love cats?"

He looked at me like he was trying to read my mind. Or maybe like he thought I had lost my mind. "I guess they're fine. I didn't know *you* liked them so much."

No help from that quarter. I turned back to the woman. "How many cats do you have?"

"Four."

"Um." What else could I say to keep this conversation from ending? Croft didn't seem interested in talking about the cats. "Any other pets?"

"No."

Obviously, our conversation was lagging, and Croft wasn't showing any sort of interest, at least not in our pretty cat-lover. His eyes stayed on me, and I decided not to pursue the conversation further.

The girl left, and I turned back to Croft, narrowing my eyes, deep in thought.

"*Do* you like cats?" I asked.

As you can tell, my thoughts were very deep.

"Well, sure. They make for some good movies."

It came to me then that I had to get to know Croft better in order for my plan to work. Once I knew his interests, I'd be able to identify a good candidate for him and steer the conversation toward common interests. That meant I had to ask him personal questions and act like I wanted to know the answers.

Why did I have to do all the work for him to find his dream girl?

I opened my mouth to ask about his hobbies, but the sight of another black-and-white-clad woman changed my plans on the turn of a dime.

"Hide me," I whispered frantically and dived under the table. My knees scraped against the floor, and I realized one second too late that I would have been less noticeable holding up a menu in front of my face. However, I didn't dare crawl back to my seat, so I tried to make the best of my hiding place, turning my back to the open restaurant and tucking my hair into my sweater to disguise its usual length. At least no one would see me unless they happened to be adjacent to our table and looked in mine and Croft's direction.

I tried to keep my breathing even. What was the woman doing here? She wasn't supposed to be here. The last time I had seen her, she was working at a restaurant on the other side of town, and she was, well, covered in spaghetti sauce. Other waiters had gotten angry with me, but no one had ever been as livid as she, out of control and yelling and throwing things. I wouldn't be surprised if she had ordered a tombstone with my name on it.

Steps continued in our direction, and then—they paused. Sweat stood out on my forehead before I heard the voice and shut my eyes. I recognized her voice all too well even though she wasn't shouting.

"Is she okay?"

"Yeah, public spaces are a little hard on her," Croft's voice answered.

"She'll work her way out from under the table over the course of the evening. It's fine."

I hiccupped at his words and covered my mouth.

"O-kay," the woman said slowly. She moved on even more slowly. I wondered if she would stop and look back. Not daring to risk anything, I stayed hidden until I was sure she had left.

Then I crawled to Croft's side of the table and straightened up on my knees.

"What did you just tell her?" I hissed, my eyes sparking.

He looked pleased, as though having me pop up on his side was a treat. Reaching for my hand, he pulled me up to sit next to him. "I had to get her to move on, right?"

"Couldn't you have chosen a less . . . nutcasey explanation?" I asked, then ducked my head at the sight of a waitress with the same hair color and length as my nemesis before realizing it wasn't her.

Phew, false alarm. But she was still in here somewhere. "Never mind. We need to make our escape. Cut a retreat." I grabbed his winter hat from next to me and pulled it on.

He looked all in, intrigued at the idea of making a stealthy getaway. Then suddenly his expression turned thoughtful, and I became worried.

"Can we just go?" I pleaded, sinking low in my seat and looking around nervously.

"So long as we get dinner elsewhere. Anywhere. We can eat in the car if you like, but I don't want to cut our date short."

I breathed out in relief. His thinking hadn't led to anything as devious as I had expected. "Deal."

He looked around, sighed, and pulled money from his wallet to lay on the table. I thought of the food we had ordered and which was being prepared in the kitchen right then. Oops.

But Croft didn't give me time to feel guilty. His duty done, his face split in a grin, and he grabbed my hand and slid from the bench with me in tow. I followed his lead, slouching a little without making it obvious we were sneaking off.

He kept hold of my hand while rushing me across the parking lot, and in our hurry, it didn't make sense for me to tug free. When he let go to open my car door, I noticed how warm my hand was where he had touched it. I started to flex it, only to have him grab it again and move me to the passenger seat.

"What are you doing?" I asked in annoyance as I plopped down. It wasn't like we were in the seventeenth century, when the gentleman handed the lady into the carriage.

"Getting away." He grinned and came around to his own side. He was laughing when he got in. "It's so fun to see you glower."

I folded my arms across my chest as he started the car.

Croft pulled onto the road and gave me a sideways glance. "Why were you afraid of her?"

There was no point in keeping it from him. "Spaghetti."

"Huh?"

I cleared my throat. "She used to work at this Italian place where I went with Frank—uh, one of the guys I've dated. I tripped. It was messy. She cursed me till doomsday."

It should have been funny. *Croft* should have found it funny.

I was surprised when he reached for my hand again.

"I'll find a way to take away the curse," he said.

An unexpected warmth worked its way through my hand and up my arm. I thought of the curse that seemed to follow me—not whatever curse the woman would have put on me if she could, but my bad luck in dating. The way I'd fall for a guy and he'd fall for me. The way he then suddenly picked someone else over me, although I seemed every bit as right for him as the new girl was.

I pulled my hand from Croft's. "You don't have that power."

He gave me a questioning look, but the spell was broken. I was done feeling vulnerable about my enemy waitress or anything else, and I was done letting him hold my hand.

Croft made a couple of turns and stopped at a city corner that sported a hot dog stand and a few outdoor chairs and tables. He looked to me for approval. "Yes?"

"Yes," I answered. Their hot dogs looked fine, but better still, the setting looked safe and free of potential drama.

A few minutes later, we sat in rickety plastic chairs, eating delicious vendor fast food, our breaths visible in the cold. I was warm enough for the time being, though. Croft had let me keep his hat and had raised the hood of his coat to protect his own head.

I felt relaxed. There was ketchup and mustard and sauerkraut, but I wasn't worried about a thing. Even if I somehow upset our table, it would only bother me and Croft. No one was using the nearby tables.

"Do you like this setting?" Croft asked. There was a light in his eyes I wasn't used to, as though eating outdoors made him happy and peaceful.

Having just taken a bite, I nodded.

Why hadn't I thought of eating out at a place like this before? Why hadn't the other guys who dated me done this kind of thing? This was a great solution to my accidents. Except . . .

My shoulders fell, and I bit back a groan. My plan for the evening was ruined. There was only one person working the stand, and he was a guy. How were we supposed to meet Croft's dream girl now?

"Then why are you frowning?"

I shook my head, still thinking. It would be nice to ditch restaurants entirely, but where could we go on our dates to meet girls? The mall? A spa?

"You—don't like being here. You do like it?" he tried again, but just then a lightbulb went off in my mind, distracting me from answering.

An ice skating rink. That was it. I could just imagine some girl coming out of nowhere and bumping into Croft. He would help her catch her balance, and they would stare into each other's eyes. Or maybe they'd both fall down together. Either way, he would be a goner, and maybe he'd end up bruised. Don't judge me, but I was heavily in favor of the second scenario.

I gathered my thoughts. "I can't even step foot in a restaurant without turning things upside down. Don't you get embarrassed being with me?"

Croft straightened. "Never. I'd brave the restaurant for another broccoli scene or an escape like today's if you wanted to risk it again. You're an adventure waiting to happen, sweetheart."

"An accident," I corrected, "and don't sweetheart me."

"Cinnamon."

I raised my eyebrows at him, though I did kind of like this nickna—

"Cinny." He made a pondering noise. "What do you think of Cinny?"

We would definitely have to go ice skating. The sooner the better.

* * *

I was stuffing my backpack the next morning when Gina approached. She wasn't quite wringing her hands, but she was clenching them together. "Um, I'm going on a date tonight."

"You're going on a date?" I dropped a folder of graded statistics homework on the table and gave her a large smile. "That's great! With who?"

She gripped her hands tighter. "His name is Tim. Croft set us up last week."

Croft set . . . ?

I fell into a chair, scraping my spine against the back. "Ouch." I rubbed the sore spot. "Croft? How?"

"He came over before leaving for Thanksgiving and asked if he could set me up with someone else who was staying in town," Gina explained. "So Tim took me to the Thanksgiving dinner hosted by one of his professors. Now he's asked me on a second date. It's dinner and a movie. I know you have your ball tonight, but I wasn't sure I'd be home by the time you got back, so I wanted you to know."

"Gina, that's great. Why didn't you tell me before? I've been home for three days without knowing about this."

Gina caught her bottom lip with her teeth. "I feel weird telling anyone. I don't want a big to-do about it. I didn't think there would be a second date, and there likely won't be a third. If I tell people, then after he stops asking me out, they'll ask about him, and I'll have to tell them it didn't lead to anything."

I tried to grasp her logic. After a moment, it actually made sense. "I think I see what you mean. I don't want my family to know about Croft. Of course, I'm not dating him in the traditional sense, but if I did want it to lead to something, I might not want to tell them about him because I don't believe it will go anywhere." History had taught me it wouldn't.

"Exactly."

"But you know, if Tim is a man worth his salt, he'll like you," I told her.

Gina blushed and giggled. "Thanks. I hope you have a good time at the ball, even though you don't love being with Croft."

"I'll have a good time, for sure. I'm excited about the dress." It was the dress that would make tonight great. Not Croft. Right?

Gina's eyes sparkled. "Your dress is amazing. I'd never dare wear it at a ball, but it's perfect for you. You're so confident."

I looked forward to showing Croft just how confident I could be.

* * *

In Stat 230, I sketched a girl on a swing using a compressed charcoal pencil while Croft leaned over every now and then to write in my open notebook. My formulas and tables were interspersed with comments such as "Surrey: Exceptional artist," "Croft: Strong and chiseled" (that one made me snort so loud that half the class turned to stare), "Surrey: Daring and adventurous," and the newest addition: "Dance the night away on clouds of glory." I smiled at the thought of tonight's ball, and I shook my head at how comfortable we were sitting together in class.

During my lab hour, in between feeding the hungry wolves (that is, helping my desperate students) and talking to Croft, I enhanced my coal drawing and realized I would need outside help. In order to make my subject's position natural, I needed to see someone on a swing. I was considering my options when Croft reminded me about joining him and his crew the next day to discuss ideas.

I laid down my pencil. "Actually, I can't go tomorrow. Thursdays are off-limits. If you want me to join, it'll have to be another day."

"What's on Thursdays?"

"Gina-day. She's barely home the other days, but I get to see her on Thursdays, and I need that girl time."

I also needed the non-loneliness time. If Croft was going to steal two or three nights of my week, they should be taken from among my lonely evenings, not the one day my roommate was around.

"Maybe I can move our meeting to Friday," he said. "I'll text the crew and see who can make it."

I nodded and returned to scrutinizing my drawing.

* * *

Following my last class of the day, I went home and knocked first on Willie's door, then on Bella Whitmer's door, with Willie in tow.

Bella's mom swung the door open. "Hello, dears."

"Hey, Sister Whitmer," I said, delighting in the chance to address her. I loved saying "Sister Whitmer." It transported me back two centuries to the early years of the restored church of Jesus Christ, making me imagine how it would be to know and live around historical figures like the Whitmer family. I imagined greeting the pioneers as their neighbor. *Why, hello, Sister Whitmer. Brother Whitmer, tell me again about your experience with the gold plates. Stay for supper? I would love to. Have you seen Brother Joseph the Prophet today?*

"I have kind of an unusual request," I began. "I was wondering if Bella would be willing to use Willie's swing for a few minutes while I take pictures. I'm making a painting of a girl on a swing, and it'll help to have action photos."

Sister Whitmer chuckled. "That *is* a request out of the normal. I think that would be fine, so long as she's okay with it. I heard a rumor you were an artist. How often do you paint?"

"Oh, I would paint every day if I could. Even when I can't, I'll at least spend a few minutes sketching."

"That's wonderful. Would you mind sending me the pictures you take? And . . . would you be willing to let me see the painting once you're done, before you show it professionally?" She looked hopeful.

"Can I see it, too?" Willie was quick to ask.

"Yes, of course." My stomach had done funny things at the mention of showing the painting professionally, but I was relieved and rather charmed with Sister Whitmer's request. "I'll send you the pictures as soon as possible. How about by email?"

Sister Whitmer gave me her email address and called for Bella.

The little girl listened patiently to the explanation about swinging and having her pictures taken and a painting made, and then she said, "Yeah, I want to go swing!"

Willie coughed to cover up a laugh. It was obvious the little girl was growing on him. Bella ran across the street, Willie followed close behind, and I soon joined them and took the lens off my camera while Willie pushed the swing at Bella's animated request.

"I love swinging," Bella sang out as I snapped photo after photo. "Can you make a swing for my yard, Willie?"

"Sorry, but you don't have any trees to hang it from. You can use mine, though. I don't use it."

"That's weird. I would use it every day. At least in summer, I would." She blew on her mittened hands, one at a time to avoid taking both off the ropes at once.

"Are you getting cold?" I asked.

"Yeah." Her large eyes grew mournful. "But this was fun. Thanks."
Willie let her slow down.

"Do you like playing in the snow?" I asked her.

She brightened. "I *love* snow. Snowmen and snowballs and running in it." With a frown, she looked around at the frosty patches left over from Monday. "It's mostly melted now."

"Yes, but hopefully we'll get some more soon, and then we can play in it."

"Yeah, with my sister and brothers," she agreed.

There was a look of faint hope on Willie's face as Bella ran back to her house. I wished it were snowing right then. At least it should be easy to get the Whitmer kids to play with Willie when the world turned white again.

I returned to my house to study and eat a quick meal. It never took me long to eat when I was alone. The food sort of got stuck in my throat the longer I spent on it, due to boredom and all.

After my solitary meal, I got ready for the December Ball, smiled at my proud reflection, and went back to studying.

That last half hour of studying, I didn't feel alone. I felt royal. Royal, elegant, and tough.

Chapter Twenty

WHEN I OPENED the door to Croft, my breath took a trip. He was dressed in white: white shirt, white suitcoat and white pants. Only his bowtie and shoes were black, making him look classy. His hair was thick and only slightly messy, and his blue eyes were as dark as ever in his tan, dimpled face.

He looked good.

Of course, anyone looked good in white, I reminded myself. I had worried he would show up in a purple suit and a polka-dot belt to punish me for not telling him what color I would wear, but no, he knew how to make an impression.

So did I. Though I was now recovered from the sight of my date, the same could not be said of him. His dimples remained almost out of sight while he gawked.

"Are you ready?" I asked and walked past him with my coat in my arms, receiving a pleasant whiff of cologne and giving him a clear view of my warrior dress.

The lacy bodice gave way to camouflage-patterned sleeves, which trailed from the white shoulders to long points that cushioned the backs of my hands. Where the front of the blouse formed a "V," I had added camo patterned ruffles with gold edges. The black-and-green pattern of my wide skirt was visible through the white lace overlay, which fell to six inches above the hem, and I had tied a gold ribbon around the waist. Finally, my hair was twisted into a braided crown and woven through with gold-edged camo fabric.

Tonight, I was a warrior-hunter-queen, and there was nothing Croft could do about it.

I stopped at the sight of the eleven-year-old boy who had taken up position in front of Croft's car. Willie faced us with his arms crossed.

Croft caught up and stumbled to a halt. "Hi, Willie." His voice sounded unsteady.

Willie didn't beat around the bush. "Where are you going?"

"To a dance." Croft looked at me and seemed to get stuck staring.

"I asked where?" A stern tone entered Willie's voice, and I found myself impressed with his interrogative style.

"Campus."

"You'll be back before midnight?"

Croft's lips began to twitch. "Yes." He started to look at me again but stopped himself.

Willie intensified his glare. "Don't make her cry."

My white prince swallowed a chuckle and raised a hand in salute. "I won't."

Willie looked at me with a grin. "You're looking good, Surrey. Have fun."

I saluted him, too. "I will. Don't stay up for me."

Willie laughed and ran home. Croft let me into the car and took a seat, scowling at the dashboard. "*I* was going to tell you you look good," he muttered.

He turned to me, blinked, and shook his head as though to clear it. "You look amazing. Out-of-this-world amazing." He paused. "You do know people will stare, right?"

I shrugged. "People usually stare. I may as well wear this and enjoy it."

He nodded repeatedly. "Yes, you may as well." The nodding continued. He turned on the ignition and, to my relief, had the presence of mind to look out the windshield before he shifted into drive.

It was the quietest drive I had been on with him. I was surprised to see him so thrown off by the dress. In fact, I had expected him to laugh when he saw me, thinking it was a joke, and I had looked forward to calmly and coolly telling him this was what I was wearing tonight.

He cleared his throat. "Where did you get the dress?"

"I made it. For an art project."

"For school?"

"No, for me." I was so excited about my dream painting, I had to tell him about it. I held up my hands and painted the scene out loud for him. "Imagine this: A woman who capably takes on the responsibilities of her kingdom, putting on an elegant façade in representing her people at international social functions, but when she's home in her wilderness country, she proves her strength, skill, and leadership as she navigates the dangerous terrain, fearlessly leading charges against rogue tribes and never shying away from driving out predators. She is wild and refined, strong and dainty. Can you see it?"

"Yeah," Croft said breathlessly and swallowed. "I can see it."

"Well, I'm going to paint her, and she'll wear this dress."

Croft looked starry-eyed.

When we arrived and walked inside, I sneaked another glance at him in his white suit. The effect was breathtaking.

"You really are a vision," he told me.

"I'm not sure everyone here will agree that's a good thing." Someone was bound to think I was making a joke of the ball, showing up in what appeared to be a costume.

He almost growled. "Everyone else can just disappear. I wish we were the only two people here. No, wait," he amended. "It's helpful they're here so I can watch the men and imitate their steps."

I halted. "Are you saying you don't know how to dance?"

"Everyone needs a weakness," he said. "What I lack in dance skills, I more than make up for in other areas."

I spoke in a dry tone. "I'm so pleased you decided to grace us with your presence tonight, Prince Big-Head."

He swept a gallant bow. "I'm likewise glad I chose to come, Queen of the Wild."

I raised my head regally and let him lead me onto the ballroom floor.

Yes, there were looks and stares from other dancers, but I became so caught up in trying to dance with Croft that I didn't spare them a thought.

"No, no," I laughed, "your left is my right, so we should step together in that direction, not in opposite directions. You need to keep your hand on my waist." He kept forgetting and dropping his hand to his side as he tried to focus on all the movements. His inability to keep things straight didn't bother me. I was laughing so much it hurt. "I can't believe you invited me to a ball when you can't dance," I exclaimed. "I'm no dance expert, but I do fine when the guy leads."

"I just want to dip you," he chuckled. "Can't you teach me how to do that?"

"If we try that, we'll both end up in the hospital. You should know a dance is the kind of thing where I'm likely to cause an accident, and with you being my partner, the chances probably increase tenfold. I think we should give up."

"Oh no, tell me again how to do this," he protested. "We can't go home yet. Look at that couple over there. We just need to sway like them. It can't be that difficult, can it?" He started swaying me back and forth so far in both directions that I felt like a ship, and we both cracked up. Let me tell you, the dirty looks from nearby people didn't help. They only made us laugh harder.

Croft frowned at the first guy who asked me to dance, and I had to explain the rules of social dance to him. We couldn't be expected to stay with the same partner all night long. My hopeful new partner led me away, his voice hoarse as he spoke to me, though he was in much better shape than our waiter the other night. He only stuttered a couple of times.

I intercepted a few glares from people who clearly thought I had no business dressing in a "costume" at a ball, but there were compliments, too. One girl came over, eyes sparkling, to say, "You should totally wear combat boots with that dress. Kick butt, girl!" Another called out as she swung past me, "Work it, girl!"

As for the guys, the ones who danced with me seemed entranced.

While I felt like an immature debutante when Croft's and my dancing efforts caused us to double over with laughter, I would be a fool not to recognize I was having tons more fun than I had ever had at a dance. The best thing about having another guy lead me away now and then was that it gave me a chance to catch my breath.

It also allowed me to watch Croft on the sly for a minute as he danced with someone else. He did his best to remember my instructions, and while it looked like he cracked a joke or two to make his partner laugh, I was somehow relieved that he wasn't as boisterous with her as he was with me.

When the last dance rolled around, Croft and I tried to stay serious. I drew in a deep breath and focused on our movements. His hand firm on my waist for once. The white clothes in front of me and the camo-sleeves trailing from my hands. His dimples and dark-blue eyes. It was kind of nice when he—

His hand began to slip, his serious expression crumpled, and I expelled my breath in another burst of laughter.

"Ready?" he asked breathlessly when the music ended.

"Yes." My throat, raw from laughter, was relieved to see the end of the night.

"You're an exceptional dance teacher," Croft chuckled as we headed for the doors.

"You're a terrible liar," I giggled.

"How did you get your hair to stay up?" He touched one of the braids. It was still firmly attached to my head. "You must have used a lot of hair spray." He slid his hand across the whole crown as if to check for the stiffness hair spray would have caused.

I felt goosebumps and tilted my head away. "No, it's the hairdo. And, well, my hair tends to stay the way I put it. Unlike London's hair. You could use twenty hair clips and hair spray, and it would still come loose within five minutes of her wearing it up."

Croft gave me a look of disbelief.

"It's true. Her hair's so fine she never uses a brush, only a comb." I touched my crown and gave Croft a pained look. "Of course, I never use a brush, either, but that's because she challenged me to go without it some years ago. There are times my hair cries out for the brush."

He laughed. "Another dare. I'm doubly amazed at your hairdo, knowing there was no brush involved. Although I have to say, I like your hair down, too."

It was strange that he had complimented me on my looks today without irony. It was stranger still that it made me feel good. I didn't get sarcastic or remind myself we weren't truly dating, at least not from my perspective. At the moment, I felt happy and peaceful and laughed out as my white-clad Prince Big-Head took me home from a terribly funny and somehow enchanting evening.

When he parked, Croft frowned at the dark house. "Is Gina out?"

"Yeah, she's probably not home yet." I let myself out and proceeded slowly up the walkway, giving Croft a chance to join me.

"Where's she at?" he asked.

"On a date. With Tim." I glanced at him sideways. "I can't believe neither of you told me about him. I just heard this morning that you set them up."

He smiled. "I thought they might both enjoy their Thanksgiving better that way. She's a very nice girl."

"She is," I agreed. "I'm surprised none of the nice guys I dated ended up with her. Sure, she's shy, but anyone who's willing to take the time will discover how incredible she is."

"You think they should have ended up with your roommate?" Croft repeated, shocked. "Didn't you think they would end up with you?"

"Well, yes, but they obviously didn't. They all found great girls, though."

"Really?"

"Forget it. I don't want to end my night on that note," I said, inserting my key into the lock. It had been such a fun evening. I was annoyed this subject had come up.

Croft lingered on the porch. "Maybe I should stay until she gets home."

I bit my lip. "I'll be fine." Truth be told, hanging out with him would be much nicer than sitting up waiting on my own.

He grinned as I opened the door. "Thanks for inviting me in, Surrey."

I laughed. "Come on, then." I gestured him inside and turned on the lights.

"Have you written your List of Ten Things for next semester?" he asked, heading for the couch while I paused by the light switch. The back of my neck prickled.

"Because if not, I have a few ideas to add to it."

I approached the table, familiar unease sweeping across my shoulder blades.

"Even if you have, I could have a separate List of Ten Things for you. You and I both like lists, don't we? Another thing we have in common."

I rubbed the back of my neck while Croft pivoted toward the glass door. My heart beat a little faster while he said something that was probably both theatrical and funny. Obviously, rubbing at my neck wasn't helping matters. I squared my shoulders and waited, but the sense of wrong in the house didn't subside. If anything, it grew stronger.

Suddenly furious with this dark feeling waiting for me after a great night, I turned on my heel and strode to the entrance. I jerked the door open, stepped outside, and slammed it hard behind me. Then I plopped down on the doorstep in despair, resting my head in my hands.

The door opened.

"What's wrong?" I had never heard Croft sound as hesitant as he did in that moment. "Should I say sorry?"

I shook my head and ran my hands across my face.

"You'll freeze within ten seconds of sitting there," he warned. When I didn't answer, he put a light hand on my shoulder and waited.

I groaned. "I just. Get. So. Tired of it."

"Of what?"

"That feeling. Like something's wrong. Like I shouldn't be in there."

He sat down and put an arm around me, warming me. I turned my head to meet his gaze.

"In there." I indicated the house behind us. "Something's off. Gina feels it, too. I'm not crazy. It only happens every few weeks, but it keeps happening, and I want it to stop."

He looked concerned. "How long has this been happening?"

"Almost two years," I said in defeat. "Maybe longer. When I first started noticing it, it was so faint. I don't think it's gotten worse. I think I've become more in tune and better at noticing it."

"In tune?" His forehead knit. "Do you think it's, like, a spirit? Bad spirits?"

"Maybe."

"Hmm. Have you thought about moving to a different place?"

I let out a frustrated breath. "We did move. We had this same problem where Gina and I lived before. And I had it in the place I lived before that." Tears filled my eyes. "If it's bad spirits, I guess they're following me around. Maybe I'm a bad person." I sniffed. "Maybe I attract evil spirits."

"You don't think that." His voice was soft.

"When I get upset enough, I do," I mumbled. "When I get mad about this and I want to wallow in self-pity, then yeah, I wonder if I'm doing something wrong. I'm not the worst person around, but I'm not the best person, either. Maybe God is punishing me for something."

Croft held me closer. "You're a good person, Surrey, and bad feelings don't come from God. Tell me, what do you do when this happens?"

"I stay away for an hour or two. By the time I go back in, it usually feels all right again. That means, what," I looked at my watch and said bitterly, "I should stay out until midnight, I guess." I clenched my jaw. Then I looked at Croft, his dark-eyed gaze visible in the light from my front porch. "Are you worthy to use the priesthood?"

He didn't hesitate. "Yes."

My heart lightened. "We've asked guys to come over before to dedicate the place, or to re-dedicate it, or to give us blessings. It doesn't keep this from happening again, but it makes the feeling go away faster." I smiled. "It was pretty dramatic once. My ministering brother was dedicating the place. He rebuked the evil in the house . . ." Croft's eyes widened, and he looked impressed. I continued, "and the lights all went off. The electricity was out for about a minute."

"Huh. Thus showing us technology is evil." Croft nodded sagely.

"No." I gave him a gentle push. "Technology is good for a lot of things, like family history and communicating with each other."

"Well." He stood and reached down to help me stand. "I'll definitely give you a blessing, and the house too, if you like."

I shivered after he pulled me to my feet. He had been right. Sitting on that stone step had chilled me. "A blessing would be great. The place has been dedicated, for all the good it does. I mean, of course it does some good," I hurried to say, "but I'd like a blessing."

"I'll give you a blessing, and I hope we'll see a greater miracle than having the electricity go out."

"I'm not looking for some big miracle." I returned inside, hunching my shoulders against the atmosphere that pervaded the house.

He put a hand on my arm, his gaze holding mine. "Having you feel peace in the next minute will be a much bigger miracle than any electric outage, and your feeling peace is the miracle I'm hoping for."

Struck by his words, I felt moisture build up in my eyes. For all his obnoxious ways, there might be a spiritual giant hidden inside this guy. Who would have thought it?

"Let's not tell Willie if you make me cry," I said.

"Deal." He searched my face. "Do you normally cry during priesthood blessings?"

"No, but I can't make promises." I had already nearly lost it.

For a moment, we stood awkwardly in the middle of the living room.

"How about this: we kneel and each say a prayer for the Spirit to be present, and then I give you a blessing," Croft suggested.

I agreed and knelt on the floor, feeling suddenly shy. Croft prayed first, asking for inspiration and for us both to feel the Spirit. After my prayer, I pulled out a chair from the dining table and sat down.

"What's your full name?" Croft asked.

"Surrey Elizabeth Witherfield."

He was learning all kinds of things about me this evening. I tried not to squirm at the thought. Even though Tuesday's restaurant date had shown me I needed to get to know him better, it wasn't in my plans to let *him* get to know *me* too well.

Just before Croft laid his hands on my head, I realized I was still wearing my warrior-queen dress and he his white suit. What a setting.

I closed my eyes, and Croft began to speak. Our prayers had helped me feel better, and the blessing helped even more. The darkness of the house still pressed in on me, but something changed. If I were to paint it, I would have showed a thin shield of light around me keeping the darkness at bay—not making it disappear, but keeping it from touching me.

Croft blessed me to find a way to bring the Spirit back into the house. He said the building would eventually be a place of security for those who lived there and that I would have clarity of mind and the help I needed when I found myself in danger. Those around me would come to my aid. This trial was not to follow me around for the rest of my life.

He ended in the name of Jesus Christ. I kept my eyes shut another moment, turning over some of the words. Danger? Where did *that* come from?

I unfolded my arms and let them rest in my lap. The promise that this disturbing feeling wouldn't stay with me, going from house to house forever, was one I very much appreciated.

"How does it feel now?" Croft asked.

I stood and looked around. The wrongness was still there, and I could feel the shield around me dispersing bit by bit. "Better, sort of. Temporarily better."

"All right, well, the blessing talked about finding ways to bring back the Spirit. What are we going to do to make that happen?"

A light came on in my mind. The answer was simple. "Hymns."

"Hymns? Singing?"

"Yes." I looked askance at him. I wasn't going to start singing with him there. I would have to make him leave before I could sing anything, but being alone would make me feel worse.

"Okay." His dimples flashed, and he opened his mouth and began to sing "I Am a Child of God."

I found myself smiling widely. I shouldn't have been surprised at his willingness to put on a show and make the house feel better, but still it warmed my heart. The song seemed a little different than usual, but I couldn't put my finger on what made it so.

He finished the verse and gave me a curious look I couldn't interpret. "Do you want another one?"

"First we have to finish this one. It has four verses, you know."

"It does, doesn't it. I only know three of them."

"So do I," I confessed.

"Here goes." He began the second verse.

I took a seat at the dining table and joined in, no longer shy. We finished the second and third verses, and then I began "I Love to See the Temple."

A couple of songs later, I sighed. "That really helped."

"That's good. I was worried I would have to apologize for making things worse," Croft said. When I looked at him in confusion, he explained, "I don't mess up the notes on purpose. I'm just half tone deaf."

"Oh, so *that's* it. I didn't know . . . Something seemed off, but I couldn't tell. Um, I'm a little tone deaf, too," I admitted.

"You are?" His face lit up, followed by a smug smile. "Just look at how much we have in common. We're the exact same person."

"I wouldn't go that far," I said dryly.

"No, really, we're twinners."

"You know what this means, right?" I raised my eyebrows at him.

"We have to start our own music group?" he suggested eagerly.

I suppressed a laugh. "We can't date anymore."

"What?" His hang-dog expression was so comical that I burst into laughter. "How do you figure that?"

I tried to give him a serious look. "We can't date because we can't get married. It wouldn't be fair."

"To whom?"

"Our children." Again, his expression was hilarious. "They wouldn't stand a musical chance. No, you and I both need to find someone musical to marry. That way, at least some of our children might have the opportunity to be a concert pianist, or a world-famous cellist, or an opera singer."

"Ah." He sat up straight and pulled at his white cuffs with a sniff. "Well, a good ear is overrated. *Our* children will adore the way our voices blend and crash."

Too late, I realized I had introduced a topic that was now making me blush hard. It had been fun to see his shock when I mentioned "our children," but I should have foreseen he would recover and turn the tables on me.

He noticed my reaction and broke into a wicked grin. "Besides, as much fun as it is for me to embarrass you sometimes, don't you think it would be fun for us to embarrass the children together?"

I stood quickly. "Um. Well. Thanks for the blessing." I should have come up with some smart retort instead of getting all flustered, but for some reason, my mind wouldn't comply. "Thanks for singing and all."

"You really didn't mind my singing?" He stood as well.

I shook my head. "It was nice. I liked it." It was true. I had enjoyed his singing, and somehow, I liked it even better knowing it wasn't perfect.

"That's two," he said softly.

I stared at him. "What?"

"That's two times you've said something really nice to me, no teasing or sarcasm involved."

I frowned. "When was the first time?"

"When you said you appreciated that I came to the reception. Just before you slammed the door in my face."

"Oh. Right."

"One of these days, I'll get to tell you my story of something I don't find funny." He didn't look excited at the thought. "Then you can tell me that's no excuse for the way I treated you, and I'll agree with you. But at least you'll know what was eating at me when we first met."

Cliffhanger, much?

I started at the sound of voices outside.

Gina's back. Gina and her date. My thoughts jumped from Croft's mystery to the exhilaration of asking Gina about her night and . . . I paused my excited thoughts to ponder whether she would welcome a post-date interrogation. My shoulders fell as I realized the answer was probably no. I looked at Croft.

"I guess this is where I leave you. Au revoir, my love." He swept a princely bow.

"You can't call me that," I said, shocked. His other endearments were, well, endearments, but they weren't as strong as this one.

"What can't I call you?" he asked, cocking his head.

I narrowed my eyes. "You won't trick me into saying it."

Gina entered, and I called out casually, "How was your date?"

"It was good, thanks. How was the dance?"

"Fabulous," Croft intercepted, and I shut my mouth tight. I had been about to use the exact same word. It was a good thing Croft hadn't caught me at it, or I would have never heard the end of us being "twinners."

Gina looked hesitant. I think she was wondering whether to hide in her room while I said goodbye to Croft, or whether I preferred for her to stay so that I didn't have to be alone with him. Since I had frequently voiced my Croft-objections to her, it would make sense for me to want a third wheel present.

Croft took my arm. "Walk me to the door?" he asked in a falsetto voice and fluttered his eyelashes at me.

I giggled. "Of course, Your Highness." I smiled at Gina. "I'll talk to you in a minute."

"Wow, a whole minute." Croft led the way. "Does that mean I need to take baby steps across the living room, or do we get to talk at the door?"

"Steps," I said. "I'm not sure you got all five hundred in at the dance."

"And yet, here we are already," he said in resignation as we stopped in the hall. He let go of my arm and searched my eyes. "Do you feel okay now? Are you sure it's all right if I leave?"

I lowered my voice. "Yes. Whatever it was, we've chased it away for tonight."

"Call me anytime you're dealing with it, okay?"

"I might just do that." There were others I could call, and of course I could usually go outside and wait for it to pass, but I wasn't averse to the idea of having Croft come help.

He put his arms around me, and for the second time, I felt myself pressed to his chest, surprised at his gesture. Heat melted through me, and my arms crept around to hug him back because it felt good—that is, because it was more comfortable that way. I wondered not for the first time in my dating history at how much a hug could make me feel.

"Au revoir, my . . ." he began and pulled away.

I scowled, partly because he had ended the hug, partly because of his words.

". . . dove," he finished with feigned innocence. "What? What did you think I was going to say?"

"Good night, Prince Big-Head," I said evenly and indicated the door.

He smiled at me and left.

I watched the dark neighborhood, butterflies in my stomach. I wouldn't have minded a longer visit. Or a longer hug. After all . . .

I caught my breath and turned away as I realized what I was thinking. No. No, I couldn't feel this. I had to work harder, faster, to find Croft's girl.

"Hey." Gina's voice startled me. She was draping her coat across a chair at the dining table. "*Did* you have fun tonight?"

My voice sounded funny as I answered, "I'll admit it. I did." I bit my lip. If Gina could ask me about my night, maybe I could ask about hers. Though she had said she didn't want anyone to make a big deal about her dates with Tim, surely a girl would like to talk over her date just a little bit. Just an *eensy*, tiny bit. Right?

An hour later, we parted ways and went to bed. Once I had started asking Gina questions while keeping my excitement for her under wraps, she had been happy to talk.

I lay back on my bed with a deep sigh. How I wished I could figure out the rest of my life the way I was figuring out Gina. However, my feelings for Croft were a whole other puzzle.

Tonight had been an anomaly. I wasn't into Croft yet, I just . . . enjoyed his company at times. But the more I did so, the more it would hurt when we parted ways, which meant I had to make our separation happen as soon as possible.

I pressed my lips together. *Ice skating, here I come.*

Chapter Twenty-One

THAT NIGHT, I dreamed Croft was dating the waitress who hated me, the one I had narrowly escaped earlier this week. He stood with his arm around her while she spoke lovingly to him.

I stood nearby, invisible and unable to walk away from or toward them. I needed to warn him about her temper, but I couldn't make my mouth function. How could I tell him he was making a mistake?

"I'm going for a walk," Croft announced, and the girl's expression changed on the instant.

"No," she cried, gripping his arm, fury in every line of her face. "How dare you, Croft."

"It's just a walk," he protested, but she would have none of it.

"It's always just a walk with you, isn't it. You never think about me. You never—"

"Wait, why is this such a big deal?"

"You dare leave me?"

"No, it's just—"

"Just nothing. You stay right here, or I'll—"

"But—"

With a howl of rage, she pulled out a bowl of spaghetti and dumped it over his head.

"HEY!" I charged toward her and woke up furious, my heart pounding, my fists clenched. I punched at my comforter, hard. How dare she treat him that way! I would tell her what was what. I would . . . defend him . . .

Gradually realizing it had been a dream, I shook my head and breathed, in, out, in, out, until my temper cooled. Croft didn't need anyone to defend him. My enemy waitress hadn't done a thing to him in real life. Easy, Surrey, easy.

I began to giggle at the image of Croft with his head covered in spaghetti. Sauce and meatballs and pasta dripping off him . . . I couldn't stop giggling. Turning over, I buried my ever-louder snorts in my pillow and tried to get a hold of myself. *Oh, no. Stop laughing, Surrey. Stop—haha —laughing. Gina will hear you.*

Finally, I grew sleepy again. The image in my mind was replaced by one with Croft dressed in white, and I'm pretty sure I was smiling when I fell asleep.

* * *

THE NEXT MORNING, Croft sent me the photos we had had taken at the dance. I emailed them to my parents with the message, "Don't read anything into this. I just thought you might want to see the pictures. This is definitely my best dress since prom."

I whistled like a cardinal and headed off to school, waiting for the Mom Explosion. She responded within minutes, but she kept her answer under wraps, refraining from mentioning Croft, gushing about how good I looked, and asking if I really ought to have worn that particular dress at the ball? But then, it looked so great on me, she concluded.

In a lull between students coming in for help during my lab hour, Croft wasted no time planning our next date. "On Saturday, how about we—"

"Go ice skating," I interrupted.

He blinked. "You want to go ice skating with me?"

I smiled sweetly. "Then you can show off your south cow."

He choked. "Do you mean the Salchow jump?"

I shook my head. "I'll be at the other end of the rink doing the north cow."

He threw back his head and guffawed until he cried tears. I was secretly pleased I could make him laugh that hard.

* * *

When I came home to Gina in her pink sweats, I was glad I had postponed my meeting with Croft's crew.

"Happy Thursday, Gina. How was your day?"

"Good." She laid down her pen and looked up, reminding me of a certain angelic painting I still needed to finish. "I've been working on a humanities paper. What about you?"

My steps faltered. "I, um . . . have a research project." This was embarrassing.

"What kind of research?"

I coughed. "Croft's videos."

She stilled. "You're watching his show?"

"I'm joining a meeting with his crew tomorrow. I figure I should find out just what it is they do."

Gina nodded slowly, recognizing the import of what I was saying. I had avoided his videos all semester. Now, at last, I was taking a look.

"Just so I can direct the team to play nicer pranks," I hurried to say.

She nodded again. "Let me know what you find out."

"Mind you, I'm not subscribing to his channel."

"Of course not," she said with a faint smile. I realized I was being overly defensive and forced myself to stop talking.

Going through Croft's channel took longer than I would have expected. His crew averaged a video every three to four weeks, and it went back nearly two years. Most of them had me laughing, and even Gina couldn't help but chuckle at the ones she watched, although she felt as bad for the victims as I did.

Not all the pranks were mean, to tell the truth. The earlier ones had been less shocking. I thought I could see what Willie had talked about, though. The earliest films and the latest ones had no particular bias, but in the videos from this spring and summer, when Croft was present and playing a role, he seemed more callous when the subject was blond. Was that a real pattern, or did I just imagine it now that I was looking for it? But Willie had had no reason to look for it, and *he* had noticed it.

My phone pinged. I opened my email and smiled at Dad's response to this morning's pictures. He wrote that he was so proud of his beautiful grown-up baby girl.

I knew he would love the pictures.

Another ping, and I opened Mom's latest message.

Just one question. Is this Croft? I won't ask anything else, I promise.

I shook my head and wondered how she had remembered the name Croft from when I blurted it out in frustration during Monday's phone call. Had she had pen and paper at the ready to take notes? She was as devious as Willie, who had so sneakily gotten the information he needed about Croft and then tracked him down on campus to teach him a lesson.

What a lesson that had turned out to be. I had had no peace since then.

My fingers scrolled to the top of the email chain, where a photo showed the white Prince Croft with his arm around his warrior-queen.

At the moment, I didn't mind that lack of peace so much.

* * *

THE ADDRESS CROFT gave me for the meeting-place the next day just happened to be at his own house. When I arrived, he let me in with a deep bow and led me to a set of canary-yellow couches where three others were seated: Tristan and Jane and a girl I hadn't met.

I stared at the yellow sofas. No one but Croft would flaunt this kind of furniture. "You know this color scheme is awful, right?"

"The rug? I did wonder if I should have gotten bolder colors." He scratched his head.

A knock at the door called him away.

I looked at the people before me. "I've met Tristan and Jane, but what's your name?" I asked the unknown girl.

"Riley. What's yours?"

"Surrey," Croft answered for me, reappearing. "And this is Poe," he introduced the newest arrival, who froze at the sight of me but then nodded and gave me a deep-throated "Hi."

"I hope you weren't planning on sitting down," Croft said as I continued to stand in the middle of the living room.

"I was just waiting to find out where you'd sit so I could strategize accordingly," I said.

"Aww, I'm so touched that you want to sit next to me." He put a hand to his heart. "How about over here next to Jane? There's plenty of room for both of us."

I sat down in the middle of the space Croft had indicated and stretched my arms in both directions. "Nope. Only room for one. Sorry."

Riley and Poe gave us funny glances, but I was enjoying our exchange.

Croft grinned and claimed a white, upholstered armchair with purple polka dots all over it. "I can see you better from here, anyway. Welcome, those of us who could make it to our unconventional Friday meeting. Some of you already know, but I called this meeting because Surrey has made me aware that I, and we, need to come up with nicer ideas for our films."

"Is this what it's like to have a teenager?" Tristan asked in a world-weary voice.

"Come again?" Croft looked confused.

Tristan held out his hands. "I've told you before that your ideas border on too mean. Now someone else tells you, and voila, all of a sudden you listen."

"Can you blame him?" Poe spoke up before anyone else could respond. "I would listen, too, if she were the one telling me something."

Croft's expression turned stormy. "I didn't listen to Surrey because she's a pretty face," he snapped. "I listened to her because she has substance."

Everyone started speaking at once.

"Whoa, and I don't?" Tristan said in mock offense.

"Obviously," Jane answered him, chuckling.

"Way to go, Surrey." Riley cheered me on.

"I didn't say she doesn't have substance," Poe protested.

"None of you should listen to someone just because they're attractive," Croft lectured, his eyes shooting daggers. "That's about the stupidest . . ."

"Oh, here we go again," Tristan sighed.

"All I was saying . . ." Poe raised his voice.

I felt bad for Croft, who was clearly upset. He had just said I had substance, which was quite the compliment.

Rather than add to the din of voices in an attempt to redirect things, I stood and walked away.

It didn't take long for Croft to excuse himself and catch up with me. The others quieted down behind us, their conversation turning more civil.

"Where are you going?" Croft asked at my heels. He sounded worried.

"To the kitchen." I passed the fridge and looked around at the large space. "I'm thirsty." I started opening cupboards until I found the cups.

"Well, um, let's see what we've got," he stammered.

It was strange to see him flustered. The question was, which part of the recent dialogue was he embarrassed about? And how quickly could I make him feel comfortable again?

"Let's." I perused the inside of the fridge as he held the door open. "I did an admirable job cleaning out your wallet the last time we ate out, but it's time to move on to bigger and better things."

He eyed me in expectation, our faces close. "Like what?"

"Cleaning out your fridge."

A smile spread across his face, and he reached over and pulled out a bottle. "Would you be willing to make do with pineapple mango juice?"

"That will do."

He started to pour for me and then for everyone else. "Sorry about that back there," he said in a low voice.

"About what specifically?"

"About Poe being chauvinistic." His jaw ticked. Then he forced his shoulders to relax. "And about me getting grumpy," he acknowledged.

I sipped my juice. "It's okay. You didn't 'blown it,' *and* your apology didn't rhyme. Do you have any roommates here?"

"You memorized my poem?" he asked in delight.

My voice turned threatening. "The worst part of it is etched in my mind. If you recite it again, I'll get mad." I could only be nice to him for so long.

He swallowed his laughter and said, "I'm the only one who lives here. My aunt and uncle turn houses, and they're renting this one to me for a puny amount, with the full disclosure that they may sell it out from under me anytime."

"So you're on the brink of disaster." I nodded as if approving of his fate and called to the others, "Come get your drinks."

We all settled in, and the team bounced ideas off each other, ranging from using some of Croft's furniture in a house-showing to having Tarzan and Jane appear in a well-trafficked forest and act out a scene among the trees. Everyone seemed at ease, getting up to use the restroom or to pace or to get another drink. Somehow, Croft ended up next to me in spite of our earlier seating arrangement. I complained at his enthusiastic gestures as he got excited about some of the topics and waved his hands in my face, but I was actually entertained.

When the meeting ended and people started to leave, I picked up two glasses and made for the kitchen.

"Well, thanks." Croft picked up another couple. "Would you mind doing the dishes, as well?"

"I would love to," I said as we put the cups in the sink and I turned on the faucet.

Croft blinked in confusion. "I was kidding. You can't do my dishes."

"*Your* dishes? Next, you'll be telling me this house belongs to you." Before he could reply, I ordered, "Go say goodbye to your friends."

"But . . ."

I brandished the wet sponge at him, sending water flying. "Go."

He fled the kitchen with laughter and a wet shirt.

I set down the sponge and opened the fridge. There was a steady rhythm to my work as I moved item after item while listening to the parting conversations at the door.

When I heard the last person about to leave, I closed the fridge and turned off the faucet. Leaving the cups we had used in the sink and unwashed, I walked to the hall and greeted Croft and the last person, who turned out to be Poe. I put on my shoes and straightened, catching a look of disappointment from Croft.

"You're not staying?" He tsked. "I have to say, you did a lousy job of cleaning out my fridge today. There's Sprite, too, you know."

My eyes widened. "Carbonation? Don't you think I'm bubbly enough without it?"

He grinned and gave me a hug, one that didn't surprise me like the other two had. A look of jealousy slid across Poe's face. The jealousy annoyed me, as it had nothing to do with Poe liking me since he didn't know me.

"It was nice to meet you, Surrey," Poe said.

I cocked my head. "You, too. But you know, Croft is right. If you want to avoid Helen-of-Troy catastrophes, you'll have to pay more attention to a woman's character than her looks."

He startled, and his cheeks turned red. "Uh—"

I had learned in my years of being gawked at that guys who didn't see past my looks could still be decent, so before his embarrassment could grow, I told him, "You had some cool ideas in that discussion. You all work together well."

He blinked and gave me a small smile. "Thanks."

"You're welcome." With another goodbye to him and Croft, I got in my car.

I made it halfway home before my phone rang. This was one call I wanted to take. I pulled over and picked up. "Surrey's Cleaning Services. How may I help you?"

Croft was laughing on the other end. He had definitely been in the kitchen. I smiled as I pictured the state in which I'd left the room. Food items were piled on the floor and counters, leaving the fridge empty—cleaned out, just like I'd promised.

"Come back, Surrey," he moaned. "Come back and clean out the freezer, too."

"Nah. Too much work in one day."

"I won't trust you the next time you offer to do my dishes."

"Oh, I wouldn't dream of offering again."

Croft laughed harder, and I smiled wider.

Chapter Twenty-Two

I ONLY HAD one item left on my List of Ten Things for the semester, and it was to cook and eat a meal I wouldn't like. Having found a recipe online, I turned on Christmas music and directed my obedient subjects into their places, looking down my nose at the spinach in spite of its acquiescence. Why would anyone want spinach in their lasagna?

Once my distasteful meal was in the oven, I returned to my room with my iPod to keep me company. By now, I had completed five paintings for the fundraiser auction, which meant I had time for other projects. I picked up my painting of Gina and scrutinized it.

Why was it so hard for me to make my subjects look like a specific person? I was so close to having it right, though. I might—I just might be able to finish it today, before going ice skating. I was only missing some finishing touches on her eyebrows to make them right. And maybe I should make a change to the chin?

My strokes were slow and precise, but what really took up time was eyeing the photos of Gina, consulting the image in my mind, staring at the canvas, and deciding on the next stroke.

I spent a good five minutes figuring out the eyebrows. It was the one on the right that caught my attention. The angle wasn't quite right. The closer I got to correcting it, the more I began to worry that the texture on both eyebrows needed work.

Jingle Bells broke my concentration, slowing me down. It wasn't a very Gina-like song, so I waited until the end before I picked up my brush again.

It was painstaking work, but it was exhilarating to see it come together. I finished the eyebrows and carefully added a line to the chin. Was that better? Yes. Wait, no. Wait, yes. But the eyelids still weren't quite right, were they?

Beep. Beep.

I ignored my phone and squinted at the painting. *Let It Snow!* played for the second time that morning, and I hummed along. My phone rang repeatedly, but I was so close to finishing the painting that I had to keep going.

That's it. I had a clear image in my mind of how to place the next stroke to correct the shape of an eyelid. I took a deep breath and slowly touched my brush across it. Then I surveyed the spot. What was missing?

It was a miracle when I became satisfied with those eyelids, especially since my phone kept ringing. If it was Croft calling to reschedule today's outing, he would just have to deal with my not answering. My gaze had snagged on Gina's chin again, and I felt certain I would be done with the entire painting once I perfected that chin.

I sneezed and wrinkled my nose at a burnt smell. My eyes traveled the canvas, up and down, down and up. I tilted my head and stepped away to look at it from a different angle.

A terrible beeping noise screamed through the house above the noise of my music and my phone. I dropped my brush and clapped both hands to my ears, then ran from my room to see what was wrong with the smoke alarm.

A haze hung in the air. It was heaviest in the direction of the kitchen.

Oh, no.

Covering my mouth and nose with my right elbow, I waved my way into the smoky kitchen like a soldier on the march with his arm chopping up and down. I turned off the oven and, keeping an eye out for flames, opened it. Heat poured out. Spinning away and coughing, I hurried to open the windows.

My phone rang again. Only, it wasn't my phone. Exasperated, I whirled back to the kitchen to turn off the oven timer I had ignored as I painted. Then I stumbled from the gaseous room.

My phone lay on the dining table. I snatched it up and opened the tools app.

My voice was irked as I recorded myself saying, "I am *not* your oven timer." I picked the recording as my new ringtone to help me get used to this very important fact.

The house grew cold, and a good deal of the smoke disappeared. I set about shutting the windows and finally removed my lasagna from the oven.

It looked black. Crusty black and brown.

I stabbed experimentally at the food with my spatula. It cut through it okay, breaking into the crunchy pasta. How appetizing.

Hadn't my goal been to make something I wouldn't like?

* * *

By the time Croft took me to the Peaks Ice Arena, I wished I had eaten something else.

"Wait a minute. Do you not skate?" Croft asked in disbelief as I grabbed the wall at the rink entrance and pulled myself onto the ice. My stomach churned, and I felt too warm in my long, white jacket and black cotton leggings. I seemed to remember telling Croft once that I didn't really skate, but either he had forgotten, or he hadn't realized it meant . . . this.

"You know what, Croft, I think you should take a turn around the rink. Don't worry about me." I put my weight on one foot and slid the other back and forth, then adjusted my grip on the railing and moved forward a few inches.

"No, that's not what you think," he said in his infuriating way while he watched me. "You know what I think you think? I think you wanted to go ice skating so we could hold hands."

"What?" I looked up at him. "No. That's preposterous," I insisted while he stole my hands away from the wall and started us moving. We glided along the ice, my legs gaining confidence underneath me as he held my arms steady. I was facing the way we were going, and he was . . . not.

"What are you doing?" I asked, worried.

"Giving you your heart's desire." He raised our clasped hands to indicate them. "This is what you wanted to do today."

"You're going backwards," I protested. "You can't see where you're going." That prospect set my nerves on edge. It made it hard to look around and scout out a girl for him.

He shrugged. "But *you* can. Think of it as a trust exercise."

I shook my head. "If I warn you you're about to knock into someone, it'll be for my benefit as much as yours. That has nothing to do with trust." I sneaked a glance toward the center of the rink, where talented ice skaters showed off their jumps and crossovers. Would Croft be more attracted to a talented ice skater or to someone who was hugging the rink, like I should be doing?

"You already love me as much as yourself?" He sounded pleased as he twisted my words. "We're making great strides tonight."

"I think you should look where you're going," I told him.

"*I* think you've moved on to flirting with me," he said, his dimples deepening. His voice became a falsetto. "'Oh, Croft, let's go ice skating on Saturday. We can hold on to each other all day.'"

That had most certainly *not* been my intention. In order to dissuade that notion, I spoke a little more harshly than I usually did. "Croft, you're an idiot."

His eyes widened. "You're swooning."

He braked and put his hands on either side of my face.

"What—" I broke off to laugh and clasped his arms to keep myself steady. "What are you doing?"

"I've got you. Don't pass out, now."

"Croft." I laughed and simultaneously shivered as he held my face. His antics were ridiculous, but they also made it hard for me to breathe.

"I'm so sorry," he murmured, stroking my cheek with his thumb and raising my heartrate. "There's nothing I can do about how strong an effect I have on you."

Sputtering, I pulled my face from his hands and hit his arm. I had a mission to fulfill, but did Croft care? "Stop distracting me."

He smiled. "From what?"

From finding your girl, I thought to myself.

"From ice skating," I said instead. "Besides, we can't possibly hold hands. You wouldn't want to do such a thing until you got married, now, would you?" I raised an eyebrow, taking another opportunity to tease him for the rule we both lived by.

"While I reserve kissing for post-engagement, one can only postpone hand-holding for so long," Croft replied. "The moment a couple laces up their skates is the moment their hands must join together."

I groaned. I should have known ice skating would keep Croft glued to my side. Well, in front of, behind, and sometimes beside me. No matter how much I encouraged him to go around the rink alone at his own pace, he stayed close. The few times he wasn't holding on to me, he circled around me, prompting me to make comments about feeling like prey, which prompted a barrage of jokes from him, which in turn prompted gales of laughter from me.

By the time we sat down on a bench to take off our skates, I felt like the floor was moving beneath me, my gliding motions from the past hour fooling my brain. It had been fun—and otherwise a complete waste of time.

Maybe I could make one last effort to send Croft after someone else here. I didn't know what type of girl he preferred, but surely *he* knew. If someone had caught his eye today, maybe I could draw his attention back to her now. All I had to do was supply some vague terms and let him fill in the rest.

I glanced at him as I untied my laces. "Did you see that girl . . ." My voice trailed off as I looked back at the rink. I pretended to be distracted as I pulled off my skate and laid it on the table.

"What girl?" Croft prompted.

"The one with the . . . hair . . . ?" I raised my hands above my head and made some small motions, indicating whatever hairdo the girl who might have caught his eye might have.

Croft raised his eyebrows.

"The . . . hair?" he repeated.

I dropped my hands. "Yes. You know, just all cute. And, uh, she had . . ." He didn't fill in the blank for me. Cripes. "Didn't you notice her?"

He pulled his skates off without taking his gaze off me.

"The one with . . ." Okay, this time, I really was going to wait until he filled in the blank. He could do that much. He had to.

"The nose?" he asked, his eyebrows still up.

I burst into giggles and nodded emphatically. "Yes, the nose." I covered my mouth with my hands.

He swung his feet forward to better face me. "And did she have shoulders?"

Somehow, he managed to ask the question in a voice that sounded nothing but curious. I coughed and shook my head.

"She didn't have shoulders?" he asked in alarm.

"Of course she did," I amended, shaking with mirth. "But back to the nose . . ."

He leaned forward, laughter catching in his throat. "Yes, what about it?"

"It was below her eyes," I managed, trying to breathe past my barely-contained laughter.

"What? You didn't tell me she had eyes." He looked around wildly. "Where *is* this girl?"

"Nooo," I moaned. "I was . . . just wondering . . . if you noticed her."

"I have eyes for no one but you," he said, scooting closer.

"You have a nose, too," I said and lost it.

Our very mature conversation ended with both of us laughing our heads off, holding onto the bench or each other to keep from falling.

I drew breath several times before I could stop. This hadn't gone at all the way I'd planned. I sighed and decided our date needed to end.

"Well. You can take me home now," I said and stood.

Somehow, I knocked my skates off the table, which wouldn't have been a problem if someone hadn't passed by right then. The skates landed in front of him, the guy lost his footing, and I reached out in desperation to grasp his arm—but as his weight was too much for me, I fell stomach-down on his back with an *oomph*.

I tried to breathe. Ohhh, my lungs, what had just happened to my lungs? Did I still have them?

Croft's arm wrapped around my waist and helped me up. "Are you okay?"

The guy who had just been attacked from beneath and above got up on his knees and then stood.

"I am so, so sorry," I told him, having apparently relocated my lungs. "Are you okay?"

He looked familiar, and it didn't take me long to realize I had just felled someone from my art class—someone I would have to see again. Lovely.

"Yes, I'm okay," he answered with a wince. "You?"

I nodded. "I'm sorry about the skates."

"That's okay." He kept looking at me. "You're Surrey, right?"

Croft stiffened beside me. I guess I could feel it because he was still holding my waist.

"Yes. And you're . . . your name starts with a J?" I ventured.

He smiled and smoothed back his white-blond hair. "My name actually *is* Jay. You're in my art class."

"Yes." I couldn't think of anything else to say. "Um, it's a good class."

Jay looked at Croft and back at me. "How's your portfolio coming along?"

He had obviously forgiven me for the accident. Grateful, I answered, "I'm pretty much done. It's nice to have a final you can finish beforehand."

"For sure."

"You're sure you're okay, Surrey?" Croft asked.

I turned to face him, stepping out of his hold. "Yes. We should have known there would be an accident before we left the building."

Jay picked up the culprits and handed them to me. "Here are your skates."

"Thanks."

"Did you just finish skating?" he asked.

"Yes. Are you just getting started?"

"Yeah." He looked disappointed. "Well, I'll see you in class."

"Bye," I said as he walked away.

"I betcha he'll ask you out the next time he sees you," Croft said in a low voice. I turned and met his dark, mirthless eyes. "Happens all the time, doesn't it?"

I frowned. "He doesn't even know me." I didn't know what to do with Croft's less-than-enthusiastic observation. Part of me wanted to reassure him he didn't need to worry about Jay, but reassuring him wasn't exactly congruous with my plans to get rid of him. I turned toward the skate rental booth to return my stumbling blocks.

"Trust me. He'll ask."

* * *

I MIGHT HAVE BEEN deep in thought on the way home if Croft hadn't turned on the radio and begun to lip sync to the music. I rolled my eyes and made some exaggerated movements to the beat. Croft responded in turn, and before I knew it, we were laughing and trying to outdo each other with ridiculous dance moves without getting in a car accident.

I couldn't help but be grateful he was still spending time with me rather than mooning over some girl with shoulders and eyes.

At home, he walked me to the door, waited for me to unlock it, and then exclaimed "Congratulations" before enveloping me in a warm hug.

"For what?" I spoke into his soft shirt, which smelled like him. Or did he smell like his shirt? Fabric softener or *eau de Croft*?

He let go. "For graduating."

I looked at him like he was crazy. I still had two semesters left.

"To hugs at the doorstep," he said and gave me another one.

This time, I was pretty sure his shirt smelled like him.

He spoke against my hair. "The shoulder-pats were okay, but this is better."

I silently agreed and gave him a weak smile when he left.

The faint smell of smoke greeted me inside. I looked at the glass pan soaking in the sink but couldn't bring myself to scrub it clean. I felt heavy, and even the memory of the girl with hair, a nose, and shoulders no longer seemed funny.

I jumped at the sound of my voice saying, "I am *not* your oven timer." Fumbling for my phone, my spirits lifted at the thought that the caller could be *Prince Big-Head*—my contact name for Croft since the ball— calling to tease me about something, maybe even to tell me he was outside my door again for some reason or other.

It turned out to be my mom.

Talking to her might dissolve my moroseness. I just hoped she wouldn't be able to tell there *was* moroseness on my end.

"Hi, Mom. Happy Saturday."

"Hi, Surrey." I felt a bit lighter at the sound of her voice. "How's your—"

"Surrey," Fairlee's voice broke in while Mom's faded away. "Surrey, I finally figured out who your date was. I knew he looked familiar."

"Fairlee, did you just steal the phone from Mom?"

"Yes, but we know who Croft is," Fairlee exclaimed, while Mom's voice from farther away said, "Give me that, young lady."

"He's the guy who pretended to call for help in that hidden camera video," my sister announced triumphantly. "Do you like him?"

I made a frustrated noise. "Fairlee, he's also the guy I'm trying to find a girl for."

"Right," she scoffed, "but do you *like* him?"

Mom's lack of protests indicated she was as interested in the answer as my sister was.

I chose my words with caution. "He's okay in doses." He was hilarious, surprisingly sweet at times, and stimulating company. In fact, those were the three things I would have put at the top of his list of good attributes if I were writing it.

The memory of how he had helped me when I found myself at odds with the feeling in my house flashed through my mind. I remembered, too, his behavior at Brody and Hanna's reception. He had been ridiculous, making it impossible for me to wallow in self-pity.

I remembered our walk in the neighborhood and how he had given voice to the overexcited dog. I snickered.

"Yes," Fairlee yelled, and I could just imagine her doing a fist pump in Virginia.

"I'm not dating him," I began, but she interrupted.

"When was the last time you saw him?"

"Today. We went ice skating." I waved a hand in exasperation. "But I'm telling you, I'm trying to set him up with someone else."

"Okay, fine," she said in an innocent tone. "But don't look too hard."

I huffed. Whether I looked or not, he *would* find his dream girl, which meant there was no reason for Fairlee or anyone else to get their hopes up. In fact, I probably should jump at the chance if Jay asked me out, in case he was meant to pick up the pieces when Croft left. My voice rose as I answered, "Just because I'm spending time with a guy, that doesn't mean I'm dating him, and it doesn't mean we'll be a thing later on. We're *just friends*. Croft will find his dream girl, and one way or another, he'll have me to thank for it." My cheeks blazed with heat, and my empty fist clenched tight.

"Hi, Surrey, this is Mom back at central control," Mom's voice came over the phone.

"Hi, Mom." I spoke quickly. "Sorry, but I have to go. Finals are coming up. Bye."

"Bye. We love y—" Mom's voice got cut off as I hung up.

I dropped the phone and burst into tears.

Sinking to the floor, I felt around blindly for my phone while I cried like an Olympic weeper. (Let's just pretend that's a thing, okay?) My fingers closed around the phone, but rather than check for damage, I threw it at the couch. Then I leaned against the wall, pulling my knees to my chest and rocking back and forth.

Why was I crying? Because Croft would stop teasing me when he left me behind someday? Surely I could get along without his cocky comments and exaggerated flirtation. I liked him now, but only as a friend. Losing him wouldn't hurt as much as losing Brody had.

I would have continued lying to myself if it hadn't made the tears come faster, disabling me from getting up and moving on. My eyes hurt, and my cheeks had probably taken on the prettiest rose color imaginable, judging by what crying usually did to my face. Each of my false statements kept me more firmly planted on the floor. Finally, I gave it up. I had to face the truth.

With a shuddering breath, I followed my high school art teacher's advice and shut my eyes, hoping it would help me see.

I had fallen for him.

I jerked forward, sniffed, and forced myself to relax and lean back again. I couldn't run from the facts. Running from them had led me to losing control of my tear ducts in the first place.

I took a deep breath. Just like I had fallen for the other guys, I had fallen for Croft. As much as I had planned for it, I no longer looked forward to the day his dream girl would show up and sweep him away. I didn't want to help him find her, and I didn't want to hurry it along. But I couldn't avoid it, and the longer it took, the more it would hurt.

It had happened too many times. After Keaton, I had thought for sure Jesse and I would get married. After Jesse, I had thought Killian must be the one. After him, I had thought it couldn't possibly end the same way again—surely Frank and I were meant to be. We had both been so in love.

After Frank, there had been Brody. *My* Brody—but no, now he was Hanna's, and I was okay with that because . . .

I sobbed and pressed my hands to my face. I was okay losing Brody, because after him, there was Croft. Croft had joined the ranks of my heart-throbs.

I couldn't bear it. Oh, I just couldn't bear it. I was so tired of heartbreak. Dating Croft should have been risk-free. I was never supposed to have gotten attached. What was I to do now that I had fallen for him?

I turned over scenario after scenario in my mind. I could keep trying to find Croft's dream girl—and probably become a walking watering pot. I could try to enjoy the time I had left with him—and face even greater heartache than I did now. Maybe I could remain friends with him after his girl came along. I would be okay not dating him, right?

Oh, stupid, stupid, stupid. I *did* want to date him. I wanted to stroll arm in arm with him at receptions, laugh my head off with him at dances, and hear him extol my virtues in ridiculous but sincere terms while offering only rare compliments on my beauty.

Come Christmas, I wanted to talk to him on the phone and know he would still be around, waiting for me, when I returned to Provo. If I lost him before Christmas, I would spend the entire vacation heartbroken and trying to put on a brave face for my family.

"Stop trying to speed up our breakup, then," I mumbled to myself and rubbed my salty cheeks.

Maybe I could set a goal. Hold on to Croft over Christmas break, and then I would let events play out as they would and be happy with the memories even after I lost him.

I let out a hysterical laugh. It would be just my luck for his dream girl to show up tomorrow, right after I'd decided to stop trying to help him find her. If she did, I would deal with it. I always did. But . . . what if she didn't? What if I could slow things down?

My mind spun. I had long believed the more time I spent with Croft, the sooner he'd find his dream girl. Maybe the opposite was also true. Maybe spending less time with him would keep her away longer.

How ironic. In order to have more time with him, I might have to cut down on how much we saw each other during the week. My mind caught hold of the idea, painful though it was. If it meant we might still be together after Christmas . . .

It would be worth it.

Chapter Twenty-Three

I MUST HAVE MADE the right decision, because God was making it happen. Croft texted me Monday morning to let me know he wouldn't be in class, and he never came to the lab, either. I missed him but told myself this was good. Things were falling into place.

The next day, Croft called before my New Testament class. It was good to hear his voice and know he was alive and well, but I was stunned when he told me he had a study group that night that he couldn't miss.

I gaped at my phone. When had we not done something on a Tuesday since I "agreed" to date him? I tried not to be disappointed, reminding myself that our relationship would last longer if we spent less time together. In fact, it was nothing short of miraculous that he couldn't take me on a date tonight. God really *was* making my new plan work out.

Or, the unwelcome thought came, had Croft already had his head turned by another girl and was now distancing himself from me?

"I can't *not* see you three days in a row, Surrey," his voice moaned with his usual feigned desperation, bringing me no small amount of relief. "Can we have lunch together on campus at one o'clock?"

I smiled but answered with regret, "I have a class then."

"How will you live without me?" he almost howled, making me giggle. "*I* have a class at noon. I bet you're open then."

I confirmed it and told him, "Sorry, Croft, but I'm standing outside my next class, and it's about to start."

"Oh. Okay."

"Bye."

Every time I stepped outside that day, it was snowing. When I walked home, the snow was soft and deep, half a foot in some places, and flurries were still coming down.

Willie was outside, his hands in the pockets of his winter jacket, his hood up. I hadn't seen him much since the weather turned cold.

"Hey!" I gave him a bright smile. "You're outside!"

He shrugged and squinted up at the cold sun. "Vitamin D." With his hood on, though, he couldn't be getting much of the coveted vitamin.

"Snow," I responded with enthusiasm and scooped up a big handful.

A snowball hit my middle, and I looked up in disbelief at my grinning neighbor.

I shaped my handful and threw it at him, only to receive another missile sent my direction a moment later.

"Hold on," I ordered and ran to my house. Unlocking the door, I threw my backpack inside and ran back to Willie, ducking to avoid another flying snowball.

It didn't take long for our snowball fight to turn into fort-building. There was an evident lack of trust between us. Instead of building a fortress together, we each built our own, facing each other from opposing lawns.

Across the street, the four Whitmer children tumbled outside, yelling about making a snowman. Bella, however, looked in our direction as her older siblings began rolling balls.

She abandoned the others and crossed the street. Her mitt was in her mouth, but she removed it to ask, "What are you building?"

"Snow forts," I answered.

"Can I play, too?"

I looked at Willie.

"Sure," he said. "Want to help me with mine?"

"Okay," she said sweetly before turning to her sister and two brothers and yelling in a voice that could wake up a bear from hibernation, "Come build snow forts!"

The others scrambled over. The two oldest Whitmer children, Jayden and Daniel, joined me. Our walls rose quickly, and it became harder to throw something at Willie, Bella, and Lena.

"We need a peephole," Jayden told me while his brother showed me where he thought was the best spot for it.

"Okay," I said, distracted from the snowball in my hand as we strategized. "So long as it's not wide enough that we'll get pummeled . . ."

Smack! Snow exploded against my arm, jerking me back. I dropped to my knees, popped my head above the wall, and yelled at Willie, "Hey! No throwing until these forts are ready!"

"Hypocrite," he yelled back. Yeah, I had no idea why.

A car drove up in the Whitmers' driveway, and Sister Whitmer came to the door to call in her children.

"Dad's home," Bella yelled, running home.

"What are you guys doing tomorrow after school?" I asked Jayden before he could follow.

"Nothing. Why?"

"Wanna test out the forts?"

"With a snowball fight? Yes!"

The Whitmers ran home. I walked over to inspect Willie's fort. It wasn't as curved at the ends as mine, but it was sturdy. "Nice," I remarked out loud.

"Bella's a good builder. Do you really think they'll come play tomorrow?"

"Yeah, why not?" I looked at Willie and realized he was worried. He wasn't used to other children wanting to play with him.

"I don't know." He kicked at the snow. "Maybe *I* won't come play."

I frowned. How could I assure Willie the Whitmers would be there? I pursed my lips, thinking. Then I smiled slyly. "I'm sure they'll come if they get invitations."

"Invitations?" He goggled at me. "You mean cards, like for a birthday party?"

I shrugged. "Yes and no. This isn't exactly going to be a party, is it? This is more like . . . a war."

Minutes later, we were on our hands and knees in Willie's living room, writing out cards.

"WE HEREBY DECLARE WAR ON YOU," the first one started out in red block letters. "BRING YOUR SOLDIERS AND MEET UP FOR

BATTLE AT THE FORTRESSES TOMORROW AT 4 O'CLOCK IF YOU DARE."

"PREPARE FOR DEFEAT," Willie added with a thick, black pen. Then he decorated the page with skulls and fallen snowmen.

From the kitchen, Willie's mom threw pleased looks at her son and grateful ones at me. I don't think she could see our artistic touches. "Who are you inviting?" she asked with interest.

"The Whitmer children," Willie answered, making some of my red text drip blood.

"That's nice," his mom beamed.

* * *

THAT'S what Sister Whitmer thought, too. "That's nice," she said when I handed her the envelopes at her doorstep. "No, the children don't have anything at four tomorrow. I'll give them the invitations to your playdate."

"Thanks, Sister Whitmer." I couldn't let the opportunity pass to use her last name.

I entered my house in time to hear my phone tell me it wasn't my oven timer. When I saw *Prince Big-Head* light up the screen, I was quick to slip off my gloves and answer.

"Surrey," Croft exclaimed on the other end.

"I know, you're surprised I'm still breathing after we've been separated so long," I filled in for him.

He gasped. "It's like you can read my mind. We're definitely twinners."

"Where were you yesterday?" I asked, curious.

He quieted. "Um, my brother was in town and needed some—help."

I frowned. Croft had skipped out on a day of school, not to mention getting to see me, for his brother? Either his brother was going through something horrible, or I wasn't that important to Croft, after all.

"Is he okay?"

"No-o-o," Croft said slowly. "But, you know, if there's anything that can fix things, it's spending time with me." The words were along his usual line of joking conceitedness, but the tone fell flat. "Anyway, this is a bad week all around. I have my study group tonight that I told you about and then a group project I'm working on tomorrow evening, and I can't miss either. I haven't seen you since Saturday. Cinny, we have to do something tomorrow afternoon. Four o'clock? We can get *lunner* if you want to try the hot dog stand again."

Lunner. I mouthed the word and shook my head. Why not, when there was such a thing as brunch?

"I can't," I told him, thinking that God had surely put his stamp of approval on my plan to spend less time with Croft. As of minutes ago, I was unavailable for tomorrow's *lunner.*

"You can't? If the calories are too much for you, we can do something else. How about a half marathon?"

"I can't. I have something else at that time."

"What?"

I fingered my gloves. Telling Croft I was playing with the neighbor kids might only make him keener to spend time with me. After all, it was the discovery of my friendship with Willie that had made him interested in the first place.

The more Croft came to like me, the more he would make us spend time together, which would make his dream girl appear faster. I didn't want that. "Just something," I repeated.

He was silent a moment. Then he asked, "A date?"

I started. Well, why wouldn't he think I was going on a date? Jay had come over and talked to me in class today. Just as Croft predicted, he had asked me out before I left, and I had agreed out of self-preservation as I pondered Croft's looming departure. My date with Jay wasn't tomorrow, but . . . Sister Whitmer had referred to tomorrow as a playdate.

"Maybe," I finally answered.

He was quiet again. "I guess I won't pry." I breathed a sigh of relief before he continued, "Today. But just wait until I see you in class tomorrow."

A smile spread across my face at the thought of seeing him tomorrow. Oh, I was far gone.

"Goodbye, Croft," I said noncommittally and hung up.

* * *

AT ONE MINUTE till four the next afternoon, all four Whitmer children ran whooping from their house.

I stood at the ready in front of my fort, and Willie stood in front of his.

"Warriors," I boomed out. "To me, anyone who wishes to win!"

Willie looked at me in surprise and then, not to be outdone, yelled, "To me, everyone who's ready to topple the towering giantess!"

I blinked. Did he think I was that tall? No, I mustn't get distracted. Bella was already running to his side, laughing. Lena grabbed hold of her brothers, who were trying to go in opposite directions.

"To me, anyone that's ready to flatten the enemy like a pancake," I yelled.

"No, I want you both with me. You can't split up," Lena whined to her brothers. "I want to be with her." She pointed at me.

Bella threw a snowball that missed her older sister. I picked up the cue and threw at the other fort, and Willie joined in, letting out a roar. Once the snow started flying and we were yelling like savages, the dividing up of teams was quickly resolved, with the three children in the middle ducking their heads and running to whichever fort appeared closest. I ended up with Lena and Daniel, but not for long. As we threw and ran and threw and tried to take over each other's forts, our teams kept changing. Soon, I was using Willie's fort with him and Daniel beside me, throwing at the other three.

A car pulled up across the street. I could see from the corner of my eye that it wasn't the Whitmer's dad come to end our game, so I paid it no heed. We continued playing and yelling insults at each other, but then my memory kicked in and made me look at the car again. I did a double take as Croft climbed out, his surprise melting into mischief. He pulled out a video camera and waved at me as if to tell me not to mind him.

At least his camera wasn't hidden. I stuck out my tongue at him and shielded my face in time to catch a snowball on my elbow.

We carried on for a good five minutes on film, with me sneaking occasional glances at our one-man audience. Willie charged across the open terrain and reached the other side only to have Daniel jump on him and wrestle him into the snow. The flurry of snowballs that flew at the two of them from my fort—that is, from the fort in front of Willie's house currently in my possession—caused both boys to scramble behind the other fort and join forces to defend themselves.

Croft must have put away his camera, because he was now walking empty-handed onto the well-trampled snow on the sidewalk, stepping onto the lawn, getting closer and closer to the fray while snow flew on both sides.

Those around me began to hesitate, and those on the other side lowered their arms as Croft stepped into the middle. Lena gave me a questioning look.

Croft surveyed the terrain with a bright smile. He raised his arms and declared, "I always knew I was invincible."

"Fire," Willie yelled.

"Get him," I shouted.

Both sides attacked, staying behind their forts and throwing as if our lives depended on it. With his arms still out, Croft shook his head as he got hit and turned from side to side in confusion, as though he couldn't believe what was happening. Lena laughed and threw faster. Between all the snow that was pitched at Croft, I could hardly make out the puzzled expression he faked.

"Nooooo." He sank to his knees with a dramatic cry, letting himself get buried. From his position on the ground, he tried to catch some of our snowballs and throw them back at us, but since they fell to pieces in his hands, his throws were useless.

"Bury him," shouted one of the Whitmer boys.

"You're done for, you snowman," Bella laughed.

"Throw your puny snowballs," Lena yelled.

"Hit me! You can do better than that," Croft yelled back. He picked up snow from the ground and threw it, now getting into the insult and threat-yelling that had started up anew.

"Your aim is off. Do you even know which direction to throw?" Willie hollered, at me or at Croft or at someone else. It was getting harder to know who each insult was meant for.

Mine, though, was directed at Croft as I shouted, "You couldn't hit a bus in front of y—"

He charged in my direction, and I froze, unsure whether he would huddle down in the shelter of our fort and join forces or whether he . . .

His eyes found mine, a wicked gleam in them as he approached at an alarming pace.

Like a startled deer, I sprang from behind the snow wall. Croft changed direction to chase after me, and I screamed and raced across the white lawn. His warrior yell behind me made it clear he was still following. No way would I let him wrestle me into the snow, so I ran screaming into my house, throwing the door open on the way in with no time to shut it behind me.

Chapter Twenty-Four

CROFT'S STEPS sounded at my back. I whirled around to see him stagger inside and stop just past the entrance to the living room, where he blocked the way and stood breathing hard.

"Oh, man. Can I stay in here a few minutes?" he moaned, stomping his feet and slapping his arms against his chest. He tipped his head up at the ceiling. "Blessed, blessed heater."

With the noise of the heater running in the background, I suddenly took in his appearance. He was bareheaded, his face and ears red. He wore a snow-splattered sweater and jeans with large wet spots from our battle. I wore about three times as many layers as him.

"Croft," I exclaimed, reaching him in three strides. "You're not dressed to be outside. How could you stay out there so long?"

His mouth opened as he debated how to answer, reminding me of a kid caught with his hand in the cookie jar. He affected the whiny tone of someone much younger than him. "I wanted to play with the other kids."

I eyed his red ears in consternation. "You're frozen. Nothing but a sweater to keep you warm." I tugged at the sweater, causing snow to fall to the floor.

"Hey, I earned that snow, fair and square," he protested, but his teeth chattered, and I could practically feel the cold emanating from him as I took off my gloves and shook more white shrapnel off his clothes. My gaze moving downward, I exclaimed, "You're not even wearing gloves." I grabbed his hands, which were chapped and jarringly cold, and began to rub them. "What were you thinking? You've been picking up snow with your bare hands. It's, like, thirty degrees out there and you were outside for, what, fifteen minutes?"

"Surrey, do you need help?" Willie's voice came from the doorway where he popped in and looked at us. I could hear the others still hard at play outside.

"No, thanks, you go on. We'll stay in here for a while." I waved him off.

Willie raised his eyebrows at us before disappearing out front, shutting the door behind him.

I strode to the couch and returned with a soft wool blanket. Croft had pulled off his wet sweater and stood turning it over in his hands as though unsure where to put it. I snatched it from him and laid it on the table, then wrapped my blanket around his shivering shoulders. "Now sit," I ordered, pushing him into a chair before I picked up his hands again and set to work rubbing them with a vengeance.

"I can't believe you just stood there and let us bombard you with snow," I scolded. "No hat, no gloves, no coat. You'll get sick. Hasn't your mom taught you to take care of yourself?"

My grumblings eventually subsided, and I worked in silence. His hands grew warmer, but I knew from the December Ball and ice skating that they weren't back to their usual temperature, so I kept going, sniffling at intervals. I honestly wasn't sure whether the sniffling came from playing outdoors myself or from being upset that Croft had let himself get so cold and wet, but I braced myself for a joke from Croft about me crying over him. It didn't come, though.

It came to me that Croft hadn't spoken a word in entire minutes. My movements slowed, and I raised my gaze to his. He was staring at me. Staring like I had grown another nose. Or was he looking at me with adoration? Really, it was a toss-up as to which interpretation was correct.

Either way, it made me nervous.

"Stop," I told him, putting the palm of my hand to his chin and gently turning his face away. Then I grabbed his hands again.

He obediently faced the back corner. I grumbled some more about how he needed to take care of himself. When he shivered, I ran my hand over his arm, unhappy to find him chilled.

"You need to go home, Croft. I don't have a change of clothes for you, and you'll never get warm until you change."

"I'd much rather stay here," he said quickly. Still looking where I had directed him, he stood and pointed at the back wall where my five auction paintings leaned against each other, partially packaged. "Did you paint those? I remember you making sketches of that front one in class." He took a step in their direction and paused. "Will you show them to me?" he asked, his teeth chattering a little.

I frowned at his still somewhat wet appearance, feeling torn. He didn't give me long to ponder, though.

With his characteristic overconfidence and winning grin, he gave me a deep bow and a "Thank you," then looped my arm through his cold one and walked us over to the paintings.

One was a landscape, one was a cute kid looking over his shoulder at whoever faced the painting, and the last three were what Gina and I had come to call world-contrasts, a combination of two different worlds in a single person or object.

Croft loved the one with the kid and insisted on likewise posing by looking over his shoulder. "Isn't it cute, though? Look." He twisted his head back again. "I could slay damsels with a look when I do this." He did it again until I smacked him on the shoulder. He did seem enthralled with the painting, though, which made me happy.

"This one's kind of different," I told him, pointing at one with a teenager taking off into the skies in a car. The back of the car was a muddy, patched-up Volkswagen, and the front was a shiny convertible. The landscape went from a dingy, polluted neighborhood to a starry night sky. "I hope someone will like it."

"Someone? You're not keeping it?" Croft asked. "I think it's super well done, and the transformation is cool."

I warmed at his praise, and suddenly I wanted his opinion on another piece. Actually, I wanted his total and complete awe as he looked at my masterpiece of masterpieces. "I have to show you one more. I have to show you the woman that was on my mind all semester. Stay here."

I carefully brought the painting from my room and turned it around for him to see. There was my elegant warrior against a backdrop of mountain forests, craggy cliff faces, and a small castle far away behind her. Her hair was a rich mahogany, and her eyes were full of fire. Her dress was a replica of the one I had sewn and worn.

I watched Croft. To my delight, he looked stunned.

"I think it's all there," he said after a moment, "everything you told me about her. Gracious when she needs to be, but she knows how to navigate her wild country."

I brightened at his evaluation and at how well he remembered my description.

"That dress." He shook his head and looked at me. "You've never been more stunning. I mean, you're always gorgeous, as you know, but in *that dress*. Wow. I'm glad you were a life-size model for your painting."

I fanned my cheeks. "Enough of that. But you like it, right?"

"Absolutely."

I gave it another admiring look and returned it to my room.

"Why are these five out here?" Croft asked after I rejoined him.

"Oh—I'm sending them to Arizona."

"What for?"

I scuffed my foot. I hadn't made the paintings so I could brag about doing something for a good cause. "A fundraiser auction." Why was I suddenly so worried about what Croft thought?

"Cool. What's the fundraiser for?"

"It's for . . . for . . ." He had a thing about children, right? I couldn't make him fall harder for me. I certainly didn't want him to think I was trying to earn his regard by contributing to a cause for children.

Then again, maybe that was exactly what I ought to do. Act like a ninny who was trying to impress him. Maybe that little bit of mischief would push him away mentally.

". . . for a charity auction to help poor children get good educations," I said sweetly. "You see, I have a soft spot for children." His eyebrows shot up. "It's one of my best attributes, don't you think?" I fluttered my eyelashes at him.

"Stop, stop," he said in a pained voice and held up his hands.

I caught my breath. This was instant success. My ninny-like behavior had disgusted him.

He continued, "I firmly believe there should only be one eyelash-flut-terer in each relationship, and in ours, I think that should be me."

"What?" I gaped at him, incredulous. "You think you're better at it than me?"

"I'm so confident in the fact that I'll let you be the judge," he answered and, resting his chin on his hands, he fluttered his lashes.

His reaction was so ridiculous that I didn't know whether to be outraged, humored, or—well, you probably would have preferred to be spared the awkward image, but there was a very real chance I would have fluttered back at him in another moment and engaged in an eyelash-fluttering competition if he hadn't spoken again.

"By the way, my hands are still cold," he said piteously and held them out.

"Ohhh!" My eyes shooting daggers, I charged at him with no clear idea of what I would do. Maybe head-butt him. *Any*thing to punish him for his unforgivably absurd behavior. He caught me in a headlock, holding fast to me while I pushed against him, the two of us staggering around in circles and laughing.

"I should be stuffing snow down your parka right now," he gasped, reminding me of what might have happened if I hadn't run in here when he came at me during the snowball fight.

I pushed harder, my giggles smothered in his grasp. He plopped into a chair, and I suddenly found myself sitting on his lap, his arms around me. Before I could take him to task for my position, he pressed his cheek against mine, and I . . . forgot everything.

"All right, I guess I can let you be the eyelash-flutterer," he said breathlessly, winding the ends of my hair around one hand. Looking at the strand, he continued, "as well as the hair-flutterer. Because I think I maybe . . . possibly . . . probably like to run my fingers through your hair more than mine." I felt goosebumps as his fingers combed through my hair. He leaned closer, his cheek pressing once more against mine, and whispered, "But don't tell the guys."

My body relaxed, and I closed my eyes and snuggled further into Croft. His breath hitched, revealing his surprise, but his tender movements continued, and my head tingled pleasantly while currents spread through the rest of me. This was what I wanted. This was who I wanted.

But I couldn't have him.

I tensed and pulled my head back, making his hand drop.

"Don't get too attached, Croft. You'll soon be going the other way," I said in a flat tone and slipped into the chair next to him to put distance between us.

"Which way?" he asked, looking stunned.

I tossed my head, feeling bitterness and hurt course through me. "Away from me and into the arms of the girl you'll marry."

He gave me a blank stare, which only got me more worked up. I pierced him with a glare and declared, "You should be thankful I'm letting you date me. It guarantees you'll find the love of your life and get married within the next year."

"We're talking marriage?" He looked like I had struck him.

"Not to me," I exclaimed. "Aren't you listening?"

"Maybe if you start from the beginning," he suggested gently.

"The beginning?" My voice went high-pitched and then broke. "That would be Keaton, Jesse, Killian, Frank, and Brody."

He recognized the last one. "The nice guys you used to date?"

"Yes, the nice guys who all miraculously found their one and only at the best point in our relationship, when I was certain I couldn't be happy with anyone else and they seemed to feel the same way." My voice was breaking all over the place now. "When I think for sure we'll get married, the other girl turns up, and," I snapped my fingers, "two or three months later, they're engaged. And you're next."

"I'm next," he repeated in a dazed murmur before his eyes sharpened with understanding. "You mean, you think I'll leave you for someone else?"

"That's exactly what I think. In fact, I was planning on it."

His mouth gaped open. "You've been trying to set me up with other girls. Gina. And our fictional girl at the rink? The one with the nose?" He didn't mention the cat-waitress, but my attempt at that point had been so poor he probably had no idea I wasn't just trying to make conversation with her.

"I figured I should speed it up." I shrugged, though my shoulders felt heavy.

"Did you try to set the other guys up, too?" he asked in disbelief.

"No, I tried to get married to them." My tone was flat. "But I know a pattern when I see it, and I don't want to wait around and get as attached to you as I was to them before you find her."

He stared. "Just how far . . ." He cleared his throat. "Did you get engaged to any of these guys?"

I blew at a wisp of hair. "Technically, no."

"Technically?"

"I happen to know Killian was in the jewelry store buying an engagement ring for me when he met Sage. They talked. She 'lit up his soul,'" I said expressively. "He still bought the ring and took it home, but he never ended up offering it to me. A couple of weeks later, they were dating."

"Ouch." Croft's eyes shone with compassion. "That sounds painful."

I let out a heavy breath. "Parting from the others was just as painful, even though none of them had gone ring-shopping. I have a problem, Croft, and I've finally figured out what it is." I stood and began to pace. I'd been thinking about this for a while. "My problem is that I fall in love too easily. I really thought it was right when I was with Keaton. And then I really thought it would happen with Jesse. And then I really, truly thought there was never a better match made in heaven than me and Killian. And each time they leave, I don't know how I'll get through it." I turned and pointed at him. "I don't want to fall for you and go through this all over again. I won't. I have to . . . to . . ."

"Suppress your feelings and ignore any sparks of attraction?" he prompted.

"Yes. Exactly."

"You mean to stop dating altogether so you don't get hurt?"

"More or less. Not forever, of course," I added unconvincingly.

When he didn't say anything, I sank back into my chair.

It was quiet for a minute as we both sat thinking. That is, *he* was thinking, and I was watching him, waiting for his reaction while my wounded passion seeped away, leaving me drained.

"You've had it worse than a lot of us," he said at last. "I don't want to downplay that. But even though it hurt, don't you see that this is what dating is?" He scooted closer and took my hand, looking earnest. "You date someone, and it doesn't work out. You date someone else, and it doesn't work out. It keeps happening until it does work out with someone." He put his other hand on top of mine. "You can't just stop dating, or try not to develop feelings for someone, or try to send them on their way with another girl just because it hasn't worked out yet. At some point, it's bound to work out. What if that's this time?"

I had a fleeting vision of my mom telling me these same exact things, but that didn't deter me from arguing.

"Yeah, but then again, what if it's not?" I swallowed. "What if after the first two guys broke my heart, when the third guy came along, I told myself maybe this was the time it would work out, maybe this was the guy I had been waiting for?" Croft rubbed circles on my hand, but the motion lost its calming effect as I continued to gather steam. "And what if, after he broke my heart and the next guy and I started dating, I told myself that surely I would be spared additional heartbreak, and as we got more and more serious, I could tell I finally had something? And what if, after *that* ended and Brody started coming around, I softened my resolve not to risk so much again and instead let myself fall in love while thinking that for sure, this time it was right and I wouldn't get hurt?" I pulled my hand from both of his. "And what if I now get too attached to you, and I tell myself that's okay because this could be it, and I need to give us a chance?" I waved my hands. "And what if, after you leave, I tell myself that again three more times, or five more times, or *fifty* more times?"

"I have my work cut out for me, don't I?" he asked softly.

I threw my hands in the air. Fortunately, nothing was within reach for me to knock down. "Or you could stop dating me altogether"—that is, if he wasn't too tempted by the fact that fate would hand him the love of his life on a silver platter if he kept dating me—"and you won't have to do any work at all when it comes to me."

He gave me a sad look. "It's too late for that. Now, I know you had to drag me kicking and screaming to our first few dates, but you've really grown on me since then."

I looked toward the ceiling in exasperation, but I couldn't help it. My lips curved upward, and a noise of amusement escaped me. "Croft. I don't get it. Why do you even want to date me?"

He looked incredulous. "Surrey, have you seen yourself? Not your looks," he said when my gaze turned mutinous, "but the way you act, the things you do. You brighten the lives of those around you."

I frowned. "Like who?"

"Like Hanna's uncle. Like your neighbors. Like those kids out there."

"Hm. Maybe so, but you didn't know about any of them when you first started pestering me to go out with you. Except maybe Willie."

"You brightened *my* life when I was pestering you." Croft grinned. "Your straightforwardness was so refreshing. There was no pretense with you, and it made me happy in a way I hadn't been in a long time. I realize now you've been thinking I would leave, and I know you're free to date others, like Jay. I actually thought you were going out with him today." He rubbed the back of his neck. "But Surrey . . . You do like me, don't you?"

I took a deep breath. "I . . . Hang on." I cocked my head. "Why did you even come by today when you thought I'd be gone?"

"Um." His gaze turned sheepish. "I brought something for you. I figured I'd leave it on your doorstep."

"What? What did you bring?"

I wouldn't let it be until he agreed to show me. He put on his sweater and, at my insistence, one of my scarves and winter hats. Then I followed him out to his car, noting the deserted snow forts on the way and the quiet street.

Croft opened the passenger door and turned around, presenting me with a luscious, red rose.

I took it. It was beautiful, but I eyed him in disbelief. "You were going to leave this on my doorstep . . . for Jay to find?"

"Uh, no. For *you* to find."

I raised my eyebrows, one higher than the other. "And Jay."

Our staring contest lasted several seconds before he grimaced. "It doesn't hurt for him to realize there's already something between us. He should have clued in to that at the rink."

I didn't know whether to be touched by the rose or amused at Croft's audacity or possibly annoyed with him. I wasn't sure what to do with his jealousy, either, not when I had tried for so long to deny my feelings for him.

Croft swallowed. "Surrey. You can obviously go out with Jay if you want to. You can even keep trying to set me up with other girls, although you know I'm on to you now. But . . . I'd really like it if you would give us a chance.

My heart hurt. So would I.

Croft lowered his voice. "Will you?"

My eyes filled with tears. It was impossible to say no when I had already fallen for him. "Just," I sniffled, "if you stop feeling drawn to me, or you start liking someone else, please—let me know right away."

Croft pulled me into a hug.

I wasn't crying. Well, I was, only I stopped as soon as I heard a door open.

"Oh," said Willie's voice.

"Are they coming?" Bella's voice sounded behind him before the door closed.

Croft and I smiled in tandem. He tightened his arms around me, but the door to Willie's house reopened.

Bella didn't have Willie's tact. "Hey! There's hot cocoa," she yelled at us.

Croft let go, his smile broadening. "Think we'd better join them?"

"Yeah." I hurried ahead of him a few steps, then remembered I wasn't supposed to plan for him to leave. When Croft caught up and took my hand, I let him. It was time to call it what it was. We were dating.

Chapter Twenty-Five

NOW, I wasn't about to be lovey-dovey or sentimental about us. Sure, I may have brought Croft's rose to school the next day, hiding it in an outer pocket of my backpack and sneaking a peek at it now and then, but I hoped our relationship wouldn't change much. I wanted us to keep having fun together.

Croft obliged. When he invited me to walk with him after lab hour, I followed him outside into the frigid air, feeling light at heart. A burden had been lifted from my shoulders with my confession yesterday and perhaps with my resolve to give us a try. I was ready to enjoy our time together.

"Longest walk ever," Croft huffed, stopping a few hundred feet from the Talmage Building.

I raised my eyebrows. "But worth it for the view," I said with sarcasm, gesturing at the slushy parking lot and waiting for an explanation.

"Right. There's someone I want you to meet. Now, he has a camera hidden in his collar, but that's just for someone else to see what's going on. Nothing's being filmed. Hey, there," he called out.

I looked over to see Jane with a brown Labrador retriever on a leash. At Jane's nod, Croft slapped his knees and called, "Come here, Pete, come here."

Jane let go, and the dog escaped, leash flying behind him as he ran to us.

His tongue lolled out when he arrived, and an excited voice came from the dog as he ignored Croft and greeted me.

"Hello, my name is Pete. What's yours? Will you be my friend?" He jumped playfully from side to side, the words coming fast. The voice was Poe's, I was pretty sure, and the sound came from Pete's collar. "I'm a good dog, a really, really good dog. I deserve a treat. Don't you think so? Do you have one for me?"

I looked in surprise at Croft, and the Labrador's attention shifted.

"Hi, Croft, you're looking good. Well, actually, you look kind of goofy, but it's nice to see you."

My unabashed laughter drowned out the stream of words.

"What do you think?" Croft grinned. "Pete will be one of our stars in the last prank of the semester. Or film, if you will. There'll be nothing mean about this one. Want to watch it take place?"

I bent to pet the dog, who wriggled with joy. "I guess I can't miss out on Pete's performance."

Croft gave Jane a thumbs up. "Thanks for coming," he told her as she came over to take the dog.

"By the way, I seem to remember you being fond of cats. Is that right?" Croft asked me while the eager Pete walked away with Jane.

"Oh, um, I was just trying to make conversation." I blushed at the reminder of my failed attempt to make him chat with the cat-waitress.

"Are you into pets, though? What kind of animal would you have if you could pick any?"

"Why do you want to know?"

"Because I want to know more about you," he said, his dark-blue eyes capturing my gaze.

I almost shivered. His undivided attention was different from Brody's and Hanna's, and it was sure to be broken up by a joke soon, but it wasn't half bad. "You're strangely serious all of a sudden," I told him and waited for the joke.

When he kept waiting, I decided I might as well tell him. "Actually, I want a rabbit someday. Like Beatrix Potter."

"Who?"

"You do know her, don't you?" I narrowed my eyes. "She was a painter. She wrote the Peter Rabbit stories." Recognition dawned in his eyes. I was relieved to see that he hadn't grown up under a rock.

I turned back toward campus. "I used to watch the Peter Rabbit movies, and they started by showing Miss Potter going to her cottage to paint and write. She had a rabbit on her table." Ah, the nostalgia those memories gave me. "I like to imagine that someday I'll do the same thing, paint while my rabbit crawls around on the desk, sitting on the brushes I'm not using and exploring everything on the table."

"Serious?" Croft's eyes were dancing as we walked along the lawn toward the library.

"Yep." It was silly, but it was a favorite fancy of mine and wouldn't take much work or money to make it happen, so why not?

Croft's smile was wide. "Do you have a List of Ten Dreams?"

"I can't limit my dreams like that."

"Good point. What are all your other dreams?"

"What?" I goggled at him. "I can't just tell you that. *All* my dreams?"

"Why not? Oh, I know." His face fell. "Because you're keeping things from me. Like when you set me up with every Tomasine, Dickette, and Harriet without telling me what you were up to." I giggled at the names. "What else are you hiding? Do you have a second roommate I don't know about?"

I folded my arms. "I'm not keeping anything else from you. My confession yesterday covered everything."

"You're sure? No guy in your attic?"

"Believe it or not, Croft, I'm all out of secrets."

"Surr," Killian's voice greeted me, and I jerked in surprise to see him standing before us, a black-haired beauty at his side.

"Hi, uh, Killian."

"Who's this?" my ex asked.

"Croft," I answered.

"Cool. Are you two, um . . . ?"

"Dating? Of course," Croft filled in, slipping his arm around my waist and giving me an amorous look. I rolled my eyes at his theatrics but enjoyed being held.

Killian frowned at him. "Surrey deserves the best."

"I happen to be the best," Croft said modestly.

I snorted, and Killian looked confused.

"Croft has his good sides," I said, not feeling the need to explain Croft's arrogant humor.

"What? *All* my sides are good. Don't you think all my sides are good?" Croft turned this way and that, which didn't help me see his other sides as his arm around me made me turn with him.

I slapped him lightly, Sage laughed, and Killian's expression lost its sternness. "In that case, I wish you the best," he said.

"Thanks, and the same to you," I responded.

He cocked his head. "You haven't changed your rule, have you?"

I shook my head and shrugged, offering a smile.

He smiled back and addressed Croft. "Stay strong. Good luck on the no-kissing rule. She's worth it."

He and Sage went on their way, and I stood as though struck.

Oops. I guess there was one more secret I had kept from Croft.

"What was that?" Croft asked, staring at me in disbelief. "What rule?"

"Umm." Was it possible he hadn't caught all of Killian's words?

"A no-kissing rule?" he pressed, and that particular hope fled.

"Well, uh. I won't kiss until I get engaged," I said and gave him an innocent look.

He gaped at me. "And you never told me? Even when I told you my rule, which happens to be exactly identical?"

I felt myself redden. "There was no point. We were following my rule without my having to bring it up."

"*Identical*, Surrey," he repeated as though I hadn't heard it the first time.

My embarrassment turned to annoyance. "So what's the big deal? It was a long time ago. Besides, what would you have done if I'd told you?" I affected a deep tone and flung out my hands. "'We're twinners, Cinnamon. We're the exact same person.'" I dropped the mocking baritone and spoke primly. "This probably isn't a good thing. In every relationship, one person should be more prone to physical displays of affection than the other." I believed no such thing, but I had to come up with something just to be contradictory.

Croft stared at me, still peeved. Then his expression softened.

"One of us *is* more prone to it than the other," he said in a low voice and lifted his hand to my face. My breath cut out as he stroked the length of my cheek, stopping just shy of my lips before repeating the caress. My whole body softened at his touch, and my heart beat in rhythm to his movements. He leaned in close, his clean-shaven cheek touching mine, and ran a hand through my hair and down my back, making wonderful sensations run through me from wherever he touched. "I just try to help you get it," he continued in a thrumming voice, "because I know that in spite of your dominant need for the physical, you're too self-controlled to ask for it."

I jumped away, my face flaming. "You're—"

He scooped me off the ground, one arm under my knees, and I squealed.

"What are you doing? Put me down."

"What?" He put me down and gave me a nonplussed look. "I thought it was a perfect romantic moment to scoop you up. Weren't you about to say, 'You're my prince'?"

"I was going to say 'despicable,'" I informed him, only to be scooped up a second time with another shriek escaping me.

Holding me against his chest, he looked into my eyes and asked fondly, "What else?"

"'Despicable' isn't a compliment," I said, glowering in his arms.

Again, he looked puzzled. "Really? From the look of love in your eyes when you said it, I thought for sure it was."

"Ohhh." I clenched my fists at him but couldn't hold back laughter.

He let me down, and I stepped away.

"I'm going home," I declared and stomped south toward the route I usually took at the end of the day.

"Don't you have another class?" he called out.

I changed direction. "I'm going to class," I said and stomped past him, fighting my own laughter. I definitely needed to sit down somewhere and take ten minutes to recover my dignity.

* * *

Saturday's date with Jay was perfectly unexceptional. We bowled. We chatted. We learned more about each other than Croft and I had shared on our first three dates combined. He took me home and walked me to the door.

I'm not sure how I survived it.

It wasn't that Jay wasn't nice, or gentlemanly, or friendly. Had it been a few months ago, I would have enjoyed spending time with him.

He just wasn't Croft.

Croft's excessive joking and constant ludicrous commentary had spoiled me. In comparison, my time with Jay seemed tame, and even if I hadn't just committed to Croft, I would have dreaded the idea of going through more dates with Jay, waiting to see if I developed feelings for him given time. When he asked about a second date, I told him thank you but no.

As I entered my house, I felt nothing but relief.

Gina met me in the living room, her brown eyes wide and pleading. "Do you think I did the right thing?"

"I'm sorry, what?"

"I ended things with Tim." She wrung her hands. "Maybe that was wrong of me. I get so few dates. Maybe I should have kept saying yes because he was interested. I was excited on our first few dates, but then I wasn't anymore," she continued, as if hoping she could give me enough details for me to make the perfect judgment.

I straightened, trying to look confident. If she thought I could help, I would try.

"He's a good guy. He's nice. He's active in the Church," she listed off. "I just don't enjoy spending time with him anymore. Is that bad of me?"

I thought about Jay. "No, it's not."

She frowned. "It seems wrong to turn down a perfectly good guy who likes me, though. What if no one else comes along? Maybe he's the only one who would ever be interested."

I winced. "No, Gina. If you're not interested, it doesn't matter how interested he is. It will hurt him a little, but it would hurt him more down the road if you kept going and he learned later that you didn't feel anything for him."

"Maybe I'd come to feel something eventually," she said, though there was doubt in her voice.

"I think we should both trust our instincts." I braced a hand against the back of a chair. "If you don't feel anything, you have the right to end it. If it's meant to be, God will bring you back together somehow as long as you're trying to do the right things, right? God wants the best for us. He won't let some dumb mistake keep us from ending up with someone we were meant for."

Gina took that in. "But he lets good people get married and divorced."

I twisted my mouth as I thought about it. "Okay, that's true. But we can't worry that we'll miss our one chance at love because we made a left turn on the way to the grocery store instead of a right turn. Or because we didn't realize right away that someone was a good fit for us. Heavenly Father's still there to help things turn out like they should."

The panic in Gina's eyes faded, and her shoulders relaxed. "You're right. Maybe if Tim *is* right for me, I'll start to miss him over the next while. I don't think I can date him again before I begin to feel something more."

"Good. There's someone out there who's right for you, and even if you don't develop feelings for him right away, I don't think it'll take you too long to feel something." Hopefully that was true. "If you dread spending time with him even though he seems great, he can't be your guy."

"So I did the right thing."

"You did."

She nodded thoughtfully and met my gaze. "Do you dread spending time with Croft?"

I blinked. My roommate was perceptive. While I hadn't begun to praise Croft to her, my complaints about him must have dwindled recently.

I don't think she was surprised when I answered, "I dread *not* getting to spend time with him."

Chapter Twenty-Six

"Places. Ready. Set."

Croft and five other crew members, among them the elusive Josh whom I hadn't seen since my demise at the beginning of the semester, sat well apart from each other in makeshift cubicles. They were equipped with microphone headsets and screens that gave them access to several different camera views at once.

I didn't know how they had arranged to rent the mall space for the day, much less how they got permission to bring animals inside, but apparently the credit went to Riley, who was fondly known as their legal manager.

As a guest of honor, I had been given equipment of my own so I could switch from one scene to another and hear what was happening.

The air hummed with excitement and intense concentration. When I caught Croft's eye, he mouthed something at me and gave me a thumbs-up. I would have to tell him one of these days that I couldn't read lips.

"Action."

On screen, the center of the mall showed the usual number of people strolling, sitting on benches, or standing around talking. Children played in the plastic treehouse. From a corridor, Riley and a crew-member I hadn't yet met released Pete the Labrador and two collies and sent them toward the benches. The collies started racing up and down the center, but the cat that Riley let out of its carrier stood stretching, not allowing itself to be shooed anywhere.

As Pete approached a couple eating on a bench, Poe's voice spoke up on a small radio hidden on the dog's collar. "Mamma mia, is that pizza?"

I quickly switched my device to the option named "Poe" in order to see the same camera angles he saw. The woman in front of Pete jerked and let out a peal of laughter. The man responded with an uncertain grin.

"You know, the best pizza around is the one with all the meats," 'Pete' said while the actual dog licked his mouth and whined, "bacon and sausage and pepperoni and just all the feels, man! Is that the kind of pizza you got? If you did, oh boy, I'm gonna have to have a taste. Which kind did you get?"

"Uh, this is garlic chicken," the man answered, choked humor in his voice.

The brown Labrador sat down and whined again. "Garlic chicken?" Poe's voice repeated, thick with disappointment. "That's good, but not good enough. Which one of you ordered?" he asked in accusation as the dog swung his head to the woman, who laughed anew.

Giggling quietly—I was trying not to distract the team—I switched to another video feed.

The guy who had helped Riley release the animals was walking around with a pug on a leash, letting it greet various people. The pug-walker and the one giving voice to the pug had an interesting job as they put on a performance together, ad-libbing with each other.

"I'm sorry, sometimes he wants to know the strangest things," the guy with the leash was saying while the short-legged dog rasped up a storm with its loud breathing and the man in front of them fought hysterical laughter.

"Mommy, can I pet him? Can I pet him?" A little boy dragged his mom over to meet the pug and threw himself down in front of the dog.

"Well, hello, aren't you just the cutest thing?" the pug asked, its bulging eyes staring into the boy's eyes, which widened and sparkled. "You can pet me anytime, mister. In fact, oops, where did you go?"

The dog had leaned its side against the boy and made him tumble over. The boy didn't mind. Giggling, he sat up to pet it. "Why does it talk, Mommy?" he asked, looking up at her.

She looked to the dog-walker, who shrugged and said, "Sometimes he just can't help . . ."

The cat suddenly made its appearance, and I heard the voice of Elly, whom I had met half an hour ago.

"Make way, make way for the queen," she said haughtily while the tabby stepped across the floor. "You there," she said as it leaped onto a bench where an older man was seated, his attention up until now on the dogs' performances. "Lend me your lap." The cat stepped onto him and purred.

He shook with laughter. "What's up, kitty?" he chuckled, petting her. "Anything else I can help you with?"

"Ooh, yes, how about a bath with Epsom salts? It would be relaxing, and you know, nothing's too good for me."

"Of course not, Miss Kitty," he rumbled, looking around in search of the person who gave voice to the feline. The cat decided to get up and spring to the floor.

"Now, what are those hooligans up to?" she asked, strutting along in the direction of the running collies, who called out to each other in Croft's and Josh's voices.

A teenage girl stepped in front of her and held out a hand, but the cat circumvented her. "Hey, kitty, better watch out for those dogs," the girl warned.

"I'll be just fine. I know them, and what's more, they know me," the wandering cat said without so much as a backward glance. "They won't put a paw out of line, or I'll make them regret it. Well, hello, Jules." That last sentence came out in an adoring voice as Croft's collie stopped to say hi.

"Whiskers," he exclaimed happily and, I might add, irreverently. "Have you come to play?"

"I have come to watch my *commoners* play," the cat said in lofty tones. "Now go back to Chomper or Jumper or whatever his name is. I have—"

"Whee-ee," Croft cried as the dog skidded on the floor, his attention already lost. I cracked up and barricaded my mouth with both hands.

The people in the mall were having a marvelous time conversing with the animals. By the time Riley and the pug-walker stepped into the middle with a large sign showing the name of their website, the crowd that had gathered burst into applause.

I sat back in my seat, spent. The whole thing had lasted less than ten minutes, but it had been hilarious, and the people around me had had to think fast as they improvised nearly everything.

Croft pulled off his headset and stood, immediately making his way to me.

"They clapped," he said, looking pleased and a little surprised. "I guess you know that doesn't usually happen. What did you think?"

I smiled. "That was very impressive, what all of you did. And you. I knew you could do something funny that wouldn't embarrass or scare anyone. You have the best sense of humor."

He started to smile, but then he stilled, his look turning serious. "Can we go for a walk?"

I looked around at the temporary studio. "Now?"

"Yes. Hey, Josh, do you guys mind cleaning things up without me?"

Josh looked up. "Where are you going?"

"Outside." Croft indicated me with a nod.

"Oh, okay."

"Thanks. By the way, you did great today. All of you." Croft gave them a wave, slid his hand down my arm until he reached my hand, and led me to the door.

Once outside, though, he dropped my hand. We left behind the parking lot and headed across a bare field behind the building, where there was little besides a narrow winding road for whatever cars wanted a roundabout way to get to the mall, I guess.

Croft was quiet. He didn't hold my arm like he usually did when we walked together.

"What is it?" I asked, premonition making me speak up. If it was bad news, I didn't want him to draw it out.

"I'm trying to think of how to start. It won't be fun telling you, but you deserve to know."

I stopped. "What's her name?"

He stopped, too. "What?"

I forced myself to look into his eyes. "You've met someone, haven't you? Just tell me. I'll leave."

"*What?* No! No, I haven't met someone. That isn't it at all. Sorry, I didn't mean to make you think that." His flabbergasted look was replaced with concern as he picked up my hand and gave it a squeeze. "I'm about to tell you why I was so mean to you when I first met you. You just gave me my third compliment back there. Remember?"

I blinked. "I did? Oh, you mean about your sense of humor? Right, okay, tell me," I stuttered, embarrassed to have shown him my insecurity like this but also relieved this wasn't goodbye.

"Sorry," he apologized again, rubbing my hand and looking down. I figured he was putting off his story. I tried not to get impatient since this was obviously difficult for him.

Finally, he raised his head and looked at me. "This is what happened. My older brother got married five years ago. They had been dating for two years. Janessa," he sounded pained as he said the name, "adored Jeremy, and they seemed perfect for each other. They got along great. He had always wanted a big family, and she badly wanted to have little children running around within her first few years of marriage." He looked off into the distance. "Their goals and everything between them seemed aligned."

I had an uncomfortable inkling I was about to hear the *buts* in their relationship.

"Time passed, and they didn't have kids. We knew how disappointed they both were, so we tried not to ask questions, but sometimes she brought it up on her own and cried because they couldn't make it happen."

He put his hands in his pockets and looked down at the dirt. "He discovered a couple of years into their marriage that she was using birth control. It turns out she'd never wanted kids at all, but she pretended because she wanted to marry him."

I stared at him, shocked.

"He didn't tell us. They continued on with their lives. When they visited, she would bring up how hard it was that she couldn't get pregnant, and he kept quiet about it while she tore up his heartstrings."

I could hear the bitterness in Croft's voice.

"Why would she marry him when she knew he wanted a family?" I asked. That made no sense. Maybe if she loved him in every other way—but it didn't make sense for her to bring up the painful subject like that if she cared about his feelings.

"She wants attention." Croft's bitterness turned to contempt. "Prestige. Money. My brother was going places with his career. Janessa loves to go to social functions with high society. Until you, I'd never met anyone as physically beautiful as her . . ." I started at the comparison, but he continued, "Not that she's even *close* to you, but she does turn heads, and she uses it. She *wants* to be eye-candy on someone's arm. And when people start giving her attention . . ."

Croft cleared his throat, and I thought he looked a little sick. "She laps it up. Her lies about how much she loves children isn't the only problem. She's . . . cheated on him." His voice cracked, and I felt terrible, wishing I didn't have to hear this. Unless it helped him to talk about it. "Not just once, and not just with one man. Once Jeremy found out . . . She wasn't even regretful or anything. It's happened again since he found out last year, and it, it's awful."

I wanted to reach out to him, but I wasn't sure my touch would do any good at this point.

He took a deep breath. "They're going through divorce now. It's been messy, but it's almost finalized. All of this has been killing him for a long time, much longer than any of us knew. He told us everything last April. It was a shock to us all. My parents are heartbroken, and my sister's really shaken. I tried . . . to still think of Jeremy's wife as a person, as someone who deserved some respect. They'd still come to our place, both of them together, and I tried not to think the very worst of her, not to scorn her and hurt my brother further. But about a month after we found out she cheated on him . . ."

He swallowed, and so did I. We were long past the unhappy ending I had feared, and it seemed there was still more.

"I was alone in the living room while the others were in the kitchen, and she walked in. She draped herself over the armrest next to me and started flirting. Running her fingers down my arm, telling me—never mind." His face was dark red now. "She was flirting, with me, the younger brother, who knew how she was going about destroying Jeremy."

His chest heaved. "I lost every ounce of respect I had ever had for her. I've never felt so disgusted or humiliated or gross." Angry tears came to his eyes. "From that moment on, I treated her with all the derision I could muster. I never let an opportunity go by to let her see how little I thought of her. I couldn't bear to be near her."

He wiped his eyes and took another deep breath. "I let it get the better of me. I shouldn't have treated her like that, as much as I hated and . . . was afraid of her. Honestly, I was terrified of being caught alone with her and having her come on to me again. But I shouldn't have . . . I became so bitter that I started seeing her in other girls. Anyone who in any way reminded me of her deserved my contempt, including you. I've been less than nice to, um, probably a lot of the blondes I've come across, and the more beautiful I thought them, the more I wanted to punish them."

He hung his head. "That's my stupid story of something I've never once found any humor in," he said in self-castigation. "It's why I acted so dumb whenever I saw you that first week. I'm really sorry. You didn't deserve any of it, and neither did anyone else I treated poorly." He looked up, forcing himself to make eye contact even though it appeared to be a struggle.

I bit my lip, my emotions churned up by his tale. "When you look at me," I said hoarsely, "do I still remind you of her?"

"No." He looked me in the eyes, his voice firm. "No. I see you. Surrey, who makes me laugh, who makes me happy, who makes me a better person. I see Surrey, who sews and paints the most stunning things and finds beauty in the world and has a zest for life that shows in her Ten Things and everything else she chooses to do. I see someone I've tortured into laughter," a glint of amusement showed in his eyes before worry lines appeared, "and who I hope I haven't pushed away."

I don't know about you, but I was touched almost to tears at his words.

I wiped my eyes. "When did you start seeing me differently?"

He smiled and rubbed his shin. "When Willie clipped me with his skateboard. I think that was God's way of hitting me upside the head. I realized you were different from my sister-in-law in at least one way: you liked kids. I had to get to know you then, to find out if you were different from her in other ways. Because if you weren't like her, then I owed you a big, fat apology; but if you were, I didn't want to be nice to you."

I stared at him. "So you attended lab to find out what kind of person I was?"

"Well, that was the plan. Only, it was clear almost right away that you were nothing like her. The whole feeling around you was so different and pure and straightforward—and funny. I should have apologized then, but it was like all the blows I got on the day I met Willie had released something inside me. After months of feeling nothing but darkness, I was finally happy, and I couldn't stop laughing at life long enough to sound sincere.

"Then we started going on dates." He smiled. "And it was so much fun. You were so guileless and had such a great wit, and I loved spending time with you.

"Then at the reception . . ." He gave me a tender look. "When you walked up to Hanna's uncle, and you made him and the little kid laugh, I just—melted. You were facing something you dreaded, but you focused on making others feel good. It was amazing."

A warm feeling spread through me. Croft's admiration made me want to do more things like that. It made me feel good about what I *had* done.

Croft took my hands again and swallowed. "Surrey. Will you forgive me?"

I took a deep breath, laced our fingers together, and looked him in the eyes. "I already have."

Chapter Twenty-Seven

He paced, his steps eating up the carpet, his lungs burning, his hands clenched.

The pictures weren't enough. The trinkets from her room weren't enough. He threw his hands in the air and growled. Nothing was enough anymore, nothing gave him what he craved, nothing could fulfill him except . . . her.

His steps slowed. With a pang, he remembered the scene from last week. She had been in the man's arms, and he had stroked her hair.

He shook his head. This man didn't deserve her. He would leave her, just like the others had done. She needed someone who wouldn't leave. Someone who had proved his commitment. Someone who worshipped her.

She needed *him*, didn't she? He touched the family portrait on her bedstand, his thumb moving across the person who stood out a mile from the others in the photograph.

She needed him to do more than adore her from afar. She needed him to be with her and to stay, to save her from heartbreak and from all those who were unworthy of her. He had waited for too long, too in awe to dare approach her, but it had cost her dearly. He must not keep her waiting any longer.

He paused and gripped the laundry basket. She needed rescuing from this humdrum life and the lowlifes who thought to date her. His fingers clenched around a pillowcase, and his resolve firmed. She belonged with him. He buried his face in the fabric and took in the smell, a smell that would be his going forward, a smell that would forever belong to him and his home.

He raised his head. Home.

He must make preparations.

Chapter Twenty-Eight

I still had Croft. I'd worried for weeks that I would be shattered come Christmas-time, that he would have found his dream girl and left me behind like a footprint in the snow. But I still had him, and that knowledge made my Christmas amazing.

Gina and I bought plane tickets together, and our families picked us up at the airport. It was a regular party as we all hugged and greeted each other.

Since Christmas break was longer than Thanksgiving, my siblings and I were allowed to spend some time in our rooms. Even so, my family got to hear my end of several phone calls with Croft. Our conversations were often long and sometimes consisted of more laughter than words.

"I haven't seen you this happy in a long time," my mom told me more than once, and I realized she was right.

Maybe in the future I would wish I'd lost him sooner, but I refused to let myself think that way now. On some mental level, I knew he and Mom were right. In fact, Croft's words from that day playing with the snow forts had seeped into my mind and penetrated my theories. Dating *did* mean having relationships not work out right up until one *did* work out. I hoped this was the time it would work. If it wasn't—well, hopefully it was.

On my return to Provo, I put a new list up on the fridge.

LIST OF TEN THINGS

1. Paint a fantasy creature from my imagination
2. Learn to fix vacuum (ask Willie)
3. Enact cardinal-whistle scene in the woods
4. Attend 3 sessions in a row in the temple
5. Drink water from a well
6. Hold a reptile
7. Call Fairlee in the middle of the night
8. Camp in a tent indoors
9. Shovel snow for Mrs. Blaine
10. Plant something with Willie and at least one Whitmer child

Number nine would be hard, as Mrs. Blaine and her husband were always on top of things, but even if there were only a few flakes for me to shovel from her sidewalk, I was determined to do it.

While Gina was busy in the kitchen, I ran a quick, secret errand to her room. Then, whistling, I pulled clean sheets from the dryer and went to make my bed.

A minute later, I popped into the living room.

"Have you seen my pillowcase? I thought it was in my laund—" I stopped, not seeing Gina. I checked the kitchen for my roommate, checked the laundry room for my pillowcase, and then went to Gina's room. There she was, staring at the painting I had hung up. I leaned against the doorway, watching her observe her portrait.

Gina turned around. "Did you . . . ?" she began in wonder.

I came over to stand beside her. "Let me tell you, that portrait was hard. But you're a worthy subject. Beautiful and interesting."

Her eyes glistened. "You really think so?" She looked at the portrait again. "It *is* beautiful. Thank you."

"I'm glad you like it," I said earnestly. "I love being roommates with you. We get to navigate the terrible and crazy ways of boys and schoolwork together. I appreciate you always being a support and a listening ear. So, thanks."

I don't know who was more surprised, me or Gina, when she threw her arms around me for a hug. She stepped back and confessed, "I don't know who else would put up with me and my busy schedule, but I really appreciate everything you do for me."

"Put up with? Your schedule may be crazy, but *you* are great."

As I left her room, I felt good. I think we both knew we got along well, but it was good to say it out loud.

My post-Christmas reunion with Croft was almost as touching.

He had asked about my first class so he could come see me. When I walked in, a pair of arms dropped down in front of me. "Surr—"

"Ahh," I shrieked. Then, recognizing a startled Croft, I leapt into his arms.

"It *is* you." His voice was muffled against my hair. "I missed you."

I pulled back. "What do you mean, it's me?"

"I almost hugged ten other people before you." He grinned. "I may have accidentally renamed them, too. You're now doomed to a class full of Cinnamons and Surreys."

He hugged me again, and all I could think was that I was glad I hadn't lost him to some other girl yet. That is, I was glad I hadn't lost him. There might be no *yet* about it.

Unfortunately, I soon found that this semester was out to kill me. I had, sappy though it was, scheduled my office hours between Croft's classes so he could come hang out, but due to my crushing homework, our dates were reduced to less than once a week.

Maybe that would help create an emotional distance for when—

No, I told myself. Our relationship would last.

We found ways to work around my workload. I hung out at his place to do homework, sometimes during his crew's planning sessions. Gina-days were combined with Croft-days as Gina and I practically moved into Croft's yellow-sofa, polka dot-armchair living room. I loved to see how spicy Gina got as she became more comfortable with Croft. He expertly brought out a sassy side of her, and it turned out she could hold her own.

"Do you think he feels ganged up on?" I asked after Croft left the room at a limp once, pretending grave injury, though his laughter contradicted the dramatics.

"He should," Gina grinned. "If he dares talk to us, he should be prepared for consequences. Your persona is blinding since you became a real artist. He should be begging for your autograph, not worrying about being unable to turn down his charm."

The fundraiser had taken place last week. I had been stunned to learn that each of my paintings sold for over ten thousand dollars. Croft, Gina, and Willie and his family had all joined me at McDonald's to celebrate with shakes.

"Real and real," I hedged. "The buyers planned to be generous when they attended the auction. They wanted to make a difference in raising money for the children."

"Real," Gina said firmly as Croft returned in the middle of what sounded like an animated conversation.

"Meet the parents," he prefaced and put his laptop in my lap.

I froze. A man and a woman smiled at me over Skype. The man had deep dimples like Croft, and the woman had his sky-colored eyes, touched with sadness yet vivid with energy.

"Hello, Surrey. It's nice to meet you," Mrs. Taylor said warmly.

"Croft never stops talking about you," Mr. Taylor said. "I'm glad to finally meet you."

Heart beating fast and furious, I looked up at a grinning Croft who had given me zero warning about meeting his parents, then over at Gina, whose eyebrows were raised, and finally back down at the screen.

I relaxed into a smile. "It's good to meet you, too. Could you do me a favor?"

"What would that be?" his dad asked.

"Would you ground Croft?"

His mom was taken aback for only a moment. "Of course. For how long?"

"Oh, at least six months."

Gina giggled.

"Done."

"Wait a minute, shouldn't we know what he's getting grounded for?" Mr. Taylor protested.

"Trust me," his mom said, and I finished with her, "he deserves it."

Both parents and Gina burst out laughing.

I turned to Croft. "Looks like your Mom and I are twinners. I'm afraid you've been demoted to not-quite-the-same-person-as-Surrey."

"That is a terrible blow." He dropped onto the couch and put his arm around my shoulders. "Mom, Dad." He paused for dramatic effect. "She's everything you've ever dreamed. But I flatter myself that I'm a close second." He waved a hand royally.

"That's quite the introduction, Croft." I raised one eyebrow higher than the other. "Did we somehow get engaged without my knowing it?"

He sputtered, and though my heart had sped up at my mention of getting engaged, I felt triumphant at having unsettled him.

"I like her," Croft's dad said with emphasis.

His parents then asked me about my art until Croft generously promised them my autograph. All in all, it was a good first conversation with his parents.

* * *

I DIDN'T WANT to face the scariest item on my List of Ten Things.

"Come on," Croft urged the following Tuesday, standing as soon as the reptile and amphibian show ended. We were at the Bean Life Science Museum, named not after beans but after someone with the last name Bean. Usually I would have come to look at the stuffed wildlife, but today, I was here for something else.

"Surrey? You're still sitting."

"Yes, I am. How very interesting." My shaky voice belied the joke.

"If you don't ask, she'll leave, and you'll have to sit through another performance and fear it all over again."

"I'm tired," I whined but let Croft pull me to my feet. I *was* tired, but that didn't matter as we walked to the handler, who was already besieged by a small group of people, all of whom seemed more eager than me to meet the snake.

"Does anyone else want to hold Tom?" the handler eventually asked, indicating the four-foot red corn snake.

Croft nudged me.

"Me." My voice cracked.

Oh, no, what had I done? Oh, no, the woman was turning to me. Oh, no, why did I have to put something so terrifying on my List of . . .

My arm tensed like a tightrope as the handler moved Tom to my shoulder. The moment his head made contact, goosebumps sprang out on my skin, and I felt my eyes grow to twice their usual size.

Croft took hold of my forearm, steadying me. "Look at those scales. So . . . reptile-y."

I gritted my teeth as Tom moved down my arm, apparently uninterested in sticking to my shoulder.

"You're doing it. You're holding a snake. Aren't you excited?" Croft kept on. "Oh, he's changing directions. I wonder if he'll try to strangle you."

"She said they can't do that," I growled and let out a shiver of discomfort. I ought to have walked away from Croft to punish him for his less than comforting words, but his hold on me helped me in turn hold on to my sanity.

"I guess he'll just drool on you, then."

In spite of the slithering slitheriness now working its way to my other shoulder, I felt a small smile on my face. "Snakes don't drool."

"They don't? Ah, I think he's shedding. He'll leave you some nice scales."

"You're not helping, Croft."

"Look at that tongue. Oh, yeah, you can't see it. If you feel a tickle on the back of your neck, it's probably his tongue. Or his fangs. I'm glad they didn't tell you this guy was poisonous. You'd be really worried right now."

"You're so not helping," I repeated, but I was laughing.

In another moment, Croft put his hand on my arm, and the corn snake obligingly moved onto him.

I sighed in relief and stepped away. Croft looked at me with admiration. "You did good," he said, and I brightened at his praise.

Then he turned an equally admiring gaze on the snake and said, "You were brave, too, Tom."

I choked and put my face in my hands as I gave in to laughter.

* * *

WHEN I GOT HOME that evening, there was a thin layer of new snow all around. My weary mind protested, but what with it being the end of January, I couldn't wait for a day when I had more energy. We might not get any more snow days, and I had vowed I would shovel snow for our neighborhood guardian and her husband.

I wrapped up in my winter gear, ignoring a small ache in my head.

Forcing myself to pick up my snow shovel, I headed for Mrs. Blaine's house, where I felt a moment's victory at the sight of her white sidewalk.

Five minutes of thorough scraping took care of it and left me exhausted. It was a good thing there hadn't been much snow. I felt chilled as I crossed the street, but I had a nice heated house and a warm bed waiting for me, I was making headway with my List of Ten Things, and I was still dating Croft. Life was good.

Chapter Twenty-Nine

LIFE WAS AN AWFUL, awful thing. I felt terrible the next morning. Gravity, among other things, worked against me, pinning me to my bed with a heaviness I wasn't used to.

I have to go to class, I thought to myself, but my brain immediately informed me I would be much better off staying home, and I decided it was right. I turned over, the movement requiring a Herculean effort and resulting in a pounding headache.

"Surrey? Are you okay?"

I opened my heavy eyelids and looked up at two Ginas.

"Are you sick?" one of them asked.

"I'mm feeeelinng fiiine," I slurred.

Her cool hand touched my fevered forehead. I was okay with that. I was less okay with her subsequent pacing and talking on the phone, although once I started coughing, I forgot to care.

The next time I woke up, I heard Croft's and Gina's voices in the other room. My room being off-limits to Croft, I was glad to know he wouldn't see me sick—until I realized I needed to use the restroom.

Somehow I managed the feat. With help. At the sound of my movements in the hall, Gina and Croft came running and assisted me on my way. I wondered hazily whether I was supposed to be embarrassed. Lucidness returned enough for me to do my business, but it seemed to leave me as I left the restroom, because I don't remember how I ended up on the couch instead of in my bed. Never mind, though. The couch was comfortable.

"Is there anything I can do for you?" Gina asked anxiously.

"Yeeess."

"What?" Croft asked, leaning over.

I raised a hand toward the ceiling. "Tttell the earthhh to ssstop moving."

"Surrey, have you ever been sick like this before?"

"Good night," I told him and let my eyes slide shut.

Fortunately, things were a little better the following day. I was achy and weary, but Gina pronounced my fever gone, and I could walk through the house without assistance, although it did help to have walls to lean on. I insisted Gina go to classes, and she felt reassured enough to do so.

She returned that afternoon, and Croft arrived soon after, bringing a delicious, soupy smell into the house.

Gina met him at the door. "I texted and asked to get off work," she told him, wringing her hands, "but they haven't responded yet."

He nodded. "Go to work, Gina. I'll be here until you get home."

"Thank you. Call me if something happens," she said, looking back at me. I sat like a ragdoll on the couch, watching her with a morose expression because lifting the corners of your mouth takes effort, I'll have you know.

"Don't worry," Croft told her. "We've got this."

The front door closed behind Gina. Croft set down a steaming pot on the dining table and came over to me.

"Hungry?" he asked.

"I think so." The smell from the table was tempting.

"Good. Gina said you can walk, so let's give it a try." He took hold of my arm, and I stood. I leaned on him as we made our way to the table, where I plopped down.

"How'd I do?" I rasped.

"Beautifully. And not a moment too soon. You wouldn't want to miss out on your reward. My exceptional cooking skills have produced a luxurious dinner of gourmet ramen noodles."

I gave him a weak smile. "That sounds good."

"I don't think you understand. It's not only good, it's positively scrumptious. Few have had the privilege of sampling my masterpiece."

I watched as he removed the lid from his concoction and ladled it up.

The soup smelled amazing. It was a beef and tomato soup with heavy helpings of onions and bell peppers.

"That doesn't look like ramen."

"It's amazing what I can do with dried noodles and a seasoning packet."

I looked at him through a bout of dizziness. "Do you want to eat with me?"

He shook his head. "I shall watch you eat my epicurean meal." So saying, he sat down, rested his chin on his hands, and stared at me.

"I'm sure it will be vastly entertaining," I said in a thin voice and picked up my spoon. My hand shook. *How strange,* I thought in detachment. Still, I managed a sip, and then another. Croft's soup was rich in flavor and warmed my insides.

"This is good," I told him, though my voice came out more tired than pleased.

"I knew it would be."

Dropping the spoon, I coughed into my sleeve, trying to face away from Croft to protect him from my germs. When I regained my breath, I said, "I hope I don't get you sick."

He scooted back in his chair several paces, leaving five feet of empty space between him and the table. "I think we're good now."

I nodded and felt my face relax into something like a smile as I picked up the spoon anew. "This is really nice of you."

"You're smiling at me," he said, clutching his chest with his hand. "My Surrey's coming back to herself."

"I called the Bean Museum," I said, watching him absently.

"Yeah?"

"I asked if Tom was okay. I might have gotten him sick."

Croft choked. "You're worried about the snake?" He shook with laughter. "Surrey, you're hilarious."

"They said he was fine."

"And sweet." Croft shook his head.

"I suppose." I frowned. The snake could be sweet, I guessed, although I wasn't sure what Croft meant by that.

After a few bites, I put down my spoon. "I'd better lie down."

"Of course." He was on his feet in a flash, helping me over to the couch and adjusting the cool, soft pillow I had been using when he arrived.

I lay down and felt a blanket descend on me. "Thank you for being here."

"You shouldn't be alone while you're sick."

"Gina's at work," I slurred.

"I know."

"Do you want to know a secret?" My voice wobbled as I whispered to him.

"I would love to."

"I love it when you . . ." I stopped and frowned, unable to remember how I had planned to end the sentence. Croft waited. Eventually, I just shortened the sentence. "I love you." Yes, that still made sense, and it sounded right.

He leaned down and hugged me. "Of course you do." His voice was unsteady. He stroked my cheek, then leaned away a little and cleared his throat. "And you think I'm hilarious, too, don't you?"

"Yeah." I closed my eyes.

"And pompous?"

"Cocky," I corrected and drifted into peaceful oblivion.

* * *

BEING sick in the middle of a very busy semester is not a good idea.

By Friday, I felt well enough to take a look at the schoolwork I had missed. However, the emails I'd sent my professors resulted in a barrage of make-up work that would have made me hide under my covers if I hadn't already spent so much time under them. In addition, my caretakers insisted on making me take breaks and move around.

"Tomorrow, you get *two* walks," Croft told me that night. "One in the morning and one in the evening."

"You're a slave driver," I groaned. He had taken me outdoors earlier, and though I had felt the difference it made to get fresh air, I was stressed about my schoolwork. "I have too much to do."

He was unperturbed. "How does nine in the morning sound for the first one? I can also help you with your schoolwork by talking up a storm all day. It'll keep you awake."

"I'd rather you sing for me. That'd keep me awake and not be too distracting."

"My singing isn't distracting?" he asked as though I had struck him. "You can't be serious. My very presence is distracting, and when I open my mouth . . ."

"Disaster is sure to follow," I interrupted.

Obviously, I was feeling better.

* * *

It was nice to sleep after a long day of homework and would have been nicer still if the monsters would have let me be.

The horse was fine until it turned into a human-sized tarantula. The clown kept laughing and laughing, and after it turned into my house's noisy heating system, it continued to laugh, making the back of my neck prickle with discomfort.

"Surrey. Wake up."

"Murg." I sat up in bed and rubbed my eyes. In the dark of the room, a silhouette stood before me. The discomfort I so often felt at home stuck around, making me shiver, but I was hopeful it would soon fade.

"Come into the living room," the figure said.

I generally don't care much for dreams within dreams, but this man and my own quiet house were an improvement over the clown-heater, so I decided this vision might be a saving grace. I stood, the floor swaying somewhat under me, and groggily followed him into the other room where the lamp lit up the dining table. It looked to be the unearthly time of day during which Gina started work on Saturdays while sane people slept in their beds.

"Sit." He indicated a chair, and I sank into it. Shadows were thick all around except at the table. I looked at the man who stood over me, and I blinked. Something in the shape of his oblong face, his almond-shaped eyes, and his reddish-brown hair reminded me of . . .

"Jack?" I asked. I remembered the first name, but not the last.

A dazzling smile spread across his face. "Yes, it's me."

I was dreaming about a random guy from my high school? One of the yearbook editors? I guess stranger things had happened in dreams.

"There's something I need you to see," he said and laid down a thick, white envelope in front of me.

I stared at it in obedience, my eyes bleary. After a bit, I found myself wondering how long I was supposed to look at it.

"Open it," he urged.

Oh. Duh, I was supposed to look at the contents, not the envelope. Embarrassed, I pulled out a stack of photos and gazed at the top one. It showed me from behind, my head turned to show off a confidential smile. My blond hair billowed across my backpack and glittered in the sun. Other backpacks and arms surrounded me as I navigated my way through a crowd of adult students, the mom-dad-and-daughter statue from the south part of campus in the background.

Strange. I put it on the table, revealing the next photo in the stack. It showed me on my couch, concentrating on a textbook. In the next one, I reached for something in the kitchen. Next, I stood in front of my easel in my bedroom, gazing at a painting in progress.

I started to feel uneasy. While in a dream it wouldn't be a big deal to have a guy, someone I passed in the hallways and shared a class or two with in high school, show up in my house and make me look through pictures of myself, in reality, it was a whole different matter. And I was beginning to feel awake.

"I don't understand." I looked up at him and felt a chill at the intensity of his gaze. "Who took these?"

"Me."

"But, how? Some of them are taken from in here."

"I have cameras in your house."

I stared at him.

"Keep looking." He pointed at the stack in my hand.

I returned to the photos with growing bewilderment. There I was, eating, my skin looking smooth and flawless. There I stood, bending over the dryer, my pose somehow striking in spite of the everyday chore. There I sat, reading in my room, a mysterious smile playing at the corners of my mouth.

I looked back at Jack. Although things were becoming more and more surreal, they also felt less and less like a dream. "Do you have cameras *all* over the house?" Not only had my living room and kitchen been invaded, but the privacy of my bedroom had been infringed upon. It came to me to be grateful I often dressed and undressed with the lights off. But what about . . .

"I left out the bathroom," he answered, his voice as natural as though he were speaking about the weather. "Out of respect for you. And there are no cameras in your roommate's bedroom."

Both omissions were a great relief.

However, I balked at the next photo. It didn't actually show much, but I was horrified to see myself changing into my lace-camouflage dress. I had done *that* during the daytime, and *Jack* had watched it and printed evidence.

I quickly laid down the photo, only to see a picture of me napping in my parents' home, our Christmas tree and fireplace behind me.

My *parents'* home?

I sped up to get through the rest of the stack. Most of the photos had been taken in my current house, but some were from my previous apartments, three were from my family's place, and several more were from my mission.

I looked up at Jack, my eyes searching his face while my mind searched for an escape route.

"Do you see, Surrey?" he asked quietly. "Do you see how I admire you? How committed I am? This is only a minuscule sample of the photos I have taken. I have devoted the last five years to watching you."

"Five—five years?" That would mean, what, since senior year of high school?

I tried to scoot my chair back without him noticing.

"All this time, I have been here for you." His eyes shone in the relative dark. "Everything I did was for you. I took a job that allowed me to stay close. Not during your mission." His voice turned petulant. "They kept moving you to a new apartment. But I flew in to see you several times, and when you came home, I took a job here. I worked home security to learn how to enter your home and install my cameras. I use the same soaps and shampoos as you so no one will notice a smell out of place after I've been here. I memorize your schedule and adjust my life around it to get the best possible shots. My world revolves around you."

I'm pretty sure my mouth was hanging open at this point. Also, I was finding it hard to breathe.

He shook his head in wonder. "I thought that was all I would ever do. Admire you from a distance." His light-gray eyes bored into mine, and he took a step closer, towering over me in my chair. My hand began to shake on the tabletop. "It took me so long to see the truth, Surrey, but now I know. No one else has stayed with you as long as I. No one else appreciates your beauty like I do. They don't adore you like they should. If anyone deserves you, it's me. Me, the one who never stopped thinking of you, never stopped looking at you."

He took a step back, and his crazed tone turned suddenly cool. "Come."

"What?" I squawked.

"You must come with me."

I had a hard time catching my breath. "Jack, I'm . . . flattered. But this is all very new to me. I don't think I can go anywhere with you just now."

"It's time, Surrey." He spoke in a tone of gentle correction.

"I, I need some time to take this in. Maybe you could, uh, leave me to think it over, and you can come back later?"

"No, Surrey. My car is waiting outside."

"I have to wait until Gina comes home," I tried, gripping my chair. "You remember Gina, don't you?"

His eyes narrowed. "You don't want to come?"

I froze. "It's not that, it's just . . . Where are we going?"

"To our last photo shoot."

"Oh. That sounds lovely," I began, trying to think of another excuse, before something in his wording caught my attention. "Last?" I asked faintly.

"Surrey, we need to go." Impatient, he reached out for me. In a blind panic, I scrambled from my chair and tried to run from the hand closing on my arm. As I pulled away, my other arm bumping painfully against the table and sweeping the photos off, he moved twice as fast, and I found myself crashing to the floor on my back. I cried out as my head hit the wood, and I looked up through a haze to see Jack standing over me with a gun pointed downward.

My head hurt, my heart pounded in agony, and—where had the gun come from? I broke out in a cold sweat. For an excruciating minute, we stared at each other.

His eyes wandered across my face, and his gaze thawed. He reached down and pulled me up by my arm, then pressed me to his side and put the gun to my ribs. "Let's go."

He had grown since high school, gaining a couple of inches on me and filling out to where it was obvious that in a battle of strength, he would win.

I followed him to the door, where he stopped. "Pick up your shoes. You can put them on in the car."

I drew breath. "But it's cold—"

He interrupted. "If you scream or try to run, someone will get hurt." He lifted his gun. "That someone might just be the neighbor who hears you."

Well, I know the basics of self-defense. Scream. Run. Never, *ever* get into the car with the bad guy. As he pulled me outside into the dark cold where no one else was out, I wasn't worried about neighbors getting hurt. I knew I had to fight at all costs to avoid entering the unfamiliar red sedan in my driveway. The sneakers in my hands just might be the weapon I needed. Determined, I tensed and—jerked, overtaken by an ill-timed coughing fit.

Jack steered me along. My coughing didn't let up until I was in the passenger seat, the door slamming shut beside me. I gasped for breath and waited as he paused, bent over my door. As soon as he began to walk around, I grasped the handle, but my door didn't budge. I locked and unlocked it, trying to open it both ways, but nothing worked.

I let go of the handle as though it were on fire the moment Jack opened his own door.

He got in and sent me a dark glance I couldn't and didn't want to interpret. Dread closed around my heart as he buckled up and backed us out of the driveway. The clock on the dashboard read 5:54.

I was very much awake, and I wanted to cry.

Chapter Thirty

WHAT TIME WOULD my neighbors step outside on a Saturday morning? How early did the sun rise these days?

I waited ten minutes to make my first request. With no idea how long our drive would last, I didn't dare wait longer for fear that we would arrive at his destination.

"You know, I'm still in my pajamas." I attempted a laugh. "Could we go back so I can change? It won't take long." And hopefully, *hopefully* someone would go outside or look out their window in time to see us. Even if I stayed respectful of the gun, walking next to Jack rather than trying to run, if someone saw us, they would have to notice I was wearing my nightgown and pajama pants and would realize something was up. Maybe Mrs. Blaine was miraculously unable to sleep and would be at her window early.

"I have a change of clothing for you," my kidnapper said, watching the road.

I blinked. "Um. We'll have to stop somewhere for me to get changed, though. I can't do that in the car." *Oh, horror!* I thought suddenly. Would he make me change in front of him? I seriously regretted bringing it up.

"You won't need to change yet. We have plenty of time."

Forcing down my panic, I focused my gaze on a blue BYU keychain lying on the dashboard. I had had one like it last semester.

I shifted in my seat. Maybe there was plenty of time before I needed to wear whatever he had picked out for me, but there was something else that was becoming more urgent by the minute.

"This is a little embarrassing to bring up," I began, although I wasn't sure he knew what it meant to be embarrassed. "I always need to use the restroom when I get up in the morning. I haven't gotten to do that yet. Could we stop somewhere? A gas station would be fine."

He gave me a doting smile and returned his gaze to the road. I waited. As we continued through the barren streets, I squirmed and began to wonder whether I would have to wet myself.

Finally, he spoke. "I will find a place."

Relief washed over me. "Thank you, Jack."

He looked at me again, his gaze fond. "Of course, Surrey."

I squirmed again. While it seemed a good idea to use his name so that I appeared compliant and friendly, I was uncomfortable having him call *me* by my name. It indicated a level of familiarity I would rather he didn't feel.

Eventually, Jack pulled up in front of . . . nothing. It was nothing but an empty road and an abandoned construction site with little to show except a hole in the ground and a turquoise Honey Bucket portable restroom.

I looked in all directions, but it was no use. There was no one around.

If I hadn't needed to go so badly, I might have thought to pull a spoiled-girl card. *Ew, those are gross. You have to take me to a real bathroom.*

Not that he gave me much time to think about it. He was already out of the car. I tried pulling at my doorhandle again before he arrived on the other side. He bent to fiddle with something. After a bit, he opened the door, immediately catching hold of my arm.

I let him escort me to the Honey Bucket, where I slipped inside and did my business. Closing the cold seat and sitting on it, I reached for the hand sanitizer on the wall and was grateful to find it not empty. I almost laughed at the fact that I could be grateful for such a small thing at such a time as this. I didn't realize I was shaking until the tremors became less frequent.

Morning sun filtered in through the Honey Bucket. Although this place appeared deserted, maybe if I waited long enough, construction workers would arrive. They might have just gotten started on the project and would continue it today. Didn't they usually work mornings, even on Saturdays? Shivering, I settled in to wait as long as necessary.

Five minutes must have passed before Jack knocked. "Surrey? Are you done?"

I hugged myself tighter and tried to retain what little body heat I had left.

Another minute passed. Another knock sounded. I rubbed my arms and coughed. I would wait all day if I had to.

I started at a noise and the sight of a silver blade appearing through the crack in the door, below the lock. I reached out too late to hold down the lock. The blade flipped it up, the door swung open, and with my forward momentum, I fell out.

Jack caught me and pulled me upright against him before pressing his knife to my neck. The pulse in my throat would have been wise to keep still at this point, but it thudded wildly as if trying to get itself cut.

"Let's go," Jack growled, moving the knife to give me breathing space before he dragged me back to the car. He was dragging me not because I was fighting but because my legs had given way beneath me. What was my high school peer doing with a knife, a gun, and a plethora of hidden cameras? How many other weapons did he have? What—I caught my breath—was up with that white gown and veil lying on the back seat?

I forgot to try opening my door this time while Jack went around to his own side. Not that it mattered. There was nowhere for me to go, and I was certain Jack could run faster than me even if I weren't sick.

We were soon on the road again, but something was different now, and it wasn't good. The air was thick with tension, and I knew it was caused by my long stay in the portable restroom. I sought desperately for a way to defuse things, but I couldn't stomach an apology. My mind bounced between the knife, the white gown, and Jack's declarations of devotion.

Finally, I got up the courage to ask, "Why will this photo shoot be our last?"

Something like pleasure melted away the worst of the disapproval in his face. "After this, I won't need the pictures anymore."

I sat in silence for a moment. "Why not?"

"Because you will be with me. We will never be separated again."

I shivered and turned my head, catching a glimpse of white on the seats behind us. My voice quavered as I asked, "Is that a wedding gown?"

"Yes. For our photos." He shook his head as if in disbelief. "I won't be hiding this time. I'll be taking my pictures out in the open."

I cleared my throat. "I think my family should join us."

He chuckled. I gritted my teeth and forced myself to keep trying.

"If we're getting married, our families should be present."

He shook his head. "We won't need a ceremony."

"I can't live with you without a ceremony," I exclaimed, letting my shock show.

He ignored my protest. "You will look otherworldly. I have the perfect place for us. If you don't try to run, we'll take the photos outside, under an arch, amidst the greenery." Satisfaction spread across his face. "Even if you do try to run, there's not much you can do in a heavy wedding gown."

I stared out the window, trying to control my breathing. "I'll have to put on makeup. Do you have any, or do we need to stop somewhere and buy it?"

"You don't use makeup." His voice was calm.

I pursed my lips in displeasure. "Not normally. On special occasions, though, it's a good idea. I ought to wear makeup for a bridal photo op."

"It would only cover up your natural beauty," he replied, rejecting the idea.

I breathed in deep again. "I've been sick this week. I don't look my best today."

He looked me over, his eyes softening. "Your illness has added color to your cheeks and shine to your eyes. And it made it easier for me to pick you up today." He appraised me with obvious admiration.

Curse it. I blushed pretty, I cried pretty, and I was sick pretty.

I clenched my hands together in my lap and watched the landscape. Deserted, that was all it was. The air was gray, the mountains shadowy, and the roads alternated between rustic and commercial in a way that kept us from seeing anyone who might be outside.

Jack hadn't been kidding when he said we had lots of time. It was past seven. Past seven-thirty. I wasn't sure how we ended up on the freeway after some of the winding roads he had picked, but suddenly there we were, well past Salt Lake City, sharing the road with a handful of other drivers who didn't have time to look in our window and notice me signal for help.

"How far are we going?" I broke the silence to ask.

He didn't answer. It looked like we were heading toward Idaho, although with some of the backtracking he had done earlier, that could change.

I reached up to rub my neck. Stopping short, I held out a strand of hair. "Should I do something about my hair before we get there? I guess I still have bedhead." Unless he felt that putting my hair into some semblance of order hid its natural beauty, surely he would agree that I needed to comb it before the "photo shoot."

"I have a comb in the glove compartment." He nodded at the space in front of me.

I opened it slowly, wondering if he might also have a weapon stored there. Its presence would scare me half senseless, but it might come in handy. Unfortunately, there was only the comb, a car owner's manual—and a familiar-looking lip balm like the one I had misplaced months ago.

I closed the compartment and eyed the keychain on the dashboard, noticing for the first time that it had a scratch in the same place as mine had had. How many other trinkets had he taken?

"Do you have a brush, too?" I asked, praying the answer was no so I could ask to purchase one at a store.

"You don't use a brush," he told me.

I frowned. I didn't, but he didn't need to know that. "When my hair gets tangled enough," I began, only to be interrupted.

"You don't use a brush," he repeated, putting emphasis on each word. "I have never seen a hairbrush in your purse or your backpack, and the brush in your bathroom belongs to your roommate," he finished, his voice reproachful.

Since I highly doubted he would reprimand me for something as innocent as not using a hairbrush, I knew he had seen through my request and was growing irritable. While Jack was clearly not a person in his right mind, he unfortunately wasn't stupid. I was losing faith that I could outsmart him, and yet I *had* to find a way to do so.

I sat back and said in a weak voice, "You know me so well."

"I revere you," he responded. "I have tried to know everything about you. I will get to know everything now, at last. I would do anything for you, Surrey."

I couldn't help asking, "Would you let me out here?"

He continued as though I hadn't spoken. "I've always admired you. I never thought anyone could be worthy of you, but now I know the truth." His voice grew more impassioned. "I am here for you, and I am right for you, because no one else is as devoted to you as I am." He paused and said darkly, "And you deserve devotion."

I swallowed. "I—I think maybe I deserve to be listened to."

He nodded. "I will listen to your voice every day."

That wasn't what I had been hoping for.

Chapter Thirty-One

CROFT ARRIVED at Surrey's house early—a whole hour early. He just couldn't wait any longer.

He rang the doorbell, smiling in giddy anticipation. Man, he loved this girl. He loved making her laugh, loved her brilliant, hilarious personality, loved *her*. And if the "secret" she had shared in the throes of illness were to be trusted—his heart beat faster at the thought—then she felt the same way about him.

Oh, he would make her laugh today. That would help her heal faster. He hoped never to see her so sick again. He would have crawled to the ends of the earth for her if he'd thought it would make her feel any better this week.

He raised his hand again but stopped short of touching the doorbell. Could she still be sleeping?

He opted for a knock. That wouldn't be nearly so rude an awakening.

When she didn't answer, he pulled out his cell phone and called her number. It rang. And rang. And rang. Then the voicemail message began.

His brows knit. What if she was feeling worse again? Starting another call, he put his ear to the door. Somewhere inside, Surrey's recorded voice snapped, "I am *not* your oven timer." He grinned at the memory of her lasagna story.

Then he frowned. Why wasn't Surrey answering? Hesitant, he tried the doorknob and was surprised when it turned. Surrey and Gina always locked the door, even when they were home.

Her phone continued speaking.

"Surrey?" he called.

Maybe she was outside. He crossed through the living room and slid the glass door open. It didn't take long to determine that no one was in the small yard.

Could she have gone for a walk? She always locked the door when she went for walks, though, even short ones around the block. Still, being sick might have affected her thinking.

Sick! His eyes widened. Surrey could be passed out somewhere.

Before the thought finished flashing through his mind, he made a run for the bathroom. It was empty.

"Surrey?" he called and ran to her bedroom. It was against the BYU Honor Code to enter her room, but this was an emergency. She could be lying on the floor, unconscious and in need of medical help.

"Surrey," he yelled, crashing through the door and looking around. He ran to check on the other side of her bed, going so far as to look beneath it. The easel and the paintings on the table made it clear this was her room, but she wasn't here.

Sorry, Gina, he thought as he hurried to the other bedroom and looked inside. He checked under the bed and even inside a closet. Biting his lip, he returned to Surrey's room and opened a small closet she would have had a hard time fitting into, but he hardly knew what else to do. Go for a drive in the neighborhood to look for her like she was a lost dog?

He did just that for ten minutes, then returned for another thorough search of her house and bedroom. She hadn't returned while he was away.

The chair beside her bed held a small pile of neatly folded clothes. Uttering another silent apology, he looked through it. Pants, a shirt, and, uh . . . His ears grew warm, and he quickly laid the clothing down, but his uneasiness grew. The change of clothing *must* have been laid out for today. But if it was, that meant—that meant she was still in her PJs. Somewhere.

Where had she wandered off to?

He was about to call her again when he remembered her phone was here. Finding it, he looked up Gina's number and called, waiting in an agony.

It went to voicemail.

"Gina," he said after the beep, "do you know where Surrey is? She's not home, but her cell phone is here. Please call me back. This is Croft."

He hung up and raked a hand through his hair. "Okay, these are the facts. She knew I was coming, but she's not here. Her car and phone are here. The door was unlocked. I think her change of clothes for today is here."

He paced and stopped again. "Her stuff is here," he repeated. "She's not. She's in her PJs."

The silence of the room pressed in on him. He raised his gaze to the ceiling and exclaimed in desperation, "She was getting well! She's *not* wandering around fevered. She's lucid. So why has she left like this?"

Not left, the words came to his mind.

He paused. She wouldn't have left like this, right? But what did that mean?

He swallowed and closed his eyes. *Heavenly Father,* he said in his mind. *What's going on? Where is Surrey? What can I do?*

Not left.

He groaned and sat down. If she hadn't left . . . If Surrey hadn't randomly decided to go for a walk, if she hadn't ignored her change of clothing and changed into something else, then he supposed she might have been . . .

Taken.

He shot up, electrified. "Heavenly Father, has she been taken somewhere?" he asked loudly.

The refrigerator hummed across the silence.

He rubbed his hands across his face. Could someone really have taken her, or was he overreacting? But something felt wrong. "Has she been kidnapped?" He felt himself turn pale. "She's—she's been kidnapped," he said, testing out the words and then listening with all his might, trying to feel the Spirit telling him whether or not that was true.

Even if it was, though—his heart clenched—the police couldn't help. Without proof, they wouldn't look for someone unless that person had been missing at least forty-eight hours. Or was it twenty-four? Either way, it was far too long to wait if she *had* been abducted. How could he get proof?

"Help me, Heavenly Father," he whispered as he paced to the kitchen and back to the living room.

Get on your knees, Croft.

He threw himself to his knees in the middle of the floor, closing his eyes and clasping his hands. His sense of urgency growing, he prayed, asking for Surrey's safety and for inspiration to strike him.

He opened his eyes and waited for an answer.

A piece of glossy, dark paper under the couch caught his eye. With nothing better to do, he mechanically reached for it and found there were several sheets—no, photos. He picked up the nearest ones and looked at them.

His throat clogged up. Why . . . why was there a picture of Surrey changing clothes? Why were there pictures of Surrey in which she seemed unaware of a photographer?

Reaching under the couch again, he pulled out more photos and checked for dust on the floor. It was clean. The photos couldn't have been there long, certainly not for months or weeks. Maybe not even for a day.

He slapped his hands down on the floor. This was the answer to his prayer. Quicker than thought, he dialed 911 and hit call.

"911, what's your emergency?"

He answered in a rush. "My girlfriend's been kidnapped by her stalker."

* * *

It didn't take the police long to find the first camera.

Croft checked his show's website fanatically. Replies to his post about Surrey were coming in fast, all of them sympathetic but none of them bringing news. Still, they showed the word was spreading. Gina had been told, too, once she called back. She was rushing home from work right this moment.

Croft paced the living room, listening to one of the officers on his phone as he put in the request to start a search for Surrey Witherfield. The other officer was in Surrey's bedroom, examining any space where a camera might have been placed. He stuck his head through the doorway and called out, "That's three so far," before disappearing from view.

At the sound of a car pulling up, Croft rushed for the door. Officer Joane held him back but allowed Croft to follow him out and greet the new arrivals, two more officers.

"Question the neighbors," Officer Joane instructed them. "Rhoades and I are searching the house."

"What about me?" Croft asked.

Joane replied with another question. "Do you know any of the neighbors?"

"I've met some of them." *Played with some of them,* he added in his mind, remembering the snowball fight. *Raked leaves for others.* Both activities seemed ages ago now.

"Join them," Joane said. "Maybe you can be of help."

They stopped at Willie's house first. His family hadn't seen anything, but Willie insisted on joining them for the rest of the interrogations. He also demanded they go across the street and talk to Mrs. Blaine right away.

That's right, Croft remembered, Surrey called her the neighborhood's watchdog. He had been introduced to her before. If anyone knew anything, it would be her.

Mrs. Blaine's response was prompt when the officers began to question her.

"I saw a red car leave the neighborhood around six," she said, and Croft caught his breath. "It wasn't the Johnsons' car or the Whitmers', and no one else here has a red car."

"Did you see who was in it?" the taller officer asked. "Did you see anyone get in?"

"No. I looked out the window and saw it drive by. It could have come from her house. It could have not."

Croft willed her to share something more helpful. Beside him, Willie was so tense that Croft felt it coming off him in waves.

"What kind of make and model was it?" the other officer asked.

"I don't know, but it was a five-seater."

"A five-seater?" The officer's forehead knit.

"A five-seater," she said, raising her brows at his confused expression. "It seats five people," she told him, lifting her brows even higher.

Croft swallowed a nervous laugh.

"It was a sedan," she said, rolling her eyes.

"Doors both in front and in back?"

"That's what I said," she answered dryly, making Croft laugh in spite of, or maybe because of, the terrible tension he felt. An image of Surrey accusing him of thinking everything was funny came to mind, and he felt tears prick his eyes.

The officer turned to his companion. "Let's get someone to look through traffic camera images at nearby intersections from around six o'clock this morning. Look for a red car. Let's hope he has her seated in front instead of hidden in the trunk where the cameras can't catch her."

Croft felt his stomach turn at the thought of Surrey stowed away in the trunk. Dismayed, he sent a penetrating prayer heavenward.

Chapter Thirty-Two

Lᴇsᴛ ʏᴏᴜ ᴛʜɪɴᴋ I hadn't prayed yet, let me assure you I had prayed silently for hours, asking my Father for safety and inspiration and help. I had carefully weighed what I said to Jack, carefully taken note of his reactions, and carefully tried to calm him down whenever I upset him. It was a fine line to walk. How obliging could I sound without motivating him to take some sort of advantage?

"What does our house look like?" I asked, stretching my fingers in my lap to keep from clenching them together. Outside, a tumbleweed blew across our path. We were on a two-lane stretch of freeway that held nothing but slush and the occasional freight truck.

Jack was pleased with the question. "It's a pretty place in the mountains. You'll like it."

Praying my petulance wouldn't set him on edge, I objected. "Actually, I like big cities." I didn't, but would he know that?

"You will like it because I will be there," he said firmly.

"Oh, right. Of course," I hurried to say, feeling the threat in his words. "That part *will* be great. I do like to have a few neighbors, though."

He made no comment, and I didn't dare push it. Instead, I made a new request. "Can I use your phone?"

He gave me a pitying look. "Surrey, I understand you're not used to me yet. I have to cut you off from others until you feel safe with me."

"It's just my mom," I protested. "I want her to know I'm feeling better after being sick. Our drive is so long, I'd like to make use of the time to chat with her."

"No phone," was his curt response.

I debated saying I already felt safe with him, but convincing him of that might encourage him to make advances.

"Think of this as our honeymoon," he said, making me blush miserably. "We'll have at least a few weeks together, just you and me. After that, we'll see whether you are ready to be around others."

"What—what about your job? Won't you need to go to work?"

"I quit last week. I'm starting a new job next month, one I can do from our home. I won't leave you, Surrey," he vowed, giving me another look that made me struggle to keep from crying.

He seemed to have thought of everything. It scared me witless when he pulled over and got out, but all he did was pour gasoline from a can into his tank. How I wished he hadn't prepared for this and would have instead refueled at the gas station a few miles ago.

He got back in and unwrapped a protein bar, the sound of the wrapper eerie in the silence. It was nearly eleven, and it came to me that I hadn't even had breakfast.

Jack chewed slowly and watched me as if I were a TV show.

When he finished the snack and started on a sandwich, I felt my stomach rumble. I shifted in my seat. Was he intentionally starving me? Or did he mean for me to ask for food and water before he would give me any?

I should ask. I would need my strength later in order to run and maybe even fight. Then the thought came to me that he might have put drugs in whatever food he was planning to give me.

I dropped my shoulders and watched him watch me until he finished his meal.

He narrowed his eyes at me as if mad that I hadn't asked for anything. I was relieved when he started the car.

Besides food and drink, I could use some sleep before we reached a place where I might make my getaway. However, in spite of getting up early, recovering from illness, and spending hours on the road, I sat wide awake, every nerve so taut I was certain I would be sore tomorrow. The thought gave me pause. Where would I be tomorrow? What awful things would I have experienced by then?

I quickly shut down that line of thought and focused on the now. What could I do now to get away?

"How's your family?" I asked. Maybe if I could get him thinking about his family and the woman who had raised him, he would grow ashamed of having abducted me.

"No family." His voice came out sharp.

It took me a moment to figure out what he meant. "Oh, I don't mean to imply they should come see us at the wedding—or the photo shoot. I was just wondering. How many siblings do you have?"

"One."

"Brother? Sister?" I pressed.

"Brother."

"Older? Younger?" I continued, feeling like a broken record.

"He's younger."

"Do you get along?"

He put his hand on the dashboard. "No family. It's just us," he growled.

I pushed out my breath in frustration. Maybe that had been the wrong tactic, though. Maybe he had family problems, and they had contributed to pushing him over the edge.

Realizing I was shaking again, I hugged myself and looked out the window.

* * *

THE SECOND RESTROOM break was as hopeless as the first. How did he find these places? Still, I might make a break for it. I said a quick, fervent prayer while Jack got out of the car. But when he opened my door, I felt a strong impression not to run. It made me pause long enough for him to get confused when I didn't so much as stand, but he wasn't one to wait. He pulled me from the car, and I walked slowly, trying to reason with the voice or thought that was telling me to do nothing. The feeling remained, and I gave in with a sigh, hoping this meant God had a plan for my escape and that this just wasn't it.

After returning to the car, I prayed and prayed, but no other thoughts came to me. I did at one point get a warm feeling, one that gave me peace for a moment. I savored it while it lasted. Still, I didn't know what it meant.

Did it mean that things would work themselves out and I could sit back and do nothing? Did it mean that things would work out but that it would require a lot of thought and effort from me?

Or did it mean that even though things would end horribly for me, God was reminding me that he loved me and that in the eternal scheme of things, all would be made fair? Was the good feeling a gift meant to help me now and meant for me to look back on later, when things were at their worst?

That third option terrified me, so I tried to focus on the other two and decided it wouldn't hurt for me to think of ways to escape.

Taking a moment to make sure I sounded calm, I tilted my head at the steering wheel. "Do you want me to drive? This is turning out to be a really long trip."

He didn't answer, but a new idea was taking hold of me. He had mentioned listening to my voice every day, but it was my looks that had drawn him to me in the first place. Well, I had met guys who were starstruck by my looks but didn't care much for my personality. Jack just might learn today that having the whole package wasn't as exciting as just looking at me had been.

"I'm a good driver. I know, I'm kind of clumsy, but I've never gotten in an accident, not while driving. I'm very safe," I blabbered. "Do you really like the sound of my voice? I hope my talking doesn't bother you. It's just, I can't stop thinking about all the things I need to do or all the things I could be doing on our road trip, so I hope you forgive me when I make suggestions. I was thinking," I leaned forward in my seat, "will we be passing by Yellowstone? I've been a couple of times, and it would be cool to go again. Jack, did you ever . . ."

He was pulling off the road. Worried, I quieted a little, but only a little. "Did we need another restroom break? This doesn't look like . . ."

My voice trailed off again as he stopped the car and turned to me, unbuckling his seatbelt and then mine in two swift motions.

"Come here," he said roughly.

"N-no," I squeaked, gripping my seatbelt and holding it in place while he tried to tug me toward him. "Jack," I protested hoarsely as one hand came around my back and another inched under my legs, attempting to lift me from my seat. I dug my heels in, trying to keep all of me exactly where I was.

We wrestled over my seatbelt. He grunted in growing agitation and tried to pull my face toward his, but then he stopped, looking out the windshield at a car that had appeared in the distance. I wrenched my head back, leaving a strand of hair to slide through his fingers, and leaned against my door, trying to ready myself for a fight.

Jack huffed and returned his hands to the wheel. "We'll have time for this later. We have to keep going." He shifted the car into gear.

My heart was going two hundred beats per minute now, and I sat quiet as a mouse, not daring to speak again. My hopes that he would keep his hands to himself at least the first few days had been dashed to pieces. After five years of being content to look at me, he should have been happy to do little more than watch me in person for a bit, right?

That hopeful fantasy was rapidly distorting itself in my mind into the nightmares I was trying to avoid.

* * *

Noon had come and passed. Twelve thirty. One o'clock. My appetite for speaking was long since gone, and Jack didn't seem to have a problem with the silence.

Scenes from my day played in my head over and over.

Photos. Knife. Driving. Honey Bucket. Photos. Gun. Photos. . . .

Photos. Something clicked in my mind. With two of his photos, I had been unable to tell where they'd been taken. Now I remembered what they reminded me of: a certain picture from my yearbook. Another idea took shape.

I took a deep breath and forced myself to speak again.

"I think you have a competitor." He looked at me. "There's a photo of me in our yearbook, before the student section. I never saw the guy who took it, but he's been stalking me as long as you have. You and I can't be together until you . . ."

The words *as long as you have* stuck in my mind. It was almost five years since that yearbook had been printed.

"What were you saying?" Jack asked with a strange smile.

I pulled myself together. "You'll have to find him and make sure he stops following me, or we'll never be left in peace," I bluffed. *Don't let it be Jack who took that picture, don't let it be Jack,* I chanted in my mind.

His smile didn't change. "Did you like that picture?" he asked warmly, and my heart sank.

"Did you take it?" I asked in a small voice.

He returned his attention to the road. "My first masterpiece," he acknowledged. "Until then, I never got a shot that gave you justice. Someone always got in the way, or you didn't face the camera. But that photo, that was the first time I was able to keep you with me in all your beauty."

We moved onto an exit ramp and entered a city. Jack reached over and took my hand, lacing our fingers together. "You're going to look straight ahead at the road," he said. "If I catch you looking at any of the cars beside us, I will pull my gun."

I think I started to hyperventilate around this time. Struggling to control my breathing, I ran through a series of self-defense moves in my head. The next time he let me out and I didn't feel a prompting not to run, I needed to be ready. If I were in a good position to kick him, I would kick. Legs were stronger than arms. If my hands were available for use, I might hit him in the eye. If he grabbed my hair, what would be the best way to fight back?

Five scenarios later, he let go of my hand and made a sharp right turn. I slid in my seat and gave him a reproachful look. He hadn't even signaled, but then, I didn't suppose I could expect a stalker and a kidnapper to obey simple traffic rules.

"Eyes straight ahead," he snapped, and I straightened my spine and faced forward even though I would have preferred to look at the cars around me, mouth "SOS," and make scared faces. Hmm. Maybe I could tap out "SOS" on the window without Jack noticing. Only, I wasn't sure I remembered the letters in Morse code. They were supposed to be simple, but all the letters in Morse code were simple. That didn't mean I remembered which one was S and which was O.

My eyes widened as we sped toward a light that had been yellow for far too long. It turned red and then one, two seconds later, we drove through it, eliciting a series of angry honks from the cars that had started to move and then quickly braked for us.

I gripped my seat with my free hand. What in the world was Jack up to now?

Chapter Thirty-Three

CROFT SAT on the front porch with his head in his hands. The neighbors and a distraught, sobbing Gina had all been questioned. Someone had taken the photos to the station to check out fingerprints. Others were looking through traffic surveillance cameras. And the officers had found sixteen cameras in the house so far.

What was happening to Surrey right now? Did she know self-defense?

He should have spent less time teasing her and more time making sure she knew the important things. Like how to fight off an attacker. Like escape tips and survival skills. Like the fact that he loved her.

"She's there! In the front seat."

In a flash, Croft was up and running into the house.

"It's a red Hyundai Elantra at the library intersection of University Avenue at six-oh-four," the officer said, showing the picture he'd just received to the other officers and to Croft and a red-eyed Gina. "We're running the plates."

"The license plate?" Croft asked.

"Yes." He switched from the photo of Surrey in the car to a close-up of the vehicle's front, which gave a clear view of the license plate. The lighting was strange, but it had been dark around that time. Croft hurried to write down the number and add it to his post online.

The officer moved to a new photo of Surrey and someone else in the car. "Do either of you recognize this guy?"

Croft gazed at the photo. It was difficult to see what the man looked like. It was easy to recognize Surrey only because they knew her and were looking for her. After a long minute, the officer started to lower his phone, but Gina reached out and gripped his wrist, holding it in place.

"Oh, sorry," she muttered when she realized the officer was staring at her.

"Do you know him?" he asked again.

She stared intently at the phone. "I'm not sure."

"Think hard," the man encouraged her.

With all his might, Croft willed Gina to recognize the perpetrator. He scrutinized the image himself, wondering if he was supposed to have seen this man before. Chills ran through him as he imagined this guy with Surrey.

"I think," Gina began and stopped.

"What?" the others chorused.

"He reminds me of someone from our high school."

"'Our'?" Officer Joane asked.

"Gina and Surrey went to the same high school," Croft explained and waited breathlessly for whatever Gina might say next.

"Just a minute." Gina whirled around and was about to enter Surrey's room when a police officer stopped her.

"We can't mess up fingerprints or other evidence," he told her.

"I just have to get her yearbook," she insisted.

He followed her in to make sure she didn't touch anything beyond the necessary. She rushed back out, opened the book, and turned to the student section.

Her finger ran down the page. "Jack Sohn. It sort of looks like him. Do you think that could be him? The picture's from five years ago."

Everyone leaned in except Officer Rhoades, who had just received another message.

"We've got news," he announced. "They ran the license plates, but we have a problem. The plates belong to a black Toyota, not our red Hyundai. Our guy switched the plates."

"Then we can't track the GPS," Officer Joane said, turning away in frustration.

"At least we can tell our people which license plate to look for. They'll keep looking through traffic camera surveillance to try to track the car, but it'll be time-consuming. Miss Witherfield and her kidnapper will have been on the road for hours unless he's already stopped. Now, what do we think, could this be our guy, five years older?"

Gina and Croft deliberated the photos, taking a seat on the very edge of the couch. Croft wanted to tear his hair out—or, better yet, tear up the guy who might be hurting Surrey even now. Rhoades checked out the photos on the sixteen cameras that had been found so far—nineteen, after three more were discovered in the kitchen—twenty-three, after a more thorough search of her bedroom. So far, Rhoades could find no pictures from this morning showing Surrey's departure or the stranger who might be Jack Sohn.

"Update from the station, "Officer Joane called out. "Jack Sohn's family has confirmed that it's him in the picture and that he owns a red Hyundai." Gina dropped the yearbook with a thud, and Croft caught his breath in an embarrassing sob. "They gave us the original plate number. Kellen, look up his car and find the GPS signal. Jergens, you look up his phone. As soon as we have a hit, we'll know where they are, or at least where he stopped before continuing on by means of other transportation."

Croft leaned back into the cushions, feeling weak. He prayed silently, thanking Heavenly Father for all they had found out and pleading that they weren't too late to find Surrey. His Surrey.

Seven minutes later, two officers called out at the same time.

"Sir, we have a GPS hit in Bozeman, Montana."

"Sir, a civilian in Montana just called her in."

Chapter Thirty-Four

MY HEART WAS in my throat from the scare of the red light and the near accident. Jack growled. Still facing forward like I'd been told, I flicked my eyes in his direction and noticed him look at the rearview mirror. In spite of his command, I moved enough to glance in the mirror and identify a dark-green car behind us. I wasn't sure where it could have come from unless it had followed us through the red light.

I shifted back to my previous position, relieved to hear no reprimand from Jack. In fact, he seemed obsessively focused on his driving, making another couple of sharp turns, including a left turn that had me reeling and grabbing the armrest.

Leaving behind the paved road, we bumped along a wide forest path, pulling some two hundred yards in among the trees before coming to a stop.

Jack unbuckled himself and opened his door. "Don't move," he told me. Gun in hand, he jumped out and slammed the door, bending next to it as he had bent next to mine repeatedly on our journey. In another moment, he ran in the direction we had come and where, I suspected, someone else had followed us to.

I gripped the sides of my seat, my mind swirling. Was my potential rescuer about to get shot? Not that the other driver had necessarily come to rescue me. How would he have a clue that I needed help?

How would he know that Jack was coming at him with a gun?

I reached over and punched the steering wheel, making the car honk. I punched it again, and then a third time. Jack would be furious, but I had to warn the other driver.

I couldn't see what was going on behind me. After trying my door to no avail, I unbuckled and leaned over to try Jack's door. It was just as useless. A violent popping noise made me start and curl up in my seat.

Another shot sounded, then a series of shots. Tears streamed down my cheeks. I prayed for the other driver and tried to look back through my side window.

With my limited view, I could barely make out Jack colliding with another man and both of them tumbling to the ground. A wrestling match ensued. They rolled out of my line of sight. Someone reappeared enough for me to see that at least one of them was standing again. I thought I heard sounds from a fistfight, but I lost sight of the action once more.

A thump sounded. Had someone fallen to the ground? My breath hitched. After a long, drawn-out moment, I heard steps. Only one set of steps.

I cowered in my seat, praying out loud, although I doubt my words made much sense. In fact, I think my prayer may have come out sounding something like, "Flibberty-really-help-floopy-please-bruh."

I probably should have searched the car for a weapon, anything Jack might have left behind that I could defend myself with, but at that moment, I felt I would die if I moved so much as an inch. If it was Jack who was returning now, he might punish me if he caught me riffling through his things.

A knock on my window made me jump. Struggling to breathe, I turned my head to look.

A gray-haired, compact man in his fifties stood outside.

I let out a whimper and collapsed in my seat. He knocked again. I pulled weakly at the handle and shook my head to signal that it wouldn't open.

He frowned and bent down. A series of tinkering noises reached me through the closed door.

A minute later, he pulled the door open.

"Surrey Witherfield?" he asked in a gravelly voice.

Why not? I thought, dazed. The entire day had been surreal. This stranger may as well randomly know my name.

"Are you all right?"

I stared at him, heedless of the tears still sliding down my cheeks.

"That's quite the trick he did on your lock," he said conversationally. "Do you think you can stand?"

The suggestion to leave behind the car that had been my nightmare today seemed like a good one. Putting a shaky hand on the interior of the car, I tried to lift myself to a standing position. The man held out a hand, and I took it and put one foot outside, then the other, before sinking down to sit on the floor of the car. That was as far as I could make it.

"You all right?" he asked a second time.

I looked behind us. Jack lay on the ground in front of a dusty, dark-green Ford.

"Is he . . . ?" I started the question and let it hang in the air.

"Just fine. I shot him in the arm and then knocked him out." As I wondered in a daze in what world being shot and punched senseless was just fine, my rescuer continued, "I called the police while I was following you. If you're okay, I'll go bind up his arm, keep him from losing too much blood."

"Did you get shot?" I managed to choke out.

He gave me a smile. "No. Don't you worry about me."

I watched him walk over to the prone form and get down beside him. A ripping noise sounded, and then he was wrapping up Jack's arm. Averting my gaze, I looked at the Ford behind them. Several decals decorated its front, and even from this distance, I recognized at least one of them as an indicator of a U.S. veteran.

Although too many decals on a car usually made me nervous about the driver, at the moment, this guy's presence and what looked to be his background made me feel far safer than I had all day.

Sirens sounded in the distance. I sat listening to them until three police cars pulled up. A couple of officers rushed to question my rescuer and see to Jack. The others ran to my side, making me tense up. I badly wished the veteran would come join me, but when I saw that two of the officers were women, I felt a little calmer.

Of course the questions came hailing down then. An ambulance arrived, and I was checked for injuries. I accepted a blanket to wrap around myself and a bottle of water to drink, but it took a while to convince the paramedics I was fine, especially after I told them the only time I could have been hurt was when I fell on the floor back home and hit my head. That pronouncement brought a renewed determination to check me out, leading them to find a bump that hurt now that my attention had been brought to it.

When they told me they were taking me to the hospital, I sighed and stood, walking on shaky legs next to my escorts.

The veteran who had saved me came to see me off. "You feeling better, young lady?"

I wasn't so sure I did, so I avoided the question. "How did you know my name?" I asked instead.

"A friend of mine watches this comedy channel online." His brows furrowed in confusion. "I guess the channel wrote up a serious notice about you getting kidnapped sometime between last night and early this morning. My friend sent a mass text with your picture and a description of the car so people could be on the lookout."

I nodded, new tears springing to my eyes. That made more sense to me than it did to him. Although I had no idea how he knew about Jack's car, Croft had helped save me.

"Thank you," I said at last, realizing I had been in too much shock to express any kind of gratitude until now.

"Anyone would've done what they could. You're in good hands now."

"Thank you," I repeated and let the medical personnel help me into the back of the ambulance.

* * *

THE AMBULANCE and the hospital were overkill. The IV was refreshing but gave me energy to think back over my nerve-racking day, which I didn't appreciate.

They took scans of my head and declared me safe. I was given granola bars, but I didn't have the appetite to eat them, and I answered another bunch of questions before they finally decided that enough was enough— for today, anyway. I guess there would be follow-up questions over the next week, and I would probably have to testify at Jack's pending trial.

During all the questioning and the hospital stay, someone came up with a solution for getting me home. I should have been elated at all the new things I got to try after my rescue: A ride in an ambulance, later followed by a ride in a police helicopter since one of their pilots was heading for Utah County, anyway, followed by a last ride in a police car to my house. I was done with excitement, though, so instead of oohing and aahing, I sat staring out the window at the nothing between me and the Rocky Mountains. Normally I would have focused on the mountains, but at the moment, all I could see was the nothing. At one point, I did make the effort to have a phone call with my family, which I kept short because I was upset and my family was upset, and I didn't have the energy to listen to my poor mom crying out her shock over the phone.

My neighborhood looked different when I arrived in the back of a police cruiser. I felt like I was wearing tinted glasses that threw shadows over the world around me. The place appeared deserted and, if you can imagine it, shocked. I saw my own emotions reflected in it.

When I got out of the car, I hadn't taken two steps before Gina yelled my name and bowled into me, hugging me tight.

"I was so worried," she cried, letting go and stepping back to look at me. Her cheeks were wet.

Croft moved in, pulling me into another tight embrace. He didn't say a word. The strength of his hug gave me a moment of solidarity after facing a world today that had been a fluid mess of unknowns. My face burrowed against his chest, I relaxed an infinitesimal amount and mumbled, "I hate hidden cameras."

He made a noise that sounded more like a sob than a chuckle. "Of course you do. Let's get you inside."

Hugging me to his side, he began to walk, Gina flanking my other side.

Willie bowled into me next, and my two escorts barely kept me from getting knocked over.

I lightly returned Willie's hug, drained. He looked up at me with sparking mad eyes and declared, "I'd like to *pummel* the guy who kidnapped you."

"Yeah." It was all I could do to get the words out. "Someone else already did."

"Sorry, Willie, but we better get her inside," Croft said.

Willie's jaw clenched and unclenched. He nodded and said, "You look dead on your feet." Something about his words struck me as funny enough that I almost started to smile.

"We've got her," Croft said and led me past police tape and inside.

"Did they feed you? Have you had anything to eat?" Gina asked, barking out the questions like orders.

"No, but I need sleep," I said and steered for the sofa, where I lay down and put up my feet, closing my eyes before I even got settled.

"They didn't feed her? Didn't anyone think to . . ."

A blanket settled over me while Gina ranted in the background about people who should have been taking care of me. My once-shy roommate was a fierce defender in that moment. I liked the contrast of personality and wondered briefly if it could be captured in a painting. With Gina's voice in the background and a warm pressure that told me Croft was sitting against the couch by me, his arm protectively across my blanket-covered self, I fell asleep.

Chapter Thirty-Five

I ALMOST RESENTED the tantalizing smell of lasagna, *meat* lasagna, for forcing me to wake up and leave my couch.

I took a small bite and looked up to find Croft and Gina watching me. Each took a bite with me whenever I did, and then they waited to see what I would do next. I looked at the wall clock and discovered it was eight in the evening.

When I couldn't stand the silence anymore, I asked, "Do you already know what happened?" There was no reason to relive the horror of my kidnapping by telling them everything if they already knew the details.

"The police removed a bunch of cameras from our house," Gina offered. I had learned that during my interviews in Montana, which gave me hope that Gina and Croft already had a good idea of recent events. "We know it was Jack Sohn. I showed his yearbook photo to the police."

It felt weird hearing his name now that I knew how often he had trespassed on our privacy in this very place.

I looked down at my lap. "He took that picture of me, that one that I hate."

Her eyes widened. "Page 22?"

"Page 22," I confirmed.

Croft worked his jaw, looking angry.

I took another bite and watched the other two do the same. I don't think they were even aware of their synchronized eating. I swallowed and traced circles on the table. "I'm sorry, Gina. You being my roommate the last few semesters means you've also had to deal with breaches on your privacy and feeling weird whenever Jack had been in our apartment or our house."

Croft picked up my hand. Gina looked downright offended.

"That's not your fault," she said.

"None of this is your fault," Croft told me in a low voice. He began tracing circles on the palm of my hand, and I felt the tiniest bit better.

Gina spoke up. "Our bishop and his wife said we could stay at their place. I thought we might not want to sleep here right now."

A weight lifted from my shoulders. "That's a good idea," I said, trying to keep my voice from choking. "When do we leave?" I asked semi-casually.

"Whenever you're ready. We can go now unless you need more time to eat."

I stood. "Let's go."

* * *

NOW THAT I think about it, it was a miracle I napped so peacefully on the couch after first getting home from my ordeal. That night, even though I was in Bishop Kennedy's large house and not the place Jack had haunted, my sleep was disturbed by nightmares. Gina, who slept in the bed next to mine, had to wake me up a few times to end my torture.

The next day after church, I felt safe enough to go in the Kennedys' huge backyard and play with their dog. The Golden Retriever was happy to retrieve her tennis ball time and again, making up for my lack of enthusiasm as I woodenly threw the ball from where I sat on the hanging sofa.

Gina must have known I didn't feel like talking, because she didn't follow me outside, but she was plastered against the window, watching me as if ready to sound the alarm should anyone show up to kidnap me.

Eventually, the glass door slid open, and Croft joined me.

I threw the ball without looking at him. Minnie ran so fast that she stumbled and did a somersault. Then she sprinted back to us, excited to now have two ball-throwers to choose between.

Picking up the wet ball again, I wanted to laugh with Croft about how gross it was, but it was like I didn't know how. With my body on autopilot, I threw and once more watched the Retriever chase after it.

"How was church?" I managed.

"Awful," Croft answered. A moment later, he thought to correct himself. "Church wasn't awful. It was good. I was just out of it. So much for teaching today."

That reminded me I wasn't the only one who had spent most of yesterday being scared stiff. Rather than turn to him in compassion, though, I looked straight ahead, not wanting to see the pain or fear that might linger in Croft's eyes.

I did have enough decency to remember I owed him a thank you. "The guy who rescued me yesterday recognized me because of a post on your channel."

"Really?" he asked, his voice unsteady. He put an arm around me and squeezed. I leaned into the one-sided hug. I guess both of us needed this.

The slobbery ball landed at my feet. Croft picked it up and threw it twice as far as I had. I had a feeling Minnie would never pick me over Croft again.

"How did he rescue you?" Croft asked quietly.

It took me a moment to answer. "He tailed us and called the police. Jack drove onto a forest path and ran out and started a gunfight with him." Croft's grip tightened. "My rescuer had his own firearm. He shot Jack in the arm. Then it turned into a fistfight. The man knocked Jack unconscious, and we waited for the police."

Croft swallowed. "I didn't know that Jack . . ." His voice faltered on the name as though it was difficult to say. ". . . had a gun. Did he ever point it at you?"

I bit the inside of my cheek. "A couple of times."

Croft's breath hitched.

"He had a knife, too," I added in a flat tone.

Croft shook his head. I still couldn't look at him, so I took a shuddering breath and watched Minnie lap water from a fountain. "I don't know how they keep their yard so nice."

"They probably pay for services," Croft replied, letting me change the topic.

I curled up next to him on the hanging couch, closing my eyes and letting him hold me.

* * *

I hadn't been forced into the wedding dress. I hadn't had to live with Jack. I hadn't been taken advantage of.

In spite of all the *hadn'ts*, I was traumatized. Depressed and scared would define my existence for the next while. I kept looking over my shoulder. I felt darkness press in around me when I tried to sleep, and I kept thinking I could hear someone else breathe.

When Sister Kennedy opened the door that evening, I hung back at a cautious distance although I knew my parents were supposed to be arriving. Mom rushed past my host to hug me, and Dad wasn't far behind.

"Surrey," Mom exclaimed, sobbing.

"We're here for you," Dad promised, deep worry in his voice.

I let them hug me as though that could take away the fear inside me. It should have, but my fear was frozen into a ball in my center, and in spite of their good intentions, they couldn't melt it.

My parents stayed nearly a week, watching movies with me while I made an attempt to do schoolwork. They assured me I could come home to Virginia if I wanted to. We could figure out school later.

It should have been a tempting offer, but my traumatized self didn't want further uprooting.

Gina seemed unsure about joining us, but Croft was constantly by my side. When my siblings FaceTimed us and Mom and Dad struggled to keep the conversation going on our end, Croft took over giving reassurances or finding something new to talk about.

Before they left, Dad found a therapist in Utah County that he trusted. He made me promise to meet with her at least three times.

When Gina and I returned to our house, where I had secretly planned to sleep on the couch, Gina suggested we switch bedrooms. We had a big moving day, carrying our things back and forth between the two rooms. It felt good to do something physically straining and to be exhausted when I fell into bed that night. I was only woken up twice by nightmares.

Even so, Croft insisted we ask to stay at the Kennedys' again the following Friday night, and I ended up being really grateful for that. I would have been almost paralyzed by fear, worrying that the nightmare from two Saturdays ago would repeat itself in the same way: Gina would leave at five for work, Jack would enter the house, and I would find myself staring down a gun and a stalker. Sleeping in the Kennedys' house helped keep me from imagining that scenario.

I spent very little time in the house Gina and I rented, instead hanging out at school and at Croft's place, though I wasn't great company. Croft showed up faithfully every morning to drive me to school, and whenever his schedule allowed it, he appeared at the end of my class and walked me to my next one, which helped lower my anxiety level. Gina gave me rides, too, and I'm pretty sure she cut down on her work hours. She was around more than usual. We received a round of dinner invitations from our neighbors, taking us to a different home every evening. And Gina let in an unexpected visitor one afternoon in late February while Croft was still at school.

I was sitting on the couch pretending to be engrossed in homework but really just going over and over my abduction in my mind when I recognized Hanna's voice at the door.

She walked right over, sat down, and pulled me into a hug. I had gotten lots of hugs since the incident with Jack, but none of them included the words that followed.

Hanna spoke into my ear. "Freshman year, winter semester. I had a stalker." I stiffened in surprise. Hanna's arms tightened. "I hated it. It was scary when I realized my anonymous gifts weren't from an admirer I wanted. I'd find roses or gift-wrapped candy or envelopes with pictures of myself. He'd leave them on my doorstep or on my car or *in* my car, both at home and when I went places."

When she let go, I moved back enough to stare at her. "*You* had a stalker?"

She smiled a little. "You'll find there are a lot of us. Everyone will start telling you their story now, and some of their stories will be much worse than mine, but I want you to know, I'm not telling it to get you to feel bad for me. I'm telling it to support you."

It was strange. My ball of fear was still frozen, but it didn't feel as painful in that moment. Everything I thought I knew about Hanna reworked itself in my mind until I came up with—the same Hanna I had always known. My shoulders began to relax as I realized this didn't define her.

"What happened to him?" I asked.

She gave a tiny shrug. "Someone figured out who it was, and he got a restraining order."

"Did that . . . work?" At least I knew Jack was behind bars.

A haunted look entered her eyes. "Mostly." She cleared her throat, and peace returned to her expression. "Actually, that's when I decided I didn't want to kiss the guys I dated—once I felt up to dating at all, that is. I didn't want anything physical with anyone when it might trigger my newfound anxiety."

"Oh." I thought about that.

Hanna leaned back against the couch. Both of us looked ahead in quiet contemplation. Then she asked, "Do you want to go for a walk?"

I tensed, insecurity rushing back in. "I—I don't know." It didn't make sense. Shouldn't I have been more afraid of spending time in this house, where Jack had intruded, than outdoors?

"I can go with you," Gina offered, appearing in the doorway.

I pictured the three of us strolling through the neighborhood. My heart was still beating fast, but I nodded. "O-okay."

* * *

HANNA STARTED COMING AROUND, and so did Brody, morphing into the role of a brother to me. I found I liked it that way. After all, I had Croft.

Croft. He was always there for me, no matter how boring or pathetic I was.

"Do you want to do something from your List of Ten Things?" he asked as we sat at the dining table one Friday evening, an abandoned board game in front of us and rare spring rain pattering on the roof. I was feeling particularly miserable, with all my negative thoughts from the past weeks accumulating into a monstrous pile of self-pity.

"Willie's just waiting for you to ask about the vacuum," Croft reminded me.

I shook my head. I hadn't worked on my list for a while. Or painted. Or anything.

"You know what?" He leaned toward me. "If you put on your warrior dress, I bet you'll be able to take on the world."

I shook my head again and rested my head on one hand.

"We can play something else if you like. It's getting close to curfew, but I'll be here early tomorrow morning and make French toast à la Croft, with berries and whipped cream."

I picked up a donkey game piece and turned it over in my hand as though it mattered. My stomach was churning. Croft had been cooking for me, driving me, escorting me, comforting me, supporting me. He was the ultimate nice guy at this point—and maybe that was a problem.

"When did you become so nice?" My voice was desolate.

He shook his head. "I'm not nice. I'm just me."

I stared at the donkey's little ears. "You've always been a good guy. I just never knew how thoughtful you could be." I sighed. "This is the point where you leave, isn't it? She's gonna come along, the perfect girl, and steal you away, just when it looks like you couldn't love me any more than you do."

Croft sat up with a jerk, causing the donkeys on the game board to topple over. "You think I'll leave you? After all this, you think I'll leave?"

"After all this," I murmured. "After all the trouble you've gone to for me. I've become a real burden, haven't I? You deserve someone happy, not someone who's always down in the dumps."

Croft leaned over and took hold of my forearms. As this made it difficult to lean my head on my hand, I raised my head and looked at him.

"Surrey Witherfield," he said, his dark eyes holding my gaze, "I am not leaving you. Do you hear me?" He shifted his grip higher on my arms. "*I am not leaving*," he vowed and moved his hands to my shoulders. "I am *not* leaving." He moved closer, drastically reducing the distance between us until he was eye to eye with me. "*I* am not *leaving.*

"Do you understand?" he asked, breathing as though he had just run a race, his eyes stormier than I had ever seen them.

Pinned to the spot by his hands and my own dull lack of movement, I stared into those eyes, watching this Croft who had teased me to distraction, who had a habit of speaking with ridiculous cockiness, who had seen to my every need and want without being asked the last few weeks.

He had stopped punishing blondes for his sister-in-law's issues and had changed the feel behind his pranks after I spoke up about them being mean. He had cheered me up at Brody's wedding reception and given me a priesthood blessing when I felt surrounded by darkness. He had known I needed help when I wasn't home that fateful Saturday morning. That day, he had kept his wits about him enough to find out what was going on and how he could help. He was sitting here now, staring me down, telling me with his all that he was here to stay.

"Do you understand?" he repeated, his voice more gentle and yet more intense than before.

Finally, I nodded. With a sigh, he slid his hands down my arms and took hold of my hands.

"I love you, Surrey. I'm staying," he said and kissed first one hand, then the other.

I watched him stand. "I'll be back early tomorrow morning," he promised. "And I'll be back every day after that. Every single day," he emphasized.

I stood, too. He gave me a hug, and I held on, trying to make it last as long as possible before I had to let him go.

Then we parted. *Just for the night, though,* I reminded myself. He wasn't leaving. Croft wasn't leaving. Croft was *not* leaving.

Chapter Thirty-Six

I MUST HAVE WOKEN up a hundred times that night, fully rested every time and surprised to find out it was still night. Every time I awoke, it was to Croft's voice saying, "I am not leaving." Real-life Croft wanted me to believe that, and obviously, Dream-Croft did, too.

At last, I woke up at a decent time and lay in bed, watching 7:30 tick by. 7:31. 7:32. Feeling lazy, I listened to the clock, the house, and the silence.

I turned onto my side, and my eyes landed on the change of clothes I had laid out for the day, a shirt on top. I thought of my veteran-rescuer and remembered the way he had torn a piece of Jack's shirt to bandage Jack's arm.

Wait! I sat up straight, struck by the memory. *He tore a piece from Jack's shirt.*

It could be done, then. It could be—couldn't it? I mean, could *I*, in spite of my failed attempt the day I was pranked?

There was only one way to find out. I got out of bed, and my blanket followed, wrapped around my foot and nearly sending me headlong onto the floor before I freed myself. I opened up Gina's—now my—dresser and looked at my neatly folded shirts.

Hmmm. I could hardly experiment on one of them. I liked them all.

I'd just have to buy one.

Minutes later, I snatched up my phone and my purse and ran outside.

I drove to D.I. and sat in my car, debating with myself and my conscience. People shopped here to get their things cheap. Maybe it was wrong of me to buy and damage an item someone else would have been happy to have. Should I go to a different thrift shop? Should I go to a shop that didn't sell secondhand clothes at all? Ugh, it had seemed so simple when I left my house.

I finally decided to enter the store. I had planned to buy a shirt I wouldn't have cared for. Hopefully, I would find something no one else would like, either.

Yeah, it didn't take me long to learn that D.I. wasn't open yet. The closed doors and the hours written on them made that clear. Now that I thought about it, the empty parking lot should have clued me in when I first arrived.

I got back in my car. Ten minutes later, I found an open clothes store in Orem.

My browsing led me to a size XXL puke-green shirt, which I promptly took to the cashier and paid for. As I walked through the parking lot, I reveled in the novel experience of buying clothes without having to try them on.

Back in my car, I locked the doors and held up the shirt. "Are you ready to—"

My phone rang, making me drop the shirt with a guilty start. Fumbling for my phone, I saw that *Prince Big-Head* was calling. I picked up.

"Where *are* you?" Croft asked urgently.

"Me?" Well, of course me. "I'm just shopping."

"You're *shopping*? What do you mean, you're shopping? Why didn't you say anything? I could have gone with you."

My face froze in sort of an "oh" expression. Poor Croft. He must have arrived at my place and was panicked to find me missing. I hadn't thought this one through. "Sorry. I didn't mean to scare you."

"Where are you? I'll come," he told me.

"No, I'm about to leave. I'll be home in twenty minutes. Don't worry about me."

"Don't worry," he mumbled as if to himself. "Okay, but you better be here soon, or we'll have the police trace the GPS on your phone."

I wasn't sure how seriously he meant the warning, but I reassured him again and hung up. My phone showed a missed call, and I felt another twinge of guilt when I realized Gina had called me despite being at work. Or maybe she was home already? She had been working fewer hours, after all. I sent her a quick text to let her know I was fine.

"All right." I picked up the shirt again. "It's just you and me." I took hold of the bottom and began to pull.

My hands strained. The fabric strained. I released the pressure and pulled hard and quick a couple of times. That didn't work. Again, I tried to tear the shirt, struggling for a minute. Stopping to rest my hands, I pulled again hard—and it tore.

Yes! I tugged at the tear and made it longer, and longer, and finally, I got the other end free and sat back with a damaged shirt in one hand and a strip of fabric in the other.

I *could* tear a piece of fabric from my clothes to use as a bandage.

Feeling inordinately pleased, I dropped both pieces on the passenger seat and started my car, humming a tune I had heard recently.

By the time I reached home, I was singing at the top of my lungs.

Pulling up to the house, I found I had a two-person welcoming committee, and they didn't look too happy. Embarrassed to have them know what I had been doing, I stowed the incriminating pieces of green shirt in my glove compartment and got out of the car.

"Where have you been?" Gina demanded, hands on her hips. Croft reached me in three long strides and took hold of my arms, looking me over as though to make sure I was in one piece.

"Shopping," I answered. A memory from Croft's and my first interaction surfaced in my mind. "My wardrobe couldn't wait," I said saucily.

He loosened his grip but still watched me with worry. I hadn't realized how often he had done that the last several weeks.

It was time to lighten up the mood around here. "If you have any items you think I should add to my List of Ten Things to Do This Summer, you'd better tell me soon," I told him, tossing my head and walking to the house. Gina fell in behind me, and Croft hurried to catch up. "I'll write up a draft within the next couple of days. My first item will be to take a first aid class. The instructor will probably fear for the life of anyone who ends up needing my help, but it's better to have the training than to not have the training, and I usually manage to get things done right when it matters, even if I do have my accidents."

I stopped, and Gina almost ran into me. I turned around and looked her in the eyes. "I appreciate everything you've done, Gina, but you can't cut your work hours for me anymore."

"Are you feeling okay, then?" she asked, her voice hesitant and hopeful at the same time.

"Yes, and I've got work to do." I whirled around. "I'm going to paint. Do you mind, Croft?"

He gaped at me in awe. "Of—of course not. You okay with me watching?"

"I'll probably be terribly boring, but you're welcome to."

"I'll probably be terribly distracting, but then, you already know that," he returned, a smirk in his voice that I hadn't heard in over a month. A smile spread across my face. I had missed this side of him. I had missed this side of *me*.

Within minutes, I had transferred my easel, a sketchbook, brushes, and a wide selection of acrylic paints to the living room.

Picking up one of my fattest brushes, I slathered it in red and drew it across the first page in a long, bold motion. Quickly cleaning the brush, I applied yellow and drew several more fat lines from one end of the page to the other.

"What are you doing?" Croft asked with a faint smile.

"Purging," I answered, my voice tinged with excitement. I snatched up the page and let it fall on the ground, barely pausing to make sure it was face-up.

Croft picked it up quickly. "You can't discard this. It's modern art." He held it up next to his face. Gina, who had seated herself in a chair facing us, giggled.

I was already tearing the next page from my sketchbook. With flowing motions, I painted green up and down it, filling out the whole thing and then putting it on the floor.

Croft held it up and stood with a "painting" on either side of his face. "That's what I'm talking about. The painting in the middle is by far the best, though."

I paused. "Which painting?"

He pointed at his face. "Why, this one."

I reached out with the brush, and he ducked away to save his nose.

We were all laughing as I picked a different brush and turned to the next paper.

I closed my eyes, envisioning the scene. Selecting a light-pink color, I mixed it with white, making it lighter still.

It was a funny way of doing it, but I filled out the page first with falling pink blossoms, and then I painted the girl on the swing in the background, allowing her to look somewhat like me. The face was partially obscured, but the hair, shape, and clothes were mine. I would have to put this on canvas. I hadn't expected to make a series of the girl on the swing, but suddenly I knew the snowstorm painting wasn't enough. I needed this painting of a girl swinging amidst a flurry of spring blossoms.

I turned to my audience, who had watched in silence. "What do you think?" My voice started out excited but ended up reverent. There was something in the stillness that felt good and something in my painting that was cleansing.

Gina's eyes shone with admiration for the painting.

Croft's eyes shone with what looked like tears. The sight shocked me, but I had no time to react before he said, "I think it's amazing" and gathered me in his arms. My face burrowed into his shirt, and I enjoyed the solid feel of him, the excitement of a new art project, and the feeling of being one hundred percent safe as he held me.

* * *

I WASN'T trauma-free from that day on, but I did start to feel much better. I watched the videos my therapist assigned me about changing from a victim mentality, and with Hanna as my example, I thought I could see how to apply those lessons. Still, I startled easily, struggled at times to fall asleep at night, and looked around with suspicion now and then in search of cameras. The nightmares didn't stop, but they did become less frequent.

I finally decided I could at least take on one more item from my List of Ten Things. Apparently Bella Whitmer had been pestering her parents about the fact that they didn't have swing-friendly trees in their yard. I volunteered to help plant a sapling.

"Are you sure that's deep enough?" Bella asked, looking into our three-inch hole.

"That's how they did it in the YouTube video," her brother Daniel reminded her while Jayden and Lena scrambled to replay the instructions on their mom's phone.

"Go ahead and put it in, Bella," Willie told her.

"That's it, all the way down. Now we cover it up." I was on my knees as we patted down the soil, our hands in each other's way and getting splashed as Jayden decided to water the tree right away.

"It doesn't need that much," Daniel protested while Lena shrieked and I reached out too late to keep a laughing Bella from putting her muddy hands to her face.

"Oh good, I'm thirsty," Croft's voice rang out behind me. "Can I have the rest of that water?"

"I'd like to see you drink it from the can," said an unfamiliar voice, and Croft stepped up beside me, followed by a stocky guy with a cowlick.

"Yeah, give him the can," Bella cheered and grabbed the spout of the watering can.

It was a miracle the sapling didn't get trampled in the uproar that followed. I laughed as Croft eventually took an apprehensive drink, and then a sensible Willie and I tried to keep all the Whitmer children from following suit. Five minutes later, Croft and his friend were both splashed, most of us were laughed out, and everyone had mud somewhere on their person.

"And that's how you plant a tree," Croft chuckled. "I hope you took notes, Jeremy."

I dropped the deer repellent. "Jeremy? Are you—"

"Croft's brother." Jeremy's dimples made an appearance, and he reached out a dirty hand to shake mine.

"Oh." I felt hot all over. How I had dreaded this moment. What would Jeremy think when he met—I paused my panicked thoughts. He had already met me, and we had just chatted and played together. A great relief enveloped me. Jeremy, the guy who had married a beautiful blonde only to have his heart crushed, showed none of the prejudice Croft had exhibited when we first met.

I breathed out. "It's nice to meet you."

"It's nice to meet you, too."

Croft shook a clod of dirt from my hair and placed a hand on my cheek. "Can you forgive me for not telling you in advance he'd be here?"

I wiped a smear of mud down his cheek and smiled wide. "Yes. It was perfect this way."

He held my hand against the smear and gave me a mournful look. "Seems like everyone's getting a swing these days. I wish you and I had one."

"Surrey knows she can use my swing," Willie said from the sidewalk, where Bella was drawing a chalk outline of his hands.

Croft's eyes widened. "What? How did I not know this?"

"I don't know. It sure took you a while," I teased.

"Come on!" He tugged me across the street, where I soon discovered a new favorite way of swinging—in Croft's lap, with his arms around me.

* * *

Just as I'd convinced myself I could pass next month's finals with some serious grit, I got a phone call out of left field. Croft watched my face during the conversation, picking up on my wonder, disbelief, and overall excitement.

"What was that about? Who was that?" he asked as soon as I hung up.

"That was a museum curator," I said, dazed. "He bought two of my paintings at the auction in January. A wing of his museum is dedicated to the work of new artists, and he wants to display my paintings if I can create several more. Do you think this is real?"

He blinked. "Of course it is. You didn't imagine the conversation, did you?"

"No, but what if it's a scam?"

"What's the name of the museum?"

Croft looked up the museum online and compared phone numbers. One of them matched the one I had gotten a call from. He put a hand on my shoulder. "I don't know how to break this to you." His eyes twinkled. "Surrey, this is real."

"Then . . . this is an incredible opportunity," I stammered, "and I . . ."

"Should take it," Croft finished.

". . . know nothing about the art business." I think my eyes looked wild in that moment.

"Aaaauugh" described my frenzied state of mind after that as I scrambled to figure out what to do in regards to agents, contracts, and more, all while trying to finish one of my hardest semesters, which had been interrupted by an abduction and ensuing trauma. One thing was for sure: I no longer had the luxury of taking my own sweet time to figure out how things worked in the art world.

My prayers were laser-focused on time management, not messing up my creative image, and not getting duped. I also had some scary but earnest talks with God about the fact that I wanted His will to be done. If it wasn't His plan for me to show my art, then I—sort of—didn't want it, either. If being a professional artist would somehow compromise my role as a future mom, I especially didn't want that. But if I could do some good, provide inspiration to others and maybe have opportunities open up to share the gospel of Jesus Christ due to my success in the art world, then it just might be His will. I prayed that He would help guide me so it could happen.

Heavenly Father answered by keeping my mind clear as I did schoolwork and by blessing me with Croft, who spent hours and hours researching how to navigate my new world. Croft also roped Riley the "legal manager" from his crew into helping.

"It says here a lot of gallery consignment agreements limit you to selling through them alone. You'd have to watch out for that," Croft told me, looking up from his computer. The three of us were sitting on his yellow sofa like three ducks in a row. "Now, the gallery owners will probably come flocking to you since you already got your work into a museum, but you should especially look into this one." He circled a spot on a hand-drawn map of galleries. "Network with them and pounce if any of them come to the museum. I think their art follows the same values as yours."

Riley finished reading the latest message in an email chain with our contacts at the museum. "Okay, you'll definitely keep the rights to the paintings they'll show."

"Yes!" I pumped my fist in the air. "I couldn't stand to lose my warrior-queen painting or the swing paintings. You guys are amazing. Do you know, I was able to work on a new painting last night practically without stress? This one shows an epic leaf fight, rakes abandoned in the background and children getting into the piles of leaves. I'd like to call it *Croft Was Silent for Once*, but I'll probably have to pick a different title especially since you're not actually in it."

"Hey, I've been silent *twice* for you," Croft protested while Riley stuffed her mouth with potato chips to hide her grin.

* * *

As the semester drew to a close, I struggled with the decision of whether to continue to rent the house that had been my home the last year and a half. Gina seemed happy to go with whatever I decided, but that fickle word, "decision," is not as easy as it sounds.

Those first few weeks after Jack's surprise visit, I had been more than ready to leave the house behind. Now, though, I thought of how much I would miss my neighbors, especially Willie. I thought of how far I had come in being comfortable in the house, so long as Gina's and my bedroom switch remained permanent. I had hopes that most of my lingering fears would wash away during the summer.

On the other hand, if I was going home to Virginia for the break, it was funky to pay rent during the summer just to make sure we still had the place in the fall.

On the third hand, though I hadn't signed up for spring or summer classes like Croft had, I didn't like the idea of being away from him for so long. I wanted to have a place where I *could* stay in Provo in order to spend time with him that summer.

On the fourth hand, I desperately wanted to spend some time with my family, too, and it would be expensive to fly back and forth during the break.

After going through far too many hands, I decided to at least stay two weeks past the end of the semester. Gina was going home as soon as she finished April finals, but I, crazy person that I was for staying all alone in a house that had brought me so much grief, stayed behind.

As spring came out with all its flowers and greenery, it was actually hard to feel scared in the house. My neighbors were constantly outdoors playing or working in their gardens, Willie was hooked on a project to create the best security system around and was always willing to talk about it, and Mrs. Blaine was extra vigilant. She came over to give me regular updates, which were usually along the lines of "Everything looks fine" but sometimes were "I saw a blue Honda Accord at two eleven. If I see it again, I'll let you know." She was studying up on car models so she could identify them at a glance. Her snickerdoodle cookies were amazing, and I came to love our visits as she started to stay longer.

Nights were still hard sometimes, but Croft was quick to give me a priesthood blessing when he noticed I was worried, and sometimes he called after he'd gone home for curfew. One night, I stayed up late on the phone with him, and we laughed away the shadows in my room.

I fell asleep smiling to the sound of his voice, happy I had chosen to stay in town for now and would get to see Croft again tomorrow.

Chapter Thirty-Seven

It was a Saturday morning when I drove to Croft's house, my windows rolled down to let in the spring perfume. I had spent a beautiful hour in the temple and had opted not to change out of my celestial-blue dress after. While I appreciated that Croft didn't often compliment my looks, I did like to look extra good for him.

Croft's neighborhood welcomed me with warm colors, red-brick walls, and tasteful landscaping. Noting Croft's car and someone else's in the driveway, I parked next to the curb, turned off the engine, and looked up at the house.

There he stood, framed by the kitchen window, slightly obscured by the curtains, holding up a ring-box to a dark-haired woman who clapped her hands to her mouth.

I froze.

The woman took the ring and held it up to the light. Croft stepped closer and reached for her hands, but she turned and held the ring up once more. When she stepped out of sight, Croft followed.

Fragmented thoughts clunked around inside my head.

He couldn't have. He wouldn't have. There was no way.

Yet wasn't that how it had happened with each of the other guys? We were both in love, and then—*wham*—New Girl had his heart.

No, this was a joke. A prank. A scene for his YouTube channel. Croft was *not* leaving.

Something spread inside me, something burning. It hurt, but I wanted it to hurt. I needed something to focus on, something different than what I had just seen. I needed something to do.

In my mind's eye, I saw myself walk up to Croft, slap him hard, and then kiss him. I could see it played out like in the movies, and before I knew it, I was unbuckling myself, slipping from the car, intent on playing out the scene I had imagined.

I slammed the door and started to move, but a pull on my clothes stopped me mid-step. Turning to see, I found myself unable to rotate more than forty-five degrees before my movement was again restricted. To top it off, my keys fell from my hands, landing on the ground with a clatter.

My long, blue skirt was stuck in the door. I put a hand behind me, searching for the handle. Finding it, I pulled, but it wouldn't open. My door was locked.

Grimacing, I tried to bend down for the keys but was forced to stop. Looking down at myself, I saw that my skirt was pulled up to just above my knees in the front. In the back, though, it was pulled up to a mini-skirt length and tucked neatly into the door. Tugging at the dress would tear it and leave me inappropriately clad.

A door opened nearby. I looked up to see Croft.

"Surrey? I didn't know you'd be here so soon," he said, sounding nervous.

Well might he sound nervous, I thought, my inner voice threatening. My mind went back over my plan: Slap him, then kiss him.

"Croft," I said in as sweet a tone as I could manage. "Come over here."

He took a step toward me and threw a glance back at the house. "Did you see anything?"

"Just come," I repeated, my voice like sugar.

He took another few halting steps. "Because, well, I wasn't going to do this just yet. I mean, I wanted to do it today, just not this morning."

I waited as he continued his tortuously slow walk. Tuning out most of his words, I focused on the only thing I could think of without pain: Slap, then kiss.

"I mean, I'm glad you came by. I wanted to spend the day with you."

Slap, then kiss. Slap, then . . . Wait a minute. Was it "slap, then kiss," or was it "kiss, then slap?" I racked my brain for movie scenes. The movies had both scenarios, didn't they?

"And I've really been looking forward to . . ."

Kiss, then slap, I recited doggedly in my mind. *Kiss . . .*

His voice as he came close melted me. Oh, how I loved this blue-eyed, messy-haired jerk. He gave me a slow smile, and I swear I turned to goo.

Slip, then kass . . . Wait. What?

He stepped within reach and opened his mouth.

I grabbed him by the collar and pulled his lips to mine.

His hands came up, and he cradled my face, deepening the kiss, leaning me back against the car that held me captive. He changed the angle, and I felt his love for me. I tried to return the favor, expressing my love and adoration with each breath, moving my hands to the back of his neck and holding on, sighing with joy and pleasure.

He pulled away too soon, and I looked at him with starstruck eyes.

"It's the wrong order," he said in a haze, and I blinked in confusion. So it *should* have been "slap, then kiss"?

Croft fumbled with his pocket, pulling out a ring-box, and I realized what he had meant. We both wanted to get engaged before we kissed.

Oops.

He snapped the box open and nearly lost his grip on it. Tears came to my eyes. He cleared his throat and dropped to his knees.

"Surrey Witherfield," he began, but I interrupted.

"No, not down there, it's not a good view. Go ahead and stand, Croft."

"Oh, okay." He obeyed, and I breathed a sigh of relief. My artificially shortened skirt didn't go well with a kneeling proposal.

"Surrey Witherfield." He stared deep into my eyes. "I love you," he said simply. Then he swallowed and asked, "Will you marry me?"

I stared at him in awe. He did love me. I had known it, and yet it was too amazing for belief. He really, truly loved me.

"Wait." I frowned. "Who was that girl in the house?"

"Huh?" He looked back at his home. The dark-haired girl stood on the doorstep with a video camera in her hands, of all things. I suddenly recognized her from some of Croft's family Skype calls. She was his sister.

"That's Calli," he said, "who, as you will notice, is filming us with a camera very much out in the open." He gave me an anxious look. "I hope you approve."

He had been showing the ring to his sister. My stomach unclenched, and a smile spread across my face. I should have known. On some level, I think I had known he hadn't found someone else, but the vengeful fantasy of playing out a movie scene had taken hold of me before logic could.

"That's fine. Ask me again."

He cleared his throat. "Surrey." His voice wobbled. "Witherfield."

My nerves danced as I waited.

He paused and then asked in a strained whisper that would never be audible in his sister's film, "Will you marry me?"

"YES," I exclaimed in a too-loud voice. (I know it was too loud. I've watched that film a bazillion times. Whenever Croft teases me about it, I tease him back and tell him we need subtitles for the part where he supposedly asks, "Will you marry me?")

"Good," he said and put his lips on mine, leaning forward so that my head rested against the car behind me while we kissed.

He picked me up and would have twirled me, but resistance in the form of my clothing malfunction stopped him. Puzzled, he set me down.

"Could you do me a favor?" I asked.

"Of course," he said, perplexed.

"Would you pick up my car key and unlock the door?" I found the key with my foot and nudged it forward, then cleared my throat. "Pick it up with your back to me. My skirt isn't as long at the moment as it's supposed to be."

He gave me a strange look and leaned over to see past me to the car door. I couldn't see his face, but I heard a sudden suspicious noise from him as he realized what was wrong. Quickly, he spun around and picked up the key.

I breathed a sigh of relief when he unlocked the door and my skirt came free at last.

Croft was grinning as I stepped away.

"Don't you dare say a word," I threatened.

Wordlessly, he captured my mouth with his.

That was as good a solution as any.

* * *

I TOOK a sudden fancy to June weddings, which meant we had just under two months to prepare.

Throughout my hours of painting, working through my List of Ten Things, and spending time with Croft, I floated on springtime clouds, coming down to earth every now and then to answer this or that question from my mom about my preferences. She was happily planning my outdoors reception, and I was happily letting her do so.

Okay, so it wouldn't be a June *wedding* since the marriage itself was taking place in the temple, but "June wedding" sounded so much better than "June reception."

When I knelt across the altar from Croft in a sacred white sealing room in the temple and listened to the ceremony, I may have cried. Even Croft looked like he might tear up at one point.

My brother and sisters just beamed at us even when we were told to kiss. I made a note to ask my parents which of them had bribed my siblings to be reverent.

Afterward, Mom took far more pictures than I liked. She insisted on getting every possible angle of us now that my tear-washed face was glowing, my nose was adorably pink, and my eyes shone brighter than before.

Like I said, I cry pretty.

I thanked her later for insisting on those photos. Not only did I look extra good, but Croft's expression—oh, he looked ecstatic. I'll admit cameras can be a good thing, because I've come to treasure those pictures.

* * *

WE BEHAVED with utmost decorum at our reception. Really, we were model citizens.

"Do you want more salt with that, Poe?" Croft asked, leaning over his friend, who was forced to hunch over in his chair while Croft shook a salt shaker all over his pasta salad.

We had abandoned the reception line fifteen minutes into the event and were now skirting the outside tables. I say outside tables because my dress was too wide to allow me to walk through the center. Both of us were dressed in white, as Croft, to my delight, had donned the same white suit he wore at the December Ball.

"No, thank you," Poe groaned, holding his hands over his plate.

Croft set down the salt shaker with a pleasant smile. "You're welcome."

I gave Poe an apologetic smile. "Sorry, Poe. There's only so much I can do."

"Ah, well. Once a prankster, always a prankster." Poe tried to pick the white crystals out of his food. "Somehow I doubt you'll have much of a calming influence on him," he told me.

"*I'll* have a calming influence on *her*," Croft said, putting his arm around me and leading me away while I smiled, not disagreeing. I looked back in time to see Poe try his food, a startled expression crossing his face.

"I'd rather have had too much salt," he called, grimacing at his now overly sweet, sugar-topped food.

We hadn't switched out *all* the salt shakers. Just a few of them.

On the other side of the pavilion, Fairlee was skipping across the grass, leading the Whitmer and Petersen children in a merry game of follow-the-leader. The sun shone bright, and the guests looked happy.

"The food looks good," I moaned, walking along the lawn. "Willie, how's your salmon?"

"It's great." He gave me a pitying look from his seat, where he had plopped down to eat and take a break from the games. "I feel sorry for you. You can't eat anything in that dress."

"Not only can I not eat anything," I huffed, warming to the subject, "but I can't even walk between the tables. This is ridiculous. It's *huge*."

"Surrey." Hanna's voice rang out, defusing my speech as she came over and grabbed my hands, Brody not far behind with two plates in his hands. "You look so wonderful. I'm so happy for you."

"Congratulations, Surrey," Brody said. "You deserve all this and more."

"Definitely," Gina said, making her way to my side. From his seat, Poe's hopeful eyes followed her. They had been on a couple of dates, and I wondered if it would lead to something. Gina would end it if she didn't feel anything, I was sure.

I gave her a fond hug before beginning another round of the outskirts of the pavilion. Croft's brother, Jeremy, looked like he was enjoying himself. He sat next to London, together with Croft's and my immediate family members, and as she talked with him, his gaze stayed on her face more than I would have expected from a casual conversation. Either the parents didn't notice, or they were doing an admirable job pretending not to. Before I could think any more of it, Bella peeled off from Fairlee's posse and hopped on the back of Jeremy's bench, chatting up a storm. He smiled broadly at her.

Distancing ourselves from our guests, my white-clad husband and I stepped onto the grass with a clear view of the awe-inspiring sky. I wasn't given long to admire the heavens, though, because Croft picked me up, heavy gown and all, and twirled around with me, making me laugh.

When he finally put me down, he lowered his head to mine and declared, "We're going to be nauseatingly happy. Half of that will be my fault because I'm irresistible and so good for you."

I widened my eyes. "Only half? You're losing your grip on your cockiness."

"I have to give credit where credit is due," he insisted, his eyes dancing and his dimples deepening. "Of course, since I was the one who recognized early on that you were good for me, by extension I can also take credit for you making me happy."

I smiled. "This is nauseating."

"Mm-hmm," he said and kissed me.

Epilogue

HEY GUYS, this is Croft. Guess what? Surrey's my dream girl. I love her to pieces and sometimes annoy her to distraction.

In this world where it's so hard to keep marriages going, I want you to know that we've stayed together and are stronger than ever. I think it has a lot to do with the bunny I bought five years ago. I mean, sure, my Cinnamon soon found out she didn't want it running the length of her desk while she painted, but once it found its niche outside her painting studio, we've all been happy with it. The kids adore it.

We have teenagers now. Can you believe it? Our growing flock of children are gonna turn heads when they grow up. They take after me, you see.

I want you to know that since the stalker, no one has bothered Surrey and lived to tell the tale. You don't believe me? I swear, it's pretty much true!

Anyway, life isn't all cakes and jokes, but I'm pretty happy, and Surrey really helps with that. Man, I'm glad she didn't marry that Brody, or I can tell you I wouldn't be friends with him today. Hey, did Surrey ever tell you her story about . . . ?

Oh sorry, gotta go. Toddler's calling. She's the cutest thing, and isn't she lucky she has me? Even if she's probably inherited my tone deafness?

Coming, Melody. . . .

Terms and Ideas Relating to The Church of Jesus Christ of Latter-day Saints

EXPLANATIONS BY THE AUTHOR

Keeping the Spirit in your home: At baptism, members of this church are given the Gift of the Holy Ghost. This means they can have the constant, uplifting presence of the Holy Ghost (also known as the Spirit) in their lives as long as their thoughts and choices invite goodness. In *Artfully Annoying*, Surrey's stalker drove the Spirit from Surrey and Gina's home, leaving behind a feeling of wrongness, but the Spirit always returned because of those who lived there. The Spirit returned faster than normal when invited through the singing of sacred hymns.

For information about the roles of the Holy Ghost, see churchofjesuschrist.org/study/manual/gospel-topics/holy-ghost

Priesthood blessings: Latter-day Saints, like people in Biblical times, are given priesthood authority to bless others with guidance, strength, and comfort and to perform ordinances, such as baptism. For blessings, hands are placed on the receiver's head. The opening and closing words are scripted, while the words in between are inspired and spoken as the Spirit puts them into the giver's mind.

For more information about the priesthood, see churchofjesuschrist.org/study/manual/gospel-topics/priesthood

About the Author

Annika Champenois grew up partly in Denmark, partly in Utah, and wholly in the world of books. Her time studying statistics at Brigham Young University gave her great inspiration for her book *Artfully Annoying*, although she never participated in any hidden camera pranks. When she isn't immersed in fiction, Annika loves to go for walks, study languages, and spend time with her family and friends.

www.annikachampenois.com
facebook.com/annikachampenoisauthor